LIVONIA CHOW MEIN

A NOVEL

ABIGAIL SAVITCH-LEW

SIMON & SCHUSTER
New York   Amsterdam/Antwerp   London
Toronto   Sydney/Melbourne   New Delhi

For the people of Brownsville.
And in memory of Wun Kam Lew.

שֶׁאֵין אֲנַחְנוּ עַזֵּי פָנִים וּקְשֵׁי עֹרֶף לוֹמַר לְפָנֶיךָ יְהֹוָה אֱלֹהֵינוּ וַאלֹהֵי אֲבוֹתֵינוּ צַדִּיקִים אֲנַחְנוּ וְלֹא חָטָאנוּ אֲבָל אֲנַחְנוּ וַאֲבוֹתֵינוּ חָטָאנוּ:

We do not say to You, in arrogance and stubbornness,
"We are blameless and do no wrong."
In truth, we and our forebears have stumbled;
we have fallen.

—Tavo L'fanecha: May Our Prayer Reach You

from *Machzor for Yom Kippur*
Temple Rodef Shalom

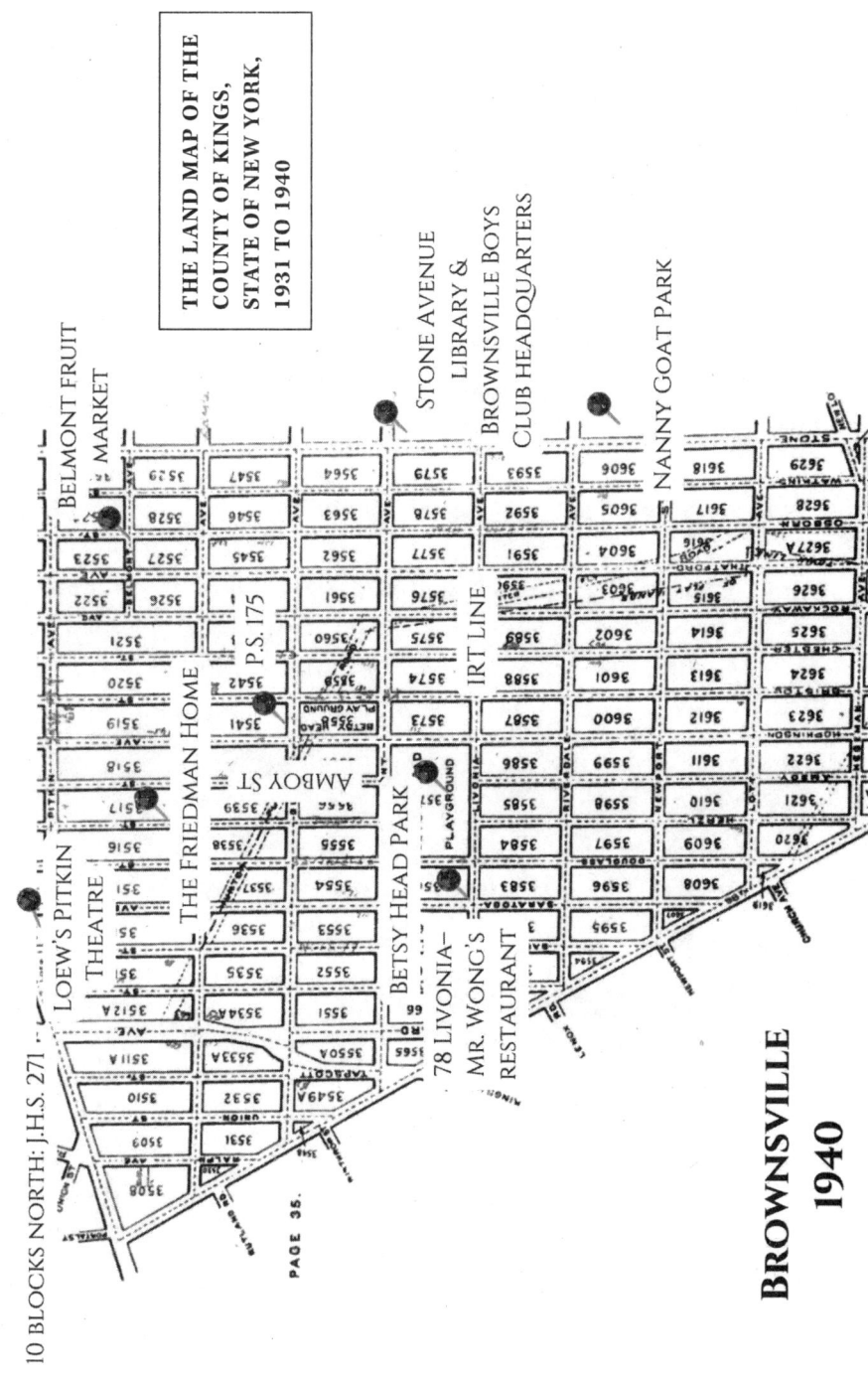

THE LAND MAP OF THE
COUNTY OF KINGS,
STATE OF NEW YORK,
1931 TO 1940

10 BLOCKS NORTH: J.H.S. 271

LOEW'S PITKIN
THEATRE

BELMONT FRUIT
MARKET

P.S. 175

THE FRIEDMAN HOME

STONE AVENUE
LIBRARY &
BROWNSVILLE BOYS
CLUB HEADQUARTERS

NANNY GOAT PARK

AMBOY ST

BETSY HEAD PARK

78 LIVONIA—
MR. WONG'S
RESTAURANT

IRT LINE

PAGE 35.

BROWNSVILLE
1940

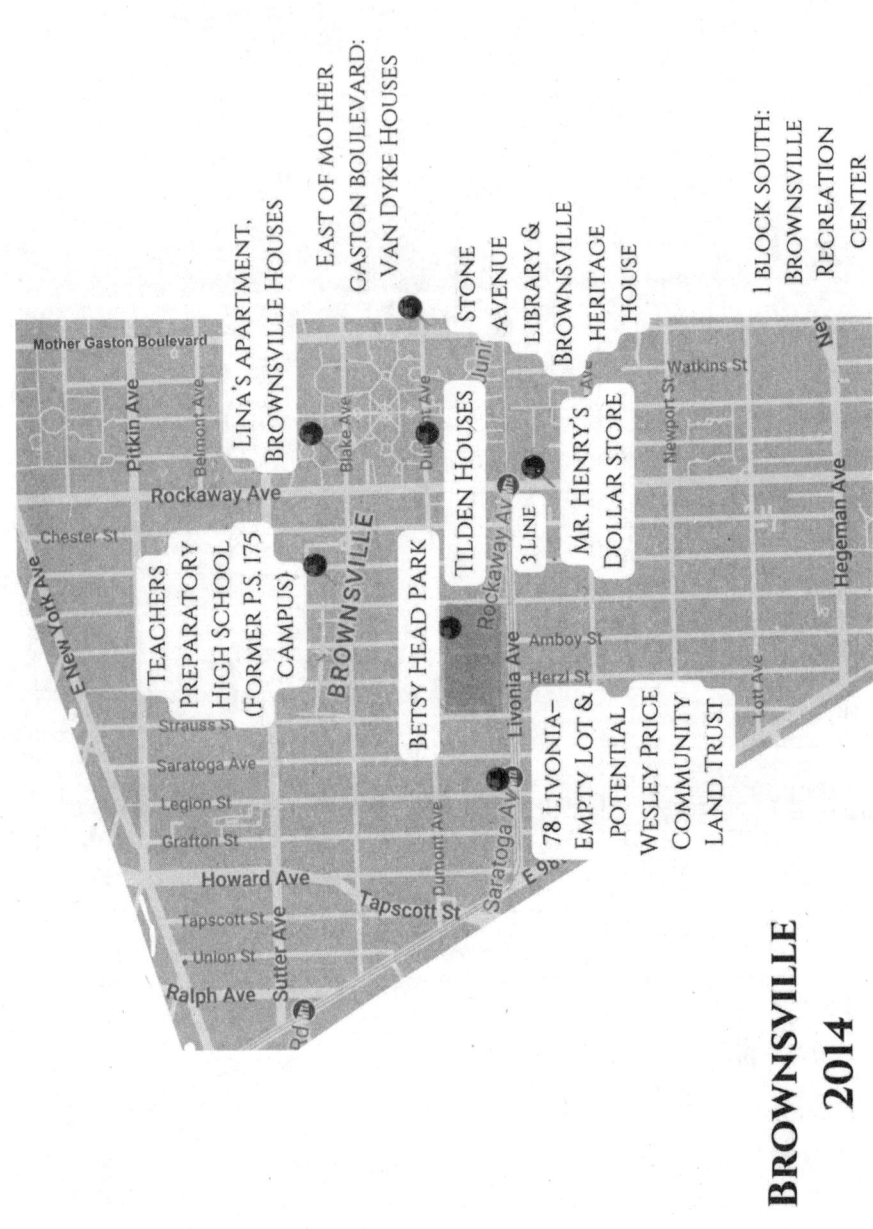

LINA'S APARTMENT,
BROWNSVILLE HOUSES

EAST OF MOTHER
GASTON BOULEVARD:
VAN DYKE HOUSES

STONE
AVENUE
LIBRARY &
BROWNSVILLE
HERITAGE
HOUSE

1 BLOCK SOUTH:
BROWNSVILLE
RECREATION
CENTER

TEACHERS
PREPARATORY
HIGH SCHOOL
(FORMER P.S. 175
CAMPUS)

TILDEN HOUSES

MR. HENRY'S
DOLLAR STORE

3 LINE

BETSY HEAD PARK

78 LIVONIA—
EMPTY LOT &
POTENTIAL
WESLEY PRICE
COMMUNITY
LAND TRUST

BROWNSVILLE
2014

GLOSSARY OF TOISANESE PHRASES

In the nineteenth and early twentieth century, the vast majority of Chinese immigrants to the United States spoke Toisanese (a relative of Cantonese). This changed dramatically in the second half of the twentieth century with the arrival of Cantonese and Mandarin speakers. Unlike Mandarin, China's official state language, Toisanese is not commonly taught, and there are few translation tools available to help English speakers learn the language. In many third- and fourth-generation American families of Toisanese descent, memory of the language is dying out.

Because novels are one means by which cultural memory is preserved, I felt it my responsibility to include Toisanese words in this book as well as a glossary to open the novel. As there are multiple dialects of Toisanese and multiple phonetic notation systems used to romanize the language, crafting the glossary required a multistep process. I adopted romanizations provided by International Phonetic Alphabet experts and Stephen Hsiao-Yi Li's online dictionary, then tweaked these—first to reflect the specific pronunciations used by my grandparents, and second, to adjust the phonetics for English readers.

It is of paramount importance to me that non-Chinese communities—especially the Black and brown communities who live alongside us in working-class, urban neighborhoods—have full access to the voices and thoughts of my Toisanese characters. Thus, this glossary is also meant as an open door, a warm welcome, and a commitment to mutual understanding.

A Bak	Great-Grandmother
an tat	egg custard tart
bai	bow (in worship or while paying respect to a deceased person)
bak diu	white beer
Bak Geng	Great-Grandfather
bak gui	white ghost, aka white people (colloquial, derogatory)
bou le	full (I've eaten to fullness)
bou wu ngoi	protect me
cha	tea
chiang fun	rice noodle rolls
Di Di	Older Sister
fat gao	steamed brown sugar cupcakes
fun sin geng dok	find new work
gen mai cha	brown rice green tea
geu biau cheng liang	time for a bath
gna toi	bean sprouts
Gu Po	Older Auntie (respectful)
Hai Pein Yiang	Big Even Sea, aka the Pacific Ocean
hak gui	black ghost, aka Black people (colloquial, derogatory)
heng bou	red envelope (used to gift money)
Hon Ngin Gai	Chinatown
hou gi	very expensive
hou hiak	delicious
hou ngai ham	very dangerous
ji ma wu	sesame pudding
jook	rice porridge
jook seing	Westernized, American-born person of Chinese descent

kui	he/she
lap chiang	sausage
mo gu gai pein	chicken with sliced mushrooms
Moi Moi	Little Sister
mou tou	shut up
Nam Gein	Nanjing
Ngen Ngen	Paternal Grandmother
Ni bong ni baba	you help your father
Ni ga doi hou	Your son's so . . .
ni het	you rest (a command)
Ni hiak fan miang?	Have you eaten?
Ni ou nai?	Where are you?
Ni so ga!	You're crazy! (Literally: You foolish melon!)
Ni to!	You sit! (a command)
no mai fan	sticky rice
On Fun	town in Toisan
siau mai	ground pork dumpling
Ting Ming	Clear Brightness Festival
to lok hui	sit down (a command)
Yia Yia	Paternal Grandfather

The pudding song, as recalled by Wun Kam Lew:

Ji ma wu!
Lek eu sa!
Liang fun yit won
Mou gong ga!

Sesame pudding!
Green pea paste!
Two cents a bowl
No discounts!

Dry summer morning, 1978. Smell of squirrel piss. Swallows chirping from a newspaper nest above a doorway. A long day ahead, on streets made into lapping rivers from the flow of unscrewed fire hydrants, below a blue sky with clouds like soapsuds. A day of chin-ups on the DON'T WALK signs.

Two boys walk home from the corner store. Cutoff jean shorts, white tees, secondhand Adidas. The older one bounces his Spalding off the brick walls; the younger one digs his fingers into a box of cornflakes for the plastic prize.

A voice calls to them from a parallel-parked car on Rockaway Avenue.

"Hey boys."

Eyes twitch over. Hands close around the Spalding, crinkle-fold the cereal bag. The two boys look at each other and then take three snailish steps toward the open window of the Lincoln, the older with his arm flung horizontal like hazard tape across his brother's chest.

"You want to make a hundred bucks?"

In the gloom of the car, a pale hand. Between two fingers, a flicker of green.

Gummed like insects on a reptile tongue, the boys are pulled toward the unknown face: a pair of thin lips etched on a marble-smooth chin, the eyes blacked out by shades.

Lina Rodriguez Armstrong saw them: two boys, no more than seven and ten, wispier than dandelion seeds, flying under the moon. From the second-floor window of her tenement, she watched as they darted from roof to roof and then crawled down the side of an abandoned house, the older one shushing the younger one's nervous cries.

It was three a.m., but Lina had been awake, cleaning up the spills and crumbs from the poster painting party. On the record player, Marvin Gaye's "Got to Give It Up" hummed loud enough to keep her eyelids open and a beat in her bones, soft enough to let the neighbors sleep. She'd fed almost twenty folks that night, and the odors of acrylics and fish fry lingered in the room. Her place had to be the most delicious-smelling apartment in Brownsville, Brooklyn: almost every day her Freedom School churned out the crispiest fish fry and the tastiest asopao in the neighborhood, and long before the Freedom School there'd been a Chinese restaurant, the essence of sesame chicken forever baked into the walls.

Now alone, she should have been washing dishes and brushes, but instead she was leaning on her elbows and peering out the window, wondering to herself if these were Sharon's boys—Sharon had been her classmate at Thomas Jefferson High—and then wondering what trouble they were up to, and if she should go after them, maybe entice them with leftovers from the Freedom Fridge.

That's when she smelled the smoke.

It was faint at first, and she sniffed the muggy night air, wondering if it was coming from a barbecue. In the light of the streetlamps, she spotted the Livonia Avenue cat—the kids called her Miss Freedom and sometimes left her bowls of tuna. Miss Freedom was now fleeing down the avenue, her mottled body almost airborne. As the smell intensified, Lina crossed to the front door of her apartment, undid the lock, and yanked the sticky door open.

Hot black smoke socked her in the face; the staircase had become a glowing, spastic frenzy.

Lina cried out, stumbling backward. Then, sucking in her breath, she hurried across the hall to her neighbor's door.

"Miss Brown!" she hollered. "There's a fire! Miss Brown!"

Annetta Brown unlatched the door, the baby on her shoulder. After one look into the hallway, she pulled Lina inside.

"Get Debbie and Kim!"

The two girls were asleep by the open window, their bodies curled like oven-hot pretzels, the sheets tossed aside. "What happened?" they moaned as Lina jostled them, dragging them onto their feet. Together, they all made for the fire escape. It shivered under their weight like it might give out and send them crashing in a shower of metal down to the sidewalk below. The baby bawled, the women and girls tiptoed, and at last Lina and the Brown family reached the ground and ran across the street. Only then did they look behind them and gasp: flames had engulfed both 78 and 80 Livonia Avenue. Smoke gushed out the windows of the two tenements like streams of ghosts, gray bodies dissipating as they ascended, losing shape in the sky above the tenement roofs. Other neighbors ran out the doors with their arms over their heads.

"This is what you did, Lina," Annetta cried, her face smeared with tears, her hair still in its bonnet. She took her children's hands from Lina's and pulled their quaking frames to her breast. "You done pushed that Mr. Wong!"

Lina looked at Annetta, looked at the girls, robbed of speech. All at once, her body became so heavy she had to sit on the curb. *Annetta blamed her.*

She realized then what it all meant—the two boys flying through the dark.

They'd lit the match.

Someone threw a towel over her shoulders. Another neighbor called the fire department. Flames ripped through the Freedom School banner, blasted the rusted Chinese restaurant sign, and licked the metal beams of the elevated rail. They lived on Livonia under the rumble of the 2 train, which came through every half hour at night, each car bombed front to back in bulbous lettering courtesy of local tagger NEVERFORGET68. Livonia itself was a street where every storefront was boarded up, or the glass shattered, the buildings stripped, and the plumbing exposed, and all around them, for blocks on end, the neighborhood of Brownsville was disintegrating: the parks littered with needles; the abandoned tenements yielding to nature, with dogs breeding in living rooms and rats crawling in the walls. The massive pool at Betsy Head Park had been closed since the Saturday a teenager had drowned in the deep end. Even Pitkin Avenue—Brooklyn's "Fifth Avenue," it was once called—was splayed like a cadaver on an autopsy table: its sidewalks littered with blood-spattered toys, muddy coats, and headless manikins. And at that moment, two boys were running east past the scarred landscape, back to Tilden Houses, looking carefully as they crossed the street—not for cars, but for stray dogs and lurching addicts.

Lina stared at the billowing flames and whispered to herself.

"They want it all. All of it. They took the junior high. Now they're taking the Freedom School."

Above the shouts and the crackling, collapsing wood, Lina heard a woman's scream from the third floor, a scratchy treble just familiar enough to twist Lina's gut.

Grandma, she thought. The old woman whom people in the neighborhood called Grandma.

"Grandma!" people cried from the sidewalk.

"Grandma's up there!"

There were no fire trucks in earshot. Lina's intestines knotted as she thought about what Annetta had said. Thought about Nellie. Had Nellie been there, she'd have wrapped Lina in her arms—held her captive. But Nellie was home, asleep.

Lina didn't have a choice. She would not be able to live with herself any other way.

Pulling her shirt collar over her mouth and nose, Lina sucked in her breath and ran into 80 Livonia.

Ducking as disintegrating tiles rained on her head, she raced up a staircase she could see only two steps at a time. One landing, then the next, hacking, eyes burning, pulled forward by that terrible pitch, she pushed through the smoke. A face charged at her—she shrieked, but it was a wall mirror and the face her own: thick eyebrows arched, Afro misshapen. She reached a room that radiated the neon red of an exit sign and crawled through it, her stomach brushing the floor, all the way to the whimpering body buried in a corner beneath a table.

"Grandma, can you hear me? Grandma, hold on to me. We got to get out of here!"

At that moment, the two boys reached Tilden Houses. *Sneaker Houses*, the older one had nicknamed it. Each of the eight brick monoliths in the complex had a yellow stripe painted up its length, the yellow interrupted by patches of brown brick, like a shoelace stitched in and out of the holes on a sneaker. That, and the buildings' whopping sixteen stories, distinguished Tilden from the other NYCHA projects directly to its north and east. On their way home through the neighborhood's west side, they'd passed heroin-starved bodies quaking into death and so many burned-down houses that their work seemed in keeping with the way of the world. The man had said: no one lived there—or, at least, no one was supposed to live there. Yet the older one was still worrying as they ran into Tilden, thinking about the little shoes he'd seen in the hallway of those Livonia buildings, the orange banner draped from a third-floor window.

— — —

"My brother! My brother!" the old woman cried between her coughs, her fingers pinched around Lina's wrist, and she pointed to the next room. Lina squinted through the smoke and the flames but could see nothing. Grandma had a brother?

"My brother! My brother!" the woman howled. Lina crawled three feet into the adjacent room, and at once, his screams pierced her. She smelled a putrid sweetness. Beside a bed, he was dancing, the wailing flesh ablaze. And that was when the ceiling collapsed.

"Grandma!" Lina cried, shielding her face from a waterfall of plaster. She backed out of the room, hurled herself toward the old woman, and lifted her by the armpits. "We got to go!"

"My brother! My brother!"

Two brothers slipped quietly into bed, side by side with their two little sisters, feigning sleep for their mother, feigning courage to each other, so agitated they would not sleep until dawn. The windows were open to the chatter on the road, the crunch of broken glass. But why be scared? They'd only obeyed orders. Only followed the steps, like a Duncan Hines recipe.

Lina tripped down three flights of stairs with the old woman in her arms, thinking she might collapse under the weight of Grandma's bones, that they might both, like the old man, be too late. She closed her eyes, swallowing her thirty-four years, and in her desperate fingers, the woman's hair became Nellie's hair. The woman's cries became her mother's keening.

Lina's feet moved before her, moved her down toward the door.

The older boy lay in bed thinking, at least it's over, at least the younger one is safe and out of trouble. The younger brother thinking, at last he's proven himself, at last he's shown the older he can be counted on. Each taking comfort in the thought of a hundred dollars.

— — —

The stairs dissolving under her . . .

A hundred dollars could buy a skateboard or *The Incredible Hulk* 225!

The crowd on the street, shrieking . . .

A hundred dollars could pay the next month's rent.

A beam of light, a spray of water. Tripping toward the light, toward the water . . .

A whole family trip to the RKO Albee Theatre!

The frame of the door, the fresh air, the crowd that took them in, gasping . . .

A bicycle! A ride at Coney Island! An escape!

Sirens, blocks away, too late . . .

A life far, far away from Brownsville.

They were Sharon's kids, as Lina had guessed: Billy and Francis. Lina would find that out later. She would hear it on the street and then she would see their picture in the *Daily News*—not their faces but their bare black backs, poking shoulder blades, and buzzed heads, hands against the wall. Spindly boys like feathers, and now to be blown far away.

The city would never find out who paid the boys, but Lina had known from the minute she'd first reached the sidewalk. She told all her neighbors, and she told the precinct captain, and then for almost forty years, no one asked her about it again.

SADIE

When NewGotham.com expanded its list of covered neighborhoods to include Brownsville, Brooklyn, the editors knew they ought to hire a Black reporter. Yet, as they sifted through the fifty applications they received after emailing their university contacts, they discovered not many Black people had applied. Of these, the editors selected only two for an interview, and by the last round, they had five prospects: four white people, and Sadie Chin.

It was a relief to the *New Gotham* editors to find her. Twenty-three-year-old Sadie had graduated in 2013 from Yale University. She didn't have a journalism master's, but she'd participated in the Yale Journalism Initiative and interned at *The New York Times*. She'd also performed well on the copyediting test, and her references sang high praise. But the thing that made the editors choose her—even over some of the candidates with the j-school degree—was that Sadie was from Brooklyn; said her family used to live in Brownsville, and even though her surname suggested an East Asian heritage, she looked kind of Latina.

That was how Sadie Chin landed her first salaried job in the summer of 2014, reporting in a neighborhood to which she'd never been. She'd only sat in the back seat of a cab driving through Brownsville on the way to JFK Airport, always with the windows rolled up because her father feared the squeegee men on Eastern Parkway. Jason Chin had spent his early years in Brownsville; his family had run a Chinese restaurant there. The Chins had been among but a handful of Chinese in a mostly Jewish, then mostly Black neighborhood. But that had been a long time ago, and Sadie had grown up miles away, in Park Slope.

Yet Sadie had also taken a bunch of urban policy and African American Studies courses at Yale, and she believed marginalized neighborhoods deserved thorough coverage of their many social issues, including everything from police violence to fresh produce access. And—as she'd added in the interview to demonstrate her knowledge of local politics—with the new mayor in office, it was bound to be an important year in Brownsville and neighborhoods like it, as the mayor had promised to implement a range of initiatives to meet the needs of working people.

On her first day of employment, she took the B train from her family's brownstone in Park Slope to the *New Gotham* office. It was in SoHo, on the second floor of a loft building that smelled like varnished wood and Windex. There was a room of desks for the reporters, along with an office for Simon Evans, the executive director, and another for the executive editor, Wendy Nilsson. It was so exciting, so *legit*, Sadie thought during the office tour. No more internships! She had a real staff job, a real press pass dangling from her neck. *New Gotham* wasn't exactly *The New York Times*, but it still got more than eight hundred thousand digital visitors per month.

Growing up, Sadie had been unsure what vocation to pursue. She'd known early on she was not destined to write poetry and fiction like her parents; she lacked the patience to sit in a melancholic gloom for hours, coming up with metaphors to describe the intricacies of her emotions. She was, rather, an information-processor, a go-getter. Then she'd discovered journalism in college, and it seemed to incorporate her varied skills. She had good syntax—this, at least, she'd inherited from her parents. She loved research and getting lost in Wikipedia. Extroverted: she liked to ask questions. One could say she'd never gotten over that kindergarten phase of poking her nose into everything. At Yale, she'd attracted boys with her ability to absorb their mansplaining on *World of Warcraft*, quantum physics, renewable energy policy, or whatever else. So, she'd enrolled in as many journalism classes as possible, applied to every paid and unpaid journalism internship in New York, and updated her Twitter bio to "investigative reporter: all opinions my own."

After her introduction to the *New Gotham* office, Sadie was expected to be in the field for the rest of the week. Her father remained uneasy about Brownsville: *How will you get home if there's an event after dark? Have you checked which streets to avoid?* It was taking great effort from her mother to calm him down and remind him that the *bad old days* were over.

For Sadie, it was the neighborhood's bad reputation that made it a draw—that and the fact that her family had lived there and was now so afraid of it. Brownsville was the underdog, the type of place she'd read about in her coursework at Yale, and she secretly wished she could claim it as her own. After all, it was embarrassing to go to Yale and say you were from Brooklyn and then, when another student from East Flatbush or Bed-Stuy or some actual Brooklyn neighborhood overheard and piped up, "For real? Where you from?" to have to admit you were just from yuppified Park Slope.

August 4 was her first day in Brownsville, and Sadie was proud to find she was not scared—most of the time, at least. On the blocks between Howard Avenue and Thomas S Boyland Street, she passed several neat rows of two-story brick homes, some adorned with garden gnomes, others with Jamaican, Haitian, or St. Lucian flags. She visited Betsy Head Park and encountered a humongous public pool brimming with children. Pitkin Avenue, the main thoroughfare on the north side, was busy and alive, people going in and out of the salons, pharmacies, and fast-food restaurants. True, she was more nervous when walking on the east side, up and down Rockaway Avenue. She'd never seen so much public housing in one place, complexes and their courtyards sprawled block after block. It was a forest of NYCHA apartments, so dense she couldn't see where it all ended. Growing up, her father had always instructed her to avoid "the projects."

And then there was Livonia Avenue. That was where, according to her father, the restaurant had been—the Chinese restaurant run by her grandparents so long ago. Sadie went in search of 78 Livonia Avenue only to discover a giant empty lot. In fact, there were hardly any buildings on Livonia at all, just vast stretches of land overgrown with weeds and choked with car parts and broken appliances. There were no people around to interview, though a splotchy cat stopped its prowling in the weeds to gawk at Sadie.

Sadie goggled at the abandonment. She was amazed Brooklyn still had so much wasted space, and she wondered whether the mayor had development plans for Livonia Avenue. It was a bit disappointing; she had been hoping to find artifacts from her family's past, ghostly remnants of the grandfather and great-grandfather she'd never met—evidence that she did, in fact, belong in Brownsville.

Sadie sent a picture of the block to her father, along with a message:

Where did all the buildings
go????

Of course, he wouldn't know. Her father hadn't set foot in Brownsville since he was seven years old. She thought about asking her grandmother, who had worked at the restaurant. Her dad worried Ngen Ngen would be upset to learn the location of Sadie's new job, but at least Ngen Ngen would have stories to share.

Walking beneath the long torso of the elevated rail was like visiting the underbelly of the suspended whale at the Natural History Museum. Sadie took a picture of a station pillar that served as a bulletin board for a range of predatory advertisements: CASH 4 HOMES and BAD CREDIT? NO PROBLEM. She posted the pic on Twitter, then checked her notifications for likes and reposts from her 207 followers.

Not everyone in Brownsville was Black. There were some Latino people, and with her waist-length black hair and round, cashew-hued face, Sadie looked kind of like one and hoped she might be mistaken for a local. Yet that first week in the field, hardly anyone was fooled. She wasn't sure what gave her away: something about her enunciation, which, like her parents', bore the sharp consonants and meticulous diction of the Ivy League educated, or her brisk gait, or maybe the denim shortalls were a tad too hipster.

Always, the men outside bodegas would stare at her, and they would not catcall; they would squint. Occasionally she'd stop to take advantage of their interest, to ask whether police conduct had changed under the new administration and what they thought of the Eric Garner case, and she'd scribble their answers in her notebook. Yet the truth was, all the stares kind of unnerved her. Wasn't she supposed to be the one doing the staring?

She didn't always understand the language. When she interviewed the woman with the cat-eye sunglasses sitting on the steps of the homeless shelter, the lady explained that she had "DV issues" and had sent her kids to live with an aunt.

"DV?" Sadie repeated. "Can you spell that?"

"This is a domestic violence shelter." The woman lowered her glasses and glared at Sadie. "You know what *that* is?"

Some people, by contrast, were too friendly—like that one guy in the red tracksuit who sat on a beach chair outside a barbershop on Mother Gaston Boulevard, hands on his long thighs. He called to Sadie every time she passed by.

"Hey miss! Miss! You need an apartment? I've got a good place for a young professional like you. Ocean Hill, right off the A!"

"I'm from here," she replied each time.

As a Brooklynite whose family had once lived in Brownsville, and as someone who had spent the last year hanging out with a bunch of millennial transplants who assumed she was just another one of them, another trust fund baby, which—as she made clear whenever possible—she wasn't, it was hard for her to accept that to Brownsville, she was just another outsider. She might not have been from Brownsville, but she'd known Brooklyn before roof gardens and thirty-dollar brunch entrées. She'd known Park Slope when Park Slope was still two-dollar pizza folded in half, motor pony rides, and Marinos Italian Ices scooped with a wooden spoon.

But there was no way to explain this to the people sitting in plastic chairs on the street. She lived for those few moments when the Dominican shopkeepers and the Puerto Rican delivery workers misidentified her as one of their own, greeting her as "mi amor." She could speak only a little Spanish but enjoyed the misimpression for as long as she could. Her Spanish was better than her Chinese, at any rate.

Her third week on the beat, however, her Chinese heritage became strangely relevant. It was a hot day in late August, and she was interviewing store owners about the difficulties faced by small businesses. For her last interview, she entered a 99 Cents store on Rockaway Avenue that lacked air-conditioning but smelled of clean plastic. Its shelves brimmed with every possible plastic import that a household could require: shower caps and pillboxes and toilet scrubbers. The owner agreed to answer her interview questions:

"How long have you been running this store?"

"What should the new mayor do to help businesses in Brownsville?"

"What are the pros and cons of running a business near the elevated rail?"

His name was Pierre Henry, and he'd emigrated from St. Lucia thirty years prior. He sat calmly behind the cash register curling ribbons with the edge of some scissors as they discussed the commercial vacancies on the block and the shooting down the street the week before. Just as they were finishing their conversation, a woman in scrubs entered the store and pushed a middle-aged man in a wheelchair up to the cash register.

"Mr. William," saluted Pierre Henry, leaning over the counter to greet the man. The caretaker disappeared into the toiletries aisle. "Summer long enough for you?"

"Summer," the customer repeated, his voice like a stuttering motor. His eyes narrowed on Sadie.

Pierre Henry nodded toward her. "She's a reporter. She's asking me some questions about the challenges of business in Brownsville."

"Good afternoon," Sadie said, extending her hand, but Mr. William didn't reach for hers.

The man was thick-bodied, with salt-and-pepper hair, and he wore a faded Earth, Wind & Fire T-shirt. His face lagged on one side and his fingers curled in his lap. As Sadie studied him, he studied her—his eyes sternly fixed on her.

"What . . . paper?" Mr. William asked.

"*New Gotham*. It's a newish paper. NewGotham.com."

"You . . . Where are you from?"

Sadie hugged her notebook to her chest.

"Brooklyn!" she answered, sidestepping what she knew he was really asking.

"Where are your people from?"

"I'm mixed."

"What's the mix?"

He would wrench out the whiteness, broadcast this news to the people of Brownsville.

"So my mom, she's, like, Jewish American. And my dad is Chinese American."

"Chinese," he said, nodding, as if he had discovered the key to her.

Relieved he hadn't latched on to the Jewish part, she smiled. Perhaps he had only wanted to know what type of POC she was. In fact, maybe he'd appreciate her family's personal connection to Brownsville.

"My grandparents used to run a Chinese restaurant on Livonia Avenue. Many decades ago."

The man gripped the handles of his wheelchair. "Wong. Your grandfather was Mr. Wong?"

"Richard Chin. Our last name is Chin. I'm Sadie Chin." She reached out her hand again, but the man only continued to glower. At this point, the nurse returned with a roll of paper towels and a box of Efferdent Denture Cleanser. She handed a twenty to Pierre Henry, who had been listening to the exchange with amusement.

When the nurse took hold of the wheelchair handles, Mr. William twisted around and hollered.

"Wait!"

Painfully, he strained against the weight of his bones and, hands on the arms of the wheelchair, raised himself to his feet. Sadie caught a whiff of the man on her breath: the smell of Tic Tacs and old newspapers.

"What's wrong, Mr. William? Let me help you!" said the nurse, touching his arm. "What do you want?"

He swatted her away.

Extending his left arm, he jutted a trembling hand in Sadie's direction and began to unclench his fingers.

"Liar!" he cried, pointing at her. "Mr. Wong! Ask your grandfather about the people he killed!"

"Wait, what?"

"Mr. Wong. The landlord. It was him!"

"What nonsense you telling that girl?" the nurse cried.

"Wait, but . . ." Sadie stuttered. "I'm not related to anyone named Wong."

"Mr. Wong is a murderer!"

"I don't know about no Mr. Wong the murderer," said Pierre Henry. "But, Mr. William, the girl already told you! She not related to that man. Her name is Chin."

Mr. William glared at the shopkeeper. "You West Indians weren't around then."

Quickly, Sadie rummaged in her purse for her press pass, and she handed it to Mr. William, hoping this proof would settle the matter.

The man took the press pass and held it an inch from his face. "Chin," he mumbled, and embarrassment quivered across his cheeks. Sadie stifled a sigh of relief.

Suddenly, Mr. William was swaying on his feet, and both Sadie and the nurse launched forward to steady him. He held Sadie's shoulder—his hand heavy, his eyes averted. Then he sat back down in the wheelchair, his pupils fixed bitterly on the floor.

"Okay, we're done," the nurse laughed. "We going home now. Time to go home and stop saying crazy things to people." She rolled her eyes and pushed Mr. William out of the store.

Sadie turned to Pierre Henry with her mouth open.

"What exactly just happened?"

Pierre Henry smiled and shrugged.

"Don't worry about it," he said, and he spun his index finger around his ear. "Something wrong with him."

"But was there actually a murderer named Mr. Wong?"

"Who can say? I've been here a long time. But he's been here longer."

Sadie unlocked her bike from the parking sign and pedaled homeward. Soon she was back on Eastern Parkway, that major boulevard connecting the east and west sides of Brooklyn, linking Brownsville to the Park Slope brownstones, her bike whizzing in the opposite direction of the cabs on their way to the airport. She passed the crowd of Hasidic Jews gathered outside the world headquarters of Chabad Lubavitch, people with whom she may have shared a distant ancestor. Yet she didn't really see any of them as, over and over, she relived the interaction at the 99 Cents store.

She was shaken, but there was no reason to be upset, she told herself. The man had probably survived a stroke. Especially in a neighborhood like Brownsville where there'd never been many Chinese people, it was natural that he'd mix her up with someone else.

When Sadie reached Park Slope, it seemed more pretentious than ever: the boutique clothing shops, the brownstones with their nineteenth-century post lights, the curated sidewalk gardens adorned with signs instructing dog owners not to let their pups pee. Add to that the obliviousness of the yuppies as they skirted around the same man on Carroll Street who'd been sitting on a stool and jingling quarters in a coffee cup for two decades. Again, she wished she wasn't from Park Slope.

Sadie strung her bike to her parents' gate and unlocked the door of the brownstone.

"Dad!" she yelled into the hallway. "Have you heard of some landlord in Brownsville named Mr. Wong?"

Then she remembered: her parents had gone to the Village to see Chekhov's *The Seagull*. She had the house to herself.

Sadie ascended the creaky stairs to the second floor. Everywhere there were shelves of books: Henry James, Tu Fu, the Brontës, Amy Tan, Hawthorne, Ginsberg—these were her parents' bibles. Yellowing pages and crumbling plaster was the smell of home. At least, she consoled herself, her parents were not like other Park Slopers. They didn't have a second home upstate, didn't use professional cleaning services. They threw Billy Joel on the stereo and danced around with feather dusters. This modesty had to count for something. Plus, the fact that she still lived in a Park Slope brownstone instead of a tenement in Bushwick like others from Yale—well, that was because she was trying to save money, to pay back her student loans.

Sadie reached her bedroom. She ran her fingers over the Lord Shiva sculpture that she'd bought at a Tibetan store, then held a staring contest with a beaded Nigerian mask from a street fair. Sadie remembered the time Aaliyah, a friend at Yale, had remarked that white people should stop buying African masks—that this was *cultural appropriation*. Sadie had nodded without telling Aaliyah that she had one at home.

In some ways, her whole life was a series of out-of-context cultural objects. Growing up, she'd eaten Ngen Ngen's fish cakes and Grandma's latkes, indulged in red heng bou envelopes and Hanukkah gelt, burned incense sticks and eight candles, bowed at the cemeteries and recited Baruch Atah Adonai. But not to any extreme: no weekend Hebrew school, no Chinese language class. The best of both worlds without the strings: two rounds of gifts in winter, two cultural New Years, everything duplicated like a Happy Meal when they've accidentally thrown two toys on your tray. Her parents had always said she was incredibly lucky to inherit two cultures.

Yet sitting at her desk, she couldn't get Mr. William's words out of her head. She searched for "Brownsville" and "Wong" in *The New York Times* Time Machine archive.

There are no results matching your search.

She thought back to the Decolonizing History course she'd taken at Yale, where she'd studied the concept of the "model minority." Perhaps this Wong dude had gotten away with murder because the police chose to believe him. Maybe it was her purpose to reveal the truth. She would find Chinese people who would talk to her because she was half Chinese. It was the story that would enlist all her identities, her talents—and in the process, she'd learn something about her own family's life in the neighborhood.

Sadie took out her journal and jotted down some notes to save for later.

THE WONGS

On the corner of Saratoga and Livonia, under the elevated rail in Brownsville, Brooklyn, there was once a Chinese sit-down restaurant called Canton Kitchen. Beef chow mein sold for seventy-five cents, sweet-and-sour shrimp for fifty cents, chicken egg soup for four dimes. Customers patted their mouths with baby-soft yellow napkins and sometimes gazed at the altar with that little red-faced, bearded warrior statue clutching a golden staff. On most nights, the room brimmed with sound—a chop suey of clinking teacups, Yiddish, and screeches from the El.

The restaurant's owner was a man named Chin Koon Lai.

Koon Lai was born in Toisan, a rural county of Canton Province, in 1903, the year of the rabbit, and even before the rabbit returned, the village knew he was the perfect candidate for America.

He learned the meaning of diligence young. So young that at the time, he needed help reaching the hen eggs at the top of the coop. That was when his mother was still alive, hobbling across the thatch house on her bound feet that looked and smelled like shriveled apples. He ate with her and the babies in the kitchen while the grown men ate in the front room. At all times, they kept wine in the glass for the statue of the warrior Kwan, and if someone fell sick, they'd believe the person possessed, and they would circle the bed, chanting and begging the demon to leave.

One day in his eighth year, a few weeks after the Spring Festival, Koon Lai heard a roar of voices from the Chin village gate. He slipped from the hut to join the crowd of men: they had gathered to greet a wagon of soldiers who brought news from the capital. Koon Lai noticed a bottle of bak diu being passed hand to hand. He watched the smaller children scurrying forward to touch the wagon. Then the village men brought their house chairs to the outdoors, and with laughter, they took turns slicing off each other's mandated braids. The Manchus were gone: no more "Lose your hair, lose your head!"

"China is free!" the villagers cried.

"China for the people!"

He was too young to understand the meaning of *democracy*, and perhaps no one did. For, as he would think years later, how could a people who had known only emperors for five thousand years grasp the concept of "republic"?

Yet everyone believed a miracle had occurred. Though their bellies still ached from the New Year's feast, the villagers threw a second celebration. They looked out at the miles of rice, sorghum, and pumpkin fields and imagined future years of bounty, and so they roasted a pig and a chicken from each household.

Decades later, the smell of squashed ginkgo nuts on the sidewalks of Brooklyn would remind Koon Lai of this misjudgment, and of the many bad harvests in the years that followed. Then, there was no meat, and the peasants ate nothing but ginkgo jook. Just like always, typhoons ripped through the paddies, landlords seized the grain, and functionaries leeched the remainder. In the year of the ox, his mother died of fever, and his father and uncles took what little they had to the teahouse in Toisan City and lost it all playing mahjong.

Koon Lai decided then that his family's survival had nothing to do with dynasties or democracies; it depended solely on the sensibilities of its able men. When he was fourteen, he hopped on a rickshaw bound for Canton City, where he peddled oysters for an old fisherman, sleeping in a rain-soaked shack along the Pearl River. In this way, Koon Lai fed his siblings and his drunk gambler of a father.

After many seasons in Canton listening to the wash of the river, watching it flow out to the Hai Pein Yiang—the Big Even Sea—his mother came to speak with him. By then, eight years had passed since the morning he had folded five hundred sheets of joss paper into golden houses and burned them for her, sending her shelter for heaven. Eight years since his father, awash in diu, had dug her hole on the muddy hill, then poured the rest of his liquor on the soil of the grave.

She arrived in the shack at dawn, dripping wet and covered in barnacles. Her white gown, the one in which they'd dressed her for the funeral rites, left a glistening stripe on the wood floor. She sat on the edge of Koon Lai's cot while he, lying prone, stared up at her, and then she leaned over and stroked his hair. She smelled of salt, her eyes gleamed like oyster pearls, and she still wore that tiny pair of lotus shoes, small enough to fit in his palm.

First son, she said, though her lips remained closed. *You must go.*
Go where?

But he knew, as soon as she left, that he needed to cross the Hai Pein Yiang.

Venture to the New World. Make money. Send it home.

The next day, he asked the fishermen how to do it. The Americans had written laws to prevent Chinese people from entering their country. To be admitted, they explained, you had to be the son or grandson of an existing resident—or at least bear papers saying you were. For a hefty sum, you could buy false papers, become someone's "paper son." And so, Koon Lai spent the next year saving up to buy himself a fake father, a fake family. In America, Chin Koon Lai would be Wong Koon Lai, the paper son of a New York merchant named Wong Man Chan.

Koon Lai left his homeland in 1922, after his nineteenth birthday. He carried little with him: a single maroon suitcase containing one change of clothes, a notebook with the correct answers to the questions at customs, a picture of his mother, and a bag of dried sour plums. "Mama, bou wu ngoi," he whispered to the photograph each night on the ship.

During the four-week boat ride to Vancouver, Koon Lai sketched in the notebook a plan for his success:

生活必需品 :   四分之一
家人必需品: 四分之一
新家建設: 四分之一
村路, 村间, 渠道: 四分之一

He would keep only a fourth of his earnings for daily expenses, and the other three-fourths would go to Toisan: one-fourth to feed his family, another fourth to commission the construction of a new house, and the last to repair the village irrigation system. No longer would his people be poor tenants on the land. He would buy the land. They would live in grand houses, and their children would be fat.

At night in the ship hold, he dreamed of his little brothers and sisters lined up hand to shoulder, playing Catch the Dragon's Tail. When he awoke, it pained him to realize all his people were far away. He was alone, adrift in a vast, blue sameness that was deeper and quieter than grief. Then, as the New World approached, he began to doubt his ability to survive. He spoke only a few words of English. He knew nothing about America's customs. Again and again, he reminded himself there would be other Toisanese men in America to welcome and guide him.

From Vancouver, he took a train east, then rode a horse-drawn wagon over the border. For four years he worked at a restaurant on Mott Street in New York City's Chinatown, bunking with six other Toisanese workers in a storage closet at the back of the restaurant. They shared a toilet with the customers.

It was not the America that Koon Lai had imagined. Still, he learned to ignore the water bugs that crawled on his sheets at night, to hold his breath while crossing the gutters stuffed with chicken feathers, and eventually, to sleep through the police raids at the gambling den and the gunshots between battling tongs.

During smoking breaks, Koon Lai and the workers stood outside the restaurant and took in the obscenities of Mott Street. Sometimes, their countrymen would stage fights in the middle of the road, smearing pig blood on their chests and pretending to be wounded with the hope of squeezing a few extra bucks from the American onlookers. Koon Lai and his fellow workers watched the bak gui watching. Bak gui, *white ghost*, was what they called the white people.

Other times, they would talk about Sun Yat-sen's efforts to unify the motherland.

"Soon the whole country is Kuomintang. The warlords can get lost," a coworker would say.

"Canton was the anus. Now Canton is the heart!"

"Get me an account in his Central Bank!"

Koon Lai said nothing, but he wondered if he had been too quick to dismiss the importance of politics. Sun Yat-sen would change the country. He would take China, a nation brittle as a shrimp chip, and build it into one as strong, unified, and proud as the United States.

There was one thing, however, that nearly broke Koon Lai, and this was the American winter: the nights he wore his overcoat and boots to bed, and still could not fall asleep; the constant tension in his shoulders; the numbness in his digits; the difficulty of knowing when the snow on the curb was hard enough to cross and when he might sink into it, soaking his trousers. His fellow workers maintained that bak gui men survived it because they had mothers, sisters, and wives to coddle them, to tend fireplaces and decorate the apartment doors with evergreen. The workers had no women of their own, they liked to gripe, for thirteen thousand kilometers.

Still, Koon Lai's industriousness made him one of the most prized young men in the community. One day, when he was visiting the Chinese Consolidated Benevolent Association, he was introduced by his paper father to Lee Jung Yu, an older man with a proud strut and a neck layered like a rooster's. Mr. Lee owned a restaurant in Brooklyn, and in his winter years, he wished to return to China and pass the restaurant to a prospective son-in-law. He invited Koon Lai for cha on Bayard Street, and as they sipped, Mr. Lee boasted about the three kilometers of rice fields he had bought for his village, now tended by laborers from San Wui. After many such cha, during which Koon Lai mostly listened and expressed admiration, Mr. Lee pronounced Koon Lai the perfect match for his daughter in Toisan. As Koon Lai nervously deflected the compliments, Mr. Lee took a red heng bou and stuck it in Koon Lai's breast pocket: round-trip tickets for the train and ship.

When Koon Lai arrived in Toisan, everyone in the village believed he was a rich man. He had already sent three-fourths of his earnings home, but the villagers goaded him for more. As he forked over the remainder of his earnings, he worried about giving away too much, but his mother said otherwise. He saw her frequently, often as a reflection in the village water well, or by the mountain stream, her white dress bubbling up like foam.

He agreed to marry the girl, who was five years his junior. In truth, he wasn't pleased that Lee Suet Fong sipped her tea before the elders sipped theirs, and he didn't love how easily she was distracted by the voices of her age-mates outside the window. But those were superficial things, things she would grow out of, he told himself. And so came the silk sedan carrying the bride, the village feast, the obligatory consummation, and after a few weeks Koon Lai was on his way back to America, to Brooklyn, to a place called Livonia Avenue in the Jewish ghetto of Brownsville.

He arrived on the elevated rail, dressed in a Western suit and a bowler hat; he blended in with the European immigrants, at least from the back. His destination was sandwiched next to the station, upstairs from a hardware store and a tailor's shop, adjacent to a row of tenements. In those apartments lived the fabric cutters and roofers and toymakers of Brooklyn, many of them from Poland, Russia, and Germany. The stone pillars of the rail advertised all sorts of jobs accessible to the immigrant. With his rudimentary English, Koon Lai

could read two of the posters: BE A DOLL—WORK FOR THE DOLL FAC-
TORY and CUT STEAK, PAY GREAT.

In the hardware store, Koon Lai met the landlord, Arnold Cohen,
who owned both 78 Livonia and the tenement next door. Mr. Lee
had spoken of the Jew's fatness and of his generosity; the man would
gladly accept rent a week late. Mr. Cohen turned over the keys and
led Koon Lai upstairs to the restaurant, on the second floor. It consisted of a large front room with ten tables that sat fifty customers, a
back room for sleeping—twice as large as the storage closet on Mott
Street—a kitchen with an icebox, and two kerosene stoves.

The location, too, was perfect, as the restaurant was easy to
spot from the Saratoga station. It helped that Mr. Lee had hung a tin
sign out the window—it announced in large red letters, CHOW MEIN
HERE!

In the years that followed, Koon Lai poured all his energy into the
success of Canton Kitchen. Business was very good at first. Every
night, the tables overflowed with cream-and-walnut shrimp, chicken
lo mein, chop suey, crunchy egg rolls, and beef and broccoli—all
swimming in thick gravy and overdressed in hoisin and soy sauce,
just how the Americans liked it. There were the laborers from the
Long Island Railroad tracks who swarmed them at lunchtime, de-
vouring multiple rounds of chow fun, and also the girls and boys in
courtship, who played footsie under the table. He even had a rabbi
who came every Monday at seven o'clock and sat in the window
reading a Jewish prayer book while sipping his favorite chicken-chive
wonton soup.

In addition to the usual specials, Koon Lai offered combos: one
vegetable, meat, and rice; or two meats, one vegetable, and rice. He
had already observed that bak gui liked to have their own plates and
grew anxious if they had to share. When the children babbled in fake
Chinese, when the young men hollered in jest, "Mr. Wong, you got
any dog on the menu?" Koon Lai would grin widely and kid them
back in his broken English.

"You like dog? Dog every week?"

The customers never asked if Koon Lai had a wife, a child, or whether his parents were in good health, but he didn't mind this, for explaining in English would have been difficult. He had a son, too, which was a wonder to him. The child's name was Dun Ho, and Koon Lai had yet to meet him.

As for Koon Lai's father, Baba had a bad liver and rotted teeth and talked of nothing but how his friends had cheated him in the mahjong tea parlors. Koon Lai's mother never visited him in America, as if even ghosts were subject to the exclusion law.

Definitely for the best that no one asked.

It went on like this for a few more years, up until the day of the stock market crash. Then the textile factory closed, and the workers abandoned the construction sites, leaving cement blocks scattered around like chunks of a bludgeoned monument. Within a few weeks, half his Brownsville customers disappeared, leaving his meats to sour. Instead, he found his bak gui standing in the food pantry lines with their bowler hats pulled low over their brows. Profits dwindled, and downstairs, the hardware store shuttered after thirty years in business.

Koon Lai went to Chinatown and learned that many of his compatriots had declared bankruptcy. Some had not survived their devastation; on Church Avenue, workers had discovered Mr. Fong dangling from the kitchen light fixtures, already two days decayed.

Koon Lai hated to borrow, but he had cut back on both his own expenses and the money he sent to China, and he still was short on rent. At the association, he found several ruined business owners smoking cigars, drinking diu, and scrambling mahjong tiles. They tried to convince him to join their game, but he stood at the edge of the four-player tables with his arms crossed, lying that he had no luck, that he would surely lose.

At last, the association president smiled and handed Koon Lai a heng bou containing a whole one hundred American dollars. Bowing with gratitude, Koon Lai took his leave and headed toward the City Hall subway station. When he made it to Foley Square, he found a crowd of bak gui swarming the roads and sidewalks. They lifted cardboard signs into the air and chanted a rhyme he could not understand.

These were the kind of men who had lost everything—their jobs, their houses—the kind who were gathering in the parks. Unshaved, in tattered coats and stained trousers, their bodies gave off a rancid odor. Koon Lai had seen some of the makeshift dwellings built with orange crates on Houston Street, and he had read in the *Mun Hey Weekly* that these men lit fires in trash cans and cooked pigeons in clay pots, just like in China.

These are bak gui, Koon Lai thought, rushing past them. *And even they think yelling makes food appear.*

Then there was a skirmish, and before he knew what was happening, Koon Lai was thrown to the ground. Pain shot through his elbows and knees, and as he cried out, he felt someone cuff his wrists. He was tugged to his feet by a police officer, rounded up with a slew of the bak gui, and slammed into a windowless truck.

Winded, shocked dumb, trembling, divorced from his arms, Koon Lai let out a garbled cry, grabbing at the few English words that came to him.

"I don't have the problem!"

Someone, everyone, began laughing.

"Seems to me like you have a problem."

A smack of spit on his neck.

He was quiet after that. They drove past the government buildings, the breadlines, the Houston encampments, the shivering prostitutes. Then they crossed a bridge to a large fort where each man was forced to empty his pockets.

He held the heng bou to his breast.

"This a gift. A gift from friend."

The police officers tore it from him, guffawed when they saw the amount, one of them pocketing it. They handled him more aggressively, calling him a thief, throwing him into one of the cages with ten other men.

Koon Lai, terrified, tucked himself in a corner and tried to make himself small. Yet there was one bak gui prisoner, the angriest and loudest of the bunch, who wouldn't leave him alone. This bak gui stood over him, gesticulating.

Then, sudden quiet.

Then, the hum of a zipper.

Then, a stream of hot piss dribbling into Koon Lai's hair.

Down his neck. Under his shirt.

Koon Lai didn't make a sound. He remained as still as the Guardian Kwan. Eventually the aggressor left him alone, as if he had concluded Koon Lai was an unfeeling object.

Koon Lai lay in half-conscious misery for hours until he woke to another putrid wetness—his own. Sitting up, he found the bak gui men asleep on the floor and on the benches, and his mind turned toward the money. He didn't know how he would repay the debt to the association or keep the restaurant afloat.

Another thought came, with the swiftness of a cook's cleaver. *I've been proud*, he brooded. He had been feeling superior to the gamblers at the association, to his father, to the bak gui—but in truth, he was just as careless.

With this self-flagellation, Koon Lai tortured himself for hours— and yet, when he looked around at the cell with all its sleeping bak gui prisoners, something kept lifting in his breast, a butterfly-fluttering of hope. He had failed, but he would do better when he got out, if he had the chance. He would be cautious with every penny. He begged the ancestors for mercy.

Still, it was terrible not knowing how long he would be kept there or what his family would do without his earnings. He regretted that he had not brought a photograph of Suet Fong to America. He wondered if she missed him or if she, too, was forgetting what there was to miss.

In a letter, Suet Fong had written that the baby at his first grab party had reached for everything in sight: the medicine balls, the abacus, the stamps, the oranges—one after the other, he scooped them up, stuffing what he could in his mouth. Chin village now joked that the baby was destined to be a businessman of international fame, or maybe the world's greatest inventor.

But he was no baby now. Koon Lai had memorized the birth date; Dun Ho was two years and eleven months old. He prayed that he might survive to hold the child on his lap.

Koon Lai was released to the streets just a few hours later. Returning to Brownsville, he begged Mr. Cohen for extra days to pay the rent. He had never availed himself of Mr. Cohen's leniency in the past, and the landlord rewarded him by granting an additional month. With double resolve, Koon Lai promised himself that he would never drink diu, gamble, or buy a woman's touch. He would keep his earnings under lock and key and slash the prices until the neighborhood returned.

During the years that followed, the textile factory reopened, and the men returned to the construction sites. Mr. Cohen filled the vacancy downstairs, and business at Canton Kitchen improved. In time, Koon Lai was able to pay his debt to the association and resume remittances to Toisan.

Yet, although he should have been satisfied by this—although he resumed his title as village hero and recovered the respect of the association—something was not well with him. He would have described it as a dry ache in his back, a weight under the ribs, a blueness in his peripheral vision. He felt it most during the Chinese New Year, or when a big family came to his restaurant, jiggling babies on their knees.

He complained to no one, confided in no one. But it was as his mother had always used to say:

Gu sin jiak yein.

A body with only a shadow for company.

It was his friends at the association who reminded him about "the seed," as they liked to call it. The seed he had planted in China the night of his wedding, the most powerful seed in the darkest, most ripe soil. This seed had grown rapidly into a fruitful plant, they pointed out, and now that plant could be seized by the roots.

Koon Lai came to agree. In the spring of 1935, the year of the pig, he paid for the boat ticket to bring his eight-year-old son to America.

LINA

Peering from her window at the courtyard below, watching the pigeons fine-dine on oxtail bones, Lina Rodriguez Armstrong knew what day it was. She knew by the quantity of glittery, windblown trash on the sidewalk, by the reshuffle of the parallel-parked cars, and by the appearance of the social worker with the Beyoncé waves who came weekly to see Debra on floor five.

It was the day after the West Indian Labor Day parade, a Tuesday—and this particular Tuesday, her last chance.

She lived in Brownsville Houses, but she'd grown up in Van Dyke Houses, the NYCHA complex across Mother Gaston Boulevard. Van Dyke was taller, and her family had lived up on the twelfth floor—they could see all the way to Jersey, and on July 4, she and her siblings would rock-paper-scissors for the best spot to watch the fireworks. As an adult, she'd lived on the second floor of the 78 Livonia Avenue tenement. She and Nellie could eavesdrop on the neighbors, on the repairman calling Mr. Wong, learn tidbits that might help with the struggle.

Yet what she had now at Brownsville Houses—the sixth floor—was her favorite. Not a city view or a street view: it was a community view. Every day she lingered by the window to see who was coming in and out, who was chasing after the ice cream truck, and who'd forgotten to pick up after their dog for the twentieth time.

Grandma, the kids called her now, like they'd once called the lady on Livonia.

Tita.

The meeting wasn't until noon, but Lina had woken with the garbage truckers at four a.m. so she'd have time to prepare. The pain was worst in the morning, and she had a regimen: ice pack to her knees for thirty minutes, a warm shower, then gentle stretches with one hand on the dresser. She'd invited the bureaucrats from the Department of Housing Preservation and Development to meet in her apartment, but they'd insisted on the Stone Avenue library. Maybe they thought if they came up to the apartment, she'd rant about repair problems that were not in their jurisdiction, that were NYCHA's responsibility—like she wasn't well familiar with the way city agencies split themselves and pointed fingers. She'd invited the HPD officials into her home because she wanted them to see the mural in her living room, to meet eyes with the heroines on her walls. She'd wanted them to look out the window the way *she* looked out the window. Maybe they'd stop gaping at Brownsville like missionaries come to save heathens.

Not to mention the arthritis. Now that she was seventy years old, walking anywhere took Lina twice as long as it once had.

Lina opened the fridge—once a teacher, never skip breakfast. She would have liked a blueberry muffin or a strawberry Danish, but she was not a niña delgada like she'd once been. Sit too much and those muffins start growing on your hips. She slurped down a bowl of Quaker Oats at the kitchen table, pulled out the leak bucket under the kitchen sink and dumped the water in the toilet, then lowered herself into her favorite chair, her mother's crocheted blanket over her shoulders.

She looked over the proposal one more time.

Starting with Mayor Dinkins, every administration had received a copy of her proposal. Dinkins had sent staff out, though after the meeting, she'd never heard from them again. But that was the summer of the Crown Heights riots and the whole administration had been going up in flames, all the whites talking about how New York's first Black mayor couldn't "control" his own people.

She'd sent the proposal to Mayor Giuliani, but heard not a word. Bloomberg: she'd received a letter thanking her for her input, explaining all the administration's innovative plans, and inviting her to participate in the Livonia Commons visioning sessions in East New York.

She wasn't talking about East New York. She was talking about Brownsville.

Her sister Sofia, calling the prior day, had been all excited to hear about the meeting.

"Oh, this new mayor is going to get things done for you, girl. This man is on the same page as you! He got a Black wife!"

Easy for *her* to say, living in Long Island on her late husband's Wells Fargo pension plan.

Marrying a Black woman and talking the big talk about the inequality in this city didn't necessarily mean you had the courage to dig for the roots, or the strength to tear them up. She was certainly glad to be done with twenty years of Republicans—and that included the elephant that pretended to be an Independent. But there was also a difference between pity and love. Some Democrats behaved like they thought Brownsville had been dozing all that time and all they needed to do was kiss the Sleeping Beauty.

By eleven o'clock she was getting restless. It was still early, but she wanted time for errands, and this wasn't the day to be late. She grabbed her black-purple beret, her cane, her purse, and was on her way.

First, Lina knocked on the door opposite hers to say good morning to her thirty-year-old mentee, Tyrell Scott. He lived in 6D with his great-aunt Kara and his teenage cousin Tima. Tyrell let Lina inside; he was helping Kara with her dialysis.

"Good morning, Ms. Kara," Lina called loudly. Kara was going deaf and senile, but she was the only person in the building old enough to remember the Freedom School.

While Tyrell pressed buttons on the filtering machine, Lina examined the library book sitting on the kitchen counter: Stephen R.

Covey's *The 7 Habits of Highly Effective People*. She'd jump-started Tyrell's reading habit with Angela Davis and Toni Cade Bambara, but now he was on a self-help kick, reading leadership books by random white men. And he was making it cool. The members of the Woo gang, who used to tease him for reading on the 3 train, now downloaded his recommended titles to their phones.

"Ty, I'm on my way to meet HPD. I'll see you at six for the Family Day meeting."

"Word. You tell them what to do, Ms. Lina."

"Papi! Don't look at me so hopeful."

"Nah," he said, shaking his head as he adjusted Ms. Kara's needle. "You're gonna win this time."

Lina hmphed in mock disapproval. "Don't forget that yogurt I bought you."

She was still trying to get him to eat breakfast. She'd recently realized that, though she'd taught him how to love his community, she'd neglected to show him how to take care of himself, and he was even worse than she'd been—he'd run for weeks on Chinese takeout and Tropical Fantasy and three hours of sleep a night before he'd suddenly crash and skirt the edge of death. The doctor at Brookdale didn't understand how the kid was still walking and talking. But that was Tyrell, a cat with nine lives.

Lina climbed down to floor five to check on Debra's baby. Descended to floor four, but Ms. Dorothy was in Alabama. Hobbled to floor three, only she and Mrs. Jameson hadn't been on speaking terms for several months. Trudged down to floor two and asked José if he'd heard back from the Gateway Center. Two years earlier, José had dropped out of high school and started roaming the streets, getting in all kinds of trouble.

Somehow, she made it, breathless, to the first-floor landing.

"They still ain't fixed that elevator," Ricky Diaz said when she'd reached the ramp. He took a drag on his cigarette and shook his head with a laugh.

"One of these days they gonna find me at the bottom of the stairs with my ankle broken. Yeah, Papi, like they found my mother at the Rockaway Avenue station in '66."

She told him, as she always did, that he had to stop with the cigarettes or he'd beat her to heaven. Then she set off for Mother Gaston Boulevard. Old-timers had lined up their beach chairs on the sidewalk, ready to spend the day lost in memories of times past. Delicious smells curled into her nostrils, floating over from the West Indian grills. Children darted through the playgrounds, crowded around fountains to fill their water balloons, or spun in circles below the fire hydrant water—as a member of the community board, she'd helped get sprinkler caps to limit the overflow.

After she bought Ajax at a 99 Cents store, Lina's knees began to bother her, and she parked her butt on a bench next to two teenage girls. They'd been chilling by that bench all summer, and sometimes a bigger group of friends would gather with a set of speakers and blare Rihanna at the highest volume.

"I ain't crashing that airplane," the permed one said as Lina sat down, and then the two girls glanced at Lina and zipped their lips.

Lina did her best to keep up with the local gang codes, but "crashing that airplane" was something new. All these kids were so young, practically babies. It wasn't like the days when gangs were after money or drugs. These children warred for territory like they thought they owned the land on this side of Rockaway Avenue—and yes, there was a war for land to be fought, but it wasn't with each other.

"What y'all doing with yourselves?" Lina asked, holding her cane with one hand and rubbing her thighs with the other. "You girls gonna pass the whole summer on this bench talking about crashing airplanes?"

The one with the perm raised her eyebrows, and she looked at her friend, who suppressed a giggle and sucked the straw in her Fanta.

"Why don't you go down to the Recreation Center and join a club. They got basketball, dance, swimming, step team. Air-conditioning, free lunch."

"Them kids jump us every time we go." Quickly, the permed girl grabbed her friend's arm and pulled her down the street, out of Lina's orbit. The friend with the Fanta couldn't contain her nervous giggle and released a dribble of juice on the other's sneakers, who playfully slapped at her as they walked.

Lina shook her head, and her breast heaved with unexpected emotion. This was the reason why her proposal made sense, why her vision was long overdue. There was nowhere for the young people to come together and squash the beef. Nothing to keep their minds engaged on these long summer days. And there was all that land on Livonia. For more than twenty years now, she'd called for the rejuvenation of Livonia Avenue, especially the reconstruction of the lots where the fire had burned down her Freedom School and a dozen families' apartments. Her proposal envisioned the development of the Brownsville Cultural Center, LGBTQ Youth Center, and Multidisciplinary Trade School. She'd worked with the Pratt Center on the feasibility study. It would include an auditorium space, a painting studio, a darkroom for photography, and two dozen dorm rooms for displaced LGBTQ youth. There'd even be a training program where young adults could get their OSHA certificates and technical degrees: plumbing, sound tech, computer coding. She'd wanted to turn to the girls and tell them what was in store for them, but truth was, she still had nothing to give, and it was unclear to her how much time she had left.

Sighing and pushing herself to her feet, Lina continued down Mother Gaston to the library. Blue scaffolding shaded half the journey. Tree roots had sliced and diced the concrete, and she recalled how as a child she'd played the game her brothers called "avoid the sidewalk cracks." Now, with the cane, those cracks were the bane of her existence.

Lina had lived almost her whole life in Brownsville. Born in East Harlem, but she hadn't liked it too much. The other Puerto Rican kids had sometimes called her the n-word with the hard *r*—her father being a Black American—and Lina had thrown some punches. She'd been a tough tomboy of a girl, the oldest of five.

But all the fights stopped when they'd reached Brownsville in 1956. Back then, there'd been a mix of Black, Puerto Rican, and Jewish, everyone going over to each other's houses, the parents watching one another's kids, no matter what the race. Of course, as she grew older, her Jewish friends disappeared from the neighborhood, often without a word goodbye. Yet even after the Jewish residents left for the suburbs, it had still been a thriving community. People seemed to forget that now—they talked like White Flight had destroyed the neighborhood and White Return was all it needed.

When Lina finally made it to the library, she was ten minutes early, but Brandon, the library intern, whispered to her that the "city people" were already upstairs in the Brownsville Heritage House. Lina rode the elevator to the third floor and found the two visitors sitting at the conference table. Olivia looked like Michelle Pfeiffer in that bad movie about the school, and Andrew, like Ross from *Friends*.

"Welcome to the Brownsville Heritage House," Lina said, lowering herself into a seat, trying not to appear out of breath. "Too bad you weren't here last Saturday. We had a jazz concert. That saxophonist— absolutely incredible. Everyone in Brownsville came out."

"How fantastic. I'm sorry we missed it."

"I'm so glad Brownsville has this venue."

The Heritage House was a large multipurpose space on the library's third floor, and it was also a museum of sorts, with all kinds of Brownsville artifacts on the shelves along the walls: family china from down South, Black Power zines from the sixties, and what had to be the city's largest collection of Black Barbie dolls.

They chatted for a bit about the library's history and future, but Lina wasn't there to make small talk. She spread her proposal before her and began, with gusto, to read it.

"*The Wesley Price Cultural Center, LGBTQ Youth Center, and Community Land Trust is a project more than twenty years in the making. In 1992, we community organizers were sick and tired of passing the empty lots on Livonia Avenue that had also become a location for drug use and the site of frequent muggings and stabbings. We knew our community was in need. Crack devastated a generation, and our young people had no one to look up to and no activities to excite them. From this, we envisioned the creation of a state-of-the-art cultural center with an LGBTQ homeless youth component. The block we selected has a powerful history: the site of the renowned Freedom School of the 1970s, an institution beloved in the community and recognized by Congresswoman and Presidential-Should-Have-Been Ms. Shirley Chisholm, before it was burned down in an act of arson that was never investigated.*

"When we thought about who should own and develop this piece of land, we realized that it shouldn't be one individual who might not be accountable to Brownsville's people. No offense intended, but we don't think it should remain the city's property. The city has let it lie in neglect for almost forty years. Our vision includes the creation of a community land trust to steward the land, named in honor of Wesley Price, a young artist from Brownsville who was taken too early from us. A community land trust, or CLT, is a community-led nonprofit that takes land and housing off the speculative market and stewards it for the public good. It's an alternative way of relating to land similar to Lenape concepts. The community land trust structure originated in the Jim Crow South, when Black civil rights leaders came together to collectively purchase land in Georgia. CLTs now exist all over the country, and in New York City, the Cooper Square CLT in the Lower East Side owns several blocks that include hundreds of affordable apartments. Today the New York City Community Land Initiative coalition is renewing a CLT movement across NYC, starting with a new community land trust in El Barrio East Harlem. We think this is the right structure for us here in Brownsville. We believe Brownsvillians must be in charge of planning, developing, and stewarding land in the neighborhood for the public well-being. We have spoken to partners who would be able to assist us with this work, including Trevor LDC, an M/WBE development company owned by Brownsville native Gregory Trevor, as well as gardeners from Salam Garden..."

Lina continued for about ten minutes, and she was so energized when she reached the end of the proposal that she could have marched all the way to city hall with a signpost in the air.

"Thank you so much, Ms. Armstrong," Andrew said. "We really respect the level of detail and thought you put into this."

"And I completely second that." Olivia nodded. "Since we're launching our Brownsville planning initiative, hearing a vision for one of the vacant city-owned properties is extremely helpful."

"Wonderful!" Lina said with enthusiasm, trying to play the good community partner. But Lina reminded herself that nothing was certain. She'd been around the block enough times to see young government types like these make promises they couldn't keep.

"So." Lina laced her fingers together. "When do you hand us the deed?"

Olivia laughed.

"Sounds like you're ready to start digging," Andrew said cheerily, fiddling with the cap of his pen.

Perhaps she'd been too direct, Lina thought, pressing her lips together. Maybe she sounded unprofessional. But what was the point of being coy? She wanted them to understand: Brownsville was waiting. Had *been* waiting. And neither Brownsville nor Lina could wait another ten years.

"We actually have some good news for you." Andrew smiled again, pulling himself snug against the table. "As we said, the administration really sees Brownsville as one of its top priorities, and this site on Livonia is just ripe with opportunity to be something better for the neighborhood." He exchanged a look with Olivia. "We do intend to release what is known as a Request for Proposal."

"An RFP," Lina said hurriedly, because yes, she knew the term. An RFP was an invitation to submit a project proposal, often for a vacant plot of city-owned land. The RFP would lay out the city's objectives and give developers a few months to write an application. If she and Trevor LDC wanted a chance to build on the lot, this was it. "So the city is thinking about an RFP, or it's actually releasing an RFP?" Lina asked. "When?"

"Later this year."

"Oh!" She kept it cool, though she wanted to shout "Ay bendito!" to the ceiling. "That *is* good news."

So many decades. So many petitions. And now they were finally going to let Brownsville build on the land. She'd have to call Greg Trevor immediately. But it was too good; there had to be a catch.

"We invite you to submit to the RFP, possibly in collaboration with the other stakeholders who have some beautiful visions for the site," Olivia said.

"Other stakeholders?"

Lina felt a knot forming in her stomach.

"There are about three or four parties who have come forward to us about the 78-80 Livonia Avenue lot."

"Who?"

Andrew glanced at Olivia. "I . . . I don't think we're really at liberty to share their names yet."

Lina sat back in her chair. So she'd been right after all. There were hyenas in the hills. They were hungry, always hungry, even hungry enough to eat Brownsville. They'd eaten all the rest of the borough and had nothing else left to eat.

"I'm sure we can agree," Andrew continued, "the neighborhood deserves a truly democratic process: all ideas out on the table, everyone discussing what the community really needs—"

"I'm not a one-woman show," interrupted Lina.

"I see you have about eighty signatures, Ms. Armstrong, but there are more than one hundred and fifteen thousand people in the Brownsville community district. And we'll be inviting many of them to the community visioning sessions that we'll be holding over the next few months."

"I'm sure you, more than anyone, understand the importance of having a groundswell of support behind your project," Olivia added. "You can prepare a presentation and try your vision on a larger audience."

Under the table, Lina massaged the felt of her beret, wondering what Nellie would have said. Nellie, the love of her life, had sewn that

hat for her decades ago; since Lina could never make up her mind about whether to wear her Young Lords beret or her Black Panthers beret, Nellie had made her a third hat, purple on one side and black on the other, split down the middle like a half-moon cookie. Lina had been wearing it for forty years, and there were holes in the lining.

She felt a sudden heaviness and wished Nellie was present to scold her for wearing her garments ragged and to strategize with her about these city officials—for the Wesley Price Community Land Trust was for Nellie too. Wesley Price was Nellie's son.

Olivia and Andrew did have a point. She couldn't claim all her people's support, not yet. Neighbors had been reluctant to get involved, too busy with their own problems. Brownsville wasn't as active as it used to be. The young people were overworked and distracted.

"Well, we're happy to make a presentation," Lina said, faking a smile.

Lina accompanied Olivia and Andrew down to the sidewalk. "May I get you both some lunch before you head to the city?" Olivia and Andrew might be on the team choosing the RFP winner, and she'd have to remain cordial.

"Oh, that's so kind of you—no, thank you so much, Ms. Armstrong."

"We should run, but thank you."

Lina accompanied them as far as Livonia and Rockaway, then watched them mount the station stairs to the elevated rail. Young Michelle Pfeiffer skipped on her heeled loafers, one arm swinging, like she'd already left Brownsville in her head, already onto the next thing. Another meeting.

"Ms. Lina!" a voice called. It was Melvin, sitting on a crate with his spine against a mail collection box, wearing pink shorts and a Mickey Mouse T-shirt. "Ms. Lina is my girlfriend!" he announced to the street. "Darling, spare me a dollar so I can get a slice of pizza?"

Lina scraped a dollar out of her pocket and handed it to him.

"You got to stop popping pizza slices, Mr. Melvin. You walk

to that soup kitchen on Newport I told you about and get yourself a full meal."

"I forgot about that, Ms. Lina." Melvin nodded. "I should go up there."

Maybe she was dreading the six flights of stairs to her apartment, but Lina found herself walking in the opposite direction, straight down Livonia Avenue. She dug a Hershey's Kiss out of her purse and peeled back the foil. Not great for her blood sugar levels, but she needed a bit of comfort.

It was from her father that she'd inherited her sweet tooth. Her righteousness. And loyalty. When Lina reached the age of eight, she'd started accompanying her father on his Saturday-morning outings. Usually they walked from East Harlem to Lenox Avenue, where he got his haircuts. Then he would send her across the street to buy Jodie's spoon bread, and at the end of the meal, he'd reach into his trouser pocket and hand her a piece of Hershey's chocolate, which in the summer was usually half-melted, making a mess in his pants pocket that her mother would scold him for later.

A few times, he took Lina all the way to the docks where he worked on the West Side, and that was where he told her about the union and about the Jim Crow Local that was fighting for better pay and better work, and about the white men who, for no God-given reason, thought they deserved the easier, better-paid jobs on the docks.

Before the docks, she'd only known her father as a quiet man. She was eleven when they shot him, when he became her first martyr. Malcolm was her second. Martin her third.

Growing tired, Lina paused by the handball courts to catch her breath. There was no one around but a couple of kids with towels draped over their shoulders, heading to the Betsy Head Park pool. Gospel hymns floated out the church door, clashing with a reggae tune from a backyard barbecue. She picked herself up and walked the last two blocks down Livonia, then stared through the wire fence at her lot.

Someone had dumped a rusty fridge on the grass. A cat eyed her from one corner.

"They better issue that RFP," Lina said to the new Miss Freedom. "And when they do, I'm getting back everything we lost. I'm going to make it right."

If she was still a niña delgada, she would have climbed the fence right then and gotten to work. To hell with the RFP. Back in the day, no one waited around for the bureaucracy. They'd carved their dreams out of brick and concrete. When the teachers stole the schools, they started their own. When the landlords left their homes to rot, they reclaimed and repaired and repainted them. Brownsville had been going somewhere back then—Brownsville had been saving itself, Lina thought.

All until Richard Wong had destroyed everything.

THE WONGS

Chin Dun Ho—Richard, he would be called most of his life—left China eager for the New World. Eight years old, he had round red cheeks that the aunties liked to pinch and a strawberry nose that the ngen ngens found adorable, but to himself he was a fearless adventurer: not afraid of the deep ocean—not afraid, even, of the bak gui.

On the day of his departure, his mother scrubbed him in the basin, dressed him in a jacket with his documents sewed into the inner lining, and packed a knapsack with a supper of shrimp, rice, and chestnuts. Next, his yia yia took him up to Cloud Hill to burn incense for the dead and offer them cuts of pork and oranges.

"And pour the wine!" he hollered, handing Richard his flask so the boy could wet the soil.

Cloud Hill, where they buried the dead, was the highest and most beautiful point in the valley. Life in Chin village carried on beneath it, consisting of forty clay huts clustered together like flies on a succulent leg of turkey, surrounded by rice paddies and sugar fields and a new canal, one irrigated at Richard's father's expense.

Everyone in Chin village and even the dead believed that Koon Lai was now wealthy. Richard imagined he would live in a house the size of four or five hovels combined, and every night would be like the Spring Festival, abounding with sesame pudding and flower jelly.

On the final day, neighbors peeked into their hut to watch their preparations. Richard was used to them. His family always had the most food in the village, and for as long as he could remember, the aunties had availed themselves of the surplus. "How do you need all these chickens, and with just one son?" they'd say, patting Richard's cheeks a bit too hard, holding out their cloth sacks so his mother could fill them with extra eggs. She usually obliged them. "He left me a bride and never came back."

Now that Richard was departing, the aunties were frantic with envy. When the wagon arrived, they and their children followed Richard, his mother, and his grandfather to the gate, whispering as they shuffled forward.

"All our children should be on that wagon," one auntie said.

"When the Japanese come, what will we do?"

Richard, not understanding their words, turned his head to gloat at their uneasy faces. Then he looked at the wagon bound for Hong Kong, and on it, he saw a boy his own age, from another village, slumped in the back with tears striping his red cheeks. Richard, who until then had felt only excitement, saw the boy's tears and froze.

Why was the boy crying?

"Go on, go on," his mother whispered, offering her palm so he could step onto the wagon. She smiled, her eyes like water buckets balanced carefully on the bridge of her nose.

For the first time, Richard realized he was leaving his mother.

He boarded the wagon, sitting as far as he could from the other boy. When he would visit the village twelve years later, the aunties would tease him for having neglected to cry or cling to his mother's neck. In truth, he longed to embrace her, to ask when she would join them in the New World, but he knew that if he did such things, he would not last the journey. He'd learned this from her. The way she took her outrage, tossed it in the well, shoved it in a pigpen. Smiled.

As the wagon moved down the road, he pretended he was already on board a giant ship and that the hill on the other side of the rice paddy was America, land of beef chunks and golden roads. The other boy would not stop whimpering. Richard ignored his snotty face. At all costs, Richard knew, he had to preserve his immunity. Locking out the sound of sniffling, the image of laden eyes—his mother's and the boy's—he pressed his thumbs and forefingers into the shape of a gun and pointed at the fields like a soldier aiming for the enemy. At the sound of the rattling wagon wheels, the half-submerged water buffalo raised their heads.

"Pew! Pew!" he cried, shooting at them.

That was how Richard Chin left for America: excited to meet his father, denying the loss of his mother, wrapped in a fantasy.

In Hong Kong, a friend of his father's awaited him. Mr. Lao reminded Richard of Uncle Gee: his teeth were yellow and mealy like corn. Mr. Lao led them on board the ship, then dragged Richard down to the bottom floors where the Chinese people slept.

"Sit," said Mr. Lao when they'd reached two empty bunk beds in the crowded cabin. He removed a little book from his pocket and handed it to Richard. "You must study the customs questions so you can prove you are your father's son."

Richard sat down on the lower mattress and flipped through the book. Squinting, he made out the name "Wong," and the characters for "Canton" and "restaurant." Again, he looked at Mr. Lao, at his dirty fingernails, crunchy teeth, and frantic eyes, and found the man uninspiring. Unable to sit still, Richard sprang to his feet.

"There were bak gui up there!"

The uncle yanked him down and handed him a metal cup. Richard drank the liquid, which was brown and bitter like throw-up.

"I want to go out!" He sprang up again.

"Aiya, your mother spoiled you! You trouble the bak gui, who's going to pay?"

Richard sat back down, disappointed. For many months, he had been waiting for the moment when he could see his country in its entirety, to grasp it in one glance like a Kuomintang pilot.

Days passed in the bottom of the ship—Richard lost track of how many. It was impossible for him to escape; Mr. Lao never slept for more than a few minutes at a time, or so it seemed to Richard. The man was often seasick and spent hours with his head bent over a bucket.

"Study your answers to the customs questions," Mr. Lao told him repeatedly. "If you don't know your answers, the bak gui will send you back. Or they can keep you in the detention on Angel Island. One woman went crazy in there. She shaved a chopstick until it was sharp like a knife and stuck it in her ear."

Richard was horrified—and intrigued. Scrunched up in a corner of the top bunk, with his shirt over his nose to mask the smell of the poop hole, Richard thought about knife-chopsticks and people trapped in dungeons. But it was never dark and never light and he couldn't sleep because he wanted to jump or break or kick something, and finally, while the other passengers slumbered, he punched a hole in the cabin wall. Water flooded the cabin, and the whole ship sank to the bottom of the ocean.

On the seabed, he met the ancestors. They were sitting on rocks in a half-circle, and they were frowning and stern, the men brushing their queues, the women nursing their tiny feet. When they recognized Richard, they scolded him, but their words dissolved in puffs of bubbles. Then he saw that beyond them, an American car floated in the ocean. It was white and gleaming, with massive wheels and headlights that illuminated the gloom. He rushed toward it, but the ancestors rose in unison and crowded around him, bubbles surging from their mouths to block his way.

Richard tore through the bubbles and dove toward the vehicle, swatting away the ancestors' gossamer forms. He pulled back the door of the car and climbed inside, gasping and victorious, and then his eyes opened to the ceiling of the ship cabin.

His encounter on the ocean floor emboldened him. The next evening, when he and Mr. Lao were eating tofu jook in the Chinese dining hall, Richard crawled under the table, combed through the diners' legs, popped out at the end, and dashed for the door. He ascended the steps all the way to the ship deck.

In the sun, he found the bak gui congregated in small groups: towering men in blazing white jackets and wide-brimmed hats, and women, almost as tall as the men, wearing dresses that flared like flowers. Richard turned around and caught a whiff of something heavenly; they were eating legs of chicken, cutting and stabbing moist chicken flesh with silver utensils. He could not remember the last time he had eaten chicken. Half-consciously, he took two steps in their direction, emerging from behind a pole, and stood exposed, the sea winds flapping in his hair.

One by one they stared, pointed, whispered. The chicken-eating women paused, and it was the older one with the giant feather in her sun hat whose eyes softened. She began to hold the fork at just the slightest angle toward him, until the younger woman snapped at her and, with a stern glance at Richard, patted down the older one's fork-holding hand.

He glanced up: bak gui faces all around, scrutinizing him, arms crossed. Yet there was one man in a bamboo-colored uniform who whistled to catch Richard's attention. The man made a funny, clucking sound in his throat, then gestured with his hand, as if calling over a puppy.

Grinning, the young man tugged Richard onto the seat beside him and showed Richard some photographs.

"Girl," said the man, pointing at the pictures, his lips spread to show his white, healthy teeth. He guffawed, slapped his knee, took a swig from a bottle at his side. Poking at Richard's chest, he laughed again. "Boy."

Girl, boy—Richard recognized those English words. He'd learned them in the village primary school.

And then he realized.

As he ogled the photographs, the bamboo man laughed, showing him others. Soft white cakes topped with hard brown walnuts.

Blond and red-haired women, naked or in lacy undergarments. Prior to that day, Richard had never thought about what lay beneath the clothes of his cousins in the village.

Just then, Mr. Lao reached the deck, and before Richard could run, his chaperone grabbed him and yanked him down the stairs.

The loss of dinner and breakfast, the spanking, the slap to his ear—these were no real deterrents. Whenever Mr. Lao snatched him with those dirty fingernails, Richard's hatred swelled, and he swore that once they docked in America, he'd run away.

The day they arrived in the harbor of San Francisco, however, the ship crew allowed only the bak gui passengers to descend to the pier, and they transferred the Chinese to a ferry. "Angel Island," Mr. Lao muttered as they shuffled on board, his fingers pressed hard into Richard's shoulder blades.

They stood on the deck of the ferry with a hundred other Cantonese as the boat bobbed forward. Richard watched the island rise before them like the hump of a beached shark, its banks flanked with long white penitentiaries. He realized then that he hadn't studied his book. In panic, he turned to Mr. Lao. "I can't read these characters."

Mr. Lao grabbed the book from his hands and began to drill him.

What was his father's name?

Chin Koon Lai?

No. He must say *Wong* Koon Lai!

How many brothers did he have?

No brothers.

No, he must say three!

Richard wanted to cry, because even when he knew the correct answer, the book required that he memorize a falsehood.

How many cooking knives did his family own?

He had no idea.

Mr. Lao told him to say the number four.

They were herded into a facility teeming with families from several ships. There were not enough benches, so people squatted on the floor, wetting their clothes in the dirty puddles under the windows, suffocating in the smell of unwashed bodies. There was rising chatter, and then the guards demanded silence. But how long were they going to keep him there? Richard watched a guard seize a woman with red pocks and drag her down the hall. Her children clawed and screamed. They were going to lock her up in the dungeon, Richard thought, and he wanted to scream, too, as if she were his own mother. Richard was still watching when someone handed him a bowl of watery oats, but when he lifted the spoon to his mouth, it tasted like something sucked up from the puddles on the floor. Mr. Lao reprimanded him—"Your father doesn't want you to cry"—"You must study" —"Eat your dinner"—now trying to stuff a spoon in Richard's mouth—"How many knives in the kitchen?"—"They'll send you back if you cry"—"How many chairs in the bedroom?"—but instead of answering, Richard howled, "Mama, Mama, Mama!" for hours, until he exhausted himself and fell asleep on Mr. Lao's shoes.

They spent two weeks in the barracks, with its four rows of three-tiered bunk beds. One morning, the guards separated him from Mr. Lao and led him to the interrogation cell. Richard faced a desk with two bak gui and a translator. Despite his terror, something coalesced within him, some strength left waiting in reserve, and he remembered his name was now Wong. He remembered that he lived in Wong village, that he had three brothers, and that their family owned four knives. He remembered their home contained three beds and four chairs, and that his father had bought his mother an ivory elephant as a wedding gift.

Lie by lie, he won their approval; by the end, he was an American.

When Richard arrived in Brooklyn, he was taken not to a sprawling house with servants, but to a tall, narrow building crisscrossed by iron ladders, its three floors crammed with people. His father's restaurant was on the second floor, and they slept with their workers in the back. Across the street was a twenty-four-hour candy store called Midnight Rose. Richard learned to say "Double Bubble" and "Abba-Zabba."

But the novelty of 78 Livonia Avenue wore off quickly. It was hard to sleep with the trains crossing outside the window, and his father was quieter, thinner, and more fastidious than the men in Chin village; he never took a nap and sometimes did not stop for lunch at all. Seeing all this, Richard reached a new conclusion. His father hadn't brought Richard overseas to fatten him. He'd brought him overseas to fatten the envelope they sent back to the village.

"We are not like the others. We have a special title," his father's speeches always began. "You are the first son—the only son. But just as I was the first son, eldest of six. And my father was also the first son, eldest of four, and his father was the first son, and his father. Which means, we inherit this family.

"You must work hard and study hard. In school you can learn English, and then one day, you can have a good, American job. You'll wear a suit and tie and go to Manhattan."

But Richard did not want to wait for Manhattan. From the restaurant window at the corner of Livonia and Saratoga, he looked down and saw bak gui boys wrestling in the gutter, bak gui grandmothers knitting on stoops, bak gui girls grouped around the iceman with his glass bottles of colored syrup, and toothless bak gui men with sardine cans, competing for the affection of the block's stray cat. He saw the dead quiet of Saturdays followed by the evening's eager rush to Pitkin Avenue, the stuffing of faces with pastrami sandwiches, the seagulls flying low for scraps.

His father confined him to the restaurant. Each weekend, Richard was forced in front of yet another Burt & Benjamin's Beginner's English Print Book, with page after page of dull gray cats, dogs, and houses, each with a wide line underneath.

"It's easy! It's a 'cat'!" he'd call to his father, and run into the kitchen to point it out, but his father would insist he write the word. And writing the word in English should have been as easy as saying it aloud, he thought—just as it should have been easy for a boy of his age to write in Chinese—but he could only stare up at the A-B-C strip that his father had pasted to the wall of the back room, his eyes whirling until he was nauseous.

Over the course of the year, attending school with the other children of Brownsville, Richard metamorphosed rapidly. As his spoken English progressed, he made friends, all of them the children of the Yiddish-speaking Jews. Richard and these boys spent their time hurling rocks from the railroad quarry at each other's noses. Or they played two-hand touch with a folded newspaper, or snuck into the Pitkin Loew's for the seven o'clock Western. Sometimes, they stood barefoot outside the turnstile of the Saratoga station, a few faking as beggars while another dipped his fingers into the pocket of a Crombie overcoat. Most frequently, the boys fought one another on the street corners, piling body on body into a thick, soft mass of prepubescence: punching, jabbing, writhing, like maggots under the sun.

The boys—many fatherless, their daddies stolen by the early years of the Depression—wanted to be mobsters like the guys who haunted the back of the candy store. Murder, Inc., wore the best clothes in Brownsville, owned the fanciest cars, and sported the finest girlfriends, and the boys aspired to be just like them. They wanted girls before they knew why, money, and big houses.

Richard learned to share their ambitions. He too yearned to be the Gary Cooper or Buck Jones of Brooklyn. But then there was his father, who began showing up outside P.S. 175 to march him straight back to Canton Kitchen so he wouldn't play with those boys, and who on weekends would drag him through the streets of Chinatown to the Chin Association, where in smoky rooms, uncles in business suits pinched his cheeks into wontons.

One summer day, a year after his arrival, Richard's irritation reached its breaking point. In the afternoon, he slipped out when his father wasn't looking and caught up with the bak gui boys. For the next couple of hours, he joined in their activities: hauling egg crates for the dairyman, teasing the Humpty Dumpty Pickle Twins, and watching the slaughterhouse workers wield their knives on a new truckload of sheep. Then the boys noticed a fresh sign.

CONEY ISLAND'S SEVEN WONDERS OF THE WORLD THEATRICALS!
10¢ A TICKET: EVERY DAY NINE TO NINE ON THE HOUR!

The boys hatched a plan: hide the challah, tell the babushka there was no more bread, make her hand over a dime for the bakery, then ride out to Coney Island to see the show. Soon they all wanted to go, and they agreed to meet at the Rockaway Avenue station the next morning.

Five, six, seven, eight of them would go, would the Chinaman?

Richard understood Coney Island was the best place on earth. He did not have a babushka, but he nodded anyway.

After the boys dispersed for supper, Richard's indignation swelled, and he felt the urge to throw something. Kicking the crumpled newspapers and soda bottles that had gathered at the curb, filled with loathing for the scrawny man who had indentured him, he sloshed globs of spit in his mouth, fomenting three English words—hurled them, loud and outraged, across the street:

"I WILL GO!"

When he reached the restaurant dining room, it was so hot, he instinctually reached to pull his shirt over his head. On days like this in the village, the children would spend all day splashing in the river. They would not be locked up behind layers and layers of brick, a human-size furnace.

Richard stomped past the mop bucket toward the kitchen. It was crowded with cooks in dove-white tunics chopping ginger and shaving carrots, the air steamy and scallion-sweet, and he found his father bent over the metal safe, accounting for expenses in a notebook.

"I need a coin to go to Coney Island tomorrow."

Closing the safe and removing his glasses, Koon Lai looked down at his son, his lips pressed tight.

"If you don't give me money, then I'm not mopping the floor," Richard bargained.

Peeved that the floor hadn't been mopped, his father sent one of the waiters to complete the task, and then he kneeled to be eye level with Richard.

"All those years in China, your belly was full," he said. "Did you ever think why?"

"I am never allowed to go anywhere!" Richard cried, swiping a pair of forks off the counter. "Bak gui boys go to Coney Island! Why can't I go to Coney Island?"

"You think you are a bak gui boy?" his father said softly, and then with terrifying, escalating volume:

"Do you have money like a bak gui boy? Can you read like a bak gui boy? Go to Coney Island when you can read like a bak gui boy!"

Richard knocked his head against the wall and groaned.

"Take the garbage to the corner," Koon Lai ordered, pointing to two black bags in the hall.

Instead, Richard bolted past the bags and down the stairs onto the street. He would get money one way or the other.

All evening at the restaurant, Koon Lai kept glancing at the door, anxious for his son's return. In such rapid time, Richard thought like an American—he thought about his own plate. Koon Lai tried to think of an appropriate punishment. In China, a misbehaving child would be beaten. But he was nervous to try; he had never beaten a child before.

He didn't like leaving when there were so many customers, but at nine o'clock Koon Lai checked the lock on the safe, inspected the supply of sodas in the storage closet, and descended to the street to look for the runaway.

As soon as he reached the sidewalk, Koon Lai heard a loud clatter and shouts from up the block. About twenty feet away, a crowd had gathered in front of a tenement, the people encircling a broken, upside-down bedroom cabinet. The cabinet, Koon Lai deduced, had just been shucked from the second-floor window. There was no sign of Richard, but he recognized the voices of the people in the tenement window: hak gui.

There was a husband, a wife, and four girl children.

He had become aware of them long before. Sometimes the girls would sit on the fire escape, dangling their feet over the street, braiding each other's hair. Once, the father and mother had come to the restaurant for a meal. His waiter had sought out Koon Lai's approval, and without hesitation, Koon Lai had nodded his assent. In any case, he had watched the two hak gui carefully that night, and they had been quiet and tidy.

Now, the four hak gui children came running down the stairs to stand under the tenement window. Maybe they thought if they stood there, the marshals would not continue to throw furniture out the apartment window for fear of injuring them—but still, a lamp shot out the window and one of the little girls ducked.

The furious crowd, mostly Jewish bak gui, appeared to be on the side of the hak gui girls. One older Jewish woman mounted the front steps of the tenement and turned to face the crowd.

"Comrades!" she bellowed. "Hear what this slum landlord does! He gets a Negro family in there, charges them double the going rent! Just to line his pockets, twice the going rent! The father of the family, Mr. Philips—he's been waiting years for a WPA job. And now the landlord wants to throw them to the streets! We can't let the Philipses be put on the streets. We must fight!"

The Jewish workers raised their fists, and together, they picked up the cracked cabinet and hauled it back through the tenement door.

But what was the use of that? Koon Lai thought. The marshal would just throw it out the window again.

He felt bad for the hak gui family, but he had enough to worry about.

Koon Lai looked for Richard in the candy store. His son, thankfully, was not there. He hiked up to Pitkin Avenue, but the shoeshine boys had left, the shopkeepers had locked their stores, and only a few knish vendors remained.

Hours went by—Richard stumbling around with his head down, scouring the streets for pennies. At a loss, he sat on the curb and watched the men on the rooftops calling home their pigeons.

And then, in the glow of the streetlamp: a dead body.

Richard made out the leather shoes first, then the crooked legs, the rise of a rump. The corpse lay in the middle of an alleyway criss-crossed by clothing lines. He moved toward it, wondering if it could still be alive. There were dark stains on the back of the jacket and on the concrete, and he thought of the Spring Festival slaughter, ribbons of rooster blood flying across the coop.

Richard prodded the body with his shoe. Nothing happened. He bent beside the corpse, listening. He tapped the body with the tip of his finger. And then he wiggled his whole hand into a jacket pocket and pried out a pack of cigarettes.

In the other pocket, there was fifty cents. He noticed three golden rings on the doughy white fingers and tried to tug them off, but the pinkie was as swollen as a frankfurter, so he took the two other rings and hurried back to the street.

They'll know, Richard thought. In a panic, he scampered back to the alley, yanked a blanket off a nearby clothing line and draped it across the body, then surrounded the mound with bags of trash.

"You little shegetz!" the dead man snapped, rolling over and throwing off the blanket. His chest was riddled with holes that spouted blood like a fancy fountain. "You think you can take my rings?"

Richard tore down the sidewalk as fast as he could, past the drunks clinging to paper bags, the night-shift workers awaiting the streetcar, stuffing his pockets with the coins and rings and cigarettes as he ran, and the dead man trudged after him, using his fist to plug the holes in his stomach.

Koon Lai saw the little boy racing down Blake Avenue.

"Chin Dun Ho!" he cried, catching him by the arm. Instead of yanking himself free, Richard wrapped his arms around Koon Lai's waist.

"There's a ghost! A ghost!"

Koon Lai could nearly have cried with relief.

"There are no ghosts in Brooklyn." He rubbed Richard's head. "The bak gui don't allow ghosts."

In fact, there had been ghosts in Brooklyn. When Brooklyn held the maize meadows of the Munsee-speaking. When whales still swam up the river. Like the Chinese, the Munsee-speakers prepared their dead for the afterlife, offering food and burying them with jewelry, arrowheads, and red-tailed hawk feathers. And even after the ancestors departed for the spirit world, they would continue to guide the living. At least those living willing to listen.

But that had been a different Brooklyn—Brooklyn before the Dutch dredged the oysters and slayed the fish; before enslaved Akan people, Senegambians, and Malagasy toiled on the plantations of Kings County.

When the new century dawned, the city-turned-borough grew thick with people. You had your Irish in Red Hook and your Italians in Bensonhurst and your Scandinavians by Green-Wood Cemetery and your Freedmen in Weeksville. And then all the way east there was Brownsville, a little Jewish factory town booming up in the middle of nowhere.

Every tribe of Brooklyn had its own leaders, its own tits for tats. At least that was how things had been until the crash. Then the assembly lines halted, and the ships in the bay disappeared. Overnight, Brooklyn was reduced to a scrabbling place, a borough of tin towns and breadlines, of frostbite and men drunk on paint-spiked milk. Some cried for revolt, raised the red flag with its hammer and sickle.

But all that was past, Mayor La Guardia had promised. He would pull the city back from the brink, put the fathers back to work, tear down the rotting tenements. Progress, the American way, would be steely and tangible: highways, airports, tunnels. Didn't matter if you were Jewish, Italian, Irish, Polish—all would participate in the realization of this vision, and all would prosper.

Coney Island was the epitome of such hope. It was the everyday man's playground, where the everyday man could indulge his desires. If he didn't like franks, then maybe he went for soft-shell crab. If he wasn't a horseback riding, Steeplechase guy, he might be a nut for the Tilt-A-Whirl. A man had to find out for himself.

As soon as his father had left for the Belmont fruit market the next morning, Richard crawled out the window onto the fire escape, skittered down the ladder, ran up the station steps, and ducked under the turnstile. Up on the El platform, the boys were scratching mustaches onto movie posters.

"It's the Chinaman," one announced.

"No tickee no shirtee! No tickee no shirtee!" said another, imitating the Chinese man who ran the neighborhood laundry.

"Look." Richard showed them the rings and cigarettes.

In awe, they reached for his treasures, but he quickly closed his hands and stuffed them back in his pockets. "I sell," he said. "At Coney Island."

Now they were full of ideas.

"If that's real, you're a millionaire," one boy remarked.

"That gold's not real," said another.

"If it's brass, you'd still get enough to ride the Ferris wheel."

"You could get a frank at Nathan's!"

"You could get a gypsy to tell your fortune."

"You could see a movie at the Pitkin Loew's. Hell, you could watch movies all day."

"Or go to Woolworths and order a hot fudge sundae."

"A banana split."

"A root beer float."

"Damn, I want an egg cream."

The train arrived and they took it west, then transferred to a line heading south to the beach. The subway car hummed with the chatter of beachgoers, and the boys stole glances at the women, many of whom were already stripped to fitted swimsuits.

"Hey Richie," one boy said, holding open a paper bag. "You want some polly seeds?"

"You ever tried halva before?"

"Hey Richie," said another, pointing to a vacated seat. "Take the window!"

Squeezed next to a bak gui man, Richard looked out the window. He could see Brooklyn stretching far and wide, the sky almost as vast and blue as the sky of the village. Below, the thousands of houses and cars looked like a classroom model constructed from papier-mâché and toothpicks. It was a world that belonged not to the Jew or the Anglo, the Italian or the Pol, but to any deserving American man.

Thirty minutes later, the train reached Stillwell Avenue, pulling up near the minarets and pinwheels of Luna Park. The boys squirmed through the crowded station and onto the street, determined to grab good seats at Seven Wonders of the World Freak Show so they could judge with their own eyes whether they were really seeing bona fide monsters.

The theater smelled of sweat and child puke, its seats spattered with sand and popcorn. One by one, the world's strangest mutations emerged from behind the curtain—first, a young girl with pigtails. She wore a long, heavy skirt and looked like an ordinary child until she lifted it. This exposed four legs—two thin ones that didn't fully reach the floor, and two thick limbs, each clothed in pink pantyhose. Richard and the boys sat on the edge of their chairs. It seemed those extra legs were really hers, and she, an actual freak. The entire crowd went wild, throwing popcorn, and Richard and the boys shouted and rocked in their squeaky seats.

Next came the Fire-Eating Man. Then the Snake Lady. Then a hak gui with elastic skin. Richard was so happy, he could have torn up all the auditorium seats with his bare hands. He could have jumped out of the El and landed on his feet—at least until the second-to-last act, when the host announced the arrival of Wee Head Wong.

It was obvious that he was Chinese, because of his tadpole eyes and black hair, only Richard had never seen anyone in China whose head was that small—so small that a teacup could've fit on his forehead like a top hat. Wee Head Wong bumbled around the stage, and then he stopped and stared at Richard. Richard twisted around, wanting to believe this, too, was an illusion. But the worst was true: Wee Head Wong had found him, and was smiling, pointing, and wagging his head like an idiot, so that the entire audience followed his finger to Richard's seat.

"Wee Head Wong! Is that your grandpa?" The boys laughed, patting Richard's head. He batted away their hands, wishing Wee Head Wong would leave the stage.

After the show, the boys descended to the streets and headed down Surf Avenue, laughing and hooting as they walked, past candy stores—ALL GOOD POPS BUY LOLLIPOPS!—cosmetic stores—WHAT MAKES AN AMERICAN MAN? HE WEARS AMERICAN SPICE!—and an accordionist with a lizard sprawled on his neck. They skipped toward the beach, sniffing up the boardwalk treats they couldn't afford to eat. HOT SAUSAGE WITH EVERYTHING! BUTTER-BRUSHED CORN! COTTON CANDY!

"Wee Head Wong, here's your sun hat," said one boy, slapping a lost baby bonnet on Richard's head.

"Look, Wee Head Wong! It's hot DOG, your favorite!"

Richard spotted a bearded bak gui with a vest full of American flags and ray guns. He showed the peddler his rings and cigarettes, and after a painstaking appraisal, the peddler offered him two dollars.

Richard agreed, then bought a frankfurter for every boy in his group.

Thanks to his generosity, they feasted on wieners that had been sitting for hours in an unrefrigerated bin on Mermaid Avenue, in buns that had been molding for months on dank shelves in Red Hook warehouses, dressed in sauerkraut bubbling with Brighton Beach bacteria. According to the *Brooklyn Times Union*, they were among several dozen Brooklynites poisoned by a sweaty, gloveless vendor on the boardwalk that day.

For Richard, it was worth it. Worth it because the boys never blamed him, and included him in their moans and groans, their vomiting out the subway windows, their storytelling for weeks after. Worth it because that frank tied his fate to all the other food-poisoned Coney Island–goers of Brooklyn, who happened to represent thirteen religious persuasions and fifteen nationalities and forty-seven occupations—everyone equalized in an identical rotation between toilet, bench, and garbage pail. Worth it because each of the dozen times Richard puked in the restaurant bathroom that night, he knew Coney Island belonged to him, as much as anyone.

SADIE

Sadie Chin had a crush on Kendrick Lamar. Raised on a diet of Billy Joel and the Beatles, then introduced to Coldplay by a college boyfriend, Sadie had never really listened to rap before, but she was starting her journey with *good kid, m.A.A.d city*. Soon she could identify the beats she heard from the cars on Eastern Parkway.

It had been more than a month since she'd started at *New Gotham*, and she liked the feeling that she was becoming more of a Brownsvillian each day. On the way back home, she would stop on Utica Avenue to buy a Jamaican beef patty or a Guyanese roti or a bottle of peanut punch, usually spoiling her appetite for whatever her father cooked for dinner.

"What's all this?" he asked one evening when she returned to the brownstone, a plastic takeout bag swinging on her arm.

Jason Chin stood before the stove, stir-frying tempeh in black bean sauce, his shoulder-length hair tied back with a rubber band. Sadie had seen pictures of his hippie years, when he'd worn it down to his waist, and she knew, too, that he'd once been so gaunt that her grandmother had complained that she hadn't come to America to have her son looking like a starved peasant. He had rounded out just a tad since then, as most fifty-five-year-olds were prone to do.

"Goat roti. I don't need dinner. I texted you."

"No, I saw," he said, trying but failing to bite back the smile bubbling on his lips. "I mean you." He nodded at her attire—she was wearing a crop top and ripped jeans. "Is this your ghetto outfit?"

Sadie nearly choked on the peanut punch.

"What?"

"Your style." He chuckled, then lowered the flame on the burner. "I think you're going ghetto."

She shook her head, dismayed. "A ghetto is an isolated neighborhood where oppressed people live. Nobody 'goes ghetto.'"

Jason, raising one eyebrow, tossed arugula in a bowl for that evening's salad. He took pride in being a versatile cook, in conscious defiance of the gender norm.

"When I was growing up, if you came from a working-class family and lived in Brownsville, you dressed very, very neatly so no one would look down on you. Black, white, immigrants—all of us. No one dressed like that."

"If I walk around in a business suit, no one in Brownsville will talk to me."

"Did you ever find out more about that Chinese guy? The murderer?"

"Nope."

When she'd asked her father a few weeks earlier if he remembered any other Chinese people in Brownsville, he'd answered in the negative. He had nothing to tell her about his childhood in the neighborhood except the sidewalk games he'd played with his friend Pete. Regretting that she hadn't gotten Mr. William's number, she'd looked for him and his nurse near the dollar store but hadn't found them, and no one else she'd met in Brownsville seemed to know about Mr. Wong.

"I should visit Ngen Ngen," Sadie said. "Maybe she'll remember the other Chinese families."

"Can you wait a bit? I still haven't told her that you're working in Brownsville."

"Still?"

"She's going to be upset."

"Because she thinks it's dangerous? Who cares, Dad."

"She's going to blame *me*, Sadie. Me." His eyes widened. "She'll say I failed to teach you Toisanese, I feed you leaves, I let you walk around with holes in your jeans like a bak gui, and now *Brownsville*, of all places!" He poked the air with his spatula for emphasis.

Sadie, dabbing her chin with a napkin, rolled her eyes at her father's antics. "Do you realize that you are being a bad son by depriving your mother of her lovely granddaughter's company?"

"Just let me talk to her first about your new job." He rocked his head from side to side, waved it like a flower in the wind, as he always did when considering one of her points. "Your ngen ngen will remember more than I do about the neighborhood. But let me figure out how to tell her the news. I'll go see her Sunday. After the reading at BookCourt. Are you coming?"

It seemed to Sadie that her father's entire world consisted of four places: the kitchen, his poetry study, his favorite black box theater on East Fourth Street, and BookCourt, that indie bookstore in Cobble Hill. These were his grottoes, and he seemed content cycling between them, never venturing beyond.

"Are you reading that X-rated poem about Mom?"

He blushed.

"No thank you." She threw her backpack over her shoulder and headed to her room.

As Sadie changed out of her crop top and ripped jeans, however, she fretted that her father might have been right.

But, she told herself, when you went to report in the field, you're supposed to dress something like the people around you. Though it was also true that sometimes she went through . . . cultural phases. When she'd had a crush on this Indian boy in her class at Stuyvesant, she'd started eating samosas and chana masala and wearing tassel earrings to school. Then, at Yale, she'd donned a kimono robe

patterned with lily pads and worn black eyeliner to accentuate the
Asian almondness diffused by her mother's Jewish blood. Given her
racial ambiguity, she really could belong to any community. Any except the Black community.

Sadie sat at her desk before her laptop, her goat roti, and her
journal. Opening to August, she reread the notes she'd taken after
the encounter with the man in the wheelchair.

A landlord named Mr. Wong
Livonia Avenue
Murderer
More than 30 years ago?

That Saturday, Sadie told her father she had tickets to see *Do the
Right Thing* at the IFC, and instead she took the train to Chinatown.
Ngen Ngen had lived in the Confucius Plaza apartment complex
since Grandpa Richard had died. It was less than a mile from Ground
Zero, and Sadie could remember her father, in a panic, dialing Ngen
Ngen on the morning of 9/11.

"Looks like China," her grandmother had mused on the phone,
watching the towers burn from her twenty-first-floor window,
sounding almost wistful. "Everybody go run run run."

Sadie loved the Confucius Plaza apartment and how completely
Chinese it felt: the rice cooker in the kitchen, the bamboo in a porcelain vase by the window, and the landscape paintings within which
tiny village men sat fishing below willow trees. The apartment
smelled like mothballs, like steamed fish. Having a very Toisanese
grandmother was, Sadie thought, something that definitively set her
apart from the millennial transplants.

On the way to the apartment, Sadie bought Ngen Ngen a magnif-
icent spread of dim sum—enough pork buns and shrimp dumplings
to leave them sleepy and semi-sick for the rest of the day.

"Ngen Ngen, I want to ask you something," Sadie said after they'd eaten. She hit the record button on her Olympus as Ngen Ngen chop-sticked another chive siau mai onto Sadie's plate. "Ngen Ngen, I'm bou le—Ngen Ngen, do you remember living in Brownsville?"

"Brownsville?" Ngen Ngen raised her eyebrows and looked quiz-zically at Sadie. She seemed to be shrinking a few inches every year, but she still dressed impeccably, in ironed pants and floral shirts with pearl earrings, never to become one of those old Chinese la-dies who stayed in pajamas all day—and never, in a million years, to be caught collecting bottles out of people's trash cans. Ngen Ngen had often reminded Sadie that she was not the daughter of farmers. Rather, her father had been the village high school teacher, and her mother, the village midwife. Sadie had always sensed that her grand-mother derived her dignity from the knowledge that she was not the lowest of the low on the world's totem pole.

"Yeah, Brownsville. What was it like living there?"

"In Brownsville, we run the restaurant. On, on . . . Livonia Avenue. Very busy."

"Did you live on Livonia Avenue too? Or somewhere else?"

"Your grandpa . . . your grandpa buy the house. On a, on a, what street, I forget." Ngen Ngen scrunched up her face, trying to recall. "Amboy Street."

Sadie jotted this down.

"Was it very different from living in Chinatown?"

Her grandmother laughed at the silliness of the question. "Very different! No Chinese people. All Jewish people. Then all Black people."

Ngen Ngen's accent was like a pizzicato take on a typically bowed melodic line, all the words in the English dictionary plucked out of the five tones of her native tongue—an instrumentation that Sadie, as they went along, couldn't help but imitate.

"No Chinese people? You don't remember anyone except for our family?"

"Oh. There is the laundry on Stone Avenue? One, two Chinese? But not so many Chinese."

"Did you know any of the other Chinese families by name?"

"No time. Just work in the restaurant. Raise the kid. Four kid. Jennifer, Julie, Jackie—then your daddy. Spoiled!" She laughed again.

"Why did Grandpa close the restaurant?"

"The Jewish move away."

"Why did they move away?"

"No one like the Black people!"

Sadie put down her pen. She'd been hoping for a bit more nuance from her grandmother, but in hindsight, that had been foolish. Ngen Ngen got her takes from *Law & Order* and *Blue Bloods*.

"What do you mean by that?"

"Hou ngai ham a! The neighborhood dangerous."

"Just because there are Black people doesn't mean it's dangerous."

"Rob you, follow you on street all the time. Your great-grandpa, he come home from the restaurant, then the Black man chase him, make him fall on the step."

"Was Great-Grandpa, like . . . hurt?"

"Very hurt! Don't walk like before. That's the Black people. Always try to rob the Chinese people."

Sadie put her face in her hands and suppressed a moan. She wondered what she could say to challenge Ngen Ngen's convictions. In college, she had learned truths—and each was as beautiful and untouchable as an artifact behind glass in a museum. She didn't know how to communicate her newfound consciousness in terms her grandmother would appreciate.

"Let's change the subject," Sadie said. "What year did you move out of Brownsville?"

"How come so many question?"

"Well." Sadie hesitated. "I got a job as a reporter for *New Gotham*. It's a newspaper. I cover Brownsville news."

"You go to Brownsville?" Ngen Ngen's eyebrows furrowed.

"Yeah. It's much safer now. I actually saw where the restaurant used to be." Sadie reached for her phone. "I'll show you a photo."

"You go to Brownsville? No good! Your father say you can go there?"

Sadie left the apartment soon after, but it was like one of those chain reaction games with dominoes to flatten, pitchers to tip, a marble swirling down a plastic spiral—the marble being the fact that she was reporting in Brownsville, which resulted not only in multiple messages to her parents' landline, but also calls to Aunt Jackie in Jersey, who relayed the news by text to Aunt Jennifer in Massapequa, who sent an email to Aunt Julie in Patchogue, who forwarded the email to Uncle Johnny. Uncle Johnny happened to be somewhat high-ranking in the New York City Police Department. He called Sadie from a 718 number the same morning she was on her way to Brownsville for a mayoral press conference.

"Sadie."

She recognized his voice right away: it had hints of her grandmother's pitter-patter along with the slurry of consonant-dropping usually associated with Bensonhurst Italians.

"For real? Ngen Ngen told you too?"

Sadie was locking up her bike—strung first through the front wheel, then through the bike frame, as Uncle Johnny had once taught her.

"Am I being charged with a crime?" Sadie said, the phone pinched between her shoulder and her ear. "Otherwise, I really have to go."

"Sadie, you gotta listen for a minute. Brownsville is one of our hardest precincts in Brooklyn. Last year: fifteen murders, forty-two rapes. I don't want you getting hurt."

He had joined the force around the time they'd eliminated the NYPD height requirement, meaning a five-foot-six Chinese boy could finally wear the badge. He was now the commanding officer of Patrol Borough Brooklyn South.

"Well, I'm not going to quit."

"Don't quit," he said. "Just listen. Go home by eight o'clock. Don't go into the projects or into people's houses."

A little boy with a Spider-Man backpack ran up to her and squinted at her press pass, then darted away, giggling. She believed her uncle

Johnny had a hard job, but she was still annoyed that he had defended stop-and-frisk for the entire decade before it had been ruled unconstitutional. They had fought about it during Thanksgiving for years.

"I'm a reporter," Sadie said as she hurried to the press conference. "I'm supposed to follow the story."

"You have to promise to follow my rules." He sighed.

She spotted what she was looking for: a group of residents gathered in one of Brownsville Houses' courtyards. She had to get her uncle off her back, or she'd be late.

"Fine. I promise."

"Be serious."

"I promise. Really. I have to go."

Shortly after she'd hung up, the mayor arrived, his head and shoulders above the rest. He shook hands with the tenant association leaders and the youth advocates, then took the mic to announce his plan for "ending the neglect of Brownsville Houses" and "reversing the racist legacy of Robert Moses."

Sadie listened, took notes, and felt zero remorse for lying to Uncle Johnny. Her relatives didn't understand what it was like to have no soil, to never fully belong anywhere. Chinese people looked Sadie in the eye and had no idea she was kin. On the high holidays, Hasidic men approached almost every white person on the streets of Brooklyn to ask, "Are you Jewish?" and she was always missed. When no one knows who you are, it becomes easy to cross borders.

She looked at the residents around her and saw mostly older men and women. Some beamed and nodded as the mayor spoke; others frowned, their arms crossed. There was also one young man. He was tall and wiry, thin wrists poking from the sleeves of his hoodie like scarecrow sticks. After a number of other speakers, the officials handed this young man the microphone.

"Good morning. I'm Tyrell Scott," he said calmly. "I was born and raised in Brownsville Houses. If you're here today, you should really see firsthand the conditions folks are living in, so I'm taking a group through 289. We have some residents kind enough to let us in their apartments, and you can also meet members of BYTE—that's Brownsville Youth for Truth and Excellence, my 501(c)(3)."

Sadie jotted down the acronym, impressed. Perhaps she could do a profile on BYTE later in the fall.

She joined the tour through Brownsville Houses. As Tyrell pointed out the broken elevators, the peeling paint on the walls, and the window cracks, the mayor shook his head and complained of the prior administration's neglect. Sadie tried her very best to focus on getting good quotes from the mayor, but she was distracted by Tyrell. He slapped the hands of every kid in the hallway, remarked on how BYTE was breaking the "school-to-prison pipeline," and helped an elder tie her laces. At the end of the tour, Sadie approached him, and he smiled warmly and shook her hand as if they'd known each other for years. She asked for his card, and since he didn't have one, he typed his cell number into her phone. She stared at it on the train ride home, aware her giddiness was inappropriate.

That night, she stayed up late writing the article, and Wendy had it posted by six a.m. the next morning. Immediately, Sadie sent it to Uncle Johnny. Maybe within a few years, the neighborhood would finally begin to flourish, and people like her uncle would change their tune.

She was proud of the piece and inspired—at least until the comment section blew up.

DoTePeters1953: This reporter just copied and pasted the mayor's press release. There's no quotes from residents. I don't think she actually knows anyone in this neighborhood.

EsmeraldaFrancois-Conrad: NEW GOTHAM THINKS IT CAN COLONIZE OUR NEIGHBORHOOD LIKE JUST ANOTHER THIRD WORLD COUNTRY BUT THE TRUTH IS BROWNSVILLE HAS HISTORY, THERE ARE CONTEXTS TO EVERY ONE OF THESE

INITIATIVES AND PROGRAMS THE REPORTER MENTIONS, ITS NOT LIKE THE MAYOR JUST THOUGHT OF ALL THESE THINGS BY HISSONERS SELF.

TyScott1ply: How does Broken Windows Policing fit into the larger plan? That's a follow-up question for the mayor.

TrevorGMWBE: "After years of total neglect, Brownsville may now see some light"—Am I the only one who finds this phrasing racist?

Melissa P: By "light," does she mean white folk?

LinaRodriguezArmstrong44: Please ask the mayor about exact timeline & budget allocations for each initiative, especially the development of vacant land on Livonia Ave. We're not interested in empty promises.

THE WONGS

Richard didn't know anything about Robert Moses. Even on his deathbed, Richard would never realize how much he owed to Robert Moses, the extent to which he was, in some way, a child of Robert Moses.

Born in 1888. Son of the famed philanthropist Bella Moses. Raised in affluence on the East Side. At Oxford, Moses wrote a thesis on the superiority of the English Civil Service, which relied on tests of merit instead of graft, bribery, or religious kinship—though in a footnote he added that naturalized Orientals from the British Raj were to be excluded: *Can the state repair the defects of heredity or of early education?*

Upon returning, and through a series of appointments that catapulted him to the highest offices in the city's bureaucracy, Moses became the most powerful man in the world's most powerful city. When Richard was a child, Moses buried the ash dumps in Queens with sod and seed to make Flushing Meadows Park. He paved over Manhattan's rail tracks so cars could glide along the Hudson. He ordered two hundred humongous trees from Long Island nurseries, had them trucked to Bryant Park and swung into position overnight. He stood up to the robber barons of Long Island, running highways through those tycoons' estates, building Bethpage State Park and Belmont Lake State Park and Heckscher State Park. He created beaches out of swampy marshland and erected convention centers, performance halls, and science centers.

In 1936, Robert Moses selected Brownsville for pool renovations sponsored by Roosevelt's Work Progress Administration, and, once the city had completed its improvements, he came to direct the opening ceremony. Hundreds of families gathered in Betsy Head Park that special night. They crowded onto the bleacher stands and on all four sides of the enormous white tarp. A city worker yanked back the tarp, revealing the transformation of their small stone pool into an Olympic-class facility as wide as the block was long. Green, pink, and blue beams of light rippled through the water, eliciting gasps from the crowd. Alderman Hart proclaimed the rebirth of the neighborhood, and a rabbi and a preacher performed blessings, reflections of the water warbling on their robes.

Then came the commissioner himself, a man like a towering monument, glowing in his white suit, stepping forward as the people chanted "Moses! Moses!" After a few remarks, he handed the shears to Mayor La Guardia.

And then the eruption! Scissors slicing through ribbons, fireworks exploding above the pavilion. The Thomas Jefferson High School band played "You're a Grand Old Flag" while Brooklyn College's swim team dove into the water. Most of Moses's opening ceremonies were elaborate, but the ones for the pools especially so. Moses liked to swim, and he saw himself in the young men who arrived at the ceremony in their suits, eager for the first lap.

Richard had grown up near the bay, but he'd never learned to swim. At the Betsy Head Park pool, he watched how the other boys kicked their feet, and he imitated them, but he was afraid to let go of the pool's rim or to leave the shallow end. Eventually, he fought through his fear and let himself float; he learned to bear the sting in his nose and the chill in his limbs. By September, he could make it across the sixteen-foot deep end.

From then on, he went to the pool every summer, especially for the free hour at ten o'clock, whether his father needed him at the restaurant or not, so that one day he would become the neighborhood's fastest swimmer. He kept to himself, for the older he grew, the more he tired of the way his friends teased him.

Below the water, Richard sometimes saw the ancestors clustered near the drains: toothless A Bak with lumps under her eyelids and frowning Bak Geng, whose long beard hung like a dog tail from his chin. They urged him to return home and help his father with the mopping. "You're not allowed here!" he'd shout at them. Whenever they made a reach for his legs, he kicked them away.

He was thirteen when a young Jewish lifeguard with a bushel of curly hair squatted at the pool's edge and offered to time Richard on his watch.

"Two minutes and thirty-nine seconds. Not bad," the teenager said when Richard returned, gasping for breath. "You ever play baseball?"

Richard shrugged.

"I'll teach you. Come find me at Nanny Goat Park tomorrow afternoon. Christopher Avenue."

The young Jew, Alan Friedman, was the cofounder of a new group called the Brownsville Boys Club, an organization created by and for the boys of the neighborhood, without any adult interference. Alan and his friends had gathered boys from every warring block and united them with the mission of securing better facilities to play ball. They'd succeeded in winning meeting space at the Brownsville Children's Library and even persuaded the board of education to reopen the P.S. 184 gyms.

They needed hardworking players on their baseball and basketball teams.

"Each member pays a penny to be in the club. Don't matter your religion, don't matter your nation of origin," Alan told Richard at Nanny Goat Park. "We follow a strict code: no stealing, no gang fights, no slurs. Those are the club's rules that we voted on ourselves—we're a democracy, we make our own decisions, just like the American forefathers wrote in the Constitution. A Brownsville democracy. You want to be a member?"

Richard said he did. From then on, he attended the practices every afternoon. He learned how to hold a bat, how to throw a black-ball, and how to dunk on a basketball court. Koon Lai, resigned to his son's lack of studiousness, felt it was better than him aimlessly roaming the streets.

The Friedmans, Richard learned in time, were respected people in the neighborhood. Alan's father owned the butchery near Amboy Street and was known for his eloquent speeches at the Labor Ly-ceum; Mrs. Friedman volunteered for the Hebrew Ladies Day Nurs-ery. There was also the daughter, Rebecca, valedictorian of the junior high, and everyone said Alan would become the first Jewish presi-dent of the United States.

When the Brownsville Boys Club newspaper came off the press, Richard accompanied Alan through the neighborhood, handing it out in schoolyards and on street corners, and in that way, he gained a new name: not Chinaman, not Chop Suey Kid, but Right-Hand Man to Founding Member of the Brownsville Boys Club. Friend to Alan Friedman.

The club obtained city grants for field trips. Richard loved every one of those adventures: to the Empire State Building, to the circus, to Fort Tilden, and, of course, to Ebbets Field. There was always a long line of people, and everyone would wait patiently for hours to cram into that tight cigar box of a stadium, to stare down at the ball-fields ringed with ads for Griffin Microsheen and Luckies cigarettes, and then finally, finally to see the muscled, gum-chewing fellows with big white *B*'s on their blue baseball caps.

In his second year in the Brownsville Boys Club, Richard made it onto the All-Star softball team that competed in citywide competi-tions. They rode the IRT dressed in ties and slacks and carried their shorts and sneakers in brown paper bags. Richard felt himself float-ing, rising. His mouth hurled new phrases free and fast: "Hold your horses!" and "Break a leg!" He was conquering the English language like he had conquered Coney Island and the pool.

One afternoon, Alan held a conference on "The Negro Question" at the Brownsville Boys Club headquarters.

"Citizens," Alan said to all the boys gathered in the Stone Avenue library. They sat on wood chairs, on the floor, and on top of the bookcases. "If we believe in democracy, if we loathe fascism, if we believe in the American way, where every one of us, of whatever nation, of whatever creed, should have a say in this society, then what would make us stop at color?"

The group clapped and whooped.

Richard was familiar enough with what Alan called "the Negroes." A few of his junior high school classmates were hak gui, and they seemed normal enough. At the same time, Richard had learned a thing or two about hak gui from *LIFE* magazine. Once, he'd come across a cartoon illustrating the world's people. The cartoon showed a mountain, and at its peak, a white man with one foot raised. Down the mountain, a man with skin yellow as egg yolk toiled on a plateau, and on a lower hill, a nearly naked brown man picked fruit off a tree. At the very bottom, a hak gui lay flat on her behind, licking the ripened fruit that had fallen to the ground.

There had also been a second yellow man in the cartoon, climbing up the side of the mountain at fantastic speed. He held an abacus, and his thin nose and spectacled eyes made him resemble a dark-haired version of the white man at the peak. "Rise of the Japanese Empire," the caption said, but in Richard's mind, this superior yellow man was himself.

All that said, when Alan asked the members to take a vote on whether "Negroes" should be recruited into the club, Richard raised his hand along with everyone else.

Over the next few weeks, the officers invited Black boys into the club space. Richard liked playing paddleball with Freddie Johnson; Freddie put up a strong defense but was always a good sport the times Richard beat him. Willy Patterson was so good at math he could help the older kids with their homework. When they went to the Italian and Irish neighborhoods and kicked the butts of the opposing teams, those kids would chase them all the way to the subway station, screaming, "Go home you kikes, chinks, and coons!"

But the Brownsville Boys were faster, and together they'd dive through the closing doors of the IRT and laugh so hard that tears fell.

During those same years, a grave silence fell over Canton Kitchen. The Japanese military had sunk its teeth into the heart of the motherland, had mashed and devoured Canton City. The restaurant workers kept a cardboard relief fund box by the cash register and bowed their heads with gratitude whenever a bak gui stuffed a dollar in the slot. Every Saturday, Koon Lai took a trolley to Chinatown for a "Bowl of Rice" fundraiser, or to donate blood, or to join a parade—a hundred homesick fathers marching the Chinese flag up and down Broadway.

"Dun Ho, your mother walked to Gui Lin. Fourteen days," Koon Lai would explain at dinner, handing Richard his mother's letters, though Richard had already forgotten most Chinese characters. "Everyone in the village has fled."

"Dun Ho, do you know what the Japanese did in Nam Gein? They killed everybody. They did terrible things to the girls."

"Dun Ho, the gum in your mouth. In China that gum could buy a dinner for a starving family."

None of the Brownsville Boys Club members seemed to know about the war in China; they never spoke of it, and neither did Richard. At night, however, he'd stumble his way onto Cloud Hill and find the ancestors sprawled in the mud, their withered bodies battered and bloodied. Sometimes his mother would be one of those battered bodies. Yet in the morning, when he was on the asphalt at Nanny Goat Park or racing across the Betsy Head Park pool, everything happening in China seemed no realer than a dream.

It was Pearl Harbor that resolved his inner discord. The night of the attack, he huddled with his father and the restaurant workers around the radio, and on their behalf, translated the president's words:

". . . A date which will live in infamy . . ." *Goi ng hui mong gi gai yi diem.*

". . . many American lives have been lost . . ." *Hou o mi gok ngin hei sha sei!*

". . . a state of war . . ." *Mi Gok nui jein!*

Now America knew what it felt like. His fathers and the workers cheered, sharing their bottles of diu with Richard.

Soon after, the city mandated air-raid drills, and it became Richard's job to turn off the lights, swathing the restaurant dining room and their customers in whispering darkness. The Brownsville Boys Club organized a scrap metal collection and attended the war effort benefit concert at the Pitkin Loew's. And the country needed its Chinese too—had finally claimed them. Now they could apply for citizenship, or work in the defense plants, or even serve under the American flag. At last, Richard thought, everyone was on the same team, a team called America, land of the free. Yet one day the dishwasher came home from the subway complaining that a bak gui had spit in his face.

"He called me Jap!" the worker exclaimed. "And I told him in English—'No, I not Jap. I Chinese, I not Jap.'"

"They can't tell the difference."

"I'll make you a T-shirt," Richard declared. "On the front, *Chinese— not Japanese*, on the back, *Believe me, I hate those nips way more than you do!*"

The workers laughed, and they said to one another that the boss's son talked like an American now, his English far better than theirs.

A week before his departure to the army base, Alan invited Richard for Shabbat dinner with his parents and sister—Richard's first invitation to an American home.

On that Friday afternoon, he hogged the restaurant bathroom to slick his hair, straighten his tie, and scrub his nails. He was sure, on the walk to Herzl Street, that his hands still reeked of scallions. It was raining, which made things worse: leaves stuck to the bottom of his shoes, and he knew that by the time he arrived, he'd look like a farmer returning from the rice paddies. When he reached the house, he stood outside the iron fence, wondering what he could do to fix himself.

Just then, Alan's sister Rebecca opened the door.

He'd seen her a couple of times, though usually from a distance, in the halls at school—she was in the year above him at Thomas Jefferson High. But getting a good look now, and in this particular way, Richard forgot all his English.

She was about his height and very slight, with a narrow face and a pointy chin. She played with the braid on her shoulder, her lips pursed, then encouraged him to hurry inside before he got sick. She took his umbrella and wet jacket, trying to assess whether he'd need to change, and touched the shoulders of his shirt. He tried to hide his incredulity, and berated himself for not bringing flowers.

"Let me give you a tour!" she said, taking one of his empty hands.

They walked to the kitchen, where a Jewish lady prepared a meal.

"This is Ima," Rebecca said, and she squeezed Mrs. Friedman's shoulders like her mother was a favorite doll. Mrs. Friedman turned around and smiled.

"Welcome, Richard!" she said, her laughter just like her daughter's. As if he were her own son, she embraced him.

They continued to the living room, where a man listened to the radio report.

"This is Abba," Rebecca said. "He's worried about the battle in Kharkov."

"Richard," said the man, looking distracted. "We'll get to talking, soon as the report is over."

They climbed the stairs. "My bedroom!" Rebecca said with delight. Her bed was so high off the floor that he strained to imagine how she climbed onto it, and there were so many novels strewn across the bed that he wondered if she slept with them in her arms.

When Alan returned, they gathered in the dining room and watched Mrs. Friedman light the candles and say the Hebrew prayers.

There were prayers for each of the young people, and Mr. Friedman offered another for the wine, but Richard was so distracted by the amused way Rebecca smiled at him and by his own hunger that he barely paid attention.

"It's your people and my people," said Mr. Friedman when they'd begun to eat. "Of course, the whole world's in chaos. But think, *think* of the millions of our people back in the old country. Our people are in the gravest danger."

"There's so much intolerance, so much cruelty in the world," piped in Rebecca. "It's the opposite of the Jewish way. Have you been to a seder, Richard?"

He shook his head.

"We should invite him, Abba. Yiddishkayt asks that we devote ourselves to tzedakah—*charity and justice.*"

She was president of a club called Students for the Protection of European Jewry. Before the attack on Pearl Harbor, the members had written letters to Roosevelt encouraging him to intervene in the war on behalf of the Jews of Europe—and for the Chinese, too, she said, glancing at Richard. Now that Roosevelt had answered their prayers, they knit clothing for Brooklyn's soldiers and held fundraisers for Jewish widows.

Richard knew he should have been listening and responding, but he was no longer his American self—jovial, loud, and eager to tell a joke. He felt weak and famished, and the more chunks of challah he stuffed in his mouth, the more he realized that bread would not satisfy him. He wanted to go upstairs with Rebecca and kiss her.

Looking up at the wall, Richard noticed that within the frames of the Friedmans' family photos, his own ancestors were creeping around: rope-chinned Bak Geng nestling his face against the fair cheek of a wispy-haired blond woman, toothless A Bak butting her head between two bearded men in ushankas. Richard gritted his teeth as a whole bunch of rice farmers tromped into a Friedman family portrait, the farmers' garments as shapeless as potato sacks, their faces sun-splotched, their straw hats consuming too much space, making a further spectacle of themselves as they sat cross-legged in front of the heavily garmented Friedmans.

Your people and my people.

Richard wanted to snap at them. *Scat!*

"Whaddaya think, boychik?" said Rebecca, and she leaned over and pinched his arm. He looked up at her, no notion of what she'd just said, but that hardly mattered. It seemed to him that, unlike any girl he'd ever met, she was eager for his attention. He nodded, smiling, and looked down at his plate.

He grew bold enough to call every weekend. He and Rebecca would sit at the kitchen table, and she would talk about her ambitions to become a history teacher, or she'd read aloud Alan's letters. Alan was with the troops in Italy. Alan had tried, unsuccessfully, to stop the execution of a Jewish family.

"Don't worry about Alan," Richard said after they'd read this. "He's got the best eye on the field."

She stared at the kitchen clock like it would tell her when Alan would come home. Richard was envious of Alan's eloquence. With each week, he felt increasingly miserable, knowing life after he finished high school would be just the same as always, his days spent toiling in the kitchen, wiping up soy sauce spills. The counselor at school had said he wasn't "college material." Even his father had stopped pretending.

Unless—he realized on his walk back to the restaurant—unless he fought in the war.

He was sixteen. If the war held out just two more years, he'd be eligible for enrollment. He'd enlist in the air force and take down Japanese warplanes, or maybe the navy, to torpedo Nazi submarines. He'd come back taller and smarter: a hero. He'd make Rebecca proud.

LINA

When Lina and Tyrell reached the school on Blake Avenue for HPD's community planning meeting, there were already a fair number of people gathered. Entering the school gymnasium, she recognized staff from the family health center and a few tenant leaders. Yet the longer she looked around the gym, the more she wondered: Who were all these others?

At the registration desk, Tyrell was assigned to table 4, and Lina to table 5. There were six others at her table, including a girl from the Department of Parks who asked each participant to introduce themselves.

"My name is Lina Rodriguez Armstrong. I'm a retired art teacher. I've lived in Brownsville since I was eleven years old, and I'll do anything for my people."

Next was Ms. Radcliff, who sat on the Community Education Council; Mr. Hernandez, the owner of an appliance store on Pitkin; and a French man who turned out to be the CEO for Bernard & Co., the real estate company behind the new condominium on Eastern Parkway.

And, by an unfortunate coincidence: Mrs. Jameson, the neighbor who had refused to speak to Lina for months. They were about the same age but rarely saw eye to eye. That past June, they had argued at the Seventy-Third Precinct community council meeting, and right in front of the cops, Mrs. Jameson had called Lina a "crazy radical lesbian police abolitionist." Lina had not denied it—she'd tried to make it into a teachable moment for the community members.

At their table, she could see Mrs. Jameson's left hand trembling like a mouse squirming in a trap. With her right hand, she struggled to hold the left one still. *She's still sitting in the hospital chair*, Lina thought to herself. Lina had experienced enough grief to recognize it right away. Mrs. Jameson had lost her grandson ten years earlier, but the wound remained fresh. She probably demanded maximum policing for the same reason Lina demanded a community land trust: remorse.

The Parks Department girl explained that the group's first task would be to use smiley-face stickers to label the map of Brownsville with the neighborhood's "assets"—places, things, or resources that were already proving beneficial to the community.

Lina laughed aloud. "You better give me my own sheet of stickers."

She stuck one smack in the middle of the neighborhood, at the Betsy Head Park pool.

"Also, the Brownsville Recreation Center. It started as the Brownsville Boys Club. I got my first job there as a summer camp counselor . . . Oh!" She threw down three more stickers. "The barbershops, because those are community centers too—counseling centers for our young men."

And Elite Salon on Pitkin, which used to be Motor City Salon back in the eighties, she thought. Back then, Lina would stop outside the window and press her nose to the glass just to look at Nellie: a goddess with her updo and white platform shoes. But this was an asset too personal to explain.

The other participants placed stickers on the libraries, the Nehemiah homes, and the charter school. Then it occurred to Lina that huge chunks of the neighborhood's east side remained sticker-less.

She plonked some smileys down on Brownsville Houses, Van

Dyke Houses, Tilden Houses, Marcus Garvey Village, Langston Hughes Houses, Howard Houses, and the others. "With the gentrification, we need NYCHA more than ever."

Next, she was thinking about all the kinds of things that happened without a place marker, that just happened in the street. All the cars decked in West Indian flags that zoomed past on Labor Day, blasting reggae and soca. Preachers on sidewalk podiums. Barbecue parties. The laughter in courtyards, on sidewalks. The way folks took care of one another.

Mrs. Jameson laid a sticker on the precinct. Lina resisted the urge to remove it, though she doubted Giuliani himself would have called the Seventy-Third an *asset*. It had been routine, in the '90s, for Brownsville's cops to shake down drug dealers, split the cash, then resell the booty to other narcos.

When the Parks Department girl asked the group to identify "deficits," Lina sighed. She grabbed a Post-it and wrote, чо Years Vacant Lot—Should Be Cultural Center/LGBTQ Youth Center, and stuck it to her lot on Livonia Avenue.

"We have an idea for this site and we're prepared to talk about it," Lina said, taking the flash drive out of her pocket.

The others at the table noted that Pitkin Avenue had too many salons and pawnshops and needed greater retail diversity. "We have more methadone clinics than fresh food grocers!" Ms. Radcliff exclaimed.

There were also playgrounds that needed fixing, basketball courts without hoops, the ever-postponed 3 to the L connection, broken streetlights, and of course the gas issue at 287 Blake, all of which Lina agreed needed attention—but why did they need to itemize these things when they were already in the community board needs list every year? And now she was starting to wonder, was there going to be a chance to play the PowerPoint?

The Parks Department girl didn't know what to do with Lina's PowerPoint, so Lina went looking for Olivia and Andrew. At the HPD resource table, another white boy in khakis said Olivia and Andrew weren't in attendance and that, no, there was no projector available.

"Well, that's a problem," said Lina.

"I'm sorry if there was a miscommunication."

"I guess I'll have to give my presentation without it, then."

"Time is pretty tight, but we can definitely consider making presentations part of the next community meeting."

He volunteered to take Lina's PowerPoint back to his office for the agency's review. Biting her tongue, Lina resigned herself to this, and they walked over to the tables at the gym's entrance so he could stick the flash drive into his laptop.

"Are you a resident of Brownsville?"

"I wouldn't be here if I wasn't."

"That's great. Do you work in Brownsville as well?"

"I'm retired," she stated, though there was no such thing as retirement when you were a community activist.

After he'd copied the PowerPoint and handed back the drive, Lina returned to her table, but she was ready to leave. They'd told her to share her ideas, make this a democratic process, and then they'd stuffed a pacifier in her mouth. It was in moments like this that she did feel crazy. That the doubt crept in. Why even try?

While her tablemates discussed the best height for new buildings in the neighborhood, Lina thought again about Mr. Wong. He must have made the big bucks, more than he'd ever made running a Chinese restaurant, she thought. He probably took it and moved to Florida.

How he lived with himself, she had no idea.

After the meeting was over and as she was waiting in the hallway for Tyrell, a girl scooted up to her, someone she'd never seen before. The young woman had a long black ponytail, an olive complexion—might have been Arab or Filipino, but she wasn't from Brownsville. At first, Lina thought she was another representative from the city come to make a promise she couldn't keep, but then the girl surprised her.

"Hi, I'm Sadie—I'm a reporter for *New Gotham*. I was wondering if you'd be willing to share your opinion of the meeting?"

"Oh. You're that *New Gotham* reporter."

In Lina's humble opinion, that article on the mayor's press conference hadn't qualified as journalism. Where was the history of the struggle? Where were the hard-hitting questions for the mayor about his timeline, the resources for his plan?

"I'm not talking to the press today."

"It will only take a second," the girl pleaded. "I really need the perspective of residents in this piece."

Lina turned and walked toward the exit of the school. She couldn't recall how many times she'd agreed to interviews, but she could count on one hand how many times it had helped. If they'd paid Lina every time they misspelled her name or mischaracterized what she'd said, she would probably be a rich lady by now. She'd have built the cultural center on her own dime.

The girl, however, followed Lina right down the steps of the school.

"Off the record?" she begged.

Lina considered it. She didn't know if she could trust the reporter, but she also didn't want her just copying and pasting the city's press release.

"Okay. If we're off, off, off the record, I'll tell you this. We prepared a presentation, and they didn't let us share it. Do they want to hear from residents, or do they just want to make it seem that way?"

The girl nodded and scribbled madly.

"I've been saying this for fifty years. Brownsville should be its own nation. Brownsville as a people should run the schools, run the Seventy-Third Precinct, and we should decide what gets built."

The girl probably knew nothing about the strike of '68. While Lina was trying to decide if she had the energy to provide context, Tyrell emerged from the school doors. He was, of course, excited that Lina had commented to a reporter—he was always pushing their "media strategy." He'd even set up a Facebook account for Lina, though she'd refused to be introduced to "Twitter" and "Instagram." At her age, one was good enough.

"Ms. Lina, you should give her the presentation, get the Livonia cultural center out to the public."

Lina gave him the side-eye. Tyrell had been pleased to see a nice description of BYTE in that *New Gotham* piece. He turned to the girl.

"I know we met. Your name again?"

"Sadie Chin."

"Sadie, glad to see you here. As I'm sure Ms. Lina was telling you, we've got our own vision for an empty lot in the community. They didn't let us present it, but you can get it out to the public for us."

"I absolutely can! And I'm happy to get the mayor's office on the record about it!"

Tyrell puppy-dog-eyed Lina until she sighed, removed the flash drive from her pocket, and dropped it in Tyrell's palm. He passed it right to Sadie.

"You have to promise to read every part," said Lina. "No misquoting."

The reporter nodded eagerly, then kneeled on the steps of the school, whipped out her shining MacBook, and plugged in the flash drive. Lina shook her head.

"You better be careful with that laptop, mami."

The child was naïve as hell. Who could say what would come of this collaboration? She and Tyrell would just have to wait and see.

THE WONGS

There was a man in Chinatown with a knack for producing imitation authorization papers and birth certificates.

They had already adapted to a new surname, and now Richard would simply have to adjust to a new birthday. Not a later birthday— there was no way Koon Lai could hold Richard back a year, as the plan depended completely on his son's cooperation. Rather, Koon Lai had been hearing from his friends at the association that when a navy boy returned home, he preened in his silly white hat and blue bow tie, but when an army boy returned, it was usually as the contents of a flag-draped box.

So, in October 1944, four months before Richard's actual eighteenth birthday, Koon Lai gave Richard the gift of adulthood, on the condition that he go downtown and sign up for the navy. That way, when Richard actually turned eighteen in the city registry, he'd already be on a ship somewhere—and some other guy would be picked for the army trenches. It was a plan that his son, so desperate to leave, would embrace.

Yet when Richard departed for navy boot camp in Key West, Koon Lai worried incessantly. Maybe he had sent the boy to his drowning death. He missed the sound of Richard's clompy feet pounding up the narrow staircase, and even the mosquitoes that swarmed them when Richard opened a window too wide and stuck out his head to holler at friends. Koon Lai was so used to his irritation that he'd forgotten how lonely he'd been before his son's arrival.

One evening about three weeks after his departure, Richard called the kitchen phone.

"Dun Ho," Koon Lai answered, his heart pounding. "Ni ou nai?"

"Still at the training base," the boy said in English. "There's nothing to report."

"Ni hiak fan miang a?"

"Twenty minutes ago. Potato and meatloaf. In the cafeteria. It was fine."

It was not the words that comforted Koon Lai, but the tone: Richard was bored. Safe. He had not left the navy base yet but was already coming to his senses. Richard was not a studious child, but at least Koon Lai could prepare him to take over the restaurant one day.

It was true that, down at Key West, the navy was not meeting Richard's expectations. So it occurred to him that the world tended to overpromise, to keep him ever-hopeful but never fulfilled.

What bothered Richard wasn't the physical toil, or even the tasteless food in the cafeteria, but the mockery—how certain boys would raise their voices in an abrasive falsetto. "Me no muscle. Too many push-up. Me don't like beef. Me want cat for dinner." He thought his age-mates had outgrown this nastiness, but it turned out Brownsville was the anomaly.

There were two Puerto Rican recruits who appeared willing to be his friends: one from Harlem, the other from Orchard Street. They always left room for him at their table in the cafeteria. But they spoke Spanish when he wasn't around and sometimes even in his presence, and he didn't like the feeling that the three of them had been disposed of, ghettoized, at the table closest to the bathroom.

One night in the showers, as he scrubbed hastily beneath the lukewarm water, he heard a cackling in the stall next to him and saw a blond, freckled recruit smirking and shaking his head, his eyes on Richard's wiener.

"Y'all got itty-bitty ones," the young man said with a Southern lilt. "Size of my thumb, I swear."

Richard, naked and dripping wet, lunged at the young man and knocked him to the ground. Next, he punched him in the jaw, busting his lip. Blood dribbled down the boy's chin like hot sauce. They fought until a junior lieutenant pulled them apart.

"Quit rolling around like faggots!"

The fight earned him some enemies but also some friends, including two Irish guys from the Bronx named Connor and Rory. He worked hard to keep their favor, which sometimes meant tossing in a few dirty jokes during supper. "Every time that Spanish guy jerks off, I think a dog got in the room," he'd whisper to his friends. Or: "When this Puerto Rican comes back from drill, he smells like a pair of old sneakers!" After about a month at Key West, Connor and Rory included him in their backslapping and shower singing, and on their jaunts to the downtown nightclubs.

Ultimately, they spent five months at sea, engaged mostly in scrubbing the deck. Then a telegraph reached the ship, declaring the war over. All the boys celebrated, and each was secretly relieved, for the more stories a young man hears about other boys rendered armless, legless, and blind, the more he dreads returning home mobile as a tree trunk.

Richard ran down the plank onto the docks of Battery Park and discovered a jubilant city—confetti everywhere and cars rolling slowly like parade floats, using their horns to ramp up the revelry. If he and his mates entered a subway car, the New York rules of silent, stony decorum fell away: little kids scurried up to touch his uniform; suited old men patted him on the back. At the clubs, bak gui girls flung their arms around his neck and begged him for a dance, and in the window of a Blake Avenue shop, he found his name printed on a sign with all the other vets from Brownsville.

He'd left Brownsville a swimmer, a baseball player, but to his delight, he had returned a man. As he masticated a wad of gum in his cheek, his navy cap tilted on his brow, Richard felt he was approaching Gary Cooper– or Humphrey Bogart–level suaveness, though of course, there was that one difference.

He hadn't written Rebecca letters from Key West, hadn't the nerve to try forming a sentence that would compare with one of Alan's, and hoped she wouldn't think he'd forgotten her. On his second day back, he strode up to the Friedman house in his cap and uniform.

"Miss Friedman!" he called when he spotted her on the porch swing. Then he realized someone was sitting beside her. Another soldier.

"Richard! Thank God you're home! Alan said you were back!" Leaping up from the hammock, she hurried to the fence, embraced him tightly, and kissed him on the cheek. A six-foot-tall GI, hands in his pockets, followed her down the steps. "Joe, this is Richard Wong, have you met Richard?"

"Don't think I've had the pleasure. Joe Salzman," said the GI.

Richard contorted his lips into a smile and shook Joe's hand.

"Richard, look." Rebecca extended her left hand. She pursed her lips, waiting for his response. "I'm going to be Rebecca Salzman."

Richard said nothing for a noticeable stretch of time.

"Well," he finally stuttered, his eyes on the pearl. "Look at that."

"The wedding is next month."

"We'll send an invitation. All her friends are invited."

"And we made a down payment today on a house in Marine Park."

The wind scraped through fallen leaves and tussled with the American flag on the porch of the next-door row house. Richard fixed his gaze there.

"Congratulations," he muttered. "I guess I should be going."

"Don't worry, boychik." She pinched his shoulder. "I'll still be around. When I finish my degree, I plan to teach in Brownsville!"

At that moment, Mrs. Friedman hurried outside to embrace Richard and invite him in for egg salad. Richard declined. "I got business at the navy office," he lied. "Got to get there before closing."

He took off down the block, wondering where he could go. A young man in Brownsville had no privacy, a young Chinese man even less, and there was no room to be weak, not even for a moment, no nook in which he could hide from the eyes of his neighbors.

He caught a train to Times Square and wandered the streets still dirty with trampled streamers, and to whoever would buy him a drink, he mumbled complaints about his father. That was how he passed the several weeks that followed, drunk on whiskey and roaming, or with the girls in the swing clubs. These were bak gui girls who ordered men like drinks, and he was on the menu.

One night, when he stumbled off the IRT in Brownsville and trudged to the second floor, his father was awake, waiting for him at a table in the dark dining room.

"Ni so ga!"

"It's you who's crazy, Ba." Richard staggered through the room until they were chest to chest. "It's you who's crazy. What do we got? Nothing. No record player. We live with our workers. You don't got even a second shirt. We're worse off than the peasants in Toisan. And all for what? So you can give all your money to the association and look like a big man."

"And what you do since come home?" Koon Lai stammered in English. "You go bar. You go dance. You do nothing."

"I can't do *this*, Ba."

"Do what?"

"Waste my life serving pork chops."

"How you live?"

"Fuck this, Ba."

"You can't get the job. You don't study."

"I'll get a job."

"How?"

Richard didn't answer, instead forcing the little man out of his way so he could make it to the sink in time to vomit. He awoke the next morning on the kitchen floor with flakes of saltines on his lips and his hair baked in Hamm's beer.

And that's when, in the desperation of his shame, he had an idea.

"Baba, I'll fix cars. I'll have a shop of my own."

"Where you fix car? No place to fix car."

But Richard applied, and the Veterans' Commission gave him a scholarship to attend an auto-mechanic school in nearby Canarsie. He rode the trolley down Rockaway to newly subdivided streets where there'd been farms only ten years earlier. Now bungalows had sprung up on all the roads, and the air was thick with sawdust and paint.

He found he liked working under the hoods and reassembling engines; he'd always been skilled with his hands. Yet the instructor, Vito Conti, rubbed him the wrong way. He played favorites with the students, and Richard was no favorite. *So fuck Conti*, Richard told himself. He showed up late one week, then skipped class altogether.

When he received Rebecca's wedding invitation, he buried it on the shelf with his father's old notebooks and tried to forget the date. It was his father's habit to hide bits of money throughout the back room, and between the notebooks, Richard discovered an unmarked heng bou with four hundred dollars.

He was nineteen, with nothing to his name.

The money was apparently to help with the funeral of a cousin, but Richard had spent it before he found this out—and there was never a better moment to own a car. Everywhere, the rails and cables of trolley lines had been scraped away to make room for the automobile.

Richard bought a map of the city's new highways and tackled them one by one. He drove himself to games at Yankee Stadium and to the beaches on the Long Island Sound. He glided from tip to tip of Manhattan, weaving his way ahead of the cabs. The only place he wouldn't go was Chinatown. His father's friends would urge him to become a bookkeeper at the Chin Association, or manager of this or that restaurant.

Like bees attracted to the bright yellow of his car, the bak gui girls appeared in droves. He'd beckon a girl into the passenger seat, then whisk her off onto the highways. If it was rush hour, the cars would be jammed nose to nose, but at the right time of day, he could take those chicks fast as a horse on the plain or a plane on the runway, conquering wide immensities.

More than anything he loved taking them to Coney Island—to the Cyclone. His date would cling to his arm, begging for mercy, and he'd laugh and tease, "Baby, why're you closing your eyes? This is the best part!" How powerful he felt, how hard he laughed when they reached the top and began to tip forward, his girl screaming for her life. Then he'd hustle through the crowd at Nathan's to order a feast of crab cakes, franks, oysters, and elephant ears, eating most of it himself since the girl feared looking pudgy.

Rumors spread back to Chinatown. A member of the Chin Association had spotted him and a blond licking ice cream and kicking heels at the South Street Seaport pier. A second cousin had seen him parked at Grand Army Plaza, tangled with a redhead. At the association meetings, they urged Koon Lai: fly the boy home.

Koon Lai sent Suet Fong a letter with detailed instructions, then bought his son the boat tickets.

"I have something for you," he said to Richard one night in the back room, and, just as Mr. Lee had done for him, he tucked a heng bou envelope into Richard's breast pocket.

Throwing himself on his mattress, Richard grinned. "You sending me to China to pick out a Chinese woman?"

"I'm sending you to see your mother," Koon Lai shot back, and Richard, suddenly quiet, rolled onto his elbow.

In the dozen years since he'd left, he had thought of his mother often, though only for a few seconds at a time, always quick to close the lid on that can. But now he had the ticket in his shirt; he could not pass up an opportunity to see her.

He flew to San Francisco, then boarded the ship to Canton. To his relief, it was not like the one on which he'd come to America. His father had paid for a bed in a better tier, and he dined in a hall with both bak gui and Chinese.

When he went to eat supper on the first night, he hesitated for a moment in front of the self-segregating groups of Chinese people and white Americans.

"We've got room for you," an American voice called to him, but when he turned around, it was a young Chinese man who beamed. The soldier was surrounded by five other Chinese men, each wearing an American air force uniform.

He'd never seen so many like himself, smiling not in the timorous way the Chinese smile, but with the beaming confidence of American men.

"Being here, you forget the way we lived," one of them was saying. "You know what I mean? No heat, no running water, no toilet. When I was in Beijing, I met these kids—poor as hell. Never seen a watch. They kept grabbing my wrist, tapping the glass, saying something in Mandarin. Honestly, I didn't have a clue what they were saying."

"Chinese women don't ask for much," said another. "Buy her a box of chocolates and she'll eat one piece a year, for ten years."

Richard's new Californian companions had been back to China already, fighting on the Pacific front, and now they were returning for wives. The American government had passed a law, Richard learned from them, allowing Chinese American veterans to bring a bride from China over to the States: a reward for their service. And so, these men were hitching to China to claim their prize. They wanted an America full of strawberry-nosed, fat-cheeked children. By the time they'd docked, and before Koon Lai's plan had begun to unfold, Richard thought he might desire the same.

When he arrived in Hong Kong, a delegation of Chins had been organized to greet him. They held a banner: WELCOM HOME DUN HO RICHARD SOLDER. He leapt toward it, and then he saw his mother.

It was as if someone had taken a soup spoon and carved the fat out of her cheeks.

"Dun Ho, aiya, you are so tall, so strong!" his mother cried, though her eyes remained dry of tears. "You're home! Are you hungry? You must be hungry!"

It was true that he was strong and that he was hungry, and he nodded and grinned, though his heart was suddenly heavy as a ship anchor.

But he had come home, which is what she'd always wanted. And she was his mother: What more could she want but to feed him?

In the smothering heat of Canton's most popular banquet house, he wined and dined with the relatives, piling his plate high with sea bass and tripe until he had to loosen his belt, paying for everything with the extra cash his father had given him.

"Is it true each man goes to university?"

"Is it true everybody has a car?"

"Is it true they eat meat like we eat rice?"

Richard grunted in the affirmative, turnip cake in his cheek. "Yeah, but sometimes they get tired of hamburgers. Why else would they eat Chinese food?"

Happy to hear their food was so respected, even in America, the peasants nodded.

The villagers had only ever taken wagons on the road, but Koon Lai had provisioned for private cabs. Like rich people, they hailed taxis and paid large sums for the ride to the country. Richard was introduced to the laborers hired to work his father's new field, and then forced to watch them whack a fish to death to demonstrate the freshness of his coming dinner.

After this, his mother laid a plate of boiled chicken on the altar and urged Richard to bai for the ancestors: Ngen Ngen and Bak Geng and the great-aunts and great-uncles who had pestered him daily in his Brownsville adolescence. He'd seen less of them since the navy, and he'd hoped they'd finally come to their senses and realized he was too American for this type of attention. Still, he was pleased when he lit the incense and the ancestors gathered quickly, their ragged spirits ballooning with the vapors of the meal. "Finally home," they whispered. "Look at him, a warrior!"

It was strange; he had long felt shame about his origins, and yet there was nothing so bad about the place.

Koon Lai had made special arrangements for the third day, but Richard's mother delayed these for as long as possible. Instead, she doted on Richard, serving him bowls of lychees, folding his blankets, washing his feet. Richard was amused at first, then unsure how to return his mother's affection, then increasingly uneasy. The longer he stayed and the more she pampered him, the sadder and weaker he became, like he was tumbling backward twelve years. It felt like if he didn't stand up and assert himself, he might crumple into a damaged thing. He couldn't risk this, and so after three weeks, he decided that his father likely needed him back at the restaurant, and told her so.

"Your baba," she responded, flat-toned. "Your baba can come to China now and find a bride to take to America. He should find a young girl. He'll like a young girl."

"Baba?" Richard was taken aback. "Baba didn't fight in the war. And he's afraid of women! He works and he sleeps."

They were both speechless after this exchange.

It was one day later that the curtained litter arrived from Ng village: a schoolteacher and his nineteen-year-old daughter.

"A nice pretty girl," his mother said. "Why not take her into town for tea?"

Richard consented, if only to escape his mother.

The girl from Ng village was pretty but very quiet. He tried to make up for the awkward silences by boasting about his exploits in the navy, and he pitied her, that she had never heard of the Brooklyn Dodgers or tasted ice cream. In two days, the Ng village man offered his daughter's hand—and what white man would ever do that for him?

The girl from Ng village did not exude sex. Having her, he knew, would lack the triumph of earlier escapades—there had been no greater victory than to have a white woman below him. Yet without a doubt, Ng Foon Wah was the kind of girl who could save a box of chocolates for ten years. For this, he adored her and became determined to provide her everything a woman could want: all the dresses and shoes and jewelry she could dream of; more excitement, in the big city, than she could even believe possible; and above all, a house of their own, in Brooklyn.

SADIE

The night Sadie figured it out, Park Slope was celebrating its favorite holiday. All up and down the neighborhood's streets, children pranced and skipped and made strange noises that threatened to break her concentration. Of course, back when she'd been younger and her relationship to Park Slope less complicated, she'd dressed up as Ariel, Sherlock Holmes, Mulan for several years, and Sarah Palin her senior year of high school.

Sadie had considered going to a party, but she'd bailed at the last minute because she'd come to a startling realization—one that, in hindsight, she wondered why she hadn't landed on earlier.

The lot that Ms. Lina was trying to develop was the same one where her grandparents' restaurant had been.

She wanted to determine when the restaurant had existed, and at what point Ms. Lina had lived there. Ms. Lina had said a fire had burned down the whole building, but Sadie could find nothing about a fire in her newspaper archive searches.

Running her fingers across a faux fur robe—she'd been planning a Macklemore-themed costume—Sadie recalled her interactions with Ms. Lina and Tyrell over the previous weeks, trying to remember what else Ms. Lina had shared. After their first encounter outside the school, Sadie had stayed up until three a.m. perfecting her article on the community planning meeting, ensuring she included a diversity of quotes as well as an accurate summary of Ms. Lina's vision for the lot on Livonia.

It was after this that Ms. Lina and Tyrell began sending Sadie issues to cover: a maternal health workshop at the library on Mother Gaston, a Family Day barbecue and resource fair. And Sadie was grateful; Brownsvillians increasingly approved of her reporting. Most recently, Sadie had interviewed Tyrell about his nonprofit, BYTE.

They'd met up on October 25 at a hole-in-the-wall diner on Pitkin Avenue. When he arrived, Tyrell gave fist bumps to the men at the counter, and an older white man came out from the kitchen to take their orders. Sadie asked for water, as she couldn't eat and take notes simultaneously, but Tyrell requested eggs over easy, sausage, grits, a bagel, a full plate of banana pancakes, and a glass of orange juice. She tried to suppress her smile, but the waiter caught her eye.

"You know about this one?" he asked, his vowels stretched, a classic Italian Brooklynese. He leaned his elbows on the red granite counter and pointed at Tyrell with his pen. "This bag of sticks comes and eats all he needs for two weeks, in one go. And then he fasts. Like a bear."

"More like a camel," Tyrell replied, adding his own elbows to the counter. "Bears hibernate. Camels live in food deserts." The others at the counter chuckled. "Anyway, Paul, be careful what you say. This is Sadie Chin, a reporter with *New Gotham.*"

"Oh, I thought she was your new girlfriend," Paul replied. "I thought the other one ditched you after you mowed down those chocolate chip pancakes."

"And that's—that's a story for another time. Off the record," Tyrell said, and he shooed Paul away so they could get to work.

Sadie blushed. She wanted to know about Tyrell's dating life, but this was not relevant to the article. Swallowing her excitement, she took out her notebook.

"I'd love to know more about BYTE's Squash the Beef campaign. What does that entail?"

"Squash the Beef is now a city-recognized Cure Violence program. The Cure Violence model comes from Chicago, but every community has an instinct for self-policing . . ."

As she listened to his answers, she tried to comprehend how Tyrell, only seven years older than her, had enough stories to fill many lifetimes—all the false arrests, all the lives he'd saved. She badly wanted to kiss him.

The way people fetishized Black men, she knew. Yet she found herself drifting off, thinking about how thrilling it would be to go out with someone so completely different from the guys that she'd dated earlier. Tyrell had not been driven to college by helicopter parents who visited every three months, the way Mike's had. He was not sarcastic to mask his insecurity, like Adrian. He was surely not obsessed with the cheese graters at Stonewall Kitchen, like Alex. All three of her former boyfriends—two white, one Taiwanese American—lacked Tyrell's sense of purpose, his clarity of vision.

"You've heard of Man Up in East New York?" he asked, and she nodded even though she hadn't been listening.

She didn't dare cross any lines. A romantic interaction would constitute a violation of the first rule of journalism: no involvement with your sources, period. Instead, she did her best to keep it professional, refusing Tyrell's offers to buy her a coffee, and always keeping the conversation focused on him, though toward the end she couldn't resist telling him that she, too, had read Robin Kelley's *Freedom Dreams*.

"So you know what we're fighting for isn't new. It's part of the long struggle for self-determination and community control. We're talking about policing, land, the schools." It appeared to Sadie that everyone in the diner was listening. "And I'm not saying, 'Let's all move back to Africa.' All that Marcus Garvey nationalist shit. Excuse my language—don't quote that. What I'm saying is, here in Brownsville, we're creating a model for Black sovereignty within a diverse urban environment."

"You make me think of the Black Panther's Ten-Point Program," Sadie added, despite herself. "Like, doesn't it talk about how Black people should be able to determine the destiny of the Black community?"

"That's right. Most white folks have never even heard of the Ten-Point Program."

"It's like the way people think what happened in Ferguson this summer was just a riot," Sadie said. "A riot with no plan, no demands. But there *are* demands. The mainstream media just doesn't report them."

"So where'd you learn all this shit?"

Tyrell looked at Sadie as if he was seeing her for the first time.

"In African American Studies." Sadie hesitated. "At Yale."

Tyrell nodded and sipped the last of his orange juice.

Paul meandered over with the check, his eyebrows raised jauntily like he'd been listening and still didn't believe they were, in fact, just reporter and interviewee. Tyrell had only finished a third of his food, and so he had it packed to go, then paid and left with Sadie.

"I didn't finish college, I had some personal stuff going on," he said then, squinting up Pitkin Avenue. "But I never stop reading. That's what I always tell these guys. You don't need a degree to read."

She picked up just the slightest hint of self-doubt in his voice.

"Thank you so much for your time, Tyrell. I learned a lot." She turned off her recorder and slipped her notebook into her backpack.

"Which way you walking?" he asked.

"Down Rockaway to the train."

He nodded, and then they were together, strolling down Rockaway.

"If you don't mind me asking, where's your family from, like your ancestry?"

"I'm half Chinese and half Jewish," she volunteered, smiling when he raised his eyebrows. "My dad grew up here."

"Chinese and Jewish." He thought about this. "Oh yeah. Ms. Lina said this whole area used to be Jewish. When her family moved here."

"It was actually my Chinese family that lived here. They ran a restaurant. And my dad grew up in a house on Amboy."

"Oh yeah?" he laughed. "I guess you got roots in the 'Ville. And you? You grew up in Brooklyn?"

She nodded.

"Which part?"

"Park Slope. But it was not as gentrified back then."

"I went to P.S. 321," he said.

"Wait, really? Me too!"

"My grandpa drove me. Finished fifth grade in, I don't know, '94 maybe."

"A couple of years before I started." She glanced at him, wanting to know exactly how he felt about her neighborhood. "Did you like 321?"

"Are we still on the record, or . . ."

"Off the record! It was a super-homogenous school," she rushed to say. "Like, super white."

"You hit it on the nail."

They stopped when they reached Brownsville Houses, but instead of going home, Tyrell turned to her.

"I'm glad I went. It gave me a perspective not every Brownsville kid gets. I saw what school could be. The teachers in Brownsville treated us like we were already in juvie. And I feel like one of the problems in Brownsville is *isolation*. We're all the way out here at the end of the 3 train, concentrated poverty, no opportunities, no friends in high places. It's important for us to be working with outside people— the ones we can trust. That's why I appreciate this opportunity to connect with you."

Disappointed to still be grouped among the "outside people," she tried to smile.

Then he touched the elbow of her sweater.

"You good getting home?"

Even after it was gone, she felt the tingling warmth of his hand and struggled not to react.

— — —

Sadie was supposed to be off from work Halloween night, but instead she found herself reliving that interaction with Tyrell, as well as obsessing over the connection between Ms. Lina's lot and her grandparents' restaurant. Scrunched up on her desk chair, Sadie tried to remember a particular database she'd learned about during her internship at *The New York Times*—a website with the deed records for each land plot in New York City.

"ACRIS," she googled. She entered 78 Livonia Avenue and converted this to an official block and lot number.

A striped table of deed and mortgage records appeared on the screen, dating back to 1980.

3/29/1986	DEED FINANCE ADMIN OF THE CITY OF NY	CITY OF NY
5/2/1984	DEED IN TRUST FOR CENTRAL BKLYN	CBMC HOUSING D
11/5/1982	DEED SEC OF HOUSING & URBAN DEVE	CBMC HOUSING D
7/5/1980	DEED SEC HOUSING & URBAN DEVE	CENTRAL BKLYN

As far as she could tell, the records indicated that the lot in Ms. Lina's proposal was a government-owned property, and had been so since 1980, at least—owned, at various times, by the federal government, the city of New York, and the Central Brooklyn Model Cities project.

But what about before 1980?

8/9/1978	DEED DUN HO WONG	78 LIVONIA AVE LLC
2/3/1967	DEED ARNOLD COHEN	DUN HO WONG

Dun Ho Wong.

Immediately, she thought of Mr. William from the 99 Cents store. Wong, the landlord.

Sadie threw open her bedroom door and, with her laptop in her arms, raced downstairs to speak with her father. He wasn't there, but Sadie found her mother sitting on the stoop with a bowl of candy in her lap, engulfed in a tidal wave of Elsas and Luke Skywalkers.

"You're home!" Her mother laughed, surprised to see her. "I thought you were out with friends."

Sadie waited for the kids to disperse.

"Where's Dad?"

"He went to the fish store. We were thinking salmon for dinner."

Sadie craned her neck down the block, hoping she could see her father among all the trick-or-treaters. "Are you all right?" her mother asked.

"I need to talk to him. Can't we just order in?" Sadie grumbled. "Why do we always have to have an elaborate home-cooked meal?"

With no choice but to wait for him, Sadie plunked herself down on the stoop, grabbed two Reese's Peanut Butter Cups from the candy bowl, unwrapped them, and popped them in her mouth.

Her mother mused, "I've been out here for ten minutes, and I've already gone through two bags of candy."

Like usual, her mom wore jeans and an old sweater, her graying hair parted evenly in the middle. This evening, however, there was a red zigzag on her forehead and masking tape on the bridge of her glasses.

"Are you supposed to be Harry Potter?"

"Correct!"

"You should tie your hair back."

"I couldn't find my scrunchies."

Sadie handed over one of the hair ties on her wrist. Her mom, who taught fiction at The New School, had never been interested in material things. She was more like a flower shedding petals, maturing naturally and without a care.

At that moment, another wave of children arrived, but this time most of them lacked costumes, though a few wore cheap plastic masks. Sadie helped her mother hand out the candy, and she knew a younger version of herself would have looked at these kids with disdain: *How can you go trick-or-treating without a costume?*

Yet it was the adult version of Sadie, the reporter, who saw them now, who discerned they were not from Park Slope.

At last, she spotted her father among the trick-or-treaters. A lump of fish swung in the bag on his arm.

"Dad!" she called as soon as he was in earshot. "Who is Dun Ho Wong?"

"Your grandfather."

"What?" Sadie jumped up from the stoop.

"My father," he said. "What's the matter?"

"But I thought his name was Richard Chin!"

"He was born a Chin. Then in the States we had the fake name Wong, so his legal name here was Dun Ho Wong. He went by Richard Wong for decades." He ascended the stoop. "I told you that Wong was our fake name, right?"

"Our *fake* name?" Sadie hugged her laptop. "What do you mean, fake name?"

"Come." He opened the front door and motioned her through it.

Leaving the fish on the counter, her father crossed to a bookshelf in the living room and selected a green folder.

The papers were yellow and brittle with age.

"Your name is Jason *Wong*?"

"Under the Chinese Exclusion Acts, they only let a Chinese person over if their father was here. My grandfather pretended to be someone else's son—to be a Wong. So, my dad became a Wong, and I was born a Wong, and then when I was a kid, we went to a government office and changed it back to Chin."

"Did you also know we were landlords?"

Rocking his head from side to side, he moved toward the kitchen and selected a cutting board. "Landlords? I guess you could say that."

"You guess?"

The smell of the salmon sickened her.

"So my parents owned a house on Amboy Street. The restaurant was on Livonia and there was a landlord we called Mr. Cohen. And then after we closed the restaurant and moved to East Flatbush, my father bought the restaurant building and rented it to tenants for a few years. So, I guess you could say he was a landlord."

"Why didn't you tell me this before? When I told you about that man who said there was a murderer named Mr. Wong in Brownsville?"

"But you didn't give me the name of the murderer. You just said he was Chinese."

"He was talking about your dad!"

Her father's brow furrowed. He rinsed his hands in the sink, dried them, then leaned his back against the counter.

"You're saying this man thought my dad was a murderer?"

"Yes!"

"Well, we know that isn't true."

"Do you know that for sure?"

"My dad was screwed up in a lot of ways, but he wasn't a murderer."

He turned to the refrigerator and removed the soy sauce and hoisin.

"You're not going to do anything about it?"

"I mean, you're the journalist, Sadie." He was facing the fridge as if looking for another ingredient. "Do you assume everything you hear is true?"

"You have to tell me everything you remember about your dad's time as a landlord."

"There's not much to tell you. It was a money-losing venture for him. So he sold the restaurant building, and that was the end of it."

She waited for her father to say more, but instead, he turned to the stove and added oil to the wok. He refused to think or speak about his childhood, and now it was standing in the way of understanding what had happened to the people of Brownsville.

"When I see something that troubles me, I look at it," Sadie snapped. "I'm not like you—I don't run away."

Sadie shut her laptop and marched up the stairs. She heard her father calling her name and ignored him. If he was going to be so indifferent, she would figure things out on her own.

With the bedroom door closed, Sadie searched in ACRIS and found 80 Livonia had a very similar deed history to 78 Livonia. She would call Ngen Ngen to ask follow-up questions, then go downtown to look at the Fire Records.

Her phone vibrated. Sadie groaned, assuming it was her mother trying to coax her downstairs to talk things over.

But it was Tyrell.

Sadie, whats up?

She answered as quickly as she could.

                                        Nothing really, you?

She found herself hoping for some sort of personal invitation.

U in the Ville?

                                        I can get there if
                                        u want me to.

No a lot of shit goes down
Halloween.

I wanted to let u know cuz ur
not from here.

For ur own safety don't come to
Brownsville tonight.

                                        Got it. Thanks.

He didn't want her to be there, she thought. He thought she couldn't handle whatever was "going down." But he also wanted to protect her. That meant that he cared about her well-being on some level, right?

Sadie wondered if she should tell him anything about her conversation with her father.

> Hey Tyrell. What would u
> guys think about an article
> on the history of the lot
> on Livonia? Maybe I can
> interview Ms. Lina and
> then write a feature.

Sounds dope.
I'll ask Ms. Lina when I see her.

THE WONGS

Ng Foon Wah could tell that Chin Dun Ho was not an *American war hero*, as the elders called him. He did not know anything about war. He was more ignorant than her child-brothers, whose laughter had echoed through the caves during the air raids. Yet she was not stubborn enough to dash her father's hopes of sending her free into the New World.

Ten years earlier, when the Japanese captured Canton, her father left to work in a weapons factory in Szechuan, and her mother took her and the younger children and fled the villages with hundreds of others. For five days, they trudged through the fields, muscles aching and shoes filling with stones. They passed abandoned villages, where other people's animals wandered in confusion in the fields. They sailed in boats up the river and caught fish, and then for four days ate nothing but fish, and at night slept aboard, awash in fish blood. Foon Wah learned how anywhere can become a home: a boat, a bean field, a clearing in the woods.

The villagers lived for several months at the generosity of the Gui Lin people, who put them up in their barns and helped them identify the edible mountain fungi. Her mother, a midwife, was always first to rise and feel the cheeks of the sick and the heartbeats of the infants. But then came the typhoon, and with it two weeks of rain that swamped the barns. Many of the children fell ill, and Foon Wah's mother tended to all of them, though she had long since run out of medicine. After this, her mother grew very tired and could not stomach the rice Foon Wah cooked. When Foon Wah tried to stay with her, her mother pushed her away, whispering, "Go mind your brothers and sister."

One early morning, the sun nestled between the mountain crags, Foon Wah discovered her mother lying motionless on the dirt floor, eyes open to the rafters, her spirit unbound.

They buried her on the hill with the Gui Lin dead. The other refugees pitied the children and helped Foon Wah learn the things her mother had yet to teach her. How to grow gna toi peas in water. How to roll taro into the burnt rice at the bottom of the pot. How, when her monthlies arrived the following spring, to spread a strip of cloth in the crotch of her undergarments.

At twelve, she became mother to her three younger siblings: hiding them when there were reports of Japanese soldiers, scrubbing them clean in the river, and when the sirens wailed, gathering them to run for the caves.

There were two caves, one to the north and one to the west, and the one to the north was their favorite, because they always projected movies on the cave walls to pass the time—movies like *Hall of the Broken Zither*, with the boy who sells himself into slavery to save his father. In the west cave, she and the adults squatted on their heels in the steamy dark while the little ones played in the mud. Sometimes her mother would be there, tucked into the shadows of the cave walls. She'd remind Foon Wah to check the little ones' hair for nits and rub the feet of the elderly.

Then came the bomb, the beautiful American bomb, the Japanese vanquished in a mushroom cloud. Their father returned and took them to Canton City. It was a city in ruins, the governor's mansion charred to its foundations, birds flying through the shattered windows of the theater house, and the hospitals overflowing with marred, raped, broken bodies. Japanese soldiers, now prisoners, dragged wooden waste carts on their shoulders through the streets. Every day, hysterical crowds poured onto the road to dump their garbage on the heads of the Japanese. Even Foon Wah did it once.

Her uncle was a tax collector for the republic, and they settled into his apartment and became his assistants. Whenever she heard the siren of a passing ambulance, she would drop everything in her hands as if it signaled another air raid.

Her siblings teased her. The past was past, they said. Her father, for his part, was determined to take her out of that wreck. Perhaps he felt guilty for all the trouble she'd faced. He spent his evenings at the homes of matchmakers, in search of a family with a son who would wed his eldest daughter and take her to America. When he introduced her to Richard, she understood that he would not find better. "Marry a young handsome brother like that? How can you ask for more?" said her best friend Mee Lai, who was arranged to marry an old man with a warty face to whom Mee Lai's father owed money. Yet the night after Foon Wah's father announced her betrothal to Richard, Foon Wah dreamed that she was in a cave—that Richard was a Japanese soldier who seized her by the wrists.

Waking with a start, she realized then that she would have been content continuing what she'd done since her mother's death: caring for her siblings, applying her tireless perfectionism to the replacement of buttons and the peeling of apple skins. She didn't want to be blown halfway across the world.

But Foon Wah wasn't the kind to disobey, and every uncle and aunt urged her to go. The Communists have taken the north, they said. And so she was fitted for a white wedding gown and a red cheongsam, at Richard's insistence.

Despite her cousins' warnings about the weather, when Foon Wah and Richard landed in San Francisco, she found it hard to believe that people survived in such a frigid climate. Their first stop was a bak gui clothing store where Richard selected a rich woman's coat with fox fur stitched to the collar. Discovering the garment cost her uncle's entire monthly salary, she pleaded for Richard to reconsider. He laughed and bought it anyway.

She was exhausted, but he was lively and talkative; he had slept for most of the twelve-hour flight, while she and the other passengers had sat wide-eyed, gripping their armrests. In fact, she'd felt responsible to stay awake for their safety—he was so foolhardy, he might have napped through a disaster.

But she was awed by his mastery of English. He could talk the bak gui into letting her use the restroom at fancy restaurants. The day he took her to dance on the San Francisco piers, he wore his navy uniform, and yellow-haired bak gui girls ran up to her husband to thank him for his service.

They astonished her: these bak gui women with bare shoulders and calves, in dresses with deep-diving necklines. They went out on the town by themselves, stood in the gutter hailing cabs, kissed boyfriends on the boardwalk, and were always eating, eating, eating— *cotton candy*, Richard called it. *Pretzels*. She had never seen grown women so intent on their own pleasure. And with the new coat—did her husband expect that she become one of them?

On the train, she and Richard shared a booth with the Goldmans. These bak gui had long noses, bony knuckles, and wide, knowing smiles, and they smelled good, like paper and ink. They were also returning to New York and thrilled to meet a Chinese American veteran, so Richard lit Mr. Goldman's cigar and they together condemned the evils of Germany and Japan. Foon Wah smiled, understanding little, trying to feign enjoyment of the beef slab and the cold, oily leaves served for lunch.

She looked through the open window at the vast American prairie and caught a whiff of home. Saw in the prairie her own sunbaked farmers squatting in smoke wreaths, and children stumbling in the dawn with poles across their shoulders. The sun had begun to set at the edge of the fields and the clouds hung pink and grubby like wet sheep fleece, like *cotton candy*, and she realized they would retire to the sleeping cars. She felt a cold pressure in the pit of her stomach, like she had swallowed a glass of what they called *ice cubes*, and she wished the sun would never set.

Her monthly was over, and she had no more legitimate excuses to delay the inevitable. When they returned to the sleeping car, she climbed the ladder to the top of the bunk and sat with her legs stretched before her, steeling herself for the worst.

In the end, it was not so terrible. He was not a Japanese soldier in a cave. In fact, what terrified her most of all was how, involuntarily, her body opened to him.

After he was done, she waited for his nightly twitch. It had come unfailingly each night since their wedding and signified that he was finally falling asleep. Then she turned to her side and cried into the pillow.

What was the use of that gnawing feeling, that unsatisfied craving in her nightgown? What was her use here? What was anybody's use in America?

In America, Foon Wah learned, a family that had made its fortune would live just outside the city in a house that was modern like a city house.

That was the kind of house Richard promised her during the taxi ride from Manhattan to Brooklyn. Koon Lai sat in front, next to the driver. They wove through traffic-jammed streets between skyscrapers, giant billboards, and flashing neon lights. Next came a bridge, one capable of bearing hundreds of cars at once, and a plum-colored river teeming with ferries, steamboats, and cargo ships.

Here was the center of the world, and it was just as impressive as it was said to be.

Brooklyn's roads were wide and smooth. On a boulevard with yellowing trees called Eastern Parkway, they passed a white building with many columns that she at first mistook for President Truman's house. Throughout the ride, Koon Lai remained quiet, and Foon Wah worried that he was upset. She'd discovered him to be a small man with a gentle, almost girlish face. He wore spectacles and walked with a slight limp. Only a moment after they'd met, Richard had switched to English and berated his father in a tone so harsh that she had to believe Koon Lai had done something awful—or else Richard was crazy.

The issue, she learned eventually, was that Koon Lai lacked the money to rent an apartment for the couple, and for the time being, she would join them and the cooks on cots in the back room of the restaurant. When they reached 78 Livonia, Koon Lai wouldn't stop apologizing.

"A new wife deserves better," he said. "This building is getting old. Cracked walls! Aiya, another crack. This mold on the window. An embarrassment!"

"Baba, don't worry." She smiled, but he remained so anxious, it was like he'd never met a woman before.

In the weeks that followed, it was always Koon Lai, never her husband, who noticed when her eyes were wet from homesickness. He liked her tripe soup, praised her and guzzled bowl after bowl of it. One evening, he took her to the Cantonese theater on East Broadway, where they played the old silent films. It would become their ongoing tradition.

Since she was good with numbers, the men entrusted her with the cash register, and she quickly memorized the phrases she would need to say to the bak gui customers. Though sometimes the little ones would tug her dress, screech "Ching chong!" in her ear, and skip away, she found that most bak gui were polite to her. When there were no chores to do, she'd amble up and down Livonia with a dictionary, attempting to read the flyers posted to the pillars of the elevated rail. "Modern Homes in Long Island," she tried to pronounce. "There's No Place like Jersey."

One afternoon, Richard returned from Pitkin Avenue with a large object and set it down in the corner of the sleeping room. It looked like a cabinet, but when he opened its doors, she saw it contained a globe of glass, a radio speaker, and six dials of different sizes. Everyone crowded around in awe—everyone except Koon Lai.

"Turn one of the dials," Richard encouraged her.

In only a second, a song began to play on the speakers and the globe spluttered into life, showing them the sweet babbling face of a bak gui infant. Richard slapped his knee and motioned that she should turn another dial. Immediately, the baby vanished, and they saw a bak gui newsman speaking from behind a table. Next, a bak gui lady encouraged them to purchase a refrigerator. Then, a ball game.

"Now you can have a movie theater right in our room."

Foon Wah clapped her hands with delight.

But she stopped clapping when she saw Koon Lai in the corner, polishing his shoes, a disappointed look on his face. At that moment, she turned pink as dragon fruit.

"The television is a wonderful device," she said aloud. "But a Chinese movie is still best to see in the theater."

Richard couldn't stand it—living with his bride, his father, and five other farting Chinese bachelors in a twelve-by-twelve storage room. Having to wait for a harmonious symphony of snores before she'd permit as much as a hand on her breast. And it wasn't just lust. He felt uneasy when his wife and father read the *Mun Hey Weekly* together and he was forced to admit he couldn't read the headlines.

He and Foon Wah needed their own apartment. No more letting the regular customers doddle after meals, no more paying the dishwasher's friends to help with side chores. And his father had to stop limping around the dining room—Richard could get the job done twice as fast.

"You should let me run the front," Richard broached the subject in Toisanese one night after closing. "Your tendonitis has gotten worse. You can rest back there and take care of the accounts."

"You're going to run the dining room?"

"Make me a partner. I am your *first* son."

Having long waited for Richard to become serious about the business, Koon Lai gave his son the keys to the money box. They opened earlier in the afternoon, hired another chef, and jammed in additional tables. Richard had never wanted to work in the restaurant, but so long as he was in charge, he could tolerate it.

Eventually, they'd made enough to rent a third-story walk-up in a tenement on Riverdale Avenue. When, four months later, Foon Wah reported she was pregnant, he decided they needed a house for their family-to-be. Following the lead of his friends from the Brownsville Boys Club, Richard looked in Sheepshead Bay and Gravesend.

"Too far from the restaurant," Koon Lai insisted. "Beach house cost too much."

"Doesn't matter. I'll get a VA loan."

"No loan. We pay cash."

Richard ignored his father, but his luck wouldn't have it. Realtors would invite him to a house showing, but when he got there, he'd receive an apology—he'd just missed his chance. Or someone's Aunt Tabatha had decided to move in. Or he must have had the address wrong.

After hearing Richard's stories during dinner, Koon Lai poured himself a cup of cha.

"No one wants to sell to a Chinese," he said.

Richard pounded the table so hard the china rattled.

"I'm an American navy vet!"

The others remained silent, chewing their tofu skins.

Another two months passed, and Foon Wah's belly swelled, but Richard had still not found a proper home. Spring arrived, and Richard went to Herzl Street to get advice from his old friend, the decorated veteran Alan Friedman. Rebecca had moved away, but Alan and his wife Eva still lived with Alan's parents.

"Have you considered Brownsville Houses?"

Alan nodded east, where the New York City Housing Authority was constructing apartments.

"You remember I was helping Milton write those letters to the city? Success. We asked for quality housing, housing affordable for a

Brownsville family, and the city is delivering. They're elevator apartments, Rich. They'll have sinks and gas stoves, a bathroom for each family. Playgrounds, laundromats, programs for the kids—the whole works. If I didn't make above the income limit, I'd apply myself."

Richard was miffed that Alan would consider him poor enough to live in those public buildings. Then he thought of Steeplechase—that rascal from the Brownsville Boys Club. His real name was Jack Schmidt, but he had a grin so wide people called him Steeplechase after that creepy face on the Coney Island billboards. Jack had followed his uncle into real estate.

"Maybe I'll ask Jack."

"I wouldn't get tangled up with Steeplechase."

But Richard didn't see what other option he had. A few days later, he found Jack Schmidt at the handball court. Schmidt made no mention of the NYCHA buildings. Instead, he threw his arm around Richard's shoulders and led him down Amboy Street.

"I've got just the right place for you."

As a kid, Schmidt had chased the girls up and down Christopher Street, trying to hit their behinds with a table tennis paddle. More recently, his wife had discovered Schmidt kept a mistress on the side, and she'd run him out of the house with a hot frying pan. Still, Steeplechase could list every house for sale in the neighborhood with his eyes closed.

"I *personally* want you to get this steal. Just think, Richie, all this and better is going to be yours." They mounted the stoop to the porch. Schmidt pointed to the plentiful windows, the wood-paneled floors. "I say you take it now. It's gonna go quick."

Richard agreed to the price of the house on the spot. It was only after they'd secured the deed that he found chipped kitchen tiles, a clogged sink, and even urine stains in the living room rug.

But Richard assured himself: he didn't need a mansion. All he wanted was what an everyday man was entitled to: something that kept him cool in the summertime and warm in the winter, with a lawn to mow and swings for children to swing on, and separate rooms for each of the activities of the American family.

Others might take that stuff for granted, but he would never. He had climbed his mountain. He'd built his life from scratch. And what makes a man an American more than that?

LINA

Halloween in Brownsville brought the two-tone moan of ambulance sirens. The taste of weak coffee in the Brookdale cafeteria. Blue scrubs. White coats. Smell of antiseptic hallways, squeak of wheels on linoleum, mothers' screams, machines beeping. Memories.

The day the U.S. Army chaplain man told them about Lou, and their mother prayed on the floor of the Van Dyke apartment with her hands over her face. 1966.

The night at Brookdale when the nurses uncoupled Nellie's hand from Wesley's. 1986.

Nellie's arm, gray and limp like a dead tree branch, dangling off the stretcher. 1987.

Or way before any of that: 1955—the day they killed her father. She, her mother, and her siblings had been in the East Harlem apartment waiting for him to come home for dinner. Then the sun dropped below the roof of the Dominican fruit market, and he still had not returned. They chalked it up to subway problems. When the police called, their mother stood by the open window with Cindy in her arms, listening to the officer speak a language that couldn't have been Spanish or English. Then she fell to her knees and dropped the phone, which swayed back and forth on its cord.

Lina caught it and bellowed into the speaker piece.

"Where's Daddy?"

"Miss, your father's been shot."

"Shot! Who shot him?"

"Your old man got into a fight down at the longshoreman's pub here on West Thirty-Fifth. He's in the Mount Sinai ER."

Lina had been too outraged to grieve. The next day, she went down to the docks, and a friend of her father's pulled her aside and told her the police had done it. A white worker had disrespected her father, and her daddy had stood up for himself, and then the white worker had come at him with his fists and her father had fought back—and so the police had grabbed and shot him.

Since that night, she'd been to the hospital dozens of times, often for what the newspapers would have called "Black on Black" crime. To her, it was more of the same. When the system starved a man of hope, they made him hungry enough to kill his own brother. This year, Kesi, her former student's grandson, had shot Andre, a member of BYTE, and then Andre's friend T. P. had retaliated, put a bullet in Kesi's thigh. Not enough had changed since 1955, and it broke her heart every day.

Tyrell was there all night too. He knew how much she hated hospitals, so at daybreak, he called a car and sent her home to get some rest.

Strange, then, to wake up from an hour of shut-eye and see an email from a different world.

Bewildered, she read it several times.

Dear Ms. Lina Rodriguez Armstrong,

I hope you are well. This is Jean Bernard, the CEO of Bernard and Company, and I had the pleasure of making your acquaintance at the community visioning session convened by the Department of Housing Preservation and Development on Saturday, September 27.

I am reaching out regarding your vision for the vacant property at Livonia Avenue near Saratoga Street.

We learned about your proposal from New Gotham's *coverage, and Olivia McIntosh was kind enough to offer me your email address. Our company, Bernard & Co., has a longstanding interest in the site, and with the city to release an RFP this month, we are eager to benefit from your insight and historical knowledge of the area.*

We would like to invite you to our Water Street offices in the Financial District to discuss a potential partnership. Please let us know when might be a good time that we can sit down with you and discuss a collaboration.

My regards,
Jean Bernard
Bernard & Co., CEO

"Thank you, but no thank you," Lina said to the screen. She had Trevor LDC, a Black-owned construction firm. She had Brownsvillians ready to establish the Wesley Price Community Land Trust tripartite board. She had dance teachers, spoken-word artists, and LGBTQ mentors. Why would she need Bernard & Co.? No— Bernard & Co. needed *her* to check off the "community engagement" box on the application.

But Lina stopped herself from writing back. With age, she'd become less impulsive. Less decisive. What would HPD say if she turned down a partnership with one of the city's favorite developers?

She knocked on the Scott family door, then wondered if Tyrell was still at the hospital, or if he'd finally returned and conked out. By four a.m., the doctors had pronounced Andre dead, while Kesi was expected to spend three days in the ICU.

But Tyrell reached the front door before his cousin or his aunt. With his bleary eyes and concave cheeks, he looked ten years older than he should have.

"Papi, you burning yourself out. Again. Don't you got that shift at Best Buy this afternoon?"

He shrugged.

"What time you got home?"

"Like an hour ago."

Irritably, he tore down the witch decal that his cousin had taped to the door.

"Can we get rid of Halloween?" he asked, leaning against the doorframe. "Just give the kids candy on Thanksgiving."

Lina sighed. "Come over, I'll make you breakfast. You got to look at something for me."

He followed her, sat down at her computer, and read the email while she scrambled eggs.

"You ever thought about a joint venture?"

"Young man, what's a joint venture?"

"A partnership between a nonprofit and a for-profit. Maybe you could partner with this Bernard guy and get your plan done."

"We working with Trevor's construction company."

"Yeah . . . last time I checked, Trevor's company don't got the balance sheet for a winning deal. Sometimes there's got to be compromises."

"Give the project to a real estate tycoon? That's not the right compromise, Ty."

"Well, at least we go meet with them."

Lina frowned, but she considered his point.

"You're a practical kid." She handed him a plate of eggs and sausage. "Let's ask the CLT steering committee during Sunday's meeting."

"Oh, Ms. Lina—you know Sadie, the reporter? She wants to write a piece about the history of the lot."

Lina lowered herself into her favorite chair and shook her head. "That reporter don't look a day over fifteen. I want to know how a child like her gets a job writing about the 'Ville."

"I thought you liked the piece about Family Day."

"She did good. That article she wrote about you was nice too. I'm just saying. We got our young adults in the high-security hamster wheel, and we got children like her deciding our reputations and our futures. I'm talking about who gets to tell our stories."

"She all right, though, Ms. Lina." His mouth was full of egg. "She grew up in Park Slope but she did her homework. She actually cares about Brownsville."

Lina looked over at Ty, and she noticed an unusual brightness to his eyes.

"What's that smile on your face?"

"Huh?"

"That smile? We talking about that reporter and suddenly, you smiling."

"Yo." Ty smushed his face with his hands as if he was wiping it clean, then raised his arms into the air. "I ain't smiling."

"What happened to you and Katrina? You ain't mentioned her name in a while."

"Katrina probably thinks I don't make enough green."

"And so you're going after the reporter who thinks you're a big shot."

"Ms. Lina!" he yelped, and to his own advantage he was too dark to blush, but she could still make out the embarrassment in the bulge of his eyes. "Ms. Lina, I ain't going after . . ."

"You better be careful what you say to Miss Sadie," she warned.

The CLT steering committee was divided on the matter. Ms. Dorothy Peters and Ms. Keesha Jones were on Lina's side, skeptical of a partnership with Bernard & Co., but Mr. Alvin Banks and Ms. Cynthia Garcia thought a Bernard & Co. joint venture might be the only path forward. It was Ms. Freda Simmons, like usual, who nimbly brokered a compromise: Lina and Tyrell would agree to the meeting, with the intention to report back to the committee what they'd learned. In addition, under no circumstances would they accept a deal that significantly diverged from the CLT's vision.

The following week, Lina and Tyrell took an Access-A-Ride to Manhattan. Lina hated Access-A-Ride. Car rides made her sick, and

Access-A-Ride was always late. She loved the subway, but it had become difficult to climb the stairs of the El.

They moved like a tortoise through the traffic, Lina sucking on a ginger candy and Tyrell cracking his knuckles. They passed that new spaceship–roller coaster of a basketball stadium and all the construction sites downtown, and also that hipster bakery on Flatbush where her former student June—now a lawyer at the New York State Attorney General's office—had treated her to a blueberry muffin.

What a difference this was from the old days when city hall wanted to wipe half of Brooklyn off the map. Now rent was sky-high, and all the Black folks were moving to Atlanta. It made sense: What's the point of paying two thousand dollars for a two-bedroom when the kids still get shot on the street? Nellie, had she been alive, would have said something like that. Nellie had possessed none of Lina's loyalty to place. Lina's loyalty to place had ruined Nellie's life—at least this was the thought that still haunted her, some thirty years later.

Maybe it had all started with her mother's prayers. It had seemed a miracle when, less than a year after their father's death, they'd won the lottery for Van Dyke Houses. At the time, Van Dyke had new appliances and not a single piece of litter in the courtyard. Lina still remembered their first Sunday service at Our Lady of the Presentation, her mother whispering, *Gracias Dios, gracias por responder mis oraciones.* Even years after Lina had left the church, she would still believe Brownsville was God's answer.

And then, how quickly Brownsville had made Lina its beloved. In her teenage years, as soon as she'd step outside, all the younger kids would run across the concrete to fling their arms around her waist and press their gap-toothed faces into her stomach. Sometimes she'd walk around with those children clinging to her like one big octopus in blue jeans. They'd loved her because she was not afraid to stand up to bullies or to fight for the boys who the others called *maricones,* and also, because of the art activities. In the winters, she'd taught them to make ice spaceships, and in the summers, go-carts with wood planks from the lumberyard on Livonia. Later, she'd become an art teacher at J.H.S. 271, which had led to Mr. Parson, which had led to the Freedom School and everything that followed—everything that, decades later, had her now stuck on the Brooklyn Bridge, trying not to vomit that morning's oatmeal.

Bernard & Co.'s office was on the forty-third floor of an Art Deco skyrise adjacent to the East River. The doorman printed name tags, and then Lina and Tyrell got lost trying to figure out which of the many different elevators would take them to the right floor. When they reached the forty-third, a receptionist led them to a conference room.

"God bless," Lina exclaimed, hobbling over to the windows, her nausea beginning to fade. She looked out at the bridges, the Statue of Liberty, the ferries hustling back and forth from the islands, and then over at Brooklyn. "I enjoyed the twelfth floor but imagine living on the forty-third," she whispered to Tyrell. "You'd start thinking you owned the borough."

"Ms. Rodriguez Armstrong, Mr. Scott. Welcome! Thank you for coming."

Mr. Bernard wore a pirate blouse, one button open at the collar. In his company were two members of his staff: a South Asian man with slicked hair and a pretty Black lady in a lavender sheath dress. He explained he had another meeting to attend, but that the two associates were there to represent him. The four sat down at the conference table, and Tyrell started them off, detailing the CLT's proposal.

"Four floors, and each has a theme. Floor one is the auditorium and rehearsal spaces. Floor two has a darkroom, a studio, a computer lab. Floor three, classrooms for certification programs. Floor four is the LGBTQ youth space. And we're envisioning an outdoor space as well, a community garden," he said. "But most important, the land would be owned by the community land trust, ensuring it never gets resold for profit. We're in the process of incorporating the Wesley Price Community Land Trust."

"An interesting concept. I think I've heard of them before," the lady said. "Like, Vermont, right? Does Vermont have a community land trust?"

"Not just Vermont," Lina said. "There are hundreds across the country. First one was founded by Black Freedom Fighters in Georgia."

"That is definitely interesting," said the South Asian guy, offering a rushed smile. "Now, our understanding is that the city's RFP is going to state a preference for affordable housing on the site, but I think there may be space on a ground floor for some kind of community center."

"They want to put *more* housing in Brownsville?"

"The RFP will be issued as part of the administration's affordable housing plan," he said. "So the housing will be lottery units targeting a range of incomes."

"I don't know where the city got the idea we need more housing in Brownsville." Lina almost wanted to laugh. "They need to remember the history of this neighborhood, the history of Robert Moses in this neighborhood. We have more public housing than anywhere in the country."

"Of course," said the man, pulling himself toward the table and folding his hands before him. "It's important not to increase the concentration of poverty in Brownsville. But the administration is trying to build as much affordable housing as possible to meet the greater crisis, and every neighborhood must do its part."

Lina pulled back her chin and glanced wearily at Tyrell.

"We get what you're saying," Tyrell attempted. "But the whole idea was to create something the community really needs. Show these kids that true investments are being made in their future."

"I suggest thinking of it this way: housing will keep many of these children out of homelessness."

Lina didn't appreciate the man's tone.

"So, this new affordable housing. How do you define 'affordable'?" asked Tyrell.

"We're planning on using the Extremely Low- and Low-Income

Affordability term sheet," said the woman, passing a printout across the table to Tyrell. "It's the city's best program to increase the supply of housing for low-income households."

"That's that AMI bullshit," muttered Lina, and all of them—even Tyrell—raised their eyebrows. "Excuse my language. But that Area Median Income metric that the government uses to define 'low-income' is ridiculous. If you're a family making fifty thousand in Brownsville, no one calls you 'low-income.'"

"We're actually going to use the city subsidy program with the deepest affordability, the program really meant for neighborhoods like Brownsville. There will be apartments for a range of incomes, from twenty thousand to seventy thousand," said the woman. She nodded, as if forgiving their mistake.

Tyrell was taking notes. "And will the new housing go to Brownsville residents?"

"All units will be advertised on the housing lottery, but community district residents will be prioritized for a percentage of units."

"What's in it for Bernard and Company?" Lina asked.

"You mean why are we interested in the project?"

"This kind of project is fairly integral to what we do," said the man, still with that lecturing tone. "You probably know us as high-end housing developers, but we also build housing for the homeless. A mixed-income project is pretty much our bread and butter."

Lina shook her head. He hadn't answered the question. "I want to know how Bernard and Co. would profit off this project. We live in a capitalist society. It's what you do."

"Well, this is the kind of work we love," said the woman, still playing good cop. "Of course, there's the developer fee and rental income. But if you're interested in a joint venture, we can offer your group a ten percent ownership stake in the property, along with management of the center on the ground floor."

"So community ownership in name only, you mean?"

The two associates looked at each other, and Tyrell jiggled his knees under the table.

Lina was sick of this already. Millionaires, billionaires, profiting off the displacement and then acting like they loved themselves some charity work. She didn't need to hear more.

"This is my point. We're not in the business of privatizing our community. We're bringing land into community control. We can't work with a developer that's drawing value *out* of the community."

The two associates nodded in silence, cleared their throats.

"We understand your concern," said the woman. "But as we see it, a joint venture provides all the ingredients needed for a successful project. As the developer, we offer the expertise, the money, while the community partner brings a good rapport with neighborhood residents."

"These days, the city thinks it can help the poor by paying rich people to get richer."

"The city needs its private developers," the man said, folding his arms. "Unless the federal government wants to build more public housing. But it won't do that, for good reason."

"I think that's exactly what the federal government should do. Just not in Brownsville."

"And we could spend a whole day on that one," Tyrell butted in before she could say more. He turned to the lady. "So specifically, how much space do you think we'd have for a cultural center on the ground floor?"

While Tyrell and the lady discussed what sort of things BYTE might like to see in a small community space, Lina dug in her purse for a tube of ChapStick.

When they finally headed to the elevators, Mr. Bernard appeared to say goodbye.

"It was nice speaking to your associates," Lina said, shaking his hand. "But we will be submitting our own proposal, separately from Bernard and Company."

Lina tried to ignore the look on Tyrell's face.

"You have an independent streak," Mr. Bernard said, grinning.

The Access-A-Ride was an hour behind schedule, and Transit Control authorized a car service ride. In a shiny black Uber, Lina and Tyrell zipped back over the bridge.

"The city wants to put more housing in Brownsville, and developers come drooling like dogs for bacon."

As she ridiculed them, Tyrell didn't laugh. He sucked his teeth and looked out the window.

"Look, I'm all about the community land trust and community control. But what about the financing? Where we gonna get it?"

"City grants. Bank loans."

"The council won't even allocate discretionary funds for BYTE at the level I'm asking. And the banks don't want to work with small fry like us."

Now, it was Lina who looked out the window. She was worried, for the first time, that Tyrell didn't believe in her. He was using this nonprofit-speak these days, and they both knew she'd never incorporated any of her own organizations—the Freedom School, the Arts & Dreams Day Care. And, of course, he was right: you couldn't erect a building foundation on barbecue fundraisers.

"Look," Tyrell said. "If we ain't working with Bernard, we need massive public support. So we get this out in the media, Ms. Lina. Big-time."

"Ah, you want us talking to that reporter you crushing on." She glanced at Tyrell to gauge his reaction, but he wasn't in a mood to be teased.

Lina took a deep breath. "Okay. We do need press. Tell Miss Sadie I accept. But this interview—you got to let me do it my way."

"Deal." Tyrell nodded.

Soon they were home in the 'Ville again, the smell of fresh bread through the window, a bass beat vibrating Lina's skull. It was three o'clock, just past dismissal time, and Lina watched the groups of kids play-fighting on the corners.

It wasn't until she was behind her apartment door that the heaviness sank in. Icing her knees, listening to the *drip drip drip* of the kitchen sink pipe, thinking about the beauty of Brownsville, Lina felt a familiar twist in her gut, her intestines tangled like Christmas lights in storage.

THE WONGS

Picture a summer day, 1956.

On Amboy Street, three little girls played in a yard: Jennifer, Julie, and Jackie Wong, seven and five and two, with matching blue overalls and red sun hats, black hair cropped to their chins. They and the hak gui were the only ones who ate their bread stuffed with pork. The only ones who went to school on Rosh Hashanah.

When no one asked to play with the Wong girls, the Wong girls played with one another. Jennifer acted the part of the mother and decided most of the plot. When her little sisters acted up, she distributed punishments: stand still for twenty minutes. No speaking for one hour. Timing them, on her imaginary watch.

Jennifer, charming like her father and industrious like her mother, won penny candy with her smile. At seven, she could recite her multiplication tables and link together the notes on a keyboard to play "Jingle Bells." She would go on to be the Wong family's first college graduate, its first with a desk job, its first to own a house with a trampoline and finished basement.

Julie was the one who loved to write her name with calligraphy pens, who waited all year for the stomp of lions on Mott Street, and who was brave enough to eat pig blood congealed in little pink squares. She'd become the most traditional of the three, and if anyone wanted to know the correct word in Toisanese for each aunt and uncle, she'd have it memorized.

The Wongs worried about Jackie's tendency to touch things that weren't meant to be touched—squirrels, and the hands and faces of beggars who waved at her. She'd be the one to spend every Sunday behind the counter of a Newark soup kitchen, to live a life of service.

On this particular Saturday, Jennifer had decided her daughter Julie deserved a pet, and they were at the shop adopting an over-eager dog named Jackie, who liked to lick Julie's knees. Foon Wah watched them from the porch, taking pleasure in the perfection of their matching overalls. Some of the homeowners hung lights along the porch rails, and others decorated their doorways with stone animals and wind mobiles. Foon Wah had chopped up the brittle soil and planted violets; her yard now fit in perfectly among the others.

Richard still wanted a boy, but this was not China. In America, a girl could go to college. Work and support her parents. She could choose who she wished to marry. Foon Wah's girls would study hard every night, attend good universities, and when they arrived in the working world, no one would doubt their worth.

The wife of the neighboring house emerged carrying a heavy cardboard box. She descended the porch steps and added it to the pile of things she had already left on the brick pathway.

"How are you?" Foon Wah ventured.

"Oh, I'm all right. Thank you, dear."

"You . . . move?"

"Yes. Yes, thank God, we're finally out of here."

"Far away?"

"Oh, just Midwood."

Something was afoot in Brownsville. The Jews whispered, pointing at the squiggles spray-painted on the synagogue door. Took new routes to avoid the projects. Mothers rummaged through the closets, yanked out suitcases, while fathers stopped in front of Kishke King to jab at the sports section:

"They're gonna knock down Ebbets Field!"

"They picked a new site yet?"

"Downtown Brooklyn, I heard."

"The city won't agree to it. They don't give a damn about our boys."

Richard was at the handball court, diving in front of another player, picking it up—a killer. Knees bent, hands on thighs. Swipe the ball, arm arched backward: a roller. He won a shutout, and the other players shook their heads. His pockets bulged with their dollars, evidence to himself that he was one of the best handball players in Brownsville.

Six games in, the eight men removed their leather gloves and passed around a pack of Murads. They breathed in the wet oak leaves, listened to the tinny tune of a passing ice cream truck.

"We made a down payment on that house in Sheepshead Bay."

"We're looking in Jersey. Any of you looked over there?"

"With all you guys leaving Brownsville," said Freddie, "who will we play handball with?"

Freddie: the only Black man in their handball group since Willy had come home in a flag-draped coffin.

"I'll miss you fellows, but Brownsville isn't Brownsville anymore."

Richard wiped the sweat from his face, turned away, tuned them out.

"Alan, where are you looking?"

"Don't ask Alan. He wants to be the last Indian."

"Alan, things are changing. Think about your kids."

Bait and switch, overpromised—that's what his life was. His first house in Brownsville, and now all his buds were leaving. Richard pointed to the falling sun and urged them back to the game.

"Richie, how come you're so sure you gonna beat us again?"

Foon Wah heard a melody on a nearby street and smiled. She'd learned what this sound meant: that soon, children would come barreling out from the doors, running and stuffing their heels into sneakers, arms flailing, quarters in their fists, hollering.

Jennifer, Julie, and Jackie had heard it, too, and turned to her expectantly, their tongues waggling in their heads.

Foon Wah fetched her pocket money from the kitchen, returned to the yard, and gathered their hands. Together, they skipped down the street to the ice cream truck and joined the long line of children. Foon Wah listened carefully to how the bak gui children ordered—"Firecracker"—"Vanilla with sprinkles"—"Chocolate in a cup, please"—until she knew what her desires were, and how to satisfy them.

"Strawberry in the cup, please."

They returned to their stoop, squatting on the steps to eat their dripping delights. While the girls finished quickly and returned to play, Foon Wah tried to make hers last as long as possible, though the strawberry ice cream turned into a cold soup. It was just like when the pudding boy came to On Fun with his wagon. All the children would grin at the sight of the pudding boy's long neck and sleepy eye and silly toothless smile, and follow his cart through the dust as he sang the pudding song:

Ji ma wu!
Lek eu sa!
Liang fun yit won
Mou gong ga!

But as she whispered the words of that song to herself, she found herself spinning, slanted, into another place, without melodies or ice cream. Suddenly, the pudding boy was shoveling mud in a rice field, and the children lining up for watery bowls of jook. She saw the oyster-slurping men wailing as they knelt on a road of broken glass, and then her uncle, standing on a platform with his eyes downcast. Her people came to her—bruised, hungry, clawing, their swollen tongues asking why she alone was so deserving. Why she alone should be so healthy, so fat.

In America, lampposts flickered on, and the street smelled not like dewy rice paddies, but like gasoline and beef brisket. Urban smog and buttered corn. She saw Koon Lai trudging home from the bus stop, bearing bags of bittermelon and bok choy from Mott Street.

Foon Wah stood.

"Geu biau cheng liang," she said, gathering the girls.

On Saturdays, the family ate in the living room, clustered around the black-and-white Philco TV set. They ate meatloaf and potatoes; Foon Wah had learned it pleased her husband to eat American food on some nights and Chinese food on others, or a mix of the two.

"Chinese refugees are flooding Hong Kong, stretching resources to the limit," said the newsman on the Philco. "The Soviets are testing a nuclear bomb . . . The U.S. is on track to launch its first satellite."

"One day we'll have guys walking on the moon," said Richard, his English garbled by mashed potato. "You kids will spend your vacations on the moon."

"In China, there is no TV," said Foon Wah in Toisanese. "In China, the Communists make people line up, and they give everybody one rice bowl."

"Long time ago, your great-grandfather start restaurant. Work hard," said Koon Lai in English, patting the pocket of his jacket where he carried the letters from their country. "Then he go back, but Communist beat him, take land, take house. He tie rope to ceiling . . ." He trailed off then, for he saw Foon Wah's eyes pleading that he say no more.

Koon Lai, however, could not turn away from the truth. After all his work to build a business in Brooklyn, his proud, octogenarian father-in-law, Lee Jung Yu, had strung himself from his barn rafters in Toisan.

Koon Lai reached into his sweater pocket and reexamined the letter from his brother. In truth, Koon Lai was relieved—that his wife and their big house in Chin village had been left alone. His cousins had taken the land and the livestock, just enough to please the revolutionaries, but they had spared the house, for they remembered the many holidays they'd eaten eggs from his barn, the tractor he'd bought for the village's use, and the new school he'd financed.

Distracted by the opening of *The Ed Sullivan Show*, Jennifer, Julie, and Jackie paid no attention to this talk. They watched as a man danced with his bangs drooped over his eyes, then thumped his pelvis in a manner that was oddly exciting.

Koon Lai thought about how wrong it was to watch such nonsense on television when your brother is eating in the dark.

"This bak gui is crazy," Richard laughed, and for once, his father nodded in agreement.

Foon Wah removed her curlers, twisted the switch on the lamp, and pulled the blanket around her shoulders, ready to settle into sleep. In the dark, she reviewed the memory of turning off the stove, then decided which mooncakes she would purchase in Chinatown. She felt shame at the luxury of such thoughts, and this shame, taut as a fishing line, threatened to drag up that barely submerged ache, to send it bobbing to the surface like a dead fish.

With the American meatloaf heavy in her stomach, sleep finally clouded over guilt.

Yet as she was drifting, she felt, sliding across the darkness, a hand. Inside the shoreline of her pajamas, along her waist, and then her stomach, snaking itself up to her breasts, cupping the left one, scooping it like a ball of ice cream. She hummed softly. Then another hand, tugging at the bottom of her pajamas, the hem of which dragged stubbornly against the bedsheets. She did not lift herself to help. She felt that cactus-shaped bulge against her backside. It humped its way toward an entry point, and at that point she swatted his hands away, twisted her body out of reach.

"I'm sleeping," she whispered.

"What about my son?"

She glanced over at him.

"Three is enough."

"I want a son."

"This isn't China."

"First son of first son of first son of first son." He chuckled as he repeated his father's trope.

"Aiya." She turned away. "Crazy. This neighborhood is not safe anymore. Look around. Everywhere, the hak gui!"

He sighed. He did not dispute it.

"And how come you know it's going to be a boy?" she continued. "Maybe it's another girl."

He reached for her hips, suffered a jab of her elbow.

Yet a few weeks later, he complained of her failure to fulfill his needs. He would wake her up in the middle of the night with his prowling hands, until she felt she had no choice but to roll over and insist that as a condition to her cooperation, he must not release himself inside.

"Take it out! Take it out!" she would cry when he reached the cliff edge of his pleasure. For many months, he complied, wiping himself with the tissue that she handed across the bed. Then a year passed where he rarely had the urge, and she thought with hope that maybe, at thirty, they'd both grown too old.

One night, he spent himself inside her. He apologized in Toisanese, laughing, and she didn't know if he'd carelessly forgotten, or if he had decided to obtain his desired son through trickery. She ran to the bathroom and squatted above the toilet seat, praying that the quiet drop she heard in the toilet bowl was all of him.

Though she went to Chinatown to see a medicine woman, though she dutifully drank the bitter tea every day for two weeks, her blood didn't come.

He had gotten what he wanted.

She was so angry she could barely speak to him, which was strange to her because she had never before shirked away from her duties. Foon Wah told herself she was being selfish and lazy. All Chinese men want a son.

One night in her second month, she dreamed of the child growing in her womb, the baby her husband continued to insist was a boy, as if he could will his wish into reality. But while the baby had a boy's name, they wore a pinafore dress and hair in two even pigtails. Foon Wah sat in the dust nearby, counting her red eggs, knowing an odd number meant girl and an even number meant boy, but she was never able to finish counting because the child would throw itself upon her lap or weave its hands around her neck. She took the child's hand and walked with it all the way to the Toisan River, where the two of them poked gingerly at the water with the tips of their toes. They climbed the path up the mountain, picking dandelion stems, blowing the feathery seeds. Then the child stood to pee.

On waking, Foon Wah knew that whether girl or boy, this child was hers, not Richard's. It had even taken her home.

In the spring of 1960, Jason was born—a wailing, whining, jaundiced banana thing with a massive tuft of black hair. When the waiters served the pig head at the one-month banquet, he stared into its hollowed sockets and screeched in terror, provoking laughter from all the guests. He was a bad sleeper, a bad eater, and as happy in a tub of bathwater as a stray cat.

Richard resolved to harden the boy the way the Depression and the war had hardened him. After his first birthday, Richard took Jason to the pool. With an early start, his son would grow lungs the size of boxing gloves and master a butterfly stroke that would break all Brownsville Boys Club records.

But Jason only grew more petulant and attached to his mother. Richard thought Jason would take better to the beach, so one summer the whole family piled into the Chevy Impala, Richard and Koon Lai in the front seats, and Foon Wah and two of the young restaurant cooks in the back, each with a child or two on their knees. In Richard's opinion, Coney Island had gone to the dogs—Luna destroyed by fire, NYCHA housing crammed all up and down the avenues—but at least the beach was still the beach, and Nathan's was still Nathan's.

But Jason was a child who cried when his elbow grazed the hot metal handle of the Chevy, and again when forced to part with his mother at the door to the men's bathroom. Down on the sand, he whined at the grittiness of sand in his teeth.

"Jay Jay, be a big boy now"—"Jay Jay, I'll hold your hand"—"Jay Jay, look, a seagull!" his sisters cooed, to no avail.

Richard tried to teach Jason to play baseball. To Richard, there was nothing better than a game of baseball at Prospect Park—a place where every twenty feet there'd be a different tribe of people, eating their traditional foods, dancing to their traditional songs, and everyone throwing down their various utensils to get on base. Yet when stationed at home plate, his son did nothing but brush mosquitoes off his arms.

"Man up!" Richard bellowed from across the field.

Foon Wah begged Richard to go easy on their son. It seemed to Richard that between her, his father, and his three daughters, Jason would be pampered into softness. A soft boy wouldn't survive in a world like this one.

One day, Richard came home from the restaurant and found Jason standing on the front porch, dressed up by his sisters in a purple lace dress and Julie's clip-on earrings.

"Ni so ga?!" Richard cried, yanking the earrings off Jason's lobes.

Koon Lai looked amused. "He'll be less trouble than you."

Richard could never get what he wanted without losing something else. He'd had a son, but the Dodgers had quit New York, Ebbets Field smashed to smithereens.

And though he couldn't always explain what, something was happening in Brownsville. Like those mornings when he looked out the bedroom window and saw a car pull up to the curb and a bak gui driver push a hak gui onto the sidewalk, the way you'd fling an overgrown goldfish into the Prospect Park Lake. Usually a nice car.

"We'll pick you up at the next corner," the bak gui driver would yell from the front seat.

It was always the same routine. The hak gui wore a soiled suit and clutched a bottle of liquor. He would stumble up the block, mumbling to himself, and throw the bottle in someone's yard, the glass shattering against the stoop. Richard saw the same thing so many times, he had a bad case of déjà vu.

Always, the expensive car depositing the soiled hak gui. Always, a few hours after, a real estate agent proceeding door to door, warning those who remained: sell now, before it's too late.

By Jason's fourth birthday, there were hardly any bak gui left on the block. Hak gui children raced up and down the street on wooden scooters. It was the same, Richard heard, in the government projects. No more "fifty percent Negro, fifty percent European," as Alan had once told him.

At first, the Jews came back on Saturdays for synagogue and stopped for Chinese food after. Then the police killed a Black boy in Harlem, and sirens blared for six nights straight. By the time it was all over, hak gui had emptied out the cigar store down the block, smashed the windows of the bicycle shop, and burglarized Mathenial Hats. Richard installed gates downstairs and a double lock on the door to the restaurant, but the Jews did not come back.

Richard checked out homes in Marine Park but could not afford them. He looked at a home in Bay Ridge, but it sold during the fifteen-minute drive to see it.

One evening after closing, Richard went to the handball court at Betsy Head Park and, finding no one there, threw the ball against the wall by himself. Half an hour later, he noticed Alan walking down Livonia in his Esquire suit. When he reached the court, Alan unrolled the newspaper beneath his elbow and handed it to Richard.

"Robert Moses." Alan shook his head with disgust. "He's the one siting a million housing projects all in Brownsville. A good idea gone bad. We said we needed better housing for struggling families. We didn't say every single poor New Yorker should live in one square mile. Can you believe it, Richard? They're planning to build another fifteen hundred government poor houses right here!"

Richard shrugged and walked off, bounced the ball against the wall.

Alan sighed, loosened his tie, and cleared his throat.

"It's good we ran into each other. I've been meaning to tell you something."

Richard hit the ball.

"We got a house. A house out in Riverhead, Long Island. A nice three-bedroom with a big yard. And an office space in the town—I'll be opening up my own practice out there."

Richard served the ball against the wall.

"Rich, you're not gonna miss me?"

Richard grinned. Laughed. Kept his eyes on the ball. "So much for loving the coloreds."

"It's not a color problem. The city doesn't give a damn!"

Richard caught the ball, took a seat on the bench, lit a cigarette.

"We've been working for years to get that vocational facility here at Betsy Head Park," Alan continued, pacing on the concrete. "And what does the Parks Department tell us? They take over the Brownsville Boys Club, fire Levine and Adelman, steal our building, and call it the Brownsville Recreation Center. Between you and me, it went down like this because of those bigots on the BBC board.

"And the schools!" Alan went on. "I don't know how my sister makes it through the day teaching at that junior high school! J.H.S. 271? There's a whole line of classrooms they can't even use because the ceiling caved in."

Letting his friend rave, Richard remained silent. A clever man could sometimes win an argument by letting the other talk himself into contradictions. And Richard felt he deserved to win, as a consolation prize. His friend was finally leaving him, and his kids' school was filled with hoodlums and falling ceilings.

Richard and Foon Wah laid off most of the restaurant staff and worked harder. Foon Wah stir-fried, Richard hosted, and Koon Lai washed dishes until his fingers turned to raisins. Yet with fewer hands, they were increasingly exhausted. A strand of hair appeared in someone's

wonton soup. A mouse nested in the cupboard. The appliances mal-
functioned; to get the burners to light, Richard had to hit the stove
with a baseball bat.

The new restaurant clientele were hak gui. They came with their
dates or for a family meal after church. Richard would lean against
the back wall of the dining room and watch them. One night, a party
of four arrived and pointed to the center table, where the Schulmans
had once sat. While most hak gui guests requested just a couple of
dishes, this group ordered a whole banquet, and Richard doubted
their ability to pay. Then they talked and laughed joyously and sang
"Happy Birthday," and when one of the women reached across the
table to playfully pat the birthday boy's cheek, she accidentally
knocked the teapot off the table.

It hit the floor and shattered, jasmine tea spilling across the
wood. The girls yelped and the men laughed, throwing their napkins
on the floor to soak up the spill.

"Waiter? I'm so sorry," the woman cried.

Koon Lai didn't want a scene; he sent a waiter to fetch a broom.
But Richard couldn't tolerate it.

"Get out!" he demanded, standing above the table. "We can't
serve you anymore."

"Oh, come on," one of the hak gui men said. "We'll pay for the
teapot. Add it to the bill."

"I said you're out. You guys are loud, you break the china. No one
can enjoy their meal!"

"No disrespect, sir, but there are no other customers here but us."

"I said get out!" Richard pounded his fist on the table. "Get out of
my restaurant!"

The birthday boy gave Richard a cold stare, and the group left in
silence with their food half-finished.

Christmas, 1966: Koon Lai found a letter in the restaurant mailbox.

He usually waited to read them at home, but it was six o'clock and there had been no customers. That, perhaps, was the most eerie change—Christmas had always been their busiest day.

He had already sent Richard and Foon Wah home, and alone, he walked slowly from one side of the dining room to the other, checking for trash and straightening tablecloths, his left knee throbbing with each step. The doctor on Baxter Street had prescribed snake oil, and for four months, Koon Lai had massaged it into his knee at bedtime. There'd been little improvement.

Koon Lai flicked off the lights and sat down behind the cash register to examine the envelope. It was addressed from Hong Kong, but he recognized his wife's handwriting. He broke open the seal. Water had penetrated the envelope, rendering a column of characters illegible.

I have taken my mother to Hong   but your third brother did not make

It wasn't hunger in the end, it was the youth   Your wealth in America is no more than a

They saw the height of the house   they saw the perfume you sent from New York, the ivory

They called us landlords   rich peasants

They took stones and smashed the windows, stole the furniture smashed the   made me walk on the glass

Your third brother they tied to a tree and whipped until he

We buried him in the

The house is destroyed.

Blood drained from the hand that held the letter. A humming in his chest, erupting on his lips as a moan.

His brother.

We buried him in the . . .

His young nieces.

The house is destroyed...

His wife, in exile.

Your wealth in America is no more than a...

And then a thought, unbearable, rose to the fore and overpowered him.

He should have insisted that they come to New York. He should have fought for the refugee visas.

Koon Lai crumpled onto the floor, panting, clutching the leg of a chair like it might anchor him. He had thought his family was safe, that they had escaped the revolutionaries' vengeance.

But children can be as cruel as a foreign army.

The lamppost outside the window illuminated the dark of the restaurant so that the tables glowed like snow-covered cars. Suddenly he was on his feet, pacing in the dining room. He had spent decades feeding bak gui, learning their tastes, smiling and laughing when they made silly sounds in imitation of his language, and all the while, he'd longed for home. And his reward? An image flashed across his eyes: his brother roped to a tree trunk. Again, Koon Lai collapsed to the floor and curled up like a child, his forehead against his knees.

A sharp silver noise shattered Koon Lai's nightmare. An explosion, he thought: an attack. He peered through the dark and saw the left window had splintered into an intricate web, glass shards falling like loose teeth.

In terror, Koon Lai thought of the masses rising in unison against him, rattling the walls and smashing the windows. They had tracked him down across the world—and if someone must be punished, didn't he deserve it far more? Far more than his brother and wife— and he saw the youth flatten him against a table in the dining room, rip off his collared shirt, and empty bottles of soy sauce on his naked back. *Si Yiu Gai! Soy Sauce Chicken!* they ordered, laughing, stuffing his face in a plate of cream shrimp, the curds dribbling down his tie.

Chunks of glass glimmered on the dining room floor. He heard a scramble of feet on the street below, then nothing.

He was afraid, but he wanted to know. Slowly, he crept toward the window, glass fragments snapping beneath his shoes.

He looked out, but there was no one below.

There, on the sidewalk: a rock the size of a melon.

He returned to the cash register, grabbed the letter and his coat, and made for the front door. He could not recall a time when the street had been so poorly lit. Once, the neon signage of the barber-shop and the cigar store had brightened the block at night. Now both were boarded up. And it had never been so silent, the only sound the tap of his shoes against the pavement. He could hear as well as see his breath, reaching out before him like a ghostly hand.

The street smelled of garbage and burning wood, and his thoughts ran like water out of a drainpipe: *The hak gui do not know how to work. And those of us who work, they tie to a tree and whip to death.*

He heard something like a step, or like Styrofoam sliding against concrete, and glanced behind him. No one. He turned the corner onto Amboy and heard it again. Stopping to look, he glimpsed what appeared to be a person, only it was thin as a stick and folded in upon itself, a body half-there, half-ghost.

Holding his breath, his eyes on the Christmas lights twinkling in their house window at the end of the block, Koon Lai walked faster. As the figure gathered speed on the outside edge of the cars, he could almost hear the tapping of shoes.

Koon Lai began to run, trying to lean on his good leg, but even so, the bad knee throbbed. He hurried onward, ignoring the searing pain, and screamed for his son at the top of his lungs. "Dun Ho!" he yelped. "Dun Ho!"

He threw open the gate of the house, but tripped on the stoop's first step. His hand still grasped the letter as he tumbled down; his elbows and knees clattered on the stone, another shattering. Koon Lai's sixty-two-year-old throat opened into a child's cry.

SADIE & LINA

With the ribs of her umbrella cracked inside-out, Sadie hurried from the Rockaway Avenue station to Ms. Lina's apartment in Brownsville Houses. There were few people on the street other than herself, just one guy dashing home, clutching a box of Tony's Pizza in one hand and using a newspaper to shield his hair with the other. She thought of Ngen Ngen's fear of rain—how even if it was only mildly drizzling, her grandmother would call and urge them to cancel all their plans and stay home. Sadie had always brushed off Ngen Ngen's paranoia, but now, in her unpadded jacket, she felt like she just might go home ill.

She was nervous. It had been easy to convince Ms. Lina and Tyrell to sit down for the interview, but difficult to prepare for it. Sadie had spent hours riffling through the files at the Fire Department archives down at MetroTech, but she couldn't find anything for 78 Livonia Avenue. Ngen Ngen, like her father, knew nothing about fires or homicides.

When Sadie reached Ms. Lina's building, she buzzed the intercom for 6A and waited several minutes.

A woman pushing a baby in a stroller rolled up the wheelchair ramp and, without bothering to pull out a key or buzz the intercom, pushed through the door into the building, the lock apparently broken.

"Is this for real?" the woman groaned, poking a dull elevator button. "I thought they fixed it." She hoisted her toddler onto her hip and looked at Sadie pleadingly, who obliged by carrying the stroller to the fifth floor.

It was only one more floor to Ms. Lina's. She heard trash falling down the shoot, smelled cat litter. Most of the doors on floor six were missing their apartment letters, but one door looked different from the others—painted green, with pink polka dots and frog silhouettes. Sadie rang the bell.

"That's our girl," she heard Tyrell say.

She blushed.

When she'd proposed writing an article about the history of the lot, Tyrell had settled the time, date, and place of the meeting with Ms. Lina, inviting himself. She liked to imagine that, once the interview was over, he'd insist on walking her to the station. Or maybe he'd invite her back to his apartment, urge her to break the first rule of journalism.

Tyrell opened the door, the left side of his mouth curling into a half smile. He wore a sleeveless white undershirt, and she found herself aroused by the sight of the fabric clinging to his lean frame.

"Sadie, what's up."

"Thanks so much for having me over. I'm sorry I'm late, I was—"

She stopped mid-speech.

A mural spanned from one end of the living room to the other. It brimmed with human faces, iguanas, hibiscus flowers, and avocados, all popping with color. On the wall next to the mural, there were posters of Black and brown heroines: *Mother Gaston. Shirley Chisholm. Sylvia Rivera.*

"Ms. Lina was an art teacher," Tyrell said as Sadie marveled.

"I always tell this to the young people: when you can't do anything about the outside, you care for the inside."

Prior to this, Sadie had only seen her on the street, hobbling with a cane, but here in her own home, her own chair, she looked like commander in chief.

"Put that wet coat on the radiator and sit down," Ms. Lina added. "They've got the heat on."

Sadie nodded and took a seat on the couch, and Tyrell sat down beside her. She withdrew a notebook with a list of questions she'd prepared. Yet before she could ask one, Ms. Lina folded her hands on her lap and began speaking.

"Miss Sadie, if you're going to write a feature about 78 Livonia, I have some things you need to understand." She nodded at the mural. "It took ten years, but I fought until I got NYCHA to okay that mural. I designed and supervised it, but it's my former students who painted it. I want you to look closer."

Sadie turned around and peered at it.

"These are my ancestors," Ms. Lina said, nodding at the figures on the left. "My people are Taíno and Yoruba. The enslavers, the conquistadores, displaced them from their homelands. And even when that ended, the cycle continued." Ms. Lina stood slowly, grabbed her cane, and crossed over to the mural. She touched its surface with her pointer finger. "Uncle Sam forced my mother's people from their farms to San Juan, then from San Juan to Nueva York. My father's people, from Nigeria to Carolina to Harlem. And I'm not only talking about my family, I'm talking about millions of families, Black and Boricua families. We're healing from generations of root shock."

Sadie nodded, hoping some of this related back to the history of the Livonia Avenue lot.

"Oh, so you heard that term before, Miss Sadie? Root shock?"

"Not . . . not really."

"There's root shock in both the Native community and the Black community."

"And these new families, they got root shock on steroids." Tyrell sighed, leaning his head back on the palms of his hands. "Brownsville is the last neighborhood people can actually afford. And hundreds of families are coming here every month 'cause they been pushed out of Bed-Stuy, Fort Greene, Crown Heights."

"And now folks are getting gentrified out of Brownsville," said Ms. Lina. "We made Brownsville livable again and now they want to take it back."

Sadie was surprised. People usually referred to Brownsville as the one part of Brooklyn immune to gentrification. That, after all, was why she'd been so interested in the job.

"Have you seen any white people living in Brownsville?" Sadie asked Ms. Lina, trying to say "white people" as casually as possible.

"Oh, all the time. I don't have a problem with them." Ms. Lina shrugged. "The problem is, people look around and they think, 'Oh, Brooklyn has changed,' but nothing's changed. Land is still money. Fifty years ago, they made money by keeping our people trapped in the cities, and now they make money by forcing us out. An investment game, same as always. They say the city is more *integrated*, but I don't see Black people, Puerto Ricans moving to Brooklyn Heights."

Sadie once again turned to the questions in her notebook. Ms. Lina had another appointment at six o'clock, and they had agreed upon an hour-long meeting. With ten minutes wasted in the court-yard and another ten discussing the mural, Sadie was anxious.

"Ms. Lina, the proposal mentions there was a fire that burned down the building at 78 Livonia Avenue. Would you be willing . . ."

"We'll get to the fire, Miss Sadie. Look, there's a reason I'm telling you this. This is why we don't need mega-developers building up Livonia. This land should belong to the survivors of root shock. It's not much we're asking for."

"How . . . uh," Sadie hesitated. "How would you counter the argu-ment that larger developers have better access to financing for com-plex projects than grassroots groups? The city gets more bang for the buck working with big developers, don't they?"

This was the question that her editor, Wendy, had asked Sadie earlier that fall when she'd first written about Ms. Lina's plan.

Tyrell nodded and sat up, his hands on his knees, his eyebrows rising with sudden seriousness. Ms. Lina prodded the inside of her cheek with her tongue and sighed.

"Where are your people from, Miss Sadie?" Ms. Lina looked at her intently.

Sadie was caught off guard.

"She's half Chinese and half Jewish," Tyrell volunteered. "Her family used to live in Brownsville. Didn't you say they ran—"

"A laundromat, yes."

Ms. Lina's eyes lingered on her. Sadie didn't know why she had lied.

Ms. Lina nodded slowly. "Well, you need to know your ancestors. Because you're the product of their dreams. And that's my answer to your question—I know it won't make sense to you now."

Sadie wasn't sure what to say. It was true she didn't know much about her ancestors. She'd always wanted to know more. And that's why she'd come to Ms. Lina, but what if the truth was shameful?

"Does NYCHA want to bake us to death? Let me crack the window," Ms. Lina said, rising to her feet. "Y'all want anything to drink?"

Rule number two: don't accept gifts from sources, not even beverages. Tyrell, however, insisted that Lina pour them each a glass of "that Spanish drink."

"Papi! Don't say 'that Spanish drink,'" Ms. Lina replied as she shuffled away. "Horchata de ajonjolí!"

"Horchata! My bad." He held his hands up in a gesture of surrender.

Tyrell and Sadie were alone then, the radiator gurgling, an old Smokey Robinson tape playing softly on the boom box. She could smell the mint gum in Tyrell's cheek, his natural sweat, and a layering of cucumber-scented detergent.

"Everyone in the 'Ville loves Ms. Lina's horchata," Tyrell said, turning to face her with his elbow resting on the back of the couch.

"I guess I should try it."

"I was at this leadership training last week and this white professor was trying to get me to say *Latinx*," he said, one eyebrow raised. "Said I was being disrespectful saying 'Spanish people.' That's what you say, Latinx? That's what they teach the kids at Yale?"

His voice sounded different from before—so fast and light on the consonants that she wanted to slip into the stream of it.

"Oh," she stuttered. "I . . . I guess my professors would say Latino, Latina. I feel like it's more recently that I hear Latinx. Like so we don't have to gender everything and everyone, you know?"

"I was talking to Ricky—Ricky's Dominican. And he was like, 'Don't come around me with those new fancy words, telling me I'm Latinx. Ain't no 'x' sound in Español, and I ain't never been Latinx until today.'"

"What does Ms. Lina say?"

"I guess she likes me to be specific. *Boricua*. But the thing that gets me is when these academics make it sound like Ricky is stupid for preferring the thing he always used. I've thought about going back, but then I'm like, what can they teach me that I don't already know about my people?"

She nodded. Was he telling her all this because he wanted her to see him as her equal? Mostly she agreed with him, but a part of her resisted this reduction of her hard work in school. She was embarrassed of this part.

Tyrell bent over and picked something up from the floor. Her hat, she realized. Placed it on her thigh. The soft crochet touched her like a hand.

Lina wondered if something was wrong with the radiator. Or maybe this was a hot flash—felt like she was going through menopause all over again. She removed her beret and wiped the sweat from her forehead.

Reaching the kitchen, she opened the window and looked down at the street. A quietness came over Brownsville when it rained. She thought of her mother Isabella, who always said it was good luck to get wet by the first May rain. Each spring, Mami would grab their hands and pull them out to the courtyard, where they'd laugh and catch droplets on their tongues, delighted by their mother's sudden whimsy. Lina would have liked to be out there now, instead of with Sadie and Tyrell and their flickering eyes. Their eyes: that's why the room felt like an oven.

With her remarks, Lina had only been trying to find a way to reach the girl, to help her understand the history and context behind their fight for the land. Then Miss Sadie had asked why the city shouldn't work with big developers, why the city should waste its time working with broke-ass grassroots groups like theirs. It was the same question that had worried Tyrell on their way back from Bernard & Company, and she'd been pondering it ever since. But the city had to think beyond "bang for the buck," she thought. It had to think about justice. About priorities. If the city didn't spend so lavishly on stadiums and military-grade equipment for the NYPD, the mayor could put funds into community groups that would construct the kind of housing and facilities people truly needed. And the community groups would do it right—they'd put their neighbors to work, hire young people to hammer and to paint, and give poor people collective ownership of the land. That was the real recipe for public safety and economic progress, in her view. That's why Lina had asked the girl about her own family. She wanted Sadie to stop thinking so hard and instead *feel*. Wanted her to remember her inheritance. Chinese and Jewish people had experienced injustice and displacement too—she needed Sadie to tap into that memory.

Bearing a tray with three glasses of horchata, Lina returned to the living room and handed Miss Sadie a cup.

"This is amazing," Miss Sadie said.

Lina had never met a mixed Chinese and Jewish person. It was hard to imagine the Chinese lady from the laundry on Rockaway sneaking over to Eastern Parkway and blowing kisses to one of the Hasid men with sidelocks.

With these thoughts, Lina had yet another hot flash, and she sat back down and reached for *Our Time Press*, folding the latest issue into a fan. There was no use speculating about Miss Sadie, she told herself again. She would have to finish this interview.

"Okay, so what do you want to know? You want to know about the Freedom School?" She sipped from her horchata. "I used to live at 78 Livonia Avenue, and I turned my apartment into an alternative school, a liberation school. We called it the Freedom School. We had a pantry, a free hair salon, art and political education classes. We even had a day care for the little kids. In the summer, we organized Black Power parades and Puerto Rican Pride parades."

"How did you fund the school?" Sadie asked.

"Donations, fish fries, art sales, rent parties."

"And how many years did the Freedom School exist?"

"About seven."

"And then what happened?"

The girl wanted to talk about the fire.

Lina sipped from her cup. "Well," she said, but she found herself struggling for words. The cold cream of the horchata touched her brain and glazed her throat, and she sat rigid, frozen. It had been so long since she'd spoken of that day.

"Ms. Lina never told me about the fire," Tyrell said, perhaps trying to buy her some time—she could tell he wanted to make eye contact with her, but she couldn't meet his gaze yet. "That was some real heavy shit, right?"

"No, no," Lina muttered, shaking off the stiffness. "I'll tell you guys about the fire."

She eyed the lower left corner of the mural. Her students had painted a young Lina there—glowing Afro, leather jacket, the black-purple beret.

"It was August 24, 1978. I was thirty-four. The building was falling apart, and we'd been in court with the landlord. There was a sign on the door that said the city was going to evict, but we thought that was some kind of mistake because the court had said the landlord had two months to fix the place up and he hadn't done any of the work yet. So, this one night, guess it was one, two in the morning, I opened the door and the hallway was already in flames. I went into the next apartment, where the Browns lived. We got the three girls out through the fire escape. But when we reached the street, the fire had spread. And some of the neighbors were trapped inside."

Lina reached for the boom box, shut it off.

"People called nine-one-one, but the trucks didn't show up. I went in the next building myself, went up to the top floor. There was this old woman. We used to call her Grandma. I wanted to get her out, but she kept telling me her brother was in the next room."

Lina clutched her stomach. Felt like she'd swallowed a live snake. "I'm trying to give you guys the facts, but I've been having nightmares about that night for forty years and it's hard to say what really happened."

Just the prior night, she'd dreamed of Grandma. The old woman had jumped out of a window, then become a monster, attacking people on the street. And two weeks earlier, Lina had locked the Brown girls in a closet to protect them from a pedophile. Then the building was on fire, and the girls still trapped inside.

Lina studied the wrinkles on the front page of *Our Time Press.*

"I didn't make it in time."

She kept her eyes on her lap.

"We had to leave without the brother, and we made it down. But by the time the fire trucks showed up, we had one dead, three injured, and sixteen people homeless."

When she finally raised her head, Miss Sadie looked like she was about to cry. Pity, likely, and Lina didn't want any of that.

"Who did it?" Tyrell asked.

"I saw the two boys who lit the match. But those kids were paid by the landlord."

"The landlord—do you remember his name?" Miss Sadie asked.

"Richard Wong."

"Was there ever an investigation?"

Lina couldn't help but laugh. "The city didn't investigate these fires! No, Mr. Wong took the money and ran."

Miss Sadie reached for her backpack, withdrew her laptop.

"I was looking at the deed record for the building." Sadie said. "I saw Richard Wong owned the building from May 3, 1966, through August 9, 1978. So August 9 is about two weeks before the day of the fire. Is it possible that someone else already owned the building by then?"

Tyrell leaned closer to the girl, squinting at the screen. Lina stared at the two of them, confused. "What deed record?" She hadn't even known a person could have access to the lot's deed record. "What's that you said?"

"August 9 is two weeks before the fire. And there's a buyer listed here—78 Livonia Avenue LLC. Do you know what that is?"

"I don't know what you're talking about."

"What about the restaurant?" Miss Sadie asked next. "What happened to it?"

"The Chinese restaurant? That was gone long before we started the Freedom School."

As soon as Lina answered the question, she knew something was off. That girl was hiding something. Tyrell must have sensed it too. He leaned away from Sadie now, glancing at Lina, his jaw suddenly rigid.

"How did you know there used to be a restaurant in the building?"

The reporter looked down at her notebook, but Lina could tell she was flustered.

"Miss Sadie, what do you know about Richard Wong?"

The girl put her head in her hands like she really was going to cry. Lina didn't want to see this. Didn't even want to know. She wished she'd never invited Sadie up to her apartment.

"He's my grandfather."

Sadie raised her face, met Lina's eyes—and Lina held the gaze, held it without moving or screaming.

"Is Richard Wong alive?"

"No. He died when I was a baby."

"You knew what he did when you came to my house today?" She tried to keep her voice flat, her face devoid of emotion.

"I . . . knew he owned the building. I knew he did something."

"And why didn't you say anything about that, Miss Sadie?"

"I wanted to know what happened."

"Your family couldn't tell you? You wanted to hear it from the victim's mouth?"

"No one in my family knows."

"Now you know what happened! Now you can get out of my house!" Unable to bear the sight of Sadie's face, Lina limped to the window.

"I'm so sorry. I was just hoping to bring this to light, to write . . ."

"Your grandpa burned down my home! And now you have the nerve to set foot in this one?"

"Maybe if you give me a chance to explain, we could work together."

Lina was appalled by the girl's audacity. She gripped the window frame with one hand. "You think after you lied to me, I still trust you enough to work with you? When I say get out of my house, you get out of my house!"

No one said anything then. She heard the rustle of coats and furniture.

"I'm really sorry," the reporter attempted once again.

Lina heard footsteps and the door slowly opening. Several footsteps—Tyrell's sneakers. He had unlocked the front door.

She looked over her shoulder—saw Tyrell with his eyes lowered and his arms folded, propping open the door, and the girl, tearing up as she shuffled into the hallway.

Once Sadie Chin was gone, Lina could tell Tyrell wanted to talk to her, but she didn't want to hear it.

She dialed a tenant organizer, reaching her voicemail.

"Rhonda, it's Lina. You know that reporter I told you about? She ain't who she said she was. Just wanted to let you know. See you Sunday."

She dialed the violence interrupter, Mr. Q.

"Mr. Q, Lina here. That reporter I told you about, don't bother with her. Yeah. I shouldn't have given her your number. You get a call from her, let it ring, she ain't worth your time."

She dialed the youth mentors, the leaders of the running club, the librarians, and a few additional community organizers Miss Sadie might have met on her own time, Tyrell watching her from the door of the kitchen.

Last, she dialed Keesha, canceled their meeting, and collapsed in her living room chair.

"I'm protecting my people," she said aloud. "I could've done a better job of that in '78. And now I'm doing it."

Tyrell sat down on the couch across from her, silent.

II

LINA

It was the Long Hot Summer of Jimmy Ruffin and The Underdogs, *Loving v. Virginia*, Newark and Detroit. Twenty-three-year-old Lina Rodriguez Armstrong stood on Livonia Avenue below a sign that said CHOW MEIN HERE!

Hands on her hips, she squinted at a piece of paper taped to the door of the building.

RESTERANT CLOSED. ROOMS FOUR RENT —
CALL MR. WONG 212-525-3959.

In high school, she'd eaten there while on a date with a guy named Ricardo. She hadn't felt anything for Ricardo, but that egg roll had been something else. All that yellow crunch, that tasty mix of carrots, pork, and cabbage—she could survive on a desert island with a bunch of those.

She looked up and noticed that one of the windows was planked with wood. Had some boys broken in and robbed the Chinese restaurant? *Shame on y'all. Where am I supposed to get my egg rolls?*

She was on the hunt for her first apartment, and what a kick it would be to live in the old restaurant. While she was copying down the number on the back of her mother's pharmacy receipt, she heard the train hurtling into the station, then the meow of a kitten. It was eyeing her from behind a pillar of the elevated rail.

"Miss Kitty!" she exclaimed. "What do ya think, should I try this place out?"

The kitten stared unblinkingly.

"I could get used to the El. I don't mind it, do you?"

Lured by the warmth of Lina's voice, the kitten gradually emerged into view and crept toward Lina until they were nearly in reach of each other. Yet as soon as Lina squatted to pet the creature, the cat darted away and across the street.

"I'll take that as a yes!"

That night, back at Van Dyke Houses, Lina dialed the number and spoke to a man who said that the "big room" was still available for rent—only fifty bucks a month. She should come by the place with her stuff next week.

It was going to be her first pad. And she'd worked for it: since graduating with her bachelor's from City College, she'd earned her teacher's certificate while also working as an assistant to a SoHo artist who made sculptures with rotted beef steaks. At least she'd earned enough from that job to pay back her mami's medical bills and save cash for a security deposit.

Now it was finally time to move out of her family's apartment. Altogether, there were eight of them squeezed into that two-bedroom at Van Dyke Houses. Lina loved kids, but not enough to take craps in the next-door neighbor's bathroom. She didn't want to leave Brownsville, though; she'd just been hired to teach art at J.H.S. 271. She wanted to be close enough to keep watch over her nieces Gabby and Tania, especially on the evenings her sister Sofia went to accounting class.

The following week, Lina packed paintbrushes and sketchbooks in a suitcase and the spare caldero in a cardboard box, then loaded up her mother's laundry cart. Dragging the cart in one hand and holding her suitcase in the other, a lampshade on top of her head, she pushed her things the ten blocks from Van Dyke to Canton Kitchen.

Lina was tall with spaghetti limbs, though her chest wasn't as flat as she would have liked. She had a frizzy Afro that her little sisters begged her to straighten, and thick arched eyebrows that Callie had said made her look like Frida Kahlo. Though she preferred a pair of jeans and sneakers, her mother insisted on a skirt and tights that morning *to make a "buena impresión" on "el lanlor."* And yes, she was a chocolate girl, though as her father had liked to say, she was Sugar Baby brown, darker than her Caramel Cream sisters, lighter than her Peppermint Patty brothers. In high school, a bunch of guys had chased her: Black boys, Puerto Rican boys—none of them could take a hint. When she told them she would rather join the Carmelites, they thought she was playing hard to get. Some still thought she was ready for the taking, and her mother wasn't helping. All summer, Isabella had been trying to pair Lina with that Boricua Sunday school teacher.

When Lina reached the block, she found the restaurant owner waiting on the sidewalk. She recognized him, had seen him taking orders. Suddenly, she found herself wanting to know everything about him. When had he come to America? Could he teach her how to say her name in Chinese, and how to write it with a calligraphy brush?

Mr. Wong was short and muscled, and with the pomade in his jet-black hair, she thought he styled himself more like an Italian than a Chinese.

"You the girl?"

"Yeah," she said, tucking her lamp hat beneath one elbow and stretching out the opposite hand. "Glad to meet you, sir."

Ignoring her hand, he rummaged in his pocket for the keys.

"This key goes in the lower lock and this one in the top lock."

It was a half-Chinese, half-Brooklynese accent, syllables sharp, but the *r*'s knocked off. "You lock both, coming in and out, and you lock the windows when you leave."

On the first floor, she heard the laughter of several brothers from the American South, then *Alvin and the Chipmunks* on a record player. Already, the place felt homey.

The building must have been a hundred years old or more—the stairs so worn that the steps dipped like spoons. She was remembering more about that date with Ricardo: the way he'd wanted to hold hands even while they were climbing the tapering staircase.

And then she remembered, her brother Lou had liked the restaurant. Lou had loved Chinese food: shrimp dumplings, beef lo mein. Before his deployment, he'd even joked that he'd be fine over there. A chance to try Vietnamese food.

Swallowing her thoughts, Lina refocused her attention on dragging the heavy suitcase up the stairs.

"Sir, if you don't mind me asking, how long have you been living in Brooklyn?"

He unlocked a door and led her inside. She realized she was getting the dining room, and it was huge, at least compared to what she was used to.

"You take this room. There's other tenants in the back room. You share the bathroom. One bathroom on each floor. Every first of the month, I'll come collect the rent. You're late, you're out."

The tables were gone, and the walls needed a paint job, but even with that one boarded window, the light was marvelous.

"So what happened to the window?"

"I'll fix it later."

"Why'd you close the restaurant?"

"You people don't eat Chinese food."

"Whatchu talking about?" she exclaimed, sitting down on her suitcase. "I love Chinese food. Those egg rolls? The best food I ever tasted!"

Paying her no attention, he scrunched down on the floor to examine a stain on the wood, then straightened himself and dusted off his hands.

"No dogs, no cats—I don't want animals damaging the wood." He motioned her over to the kitchen appliances. "You turn the lights out when you go to work and you make sure the faucets are off. Water's not cheap. Make sure the gas is off when you leave the house. The ceiling fan works, but don't keep it on the first setting. I don't want the ceiling to fall down."

He suddenly turned to look at her, his narrow eyes narrowing farther.

"You got kids?"

She closed her lips, breathed out through her nose.

"Not one child," she replied dryly.

"No guests. I don't want to hear about guys coming in and out all day and night. You'll get me in trouble with the city."

"Sir, I can assure you, there won't be no men."

The two waited as the train screeched into the station, and then Mr. Wong put the keys on the kitchen counter and descended the stairs without a nod goodbye.

In any case, Lina wasn't giving up the apartment. She would paint the walls. Yellow and pink, fruit salad colors. She lugged the rest of her stuff up the stairs, then took a slower, self-guided tour of the apartment. On the back of the door, she found a red knot with a long tail of silk tassels, and under the kitchen sink, a pot shaped like the bell of a horn. In the bathroom, there was a wall calendar. Someone had etched five little dots between March 2 and March 7, and then another five dots twenty-eight days later, from April 4 to April 9. For several minutes, Lina stared at the dots. Then she realized it was a language she knew, a language known to half the world.

Mr. Wong had a sister, or a wife.

As she danced around the apartment and planned out her wall murals, she stubbed her toe on a piece of plastic: a tiny, white-clad, yellow-skinned nurse doll with a medical cross on her removable cap and a head that could be rotated through a series of facial expressions.

She opened her suitcase, threw off the dress, unhooked her bra, and changed into her paint-splotched jeans and Danny's T-shirt—her baby brother was exactly her height, and she often stole his clothes.

Her next-door neighbor didn't answer the door, but she managed to introduce herself to the two households on the top floor and the two on the bottom. In 3R lived fortysomething-year-old siblings, Sam and Sylvia Jenkins, both fresh up from Florida and on the superstitious side—they didn't like the black cat that climbed up the fire escape and peeked in the window. In 3L lived old Patricia Taylor, who wasn't fretting over no fire escape cats, and her six grandchildren, who enjoyed feeding the cats one another's hash browns. On floor one, Lina met Harry Eugene, a WWII veteran with an amazing memory, and also John Coleman, "Daddy J," from Baltimore. She offered a hand to everyone.

Up and down the sidewalks of Livonia, trash bags formed a human-high barricade—it had been over a week since the Sanitation Department had acknowledged Brownsville's existence. She waved to a group of children playing stoopball, then at the old man in the window whom everyone called Jewish Pops, since he was one of the few left.

A white lady in a tan dress suit knocked insistently on the Garcia family window at 80 Livonia. Child welfare, Lina figured. She hoped the woman had not come to break them up. It had almost happened to the Rodriguez Armstrongs back in East Harlem, about a dozen years earlier. Lina had answered a few questions, then realized what they wanted and slammed the door in the social service worker's face.

Even if Evelina had her issues, Lina thought, those kids were better off in the reach of people like Mr. Angel Rivera of the Puerto Rican Organization of Brownsville and East New York, or like Ms. Delores Torres from Christians and Jews United for Social Action.

But the Garcias didn't answer the door, and the white woman made a mark in her file and descended the stoop. Lina took a deep breath and continued on her way to Mr. Dachensky's deli.

When she reached it, there were three kids trying to insert rocks into the gumball machines. She gave them quarters, then headed down the produce aisle.

"Cabbage?" said Mr. Dachensky as he rang up her items. "I thought you said you hated cabbage."

Mr. Dachensky liked to tease her.

"No, sir, I like the taste," she corrected. "It's the shape that's the problem. Like I'm cooking someone's head!"

She bought diapers to drop off at the Garcias' and a box of Dippy Canoes for the kids playing stoopball, then strolled back to the new apartment, snacking on a Hershey's bar as she walked. Hershey's had been her father's favorite, and she'd been missing him more than usual—and now her mother wasn't around to admonish, *No hay postre hasta que termina la cena!*

Even their mother, when she got all soft and talked about their father and how he'd wooed her, never failed to mention the candies. They'd met on the IRT, when Isabella Rodriguez was new to los Nueva Yorks and prone to getting lost. Paul Armstrong had offered her directions, and then a Fifth Avenue bar, and she'd reciprocated, offering the "big moreno" a square of budín de pan.

Lina loved when her mother told this story. There was an innocence to her parents' love that seemed impossible to replicate in her own time.

When she finally reached the CHOW MEIN HERE! sign and climbed up the staircase to her apartment, she ran into a young woman with a baby on her hip.

"You just moved in?" the woman said. "Annetta Brown, and this is Deborah."

"Good to meet you, Miss Brown and Deborah," said Lina, reaching out to shake the baby's hand. "I've seen y'all around. Y'all used to live at Van Dyke?"

"No, but we go to Presentation. Ain't your mama that little Spanish lady?"

"You know my mama, huh."

"2R is small," Annetta said. "Tight, but that's all I can afford right now. You got the big space." She nodded toward Lina's side of the floor with her lips pursed and her eyebrows raised, an expression that was almost begrudging.

"Yeah," Lina muttered, scratching her head. "I got to do something with all this." She smiled at Deborah's wide-eyed stare. "Maybe something for the kids on the block!"

"Ain't Mr. Wong tell you no guests?"

"Oh, he said a lot of things. But I'm trained to work with kids. I was just hired to teach art at J.H.S. 271. Right on time for community control—you know about community control?"

"Community control?" Annetta raised an eyebrow. "What's that?"

"Folks here in Brownsville, we taking over our own schools. It's going to be education for, by, and about our people—Black people, Puerto Ricans. They'll teach young people like Deborah how to be strong and proud. You know the board of education office on Livingston Street? We occupied the hall for three days."

It had been incredible to be there. The activists had declared themselves "the People's Board," and held an impromptu hearing on the conditions in slum schools. Dozens of folks from Brownsville, the Lower East Side, Harlem, and the Bronx had shown up to speak their truths. When the police surged the hall and made arrests, Lina had scrambled out—she couldn't afford to go to jail. But the amazing thing was, in the months that followed, the city had responded to their demands. Mayor Lindsay, with the state legislature's support, appointed a task force to create an education "decentralization" strategy for the city, starting with a pilot program in Brownsville, Harlem, and the Lower East Side. Each of these neighborhoods would elect a governing board of parents and community leaders and appoint a local superintendent to transform the neighborhood's schools.

And of course, Brownsville being Brownsville, her people were going to take this opportunity by the reins. Brownsville wasn't asking for no decentralization, they were asking for the power to overhaul their broken schools. *Stop saying Decentralization, start saying Community Control!* That had become Brownsville's mantra of the summer, and Lina made sure to teach it to Annetta.

"Community control. All right now. But I really got to be going." Annetta forced a smile and headed for the staircase.

"Right, sorry about—"

"Have a good evening."

"All right now."

Lina returned to her apartment. She washed and chopped the cabbage and tried to light the stove, but none of the burners would ignite. She searched the cabinets until she found a match, but even then, she only got one of the burners to spark. She had to cook the cabbage first, the beans second, and the rice third, and she had devoured the whole Hershey bar before the rice finished.

When she called Mr. Wong, he didn't pick up. "Mr. Wong, I have a question about the stove. Call me back when you can."

It was nighttime and the windows curtainless and screenless, moths circling the overhead light and mosquitoes eyeing her from the walls. She might as well have been camping. And until Danny got his ass together and brought her mattress over, she would have to make do with piling blankets on the floor.

She hit the light, crawled on top of the blankets, and tried to imagine it. Imagine *her*—a *she* who knew when to be safe and when to take a risk. So far, Lina had only known Callie. She rolled over on the hard floor, restless, wondering if Callie ever thought of her.

They'd been classmates in the art department at City College. Lina had always thought artists were daydreamers, but these ones spent more time striving for inclusion in Manhattan's sophisticated circles. Lina took a more whimsical approach to her work and seesawed between a desire to laugh at their seriousness and the worry that maybe she didn't deserve to be there.

But Callie Franklin had been different.

They first spoke in sculpture class. Callie, on her way back from the women's room, leaned one elbow on the back of Lina's chair and asked, with glee, if the tubular shape in Lina's hands was "supposed to be phallic?"

"It's coquí!" Lina protested, her hands caked with clay. "A frog from Taíno culture!"

Lina was offended, but then she began to notice the way Callie eyed her from across the classroom, hand on chin, as if studying her features for a portrait. Though all her life Lina had stared at other girls, the reality of Callie with her short blond hair, jean jacket, and flared jeans was enough to make Lina want to switch majors. But when Callie invited her to climb trees, she didn't say no.

Central Park had many trees worth climbing, Callie insisted. Lina had never climbed a tree before, but Callie coaxed her into it, and once they arrived, they pressed their bodies against the rugged trunks, flopped over branches and pulled each other up, found perching positions on various tumors and completed their sketchbook homework ten feet off the ground.

"No longer a virgin," Callie said. "In tree climbing, at least."

It was Callie who showed her the Village, who introduced her to Dalí, to red wine and Brie cheese. Who taught her how to touch a woman, then how to touch herself. And who, once they graduated, found Lina the job with the SoHo beef steak artist.

In their three years together, Lina never took Callie to Brownsville, but there was one time, toward the end, that they ended up in Bed-Stuy. Callie and her friends wanted reefers from Nostrand Avenue. When the car reached the block and a Black man approached the vehicle, Lina wished she had a blanket to throw over her face. Instead, the man spotted her in the back seat, and his mouth twisted with amusement.

What you doing with these white chicks? said his expression. *You back there like they abducted you.*

As the girls paid him, Lina nailed her eyes to the back of the seat in front of her.

"Bed-Stuy is a lot more than this. We have the Club Baby Grand,"

Lina mumbled as they drove away, though she hated herself for trying. "And there's Doctors' Row, Preachers' Row . . ."

"Oh, I love Brooklyn," the friend in the passenger seat said. "My ex took me to the Club Coronet"—and she twisted her head over her shoulder to meet Lina's eyes, as if she deserved praise.

In the days that followed, Lina was sullen. Callie bit Lina's neck and stuck a hand under her bra, but Lina pushed her away: she didn't want sex. And yet she couldn't figure out how to explain herself or pinpoint exactly where Callie had been at fault. Callie, oblivious, offered Lina the chance to live for six months in the Village; a family friend was going to London and needed someone to watch the cat. "You feed the cat, we fuck," Callie said. "No more subway rides at two in the morning."

An apartment all to herself in the Village, just blocks from Kooky's Cocktail Lounge—it held an allure. But then came the day that changed everything, the day the army chaplain knocked on their apartment door at Van Dyke.

Like the foliage of Brownsville's ash trees, which crumbled all at once in the first autumnal storm, the family, so optimistic, so admired in the community for their resilience, blew apart at the news of Lou's death. Their mother stumbled at the Rockaway Avenue station, tripped down a flight of stairs, and broke both her ankles.

Lina took care of her mother during the four-month recovery period. She cooked asopao for her sisters. She went out each night and hunted for Danny. Never tiring, never showing a hint of her own grief—only late at night, sneaking candy button after candy button, cleaning the white strips of paper of their color drops.

After the news about Lou, she saw Callie much less. The time she did attend one of Callie's artist salons, she drank the red wine, ate the Brie, and watched Callie laugh with a friend about a professor's ugly affair. If Callie noticed how quiet Lina was, how distant she'd become, Callie played it cool. Lina was not usually conflict-averse, and preferred to handle any tension face-to-face, but she had discovered that, bold as Callie might have been with a paintbrush, Callie was a white girl. Lina could not love a person like Callie, and so she decided she would simply disappear.

Yet lying on her back with her hands behind her head on the floor of what had once been Canton Kitchen, Lina feared that she would never find her. Not Callie: the *she* who would feel at home in her messy bedsheets on Livonia Avenue.

A few days later, Lina discovered a puddle of water by the radiator pole. The toilet kept clogging. Also, someone had run off with the downstairs doorknob.

She called Mr. Wong again. Then every day for the next three weeks.

He showed up on September 1, at seven thirty in the morning, with a bang on the door. After collecting the rent, he replaced the knob, accused her of flushing her sanitary pads down the toilet, and finally mumbled that he'd send a plumber.

On the first day of school, the United Federation of Teachers called a citywide strike. Brownsville's parents tied the shoes of hand-me-down loafers and tugged at the malfunctioning zippers of Salvation Army backpacks and wondered how their kids were going to learn anything worthwhile with the majority of the faculty absent.

Early that morning at Canton Kitchen, Lina listened to the radio and shook her head at the news.

"Oh, come on," she muttered. "On the first day of community control?"

She hadn't officially joined the UFT yet, and although she usually supported union activism, there was no way she was going out on strike that day. Instead, she pulled on her pantyhose, her best skirt, and a half-sleeve white blouse. Catching a glance of herself in the mirror made her nervous. She had such hairy forearms and ashy elbows that Danny called her Gorilla Girl.

Just a decade earlier, when she'd been a student at J.H.S. 271, there had been no teachers who reminded the Black students of themselves. She'd had Mrs. Solomon, Miss Neumann, and Mrs. Baron. They'd insisted all the *ain't*s be *isn't*s and assigned chapter books about children you were oh so close to becoming if only you were blond.

Now there was not a single white kid left in the junior high, and it was about to change even further. Over the summer, Lina and others had hauled in crates of books and set up an Afro American and Puerto Rican library. A few of the other community activists had developed a plan to stand on street corners throughout the neighborhood each morning to ensure every child made it to school.

Lina arrived with a few other teachers—some new young hires like herself, some older ones who didn't care to strike, and a bevy of new parent volunteers. Her schedule would be busy that week. Mr. Devin, the other art teacher, was out on strike, and she would be covering his classes too.

She recognized many of her teachers' faces in the pictures on the bulletin and wondered what they'd say to her. She knew she had been considered "smart for a Negro," if "troublesome" like the rest. Once, Mrs. Romano had sent her to detention for saying Christopher Columbus was a murderer. She was now one of the assistant principals.

Lina led her first class upstairs from the auditorium. The ones who recognized her from the Brownsville Recreation Center went berserk.

"Lina!" Walter yelled, trying to squeeze past the others to the front of the line. "Why you in the school?"

"It's Miss Rodriguez Armstrong to you, Mr. Rodgers."

"You a teacher?" he exclaimed. "I thought you just a camp counselor."

Walter had been one of the more rambunctious kids at the BRC; at the age of eight, he'd gotten down on one knee and proposed to Lina. She'd told him she would accept his hand in marriage if he gave her a billion dollars.

She brought the students inside the classroom, where instead of taking their seats, they sprang in all directions like cats chasing balls of yarn, shrieking and knocking over chairs. As Mrs. Jacovitch, Lina's eighth-grade math teacher, passed down the hall, she stuck her head in the room and shot Lina a look of reproach.

"I'm the new art teacher," Lina said, assuming a professional tone. She moved toward Mrs. Jacovitch and reached out her hand.

"Whatever you do with them, please be sure to keep these kids quiet. I'm one class down and I'm very sensitive to noise."

Lina waved goodbye, closed the door on Mrs. Jacovitch's concerned face, and turned around. She took in the scene before her: so much unused energy, the students buzzing around like atoms above a Bunsen burner. This was not good.

She knew how Mr. Devin began the year: handing out textbooks and asking the students to paint a replica of the Monet on page 16 or the Monroe on page 19. Instead, Lina picked up a chunk of chalk in her shaking fingers and drew a figure on the blackboard.

"What you drawing?"

"It's a ladder," one boy surmised.

"Skeleton," said someone else.

"It ain't all that," said a girl. "It's a building. It's a map of the school."

"Shut up, Holes."

Lina looked at the girl, whose name tag read *June*. Her beady eyes were not afraid to meet Lina's. Her hair was coiled tightly on top of her head, her tights scarred with stitches. Just as Lina herself had been, June was poor and bold. She gave the girl a high five, confirming her hypothesis.

"It *is* a map," June repeated, excited.

"Why you drawing a map, Lina?" asked Walter.

"*Miss Rodriguez Armstrong.* And I'm only going to explain it once," Lina said.

She waited while the students corralled one another into silence.

"A lot of you know me from around the neighborhood, but now summer's over and we're here in school. How many of you like school?"

One or two began to raise their hands—June included—then quickly shoved them down.

"How many of you hate it?"

Hands shot up across the room.

"And how many months each year do you spend in school?"

She saw minds working.

"Nine," a student said, and then corrected herself. "Ten. Or, like, almost ten?"

"There are almost ten months of the year in school and only two months of summer. So why do you spend ten months of the year at someplace you hate?" she said. "What's the sense of that?"

"We can go?" asked Walter, pointing to the door. The others laughed and watched Lina. They'd never heard a teacher sanction their hatred of school.

"If you're going to spend ten months of the year in this building, it has to be meaningful, right? You have to feel like you're doing something important and interesting. Maybe it's not fun all the time, but you have to feel like it's worth your attention, right?"

They eyed her, unsure. She pointed to the blackboard. "This here is the shape of your school. The floor plan. Now take a piece of paper, some markers or pencils, copy this structure on your paper, and fill it out for yourself. Show me what a good school would look like."

It became clear to them they had been lured into an assignment, but some appeared willing to give it a try, and the rest followed suit. They each took a sheet of easel paper and began copying her model from the board.

"You can't hate school without telling me what a good school looks like. What do *you* want? Walter, I know you like the pool. So what you gonna do about it? Turn our stairwells and hallways into a water ride? Row to English on a canoe?"

The kids laughed. One student drew spaceships launching from the roof; another, a class where students learned to construct toys; and Walter, a reward station where they could win prizes like at an arcade. June drew teachers with faces as black as her own, and Veronica, a garden where her grandmother could train students to tend flowers and plants. A quiet boy named Hank wanted a row of dormitories in the school building.

By the end of the period, Lina had collected dozens of drawings and was elated at her success. Then Assistant Principal Mrs. Romano called her into a second-floor office.

"Miss Lina, we are happy you are here. But I must ask you to keep your class quieter. Mrs. Jacovitch is very sensitive to noise and already has a migraine."

"I..." Lina squashed her emotions and again affected a deep concern. "I am so sorry to hear Mrs. Jacovitch isn't feeling well."

"You've been hired to teach art, Miss Lina. And if I remember correctly, one can usually make art in silence."

Mrs. Romano turned away toward the papers on her desk, and though Lina would have liked to run a red marker over the education certificates on the wall, she instead lifted her cheeks into a smile nearly as cloying as Mrs. Romano's.

When she got back to her classroom, Lina bit her lip and watched her next class tumble in. She wondered if the kids would accept the idea of a talking stick: only if you're holding the silver marker can you speak.

She skipped lunch to clean the classroom. Seventh period, she descended to the auditorium for the First-Year Faculty Orientation.

"Don't worry too much about your training. You will certainly know more than the kids," said Dean Bianchi. "Most of them are illiterate, and most will be incapable of earning more than Cs."

Lina dug into her purse and popped a caramel in her mouth—to gum up her teeth, so she couldn't say anything. With these old teachers and supervisors still in the buildings, community control was off to a snailish start.

The striking teachers returned after two weeks, having gained salary and benefit increases. Yet for the rest of the year, on any given day, it appeared that half the faculty had the flu. Or teachers would arrive late, complaining they'd missed the bus from Canarsie, Midwood, or Nassau. Lina often heard them gossiping in the lounge about the decentralization experiment: they didn't like seeing so many parents in the school building; they thought Rhody McCoy, the local superintendent appointed by community leaders that summer, was unqualified for the job.

After Christmas break, almost a fourth of the faculty and administration disappeared from J.H.S. 271; they'd requested transfers out of Brownsville. And good riddance to them, Lina thought. If they didn't want to teach Brownsville's kids under the direction of Brownsville's community leaders and first Black superintendent, Brownsville didn't want them either. Superintendent McCoy hired a new principal for J.H.S. 271 and a number of replacement teachers.

One was Mr. Parson. A Black man from Chicago, he had taught history in Harlem before arranging his own transfer to Brownsville, and he and his wife had bought a house on the Ocean Hill side of the neighborhood and were quickly making themselves part of the community.

When she had a free period, Lina attended Mr. Parson's history class. He was teaching the eighth graders about the kingdoms of ancient Africa, the Harlem Renaissance, the sit-ins down South, and the Black Panthers in Oakland. Mr. Parson did not tell his students which way was right, only that there were many possible paths to liberation, each of which must be properly understood and assessed.

It was her first time considering the idea of a separate Black Nation within the United States of America. On some level she liked the idea, but if African Americans had their own nation, on which side of the border would the Puerto Ricans live?

Later, Mr. Parson dedicated a whole two weeks to Puerto Rican history, and it was during that unit that Lina realized not only her father, but her mother, too, descended from Africans, at least partially. She also learned about the maroons, the movement for Puerto Rican independence, and Arturo Alfonso Schomburg. The day Mr. Parson described the genocide of Native peoples, she got up to close the classroom door, afraid that Mrs. Romano would fire Mr. Parson on the spot.

"Sir, I'm just looking out for you," she explained after class. "We have some supervisors here that I know would take issue with the stuff you're teaching."

"You don't need to worry like that." He leaned back in his seat. "Principal Harris knows who I am and how I teach. This is an unprecedented moment. No use wasting it."

She went back home and thought about Mr. Parson's words all evening, inspired by him, and frightened. Her pride in her people, Black and Puerto Rican, was like her love for women: kept in the closet.

On parent-teacher conference night, one of the neighborhood activists ran down the third-floor hall. From her classroom, Lina saw him whip past and mistook him for a student. She poked her head into the hall to scold him and then realized it was George Furman from the Brownsville Community Council, and that he was dashing into Nick Parson's classroom.

"The King."

It took a moment for everyone to understand. Then he told them where and how, and the significance of each fact reached them, and everyone began to break down.

Lina didn't need to hear the radio. She believed it, was not surprised, and she was gripped with that all-too-familiar rage, the one that had sent her, at eleven years old, walking all the way to the docks to find answers on the night the cops had killed her father. She embraced every student within reach. Their bodies hung limp like wilted plants in her arms. Principal Harris came onto the loudspeaker and announced the rest of the night's conferences canceled.

Lina ran into Nick Parson on the stairs, and he gave her what she needed most: an invitation to the Parson home in Ocean Hill, and an umbrella to share on the walk there. She didn't want to be in her apartment that night, reminded of the hate of the world by the orange mold on the bathroom ceiling, the inconsistent hot water, and the boarded window, which, more than eight months since she'd moved in, Mr. Wong still hadn't repaired. She intended to move out as soon as the school year ended.

In Mr. and Mrs. Parson's house, they watched the *ABC News* report on the little TV.

"Here in Memphis, of course, a great deal of shock, a great deal of confusion and some violence, I can't say a great deal because I don't really know . . ." one newscaster said. "There is some rock throwing and some fires recorded and some shooting . . . The full curfew has been imposed . . ."

"Turn it off, Nick," said Mrs. Parson. "The white man won't tell us anything new." She was a buxom, deeply black woman, and the oldest woman Lina had ever met who wore her hair natural.

"Tell us what you are feeling, Miss Lina," said Mrs. Parson.

Lina closed her eyes. "Like I always knew it would happen."

"This is what I've been trying to say," said Mr. Parson, his eyes on his wife. "It's not about asking to be loved."

It was around then that the sounds began in the street. Above the gush of rain, they heard wailing and cursing, then the shattering of glass, the drowned-out protests of someone's mother.

Lina put her forehead against the window glass and saw young brothers hurtling toward the avenue. She recognized one of her students, Derek, an older boy who'd been left back; he was charging down the block, a rag-stuffed bottle in his hand. Without an umbrella or her coat, Lina pushed the front door open and dashed down the street.

"Derek!" she shouted, running toward him, catching him, grabbing his arm. "Where you going, Derek?"

"If they asking for war, I'll give them war!"

He was strong but she held him. Urged him to return to his apartment and take care of his mother and sisters, told him setting fires in his own neighborhood wasn't going to bring their people healing or justice. Rain pummeled their hair, and their feet skidded over the slippery asphalt, the tar moist and shining like cake. The blockade of his body served dually as a restraint to stop herself from tearing shit down.

The next morning, the city churned on like nothing had happened. The residents of Brownsville read about the arrests in Harlem and on Fulton Street, but their eyes were too tired to make tears. When Brownsville returned to school, an uncanny stillness pervaded the classrooms of J.H.S. 271. Students sat with their elbows on their desks and their cheeks in their palms, unable to summon the energy for the usual, feisty rebellions. Principal Harris held gatherings in the main office for distressed parents, and even the white teachers grieved: Mrs. Rebecca Salzman, red-eyed, dabbed her nose with a handkerchief.

Lina had her students paint posters in honor of MLK, and in her every spare moment, she sat in on Mr. Parson's classes. She wasn't alone: ninth graders skipped their lunches to attend his eighth-grade seminars. During any given class period, there would be a dozen students, teachers, and parents crowding on top of the bookshelves at the back. They all needed him more than ever.

Mr. Parson offered no easy answers. Mostly, he sat on his desk at the front of the classroom with his hands folded on his knee, and he asked questions.

"What do you think about the looting on Fulton Street? The fires on Sutter Avenue? Were they justified?"

Some guilty eyes shifted to the floor.

"We angry." Walter shrugged.

"My mama said it ain't right," said Veronica, turning sharply in her chair. "You think King wanted us to go out and burn down our neighborhood?"

Hank, who never said anything in class, leaned forward on his desk.

"You fixing to say something?" asked Mr. Parson.

"I don't know what kind of stores got looted," Hank said. "If it was white people's stores, then I get where folks was coming from."

"It don't matter whose stores," retorted Veronica. "You robbing people, that ain't right. And it looks bad for the race. You get a new pair of shoes, and they treat you like a wild animal for the rest of your life, is that what you want?"

"Those people was taking advantage of the situation."

"Those people are po'," said June. Her voice was firm enough to scatter a flock of pigeons. She never evinced any shame, and over time, the other kids had come to respect her.

"Rich people," June continued, "wouldn't need to take advantage of the situation because they already got all the food and clothes they need."

The arguing continued for a while, and then Mr. Parson stood up and moved to the chalkboard.

"Tell me three actions President Johnson should take right now, in response to the King's assassination."

"Civil rights," someone suggested.

"They already passed the Civil Rights Act," said another. "He gotta jail all the people that be killing us. Jail the KKK."

"It's not just the KKK. The police be killing us."

"Poverty. Poverty be killing folks."

"I don't need nothing from President Johnson," Hank said. "If we can take over the schools, we can do anything."

"What else shall we take over?" asked Mr. Parson.

The young people went quiet. They'd been stunned by the question and by its myriad possibilities.

The bell rang.

Mr. Parson nodded quickly.

His students, overwhelmed, did not move from their seats. Mr. Parson had brought them to the edge of something beautiful and terrifying. To return to normal routines seemed senseless.

"Black Power!" one of the students yelped, jumping up from her seat. It was June again, hurling this phrase toward Mr. Parson like a command.

One of the boys took it up, and then others, and then almost the whole room. As they gathered their books and sweaters and headed toward the door, it became a unified chant. Tepid at first, the handful of Puerto Rican kids joined in.

Lina and Mr. Parson watched from the door as the students paraded into the hallway. Other students, emerging from classrooms, stared at the parade in bewilderment, then gradually adopted the chant themselves. Dean Bianchi appeared, wobbling in the sea of students. Shouting into a cone, she demanded silence, but no one paid her mind. The young people stormed forward as one, lurched down the hall, heads held high and fists in the air, until every teacher had hurried to their classroom door to witness the spectacle.

"Mr. Parson," Lina whispered. "They gonna arrest you for inciting a riot."

"This came from them," he said calmly. "Their idea. Come watch."

She joined him by the windows, from which they could see the students marching in pairs down the street like the Freedom Fighters of Selma, wrapping around the school building in the direction of Betsy Head Park, not an adult in sight: a bunch of twelve-, thirteen-, and fourteen-year-olds deciding they'd had enough. It was the most amazing thing she'd ever seen. This was the generation that was going to change the world.

But the sound of an argument outside the classroom pulled Lina's attention away from the window. In the hallway, she found Mrs. Rebecca Salzman facing an irate Janet Thomas.

"It ain't fair! They all left the building!" the ninth grader cried. "I'll do detention tomorrow."

"This was a hard day for every one of us," said Mrs. Salzman, employing her most soothing voice. "But that doesn't mean all the rules have changed."

"Fuck you, white lady!"

"Janet, your language."

"You're just scared!" Janet seethed. "You're scared of Black Power!"

Janet raised her arm and slapped Mrs. Salzman's cheek.

Lina couldn't believe it.

By the time she and Mrs. Salzman had overcome their shock, Janet was already plunging down the stairs. Lina leapt after her, but the girl ran faster.

"Janet—stop!"

But Janet cut past the security guard and darted out the main doors.

Lina returned to the classroom to find Mrs. Salzman sitting in her desk chair with her face turned toward the window, one hand still on the injured cheek.

"Mrs. Salzman!" Lina reached for her shoulder. "Are you all right? You should tell Principal Harris!"

Mrs. Salzman slipped away from Lina's touch. Without a glance at Lina, she stood and began packing her briefcase.

"He wouldn't believe me," she said. "Or care."

"What?"

"I'm on the side of the enemy."

"Why would you say that?" Lina was flabbergasted.

"It's not just Janet. It's all of you," Mrs. Salzman said, waving her hands with exasperation. "You set these children on us, and then you stand and watch."

"No one ever said . . ."

"Teaching them to hate what you call 'white people.'" Mrs. Salzman tucked her long braid into a hat and glared at Lina, a tight fury in her wet eyes. "That's what you all are doing. The opposite of what the Reverend King believed. You and your new colleagues—you're teaching these children to hate. And you think you are the only people ever to be mistreated on this earth, but I'm a Brownsville girl. I grew up right here, and my brother started the Brownsville Boys Club. And things weren't easy. You're too young to remember, but six million of my people were murdered in Nazi concentration camps by hateful people who raised their fists in the air and declared themselves the fittest race on earth. And now my colleagues promote the same kind of behavior."

"We don't promote violence against other people."

"Why does Nick Parson have Malcolm X posters all over the hall-way? Why are there drawings of pale faces in cages?"

"That was Veronica, she was drawing her vision of justice for—"

"I have never seen color. I don't understand why you'd want the children seeing it."

Mrs. Salzman seized her briefcase and marched out of the room.

Lina stood stock-still in the empty classroom, thinking she would explode from all that she still wanted to say. She wanted to correct Mrs. Salzman—she wanted to assure her, but also to enlighten her. Or maybe she was sick of assuring and enlightening white women. Maybe she just wanted to scream.

She never had to make the choice: that was the last day Mrs. Salzman came to Brownsville.

The war began in May. The Battle of Brownsville, Lina called it. That was when Superintendent McCoy and the Brownsville Governing Board voted to transfer six administrators and thirteen teachers out of the district for their efforts to sabotage community control.

Albert Shankar, president of the UFT, slammed McCoy and the Governing Board, declaring they lacked the authority to make such transfers and that the faculty should report to work as usual. Browns-ville's parents and community leaders poured out to the streets to block the dismissed teachers from returning. It was like 271 was a citadel and they its soldiers—and besieging them, the dismissed teachers, and enclosing them all, a moat of two hundred police offi-cers. Mayor Lindsay, afraid to act on either side's behalf, declared 271 closed for the day.

Shankar called another citywide strike. Picket lines crisscrossed the five boroughs, inescapable as white picket fences in Levittown. The strikers were gone for the remainder of the school year, and the loyal teachers, with parent volunteers, kept Brownsville's schools open but barely functioning. One morning, Lina found herself su-pervising an art class of one hundred students. They had to move

to the auditorium, with groups of six kids sharing one palette of wa-
tercolors. Almost a dozen students asked her permission to use the
bathroom, none of them returning. For all of that month, she went
home to her apartment after nine p.m. each night, collapsing on her
mattress as soon as she walked in the door, waking only when her
alarm rang at five the next morning.

Superintendent McCoy wouldn't take back any teacher who had
abandoned Brownsville, and over the summer, he hired three hundred and fifty new teachers of his own, people willing to cross the
picket line and defend community control—hippies and draft evad-
ers, Black and white and Jewish, some of whom had never taught a
day in their life but were down to try. *The Brownsville X-Men*, Walter
called them.

Lina had intended to move that summer, but then 78 Livonia became a ground base for the movement. Mr. Parson held
consciousness-raising meetings for the new teachers there, and Lina
cooked giant community meals on the stove that had once churned
out egg rolls—if you hit the left side of the appliance with a snow
shovel, all the burners came on.

On the first day of the new school year, Lina wore jeans and a
black leather jacket, a Puerto Rican flag over her curls. She devoted
her first lesson to the arts and culture of Puerto Rico, and down the
hall, an English teacher assigned Baldwin's *Go Tell It on the Mountain*.
A math teacher wrote "Black-Owned Business" on the board. Instead
of reciting the Pledge of Allegiance, the students chorused "Lift Every
Voice and Sing."

Over the following weeks, as the entire nation caught wind of
Brownsville's experiment, all the most distinguished Afro Americans in the nation—a linguist of African dialects, an Afro Dominican
NASA mathematician—dialed McCoy and asked how they could assist. McCoy invited them to visit and speak to the students. He welcomed Ghanian drum troupes, Kenyan dancers, and Jamaican poets
so the young could witness the creativity of their people. The students devoured it all.

But they remained under siege. The board of education sent the dismissed teachers back to Brownsville, escorted by a team of police who swung their clubs at any parent who stood in the way. A half dozen Brownsville parents were hospitalized for concussions and bruising. Mr. Devin strode into eighth-grade art and took a seat at Lina's desk as if he didn't see her roaming the classroom, assisting students with papier-mâché masks.

"Class," he said, "clean up this mess, and each of you get a fresh sheet of paper."

Her students looked up, at first confused, and then, with their hands still dripping with batter, they pushed back their seats and leapt to their feet in protest.

"You ain't our teacher anymore!"

"Go find a different job!"

Later that day, Mr. Devin would lodge a complaint that the students had "assaulted" him.

Growing up, she'd always thought wars happened in jungles and mangrove swamps. But maybe when people talked about revolution, *this* counted just as much. Coke bottles and rotten groceries hurled over the cracked sidewalks of Brooklyn. Defending the streets with your hands still stained with acrylics. This was war for people who were penniless, weaponless, and wanted nothing except a fair chance for their children.

A war they would lose. It was around then that the teachers union began circulating an anonymous leaflet, supposedly written by someone in Brownsville. It called the UFT teachers the "Middle East Murderers of Colored People," "the Money Changers," and the "So-Called Liberal Jewish Friend." The teachers union had it copied and printed by the thousands, and they passed it out on street corners, in subway stations, and at their massive city hall rallies, so that the people of New York could see it for themselves:

This was not a labor dispute. Not a matter of Black sovereignty, of community control. This was an attack against Jews.

A potent rallying cry. In November, the state education department announced it was taking over the Ocean Hill–Brownsville school district. The state suspended McCoy and the new principals, then offered class assignments to any UFT teacher who asked to return to Brownsville. Some did, and immediately, the students fell back on their old rituals of protest—drifting into class late, refusing to follow instructions, fighting in the hallway, throwing chairs out the window.

This was why, years later, it would irk her when the media made it sound like the 'Ville hadn't done anything. Like they'd all been lazing around, waiting for the white people to come home to Brownsville.

No. It wasn't that they hadn't tried.

It was that they'd been crushed.

THE CHINS

In the beginning, in a land of vast sidewalks and flying trains, there was a little boy named Jason. Jason had a friend named Pete. The two shared a love for butterflies, pizza, and jetting through outer space, and together, they spent many hours watching the ants migrate through sidewalk cracks. They put their ears to the manhole cover on Blake Avenue and listened to the whining of the sewage alligators. Paid acorns to the fire hydrant that dispensed magic blueberries.

Brownsville smelled like the lilies his mother planted in the front yard. Like the chlorine coating his sisters' skin when they returned from the Betsy Head Park pool. Like clouds of soy sauce-ginger-sesame oil, and the wet wood of the pushcarts on Belmont, and the pies in the windows of Sweet Carolina's, where a woman in an apron offered him free bites of peach crumble.

Next came everything he would wish he didn't have to remember, everything that—fifty years later—a parent to a twenty-three-year-old daughter, Jason would not be inclined to share.

Four years old. Folded in his mother's lap. Eating pistachios on a beach blanket. Then Baba yanked him by the arm, dragged his bare feet through the scalding sand, hauled him over a brawny, red shoulder, and pitched him like a football into the surf.

Swallowed in ice water. Screaming, flapping for help. Water seared up his nostrils, salt burned his throat. With his eyes clamped shut, he imagined fanged sharks and ghoulish jellyfish. Then he sank, lungs burning, eyes open to the acidic, green, cloudy water, and through the gloom, saw . . . not a shark, but his father's calves, shining like dead fish.

Of course Baba rescued him. His sisters called it silly that he cried for hours after. But he was like their mother—afraid of water. The way it separated them from the place she called home. To strive to conquer water was the worst sort of hubris. Perhaps this was why, in his adolescence, he frequently biked alone to Jamaica Bay. Robert Moses had intended to remake Jamaica Bay into a waterfront that rivaled Battery Park, but he hadn't gotten to it, and the shores remained knotted with old fishing boats and tar pits.

To Jason, Jamaica Bay was perfect in its oily, untamed wildness.

One morning when he was six, his mother woke him with welcome news: they would skip school that day and take a trip to Manhattan. America was so impressed by the obedience of its Chinese residents that it had decided to adopt them.

"Before we hide, use fake name," his mother explained to him on the 4 train. "But president see Chinese good. We don't have to hide. We use real name. No more Jason Wong. Now, Jason Chin."

They hopped off at Brooklyn Bridge–City Hall and entered one of the limestone towers. In a thirteenth-floor office, each of them signed their new names in a government book with a government pen.

Then they went to Chinatown for a feast, and Jason knew he was supposed to feel happy, but mostly he felt confused.

On Christmas, his grandfather fell and broke his leg. Jason watched over Yia Yia as he slept like a baby beneath the blankets on the couch. Yia Yia didn't like lying down, he told Jason. Yia Yia liked working at the restaurant. Yia Yia said what was the point of life if he couldn't even move? Sometimes, his grandfather would declare himself healed and try to stand.

"Mommy!" Jason would call into the kitchen, and his mother would rush over.

"Ni het," she'd insist to Yia Yia. Or, she warned, he might never walk again.

In the many weeks that followed, Yia Yia turned away from food, and in his chest, a shuttering, like maybe he'd accidentally eaten the butterflies Pete had been chasing at Betsy Head Park, and then, Yia Yia's face against the pillow like he didn't want anyone to see. But one day, when Baba came into the room, Yia Yia sat up and Jason saw everything: the red eyes, the scrunched cheeks, the runny-nosed knot of hurt.

He realized then that even old men can cry.

Against his grandfather's wishes, Baba decided to close the restaurant for good. One day, their mother took Jason and his sisters to Canton Kitchen to say goodbye. With all the tables and chairs gone, the dining room looked gigantic. Someone had installed wood planks over the shattered window—the growl of the elevated rail was especially loud on that side. And someone had confiscated the cat food bowl he and Jackie had left on the fire escape, and the gna toi peas they'd been growing in a glass jar on the kitchen windowsill, and the pigeon cage on the roof.

Mourning, Jason sat on the wooden floor, handing his mother and sisters pieces of Scotch tape, which they used to bind the china in Bubble Wrap. He mourned for his grandfather, for the gna toi, the cats, the pigeons. There was nothing he could do to save them all.

"What will you and Baba do for work?" Jennifer asked their mother.

Remembering now that the restaurant had not only fed the neighborhood, but them, too, the rest of the children looked up.

"Fun sin geng dok a," their mother said, her eyes on the teapot in her hands.

Two days later, Baba pulled up in front of the house in a used truck. He insisted they take a ride, he in the driver's seat with Julie on his knee, and Jennifer in the passenger seat with Jackie and Jason on hers.

"Son, when you make an investment, you got to think about the market," he said as they jerked around the block. "Where's the demand, who's looking for a bargain. I said to myself: all those Jews, Italians, they're moving out. People need a moving company." He took one hand off the wheel to tap his head. "That's called thinking like a businessman."

But Jason's sadness had evolved into nausea, and before they could make it home, he barfed on the dashboard.

"Aiya," his father groaned. He parked the truck and hurried over to the passenger side to carry Jason to the sidewalk. Baba ordered the sisters to clean up the mess, and gently, he leaned Jason over the street gutter and rubbed his back until the vomiting stopped. Yet if there was any tenderness in the hands that held him, it was drowned in the meanness of the rebuke.

"How come you always get sick in the car? Your sisters don't get sick!"

Years later, Jason would not remember what had happened to his father's moving business—he'd think of it as the first of Baba's many failed ventures.

There was a door-to-door knife sales company. Then a life insurance business. At some point, his father bought the restaurant building and the one next door from their longtime landlord, Mr. Cohen. He got a good deal because no bak gui wanted to buy property in Brownsville anymore.

Baba's favorite job would be the one waiting tables at the lounge on Wall Street. Big shots dined there, he would tell the kids a thousand times: millionaire stockbrokers, movie stars, politicians. Baba had to dress in a suit and tie, and sometimes, instead of cash tips, the patrons would give his father tickets to a Mets game, or to Loew's Kings Theatre, or to Jason's favorite, the Brooklyn Zoo.

But even during the best of times, Jason and his sisters could not risk annoying Baba, for their fates were subject to his moods. If provoked, he could flush those tickets right down the toilet or leave for a Mets game without them. Their mother, especially, would suffer.

After the restaurant closed, she took one of those factory jobs in Chinatown, the kind Baba refused to consider. One school holiday, the sisters decided they would make a surprise visit. Jennifer had already memorized the subway station names and had earned enough pocket money from babysitting the Lebovitz kids to afford the cost of two tokens for Julie and herself. Jackie and Jason remained small enough to duck under the turnstile.

He wanted to see his mother but didn't like going to Chinatown. This was one thing he shared in common with his father. For Jason, it was a cruel place—all the haggling and shoving and the crabs scraping their pincers against the bins. It upset him when cooks grabbed the fish right from their tanks, the salmon flopping screamlessly all the way back to the kitchen. He too felt like a fish swimming in an overcrowded fish tank as they hopped over gutters clogged with sewage thick as eels and passed bakeries where the locals battled like guppies for flakes.

At last, they arrived at their mother's sock factory. Trying to spot their mother among the others, Jason and his sisters peered through the narrow window into the basement. It was hard because the window was small and, sitting in rows at their sewing machines in the cramped room, all the women looked the same: shoulders hunched, heads bent, bodies curled inward.

"In the back!" Jennifer exclaimed, and Jason tussled with his sisters for the view. Yet when he picked out his mother, she did not look right. Her mouth was lopsided, like someone had drawn a frown on her face with a crayon.

"Why does Mommy look like that?" Jason whimpered.

"She misses us," assured Jackie, and the four children hurried inside. As they approached, their mother's eyes widened. Jason threw his arms around her waist, and Julie presented her with a bag of dragon eyes from the vendors on Canal Street. But not a moment had passed before their mother urged them all to leave. Her Toisanese spilled out in a panic.

"Aiya! Ho ngai ham a!"

After that day, he noticed that, with increasing frequency, it was the factory version of his mother who came home from work. In the lines of Factory Mommy's forehead was an unending script of worry. Jason loved helping her in the kitchen, peeling shrimp scales and removing the strings of pea pods. Yet Factory Mommy's hands were shaky, and she often burned herself on the pot.

Factory Mommy reminded them not to talk to strangers, to spurn offers of candy. If there was a stranger coming down the block, she would yank Jason to the opposite side of the street. Fear was like chicken pox, and soon Jennifer, Julie, and Jackie caught it too. Passing a haunted house, Jennifer made them hold their breaths until it was far behind. In Julie's make-believe games, there was always a girl murdered by a bad man. And at night, after their mother had put the four to bed, Jackie would creep downstairs to check the locks on the doors. Sometimes, she'd go down there three, even four times.

Jason didn't like Jack Schmidt, the man with the Cheshire cat grin and the honky voice who came to slap backs with his father and always called his mother "Foo Foo." At dinner, Mr. Schmidt spoke of lawns and big bedrooms like an ad man on the television. Baba loved this kind of talk. He grinned and served Jack leg after leg of soy sauce chicken until there was none left for their lunch boxes.

It wasn't until seven-year-old Jason found his toys sealed with duct tape in a cardboard box that he realized Schmidt had sold his father a new house. The women nestled into the back of the truck with the boxes, and Jason sat in front with Yia Yia and Baba. Their father drove by the pool and the playground. Out the window, Pete rolled by on a wooden scooter, maybe coming to look for him. He would never see Pete again.

They drove past the haunted houses, which seemed less scary, more sad in the morning light. Then they were in unfamiliar territory, merging into the flat expanse know as Kings Highway, above them a wide, cowboy-prairie sky. Though in truth it was only about a mile to East Flatbush, it felt to Jason like they had traveled an eternity when they arrived at the new house.

As Jason would realize later, Richard was chasing the receding edge of bak gui Brooklyn.

Richard was in one of his best moods that day. The new neighborhood, he said, was "just like Brownsville used to be." In their new house, there was a washing machine and a walk-in closet. The sidewalks were clean, and there were no haunted houses on the block. In the weeks that followed, their mother fixed the garden, and their father ingratiated himself with the neighbors, each week barbecuing hot dogs and hamburgers on the grill until all the bak gui followed the scent into their backyard. The Chin sisters befriended the Hoffman girls and introduced Jason to the Hoffman boy. Yet as soon as the girls disappeared into the house, the Hoffman boy took two fingers and pulled up the corners of his eyes.

"Guess what I am!" the boy, Lucas, shouted. "A Chineeeee!"

Jason stood still, suspended in time. Then understanding cleaved him clean and wet like chives on a cutting board, and his eyes grew spicy. "I'm not Chinese!" Jason cried, but that wasn't what he meant, and not knowing what to say next, he bolted into the house, into a dark corner where he could be alone with Layla the Stuffed Bunny and his daydreams.

At the end of the summer, he enrolled at a new, prettier school, with freshly painted walls and working bathrooms on each floor, and a woodwind instrument gifted to each second grader. Even so, he missed his old school in Brownsville.

"I want to go home," he whined to his mother.

"Don't you remember what I said?" Foon Wah replied in the language he could somewhat understand but barely speak. "When I was a girl, we had to leave our home with nothing. When the Japanese threw the bombs, we had to hide in the caves. That was where my mother died, and I had to raise my brothers and sister on my own."

Jason began to keep his feelings to himself.

It took about a year to accept his new home. Maybe this was just a gradual surrender, a coming to terms with loss. Or maybe it had to do with the new family moving into the house next door, an event that prompted his father to grumble, "Here we go again."

One morning, Jason was playing with Layla in the grass of the backyard when suddenly he felt, in the crook of his neck, a cold and tickling buzz. He yelped in shock, touched a hand to his neck, and heard a giggling from beyond the bushes. He approached gingerly, until a stream of water sprinkled his shirt, and then he saw the tip of a plastic water gun poking through the wire.

There, he discovered his assailant's face nestled within leaves: another little boy, no bigger than him, maybe even smaller, and smiling.

He said his name was Macon George, but Jason grinned because he looked like Pete.

Jason's imagination had always been his house of refuge, but after meeting Macon, all the windows and doors of his house swung open. Extracting the jokes from *Alice in Wonderland*, the moodiness from *Peanuts*, the magic from *Snow White* and *Cinderella*—all the books and movies Jason had consumed during his friendless year, sitting in front of the black-and-white Philco—he produced story plots unceasingly, and found he had the power to enchant Macon, to wrap him up in the fabric of his fantasies.

Foon Wah noticed with what care the hak gui boy double-bowed his shoelaces, how perfectly his mother pressed his clothes, and how patiently he awaited Jason on the stoop, and so eventually, she welcomed Macon to the kitchen table and subjected him to squares of sesame jelly, which he politely consumed with quivering lips. Jason visited the Georges and gladly gobbled up the sweet potato pie, baked fish, and collards.

— — —

For as long as he could remember, he had watched the news each Saturday night with his family. He'd seen the young men sitting quietly at the lunch counters while others broke plates on their heads.

His family gawked at these news clips, but never discussed them, as if all that bak gui and hak gui craziness was no realer than the spaghetti Westerns on channel four. When his parents talked about America, it was the America that they'd been sold: paper turkeys on the windows, handshakes and saying, "Break a leg." Yet all that time, there was still the America of bak gui–hak gui craziness, and it was coming closer and closer, rattling the walls of their America.

One day in bak gui–hak gui America, the teachers decided to stop teaching. Instead, they marched outside the school buildings with signs that said, END MOB RULE! Jason didn't know what this sign meant, only that as a result, he and all the children of East Flatbush were herded into a church to watch a film about Eleanor Roosevelt projected dimly on a white sheet. It was drafty in the church and impossible to hear the documentary above the screaming children.

He searched for Stella, a girl in his class with strawberry blond Rapunzel hair, but when he found her, he lacked the courage to speak. Instead, he grabbed Macon, and they squeezed beneath a pew in the back and, lying on their stomachs, filled a notebook with stories about the blue, green, and pink fairies.

"You're not blue, Jason. You're yellow."

"I'm blue!"

"You're yellow. You're Chinese."

"I'm not yellow! How is this yellow?" Jason shouted, shoving his arm in front of Macon's face. "What color is this?"

"Oh yeah! You're not yellow." Macon grabbed hold of Jason's arm and began examining it. "You look like sand! No—like this wood. Wait—you're an apricot!"

"I'm an apricot," Jason agreed. "And what are you? You're not black."

"Yeah, how about me?"

"You're hoisin sauce. You're a chestnut shell."

"Hi, I'm Macon and I'm a chestnut."

"Hi, I'm Jason and I'm an apricot."

Three months later, when the strike concluded, Jason didn't want to learn about long division or the science of magnets. His sisters already knew these things and had received straight As on their report cards. Class bored him, and he didn't see why he should have to go to school when adults could leave their jobs whenever they wished. Instead, he once again took refuge in his imagination.

In his fantasy worlds, he was not Chinese. He was not a bak gui or a hak gui either—he was nothing. He understood how Tarzan felt when, looking into a reflecting pool for the first time, the Jungle man encountered not a soft and fuzzy ape, but an elongated face in a stringy mop of hair. Jason, too, was always surprised to catch a glimpse of himself in a mirror and discover his strawberry nose, full lips, wide cheeks, and ink-black hair. He had his father's massive calves, "the genetics of rice pickers," the gym teacher had said, and his mother's petite frame. These were the things others saw. This was why the Hoffman boy pulled up the corners of his eyes.

He reached his breaking point at the age of twelve, the year he started junior high. Like usual, he was the only Chinese fish in a Black and Jewish ocean, and he had no friends—Macon was in the grade below, still at the elementary school. At the end of his first week, Jason received a form asking him to choose between two electives: Visual Arts or Drama.

"Choose Visual Arts," Jennifer instructed. "We all took it. Mrs. Sanders will know who you are."

"She's very nice," Jackie added. "She'll make you feel comfortable."

"And you're too shy to act onstage," laughed Julie.

He marked Drama, despite their protests. He and Macon had outgrown their make-believe games, but he often missed the wonder of those earlier years.

"You go acting class, then go cry cry after?" his mother asked, shaking her head, and with reluctance, she signed her name on the form. When no one was looking, he crossed out her Chinese characters and wrote "Mrs. Chin."

On the following Monday, he discovered that despite his selection on the form, he had been placed in Visual Arts anyway. Though he hated speaking to adults, he went right up to Mrs. Sanders and pointed out the mistake.

"The Wongs have always been my best students," she said, but he shook his head and refused to return to his seat.

She sent him to the dean, who asked him to speak to the guidance counselor, who referred him to the assistant principal.

"I'll tell you a secret, Mr. Wong," Mr. Gruber said, leaning forward in a confidential manner. "As you know, you're in our Gifted program. This year, it's mostly the other kids taking Drama." He winked. "Our gifted students usually take Visual Arts, as your sisters did. I know you Wongs are smart, quiet kids, not like some of the others."

"It's Chin," Jason replied, not daring to look up at the assistant principal's face.

"Chin! My apologies, Mr. Chin. It's not every day that a family changes its surname." Mr. Gruber laughed.

But Jason did not belong in Visual Arts and wouldn't go unless they dragged him there on a leash, and so the assistant principal, relenting, signed the form to correct Jason's schedule.

On his way to Drama, Jason felt a desire to sing loudly in the hallway, or to slide down the stair banisters hollering like Tarzan. He thought about using the girls' bathroom or opening the windows in the gymnasium and letting the squirrels inside.

He wanted to be bad because nobody thought he was capable.

And yet he stayed good, out of pity for his mother.

It was true that Jason was shy. He avoided auditioning for the big roles and was given the part of Second Watchman; he only needed to announce having captured Balthasar. He and the other side characters spent most of class behind the curtains, where it was dark and smelled like preteen sweat.

Jason liked watching Elaine McIntosh through a slit in the stage curtain. He adored the way she burst onstage and, hands under her chin, whispered, "Oh Romeo, Romeo, wherefore art thou Romeo?" He was riveted when she drugged herself with imaginary poison and lay shaking into death.

A boy named Caleb Levine played Romeo—he and Elaine were among the handful of bak gui in Drama. During each rehearsal, Caleb and Elaine would hold hands tenderly, and even real-kiss, because Mr. Youdelman insisted that real actors should not be afraid to real-kiss. Jason knew through the grapevine that Elaine had ambitions to be a real actress one day.

One afternoon, Mr. Youdelman asked the class to sit in a circle for a lesson on the Shakespearean sonnets. When Elaine settled beside Jason, he forgot how to breathe. She had candy lips of such a bright red that it looked like she'd eaten a cherry ice for breakfast.

He struggled to pick out a few words worthy of her attention.

"You want to be an actress, right?"

"Yeah," she said, barely looking at him.

"If you were going to act on Broadway, which play would you pick?"

Elaine put her hand on her chin and pondered the question, her eyes twinkling. "*West Side Story.*"

Jason had seen the movie multiple times.

"Well, you're already Juliet. You could play Maria."

She nodded, glancing at him now. He felt called on to amuse her, to perform. Before he could overthink it, he launched into song, in what he hoped sounded like a Puerto Rican accent.

"I like to be in America! Okay by me in America!"

"Everything free in America!" she sang back. "For a small fee in America!"

They laughed, and might have continued, but Mr. Youdelman clapped for the class's attention. Jason felt his chest turn into a cage of pigeons, and he knew that if someone broke the lock, they would flap out and cover the entire auditorium.

After that day, he could no longer stand to watch Elaine and

Caleb onstage, for he feared they would forget the boundary between character and self. He asked First Watchman to come get him whenever his one line was coming up and spent almost entire rehearsals buried in the prop closet, refining his iambic pentameter.

He was reading *The Scarlet Letter* when his bedroom window was attacked by a barrage of stuffed animals.

"Chinny Chin Chin!" He heard Macon calling from outside. "Chinny Chinny Choo Choo . . ."

Jason opened the window and looked down.

"You want to play?" Macon called. He dribbled a handball.

"Nah, I suck." Jason smiled and put his elbows on the windowsill. It was nice to be wanted, but he had reached the part where Dimmesdale and Hester reunite in the woods. Here was a book about made-up people from the 1600s, but they understood his suffocation better than anyone.

"Come on. I never see you anymore."

Jason sighed, grabbed a jacket, and headed down to the porch to meet his friend.

"How come you're always so busy now?" Macon complained, rolling the Spalding between his palms. Jason sat down on the stoop, wondering whether Macon was old enough to understand what he was feeling.

"Hey, you ever liked a girl before?" Jason mumbled.

Macon froze. Something like fear flickered in his eyes.

"You got a girlfriend?" he accused.

"What? No!" Jason laughed. "My sisters aren't even allowed to have boyfriends."

"You're always staring at some girl. Who is it now?"

"Elaine McIntosh."

"Never heard of her," Macon said, as if this decided the matter.

"She wants to be an actress."

"Little boy!" Macon put on a high voice in imitation of Jason's mother. "No time for girl! One day you grow up, find nice nice Chinese girl, okay?"

"Shut up, Whopper-head," Jason returned. "There's no Chinese girls in East Flatbush. And you didn't answer the question. Did you ever like a girl?"

"Yeah," Macon said, shrugging, like this was obvious. "Of course."

"Who?"

"Diana Ross. She's gorgeous. Especially when she's singing 'Baby Love.'"

"She's not a kid."

"I like myself some older women."

Jason laughed, but then he remembered that Macon's cousin had said the exact same thing about "Baby Love" on Thanksgiving the prior year. Macon had just gotten it from him.

Later that week in the library, Jason discovered *Leaves of Grass*. There were many sentences he didn't understand, and he looked up dozens of words in *Webster's Dictionary*.

> *You shall no longer take things at second or third hand, nor look through the eyes of the dead, nor feed on the spectres in books,*
>   *You shall not look through my eyes either, nor take things from me,*
>   *You shall listen to all sides and filter them from your self.*

He said: experience the world, don't take my word for it. And he wasn't confined by the body he was given: he didn't want to be just a man. Whitman sometimes called himself a man-child, sometimes a mother. Whitman wanted to be everything, and he didn't care about money.

Jason yearned to share in this openness, this expansiveness. He didn't want to be a boy; he wanted to be a fairy godmother, a woman condemned to wear a big red *A*, a hairy man raised by apes. Even without understanding all the poems, Jason knew he had met a kindred spirit.

I celebrate myself and sing myself, Jason thought each day of that summer as he biked around East Flatbush, passing Jewish girls rotating their waists to keep Hula-Hoops in orbit and Black girls selling bracelets and lemonade.

What did that mean, celebrate himself? This was beyond cake and cone hats. His mother had told him that in China, people didn't celebrate all their birthdays, that only American kids were showered in presents every year. "American kid like to party party!" she often said, and then she'd glance at her American-born children, her *jook seing.* "Now the jook seing too! Spoiled!" And even though she bought him sheet cake from Lords Bakery every year, she was never joking when she said this. Yet how could he help it if he liked birthdays? How could he help his desire to sing?

Jason read books on the way to and from school. He read while his sisters studied for exams and his father watched *Bonanza.* He wrote more poems, relishing how words gave him a place to talk about the secret, the better-left-unsaid, the laundry list of things his mother would deem unrespectable. How much rice noodle rolls resembled condoms, for instance. He wrote in the margins of his school notebooks in class and on the backs of heng bou envelopes during Chinese banquets.

On Jason's thirteenth birthday, Koon Lai announced he had a surprise for his grandson, and that they would have to take the bus to Bedford Avenue. Just the two of them set out, holding hands at the crosswalks, saying little. There was something about Koon Lai's silence, his blueness, that Jason understood without words. Koon Lai had never gone back to work, and he spent most of his time alone in his room, preparing visa applications and refugee appeals for whoever needed.

When they reached Sears, Koon Lai took Jason to the typewriter aisle.

"Pick."

Jason chose a teal Olivetti, and it was the best gift anyone had ever bought him. The only problem was that he could not keep the pages hidden, and one day, when he was writing in the living room, his father grabbed a half-finished sheet right out of the top.

"Put it back," Jason growled. Baba crumpled the paper and passed it back and forth like a ball between his hands.

"Go outside. Go to the handball court," he said, gesturing to the window, and, stretching his elbow back, he simulated a serve, nearly lobbing the paper at the glass. "Stop fooling around all day with that typewriter."

"I'm not finished."

Baba shook his head and sat down on the lounge chair.

"Kids at school know about this? All the kids at school know you sit around all day, you don't have friends—"

"Macon."

"You don't have friends, they gonna say you're a queer." His father twisted in his chair and looked pointedly at Jason. "You know what that means?"

Someone had once called Macon a queer. Any soft, kind boy, they'd call a queer.

"A faggot," his father said, almost relishing the opportunity to say the word, it seemed to Jason.

Jason waited for his father to leave him alone. Then Jennifer, Julie, and his mother appeared in the kitchen, and his father brought his complaints to them.

"Ni ga doi hou lazy," he said to their mother. "Kui just sit around all day playing with the typewriter. Kui no social skills."

"Ni bong ni baba," his mother called tiredly into the living room.

"He didn't ask me for help!" Jason cried. "He doesn't need me to *do* anything."

"Well, come wash dishes, then," Julie yelled back.

Jason debated whether he ought to assist in the kitchen or run upstairs to escape. His mother appeared in the doorway of the living room and, saying nothing, sat down beside him with a bowl of snow peas in her lap. Pod by pod, she peeled the strings. Swallowing, he set aside the typewriter and gathered a handful from the bowl. Together, they cracked the pod tips, tugging the threads across the pods like jacket zippers, piling the strings on the coffee table.

"What you do today?" she finally asked in English.

"Write."

"Why you write?"

"I'm a writer," he said.

The answer came unexpectedly. Never before had he claimed the title. He wondered if he was allowed to say this. If he was good enough.

But he had loved saying the word, and he would not take it back.

He looked up at her. His mother remained quiet, which made his heart thump. She gave him another handful of snow peas, and when they'd finished, she put the bowl on the table and took Jason's hands in her own.

"You're going to be a man soon," she said softly in Toisanese. "And then you are not a child anymore. It is okay to play when you are a child, but when you are grown up, you must think about your future. Think about a job. You are good with English, so you can use your writing to get a good job. You can be a lawyer. You can't make money writing silly things. Can you feed children on poems?" She laughed, pinching his cheek. "One day Baba and Mama will be old! Can you take care of your parents writing poems?"

Jason held her cold, damp hands. He gestured with his chin toward his sisters in the kitchen.

"They'll make money. Can't they take care of you?"

He was being serious, but she laughed. "Aiya," she cried, tousling his hair.

He winced, felt a blueness seep across his chest. Either they would smother him, or he would betray her. It was only a matter of time.

— — —

His English teacher made him Elaine's desk partner, and when Valentine's Day approached, he panicked. It was his chance to make his feelings known, but he didn't know how. He'd never seen his father buy his mother a bouquet of flowers, had never heard them say "I love you."

He decided he would give Elaine a collection of poems. He was in the midst of composing them when another blitz of stuffed animals battered his bedroom window.

Jason wished Macon would call ahead on the phone; it was frustrating to interrupt his process mid-thought.

"You don't remember?" Macon eyed him when he reached the porch.

Then it hit him. He and Macon had made plans to see *The Street Fighter* at the Kings.

"You were supposed to meet me at the B8 an hour ago!"

"Sorry." Jason crossed his arms, shivering. He'd left his jacket upstairs. "I was working on something."

"On what?" Macon leaned his back on the porch rail.

"A present for someone."

"Oh, come on. You're still crushing on that Elaine Mcwhatever? You're stupid as hell. She doesn't *like* you. Everybody knows she's crushing on Ronny Stein."

Ice water seeped across Jason's chest.

"Forget about her, man. She's the same as the others. She doesn't see you. Your problem is, you have a white-girl fetish."

"What?" Jason scowled. He hadn't expected so many assaults. "No I don't!"

"Stella, Hannah. You're so obvious. You liked white girls before you could add fractions. Maybe you watch a little too much Hollywood and it's gone to your brain. Soon as a white girl passes you by, your eyes pop out of your head."

The accusation angered him. He liked who he liked.

"Well, what about you?" Jason shot back. "Remember how you ignored Donna Harris? Who's the self-hater now, huh?"

This time it was Macon who clammed up. Yet when he met Jason's eyes, it was an expression Jason had never seen before, tight with repressed emotion.

"Jason, do you even know who I am?" His voice was different now, serious and low. "You think I'm your sidekick who shows up to give you relationship advice."

He brushed past Jason and stepped down the stoop. "I'm going home."

"Let's see the film tomorrow."

"Nah, you'll be busy. I'll see it by myself."

They avoided each other in the hallways at school. When he awoke on Valentine's Day, something was not right.

It was one of those brutal days in Brooklyn, the wind so cold it burned, the curbs slicked with black ice. The poetry collection was in his backpack. In the school lobby, the Cooking Club sold roses and cupcakes. He glanced at them in fright and continued walking.

In English, Elaine bit the tip of her pencil, her eyes on the door. He could hear her breathing. He felt every blink of her eyelashes. He had memorized each of the charms on her bracelet, could spend an hour just going around and around her wrist: *trumpet, ballet shoes, tragedy mask, teapot, kitten . . .*

He thought about what Macon had said.

To give her the poems, or not give her the poems. That was the question.

Halfway through the period, someone knocked on the classroom door and turned the handle, disrupting the lecture.

"Mrs. Palmer, may we interrupt for just a minute?" begged a Cooking Club member. "We're making a delivery."

When Mrs. Palmer relented, the two girls entered the classroom, their arms full of separately wrapped roses, and their elbows strung with shopping bags full of cupcakes.

"You got one for me?" someone shouted from the back of the classroom.

"Buy me a cupcake, Mrs. Palmer!" another student jested.

Jason held his breath. Birds pecked at the flesh of his rib cage. He had wrapped the poetry collection in red tissue paper and hid it in his desk cubby.

"One rose," said the Cooking Club member, and she read a tag attached to the flower. "For a . . . Elaine McIntosh?"

Everyone turned to look at her, and Elaine's cheeks flushed.

"Ooooooo," the room cooed as the flowers made their way to her desk.

"Who's it from?"

"Is it from Caleb?"

"Nah, it's Ronny Stein, right?"

"Are you and Ronny going out?"

Elaine took the plastic-wrapped rose and read the label on the stem. A tender smile crept across her lips. She cradled the rose against her breast, her care for it reminding Jason of the way she'd held the limp, fake-dead hand of Caleb-as-Romeo. He could not see the label, but he didn't need to.

Jason tucked the poetry collection back into his backpack. He would have liked to cry, but instead, he studied a dried splotch of gum in the cubby. It was a green brain, a tiny map of a fantasy island, a foreign planet.

Who cared if he was good or not. Turning inward, he was safe. He would retreat there—as he would for decades onward—to forget about what hurt him.

SADIE

When Sadie reached home, her parents were sitting in the living room, reading aloud articles from *The New Yorker*. She avoided their eyes. "I just need to change," she muttered. The wind at Grand Army Plaza had sucked the last life out of her umbrella, and in her room, she peeled off her sweater, jeans, shirt, and bra. It was like peeling off a layer of skin. Buried in her comforter, eyes closed, she saw the moment when Ms. Lina had told her to leave.

She'd messed up.

No, she would not tell her parents what happened, not yet. And she couldn't talk to her friends from *The New York Times* internship—didn't want to admit to them she'd gotten herself thrown out of an interview. Her transplant friends from Yale would be the most sympathetic, but she didn't want their kindness. They wouldn't really get it.

Of course, she couldn't speak to Wendy or another reporter at *New Gotham* because the truth was, she should never have been reporting on a story of personal significance in the first place.

Thinking about Wendy, Sadie realized she had an article due the following day, a piece about a healthy-eating initiative in Brownsville. She sat up immediately in bed and grabbed her laptop. No more dwelling on what had happened. There was no time.

She stayed up till one a.m. drafting an outline for the healthy food article, and the next morning, she tried to contact a few sources. It was more difficult than usual. Ms. Charlene, one of Brownsville's nutrition gurus, almost always picked up her phone, but that morning, she didn't answer. Sadie had arranged an interview with a local children's advocate for ten a.m., but that source emailed her at the last minute. *Sorry, something came up.* Sadie tried several other numbers, but people either failed to pick up or dismissed her curtly. She wrote to Wendy for a twenty-four-hour extension.

At two p.m., Carl Baker, a parent on the PTA at P.S. 401, sent an email that confirmed her worst fears.

> *Please stop emails to me and any others in Brownsville who you may be in contact with. Peace be with you.*

Once again awash in the anxiety that had choked her the prior night, Sadie stared at the email, now completely at a loss. She was almost afraid to bike to Brownsville and see what people on the streets would say to her.

The following day, she biked there anyway, and when she arrived, there were no activists waiting to throw her across Utica Avenue. A Dominican man, smiling warmly, sold her a beef patty. Like always, the children gaped at her press pass. It was not until she found Ms. Davis, the director of a NYCHA senior center, that she was able to speak to someone in earnest.

"Miss Sadie, I'm going to be honest with you, I liked the article you wrote about the senior center last month," Ms. Davis said as she opened boxes of applesauce in the center's kitchen. "I don't know what you did to make other people mad, but you sure did make them mad. A lot of people here don't trust you anymore. How come you're reporting in Brownsville, anyway? You report in other neighborhoods? Maybe you should try reporting in a different neighborhood."

Sadie blew her breath out and leaned her hands on the metal countertop. As she'd always been a good student, this would be the first missed deadline of her life.

When Sadie left the senior center, it was snowing, the first flurry
of the year, the flakes light and wispy like puffs of laundry lint. Ms.
Lina and Tyrell's building was a few blocks away. Out of desperation,
she reached for her phone, wiping it with her reddening hands each
time a flake curtsied on the screen.

> Hey Tyrell, I'm in the area.
> Can we talk?

Waiting for a reply, she walked up and down Rockaway Avenue,
watched the snow kiss the car hoods. A NYCHA janitor spread salt
on the sidewalk, the chunks as big as fish tank pebbles.

No response.

Sadie snuck into their building quietly. On the sixth floor, she hesitated, unsure which door was his and afraid Ms. Lina would discover
her standing there. Sadie picked the door with a bumper sticker
shaped like a skull and bones. CRACK IS WACK, it read.

She knocked.

Footsteps. An eye in the peephole, widening. An awkward pause.

"Tyrell, is that you?" she whispered. "Can I please talk to you?"

She heard him cursing beneath his breath.

The scraping of the chain lock. He opened the door just a few
inches and glanced beyond into the hallway, looking for Ms. Lina.

"What the hell are you doing here?" he whispered.

"Can I come in?"

"No," he snapped, and then he swallowed, his forehead creased.

"Please, I really need to talk to you. Just for a second."

Warily, he unchained the door, let her through the entry, and
closed it behind her.

"What did you want to say?"

"Could we . . . sit down for a second?"

He bit his lip, and without speaking, led them to two separate
chairs by the TV. In one corner sat a white machine that looked like

something you might find in a doctor's office, and near it, a table stacked with Clorox wipes and blue pads.

All of the warmth of their earlier interactions was gone, and more than ever, she felt like an outsider.

"Look, I didn't mean to hide something—I didn't expect any of this would happen."

She waited for a sign of understanding, but she could not read his expression.

"I didn't know anything about the fire when I started this job. I knew my grandfather ran a restaurant. And I was shocked when I learned the connection."

"How can we trust anything you say?"

He pinched his temples as if he had a headache.

"Tyrell, can you please convey my apology to her?"

He leaned forward, his elbows on his knees, and cracked his knuckles. "I know you didn't mean to hurt her, but tell you the truth, I haven't seen her like this before."

"What do you mean?"

"I know she's been through a lot, like stuff she hasn't even told me about. And you know, she's a strong lady. Always keeps looking forward. But I feel like, talking about the fire, that landlord, your grandpa, it got to her. She usually knocks on my door every day, and she hasn't left her apartment since that night."

Sadie put her hands over her face.

"She'll be all right. But I can't help you."

"I feel so guilty," she exhaled.

"We don't need your guilt, Sadie."

She felt a lump in her throat, like she'd gulped a salt pebble.

"Go home," Tyrell said calmly. "Ask yourself if you're here for the right reasons."

She looked at her lap. Put on her hat and walked to the door.

"I fucked up," Sadie whispered. "I'm sorry."

When she reached the stairs, Ms. Lina was still locked away in her apartment.

— — —

The following week, Sadie met with Wendy and Simon in *New Gotham*'s conference room and told them the full story. Beyond its glass walls, a half dozen reporters worked cheerily away at their assignments— reporters, she imagined, who would never have made a mistake as grave as hers.

"We've talked about it," said Wendy, "and we think it's a good idea to transfer you to Sunset Park."

Sadie nodded. A part of her had hoped her bosses would assure her it was no big deal, but they hadn't done so. At least they hadn't fired her.

"We need a reporter on Sunset Park," Wendy continued. "And we recently met an *amNewYork* reporter—Brian Parker. We'd like to offer him the position in Brownsville."

"What about the story of the fire?"

Sadie didn't mean to be so forward. She only wanted to know whether they were giving that to Brian too.

"There might be a story there," Simon said, "and we can have Brian take a look at it, but you understand it really shouldn't have been you pursuing this story by yourself, given the conflict of interest, and definitely not without informing us."

For the rest of the day at the office, Sadie tried to keep it together. Stuffing her face with the coworking kitchen's free almond croissants, she googled Brian at *amNY* and found that, as she had guessed, he was a Black man, and he had ten years working in the field.

Waiting at Broadway-Lafayette for the Brooklyn-bound F train, she thought to herself how much she'd wanted Brownsville to claim her as its own. But Brownsville had never needed her help. Maybe that had been some white savior shit. *And yes, you are also white, in case you forgot,* she told herself. *And you're not the first white person to try to fool themselves into a state of innocence.*

The F train blew into the station. She grabbed a window seat and watched the tunnel lights loom and loom, disappearing right as they blinded her. For a moment, a train sped parallel to hers, and she could see herself in the reflection of its windows. It was a train kaleidoscope, blurry versions of herself rippling out like ghosts, and she wondered if you could talk to the dead this way, trapped in a transit layer cake.

At dinner, she told her parents everything: about the argument at Ms. Lina's house, her struggles reaching her contacts, and that she'd been transferred to Sunset Park. She tried to eat enough of her dad's chicken to make it look like she was okay.

"Honestly, they shouldn't have hired me to begin with," Sadie declared when she'd finished explaining.

"I don't think that choice was yours to make, honey," her mother said. "Your responsibility was to do the best job you could."

"My best job wasn't good enough."

Sadie pronged the bok choy.

"Well, Sunset Park. That's a lot closer," her father said.

Of course, he would be happy that she was in Sunset Park: no more panicked calls from Ngen Ngen each time *NY1* covered a shooting in East Brooklyn.

"Do you believe it now?" Sadie asked, looking quickly at her father and then back down at her plate.

"Believe . . . ?"

"Believe Grandpa burned down those buildings."

They ate, no one speaking. When she looked up again, she saw he wasn't chewing but had his elbows on the table and his chin on his hands.

"You think he did?" he finally asked.

"Probably. I don't know. The buildings burned down two weeks after he sold them. At least according to the deed. I don't know what that means."

She waited for him to say something, but he did not; he resumed eating. Before, she would have been angry with him, but humbled by her own bout of dishonesty, she felt she had no right.

Sunset Park was easier for her. Within the first week, she wrote three pieces—one about Eighth Avenue's Lunar New Year festivities, another about the city's first commercial-scale wind turbine, and the third on a developer's proposal for Industry City.

She wondered whether anyone of her background could be a good reporter in a neighborhood like Brownsville. It wasn't like the African American Studies classes she'd taken at Yale were enough to give her the perspective of a Black person. What was the morality of writing "objective news" about people of color when you're not, really, a person of color, at least not by everyone's definition?

Or maybe, she didn't need to get so theoretical. Maybe she'd just done a terrible job.

In Sunset Park, Chinese people didn't always recognize her as Chinese, but when she explained that she was half Chinese, they grew intrigued: *Your mother or your father is Chinese? What about your mother? You don't speak Chinese? You visit China before?* The more she talked about herself, the more they'd talk about their own lives, and so it was easier, at the end of the day, to establish some level of connection.

She went to a Department of Education town hall at M.S. 136 where several Chinese parents expressed unease about the mayor's intention to change the high school admissions process for the city's specialized high schools. The mayor had sided with the educational equity advocates, who believed the specialized high schools' reliance on a single test—known as the SHSAT—was unfair and placed Black and Latinx students at a disadvantage.

After the town hall, Sadie approached one of the more passionate young Chinese mothers in the hallway.

"What would you say to the concerns of Black parents that the test is biased?"

"I heard the concern, but I think this is the mistake. The test is not biased. A test cannot be biased. You have to learn how to take it." The lady wore her bangs cut straight across and an apron with the logo for Angel Nails Salon. "The problem is the Black and Spanish students don't know how to test. Maybe they don't have good middle school, their parent don't look for the after-school class."

"But what do you think of the argument that we need more diversity in each of our schools?"

"Where you go to high school?"

"Stuyvesant," Sadie readily admitted. "And it was like seventy percent Asian students when I was there."

"Because Chinese student work hard. This is all Chinese parents want. Ask your parents. They want you to succeed in the world. Where did you go to college?"

"Yale."

"Yale! You see. You go to a good college because you go to Stuyvesant."

She saw the mother only wanted the best for her son, but such simple arguments erased centuries of history. Black Americans had been denied access to education for hundreds of years, until one day it was assumed to be "the way things were"—or worse, the fault of Black parents. That she couldn't convey all this in a five-hundred-word article for *New Gotham* frustrated her.

Sadie covered a protest held by Chinese groups in Cadman Plaza to denounce the indictment of a Chinese rookie cop who'd killed a young Black man in East New York. The Chinese protestors told Sadie that they had common cause with the Black community; the NYPD was scapegoating the Chinese rookie for all the vicious, unpunished crimes of white police officers across the nation. The Chinese rookie wasn't racist—he'd only shot his gun by accident—and while the young man's death was a terrible tragedy, the rookie deserved forgiveness; it was only fair.

And yet, it was disingenuous to say they had common cause with the Black community, Sadie thought. Their goal was simple: that the Chinese rookie enjoy the same impunity as the white ones before him.

Not everyone in Sunset Park liked her article about the protest. Some readers called her "self-hating" in the comments. It had taken her a while, but now she understood: you don't become a journalist

because you want people to love you. You become a journalist despite your need for love.

Still, in the months that followed, she couldn't stop thinking
about Ms. Lina and Tyrell. Brian, the new Brownsville reporter, was
doing a great job covering the neighborhood, but he'd set aside the
story about the fire. Ms. Lina had refused to answer his calls, and
Brian said it was difficult to pursue a story with so little material.

Sadie understood, but she couldn't let it go.

LINA

Lina Rodriguez Armstrong had decided to turn Canton Kitchen into a Freedom School.

Every leader and lover of Brownsville who the newspapers had labeled a radical extremist or an anti-Semite, or who'd been fired or quit at the end of the Brownsville decentralization experiment, ended up teaching in the Freedom School. There was the Decolonize Your Mind evening history class and Music of the People on Saturdays, the arts enrichment after-school program and the Altogether Now Day Care. Her school gave out Little Red Books and copies of *The People's Voice*, along with hot meals, fresh lemonade, toilet paper, and sanitary supplies. Presidential candidate Shirley Chisholm dropped by one night to offer her blessings. And so, community control was back in the house—unfunded, unrestricted, off-the-grid: a sweat-equity project.

Mr. Eugene trudged upstairs for the hot meals, and Patricia Taylor's grandchildren raced downstairs for the music classes. The most persistent cat of the block, who the kids nicknamed Miss Freedom, received her daily tuna can courtesy of the Freedom School—in exchange, Lina hoped, for keeping rats away from the building. Lina told her old students about the school, and she paid visits to the families in 80 Livonia, the tenement next door. Mr. Wong owned that building, too, and had subdivided the existing apartments to pack in more tenants. She listened to the residents' stories and encouraged them to come speak about their experiences and share their insights with the community.

Her people had so much knowledge they didn't know they had. They had been told all their lives that their experiences represented nothing but deviations from the true story of American greatness, when in fact they *were* America, the very foundation of it.

The building still had problems, but her team took maintenance into its own hands: repairing leaky sinks and toilets, sweeping the sidewalk, clearing leaves out of the roof drain. Her former student June was especially devoted to the school's success. She designed a big orange banner that said, BROWNSVILLE FREEDOM SCHOOL, which they hung out the window, though Lina also kept the restaurant's CHOW MEIN HERE! sign. It was a good landmark, a way to help people remember her school's location. Some people even started calling it the Chow Mein School. And Lina insisted every visitor touch the red silk knot on the back of the front door—it was the Freedom School's official good luck charm.

Lina was the founder and organizer, but she was also one of the students. It was during Mr. Parson's Decolonize Your Mind seminars that Lina realized the struggle was no longer Black against white. Now in Brooklyn, you could find Black and Puerto Rican cops and Black and Puerto Rican politicians willing to terrorize their own people. Community control in Brownsville had devolved into one Black politician's fiefdom, a quid-pro-quo machine to sugar up a few and disenfranchise the rest, negating everything they'd been trying to do—and all this while the pangs of hunger sharpened, the young men roamed the streets, and the city offered nothing but broken promises. It had promised to fix the crumbling homes and abandoned buildings, to build new homes and recreation centers and schools, but instead it let the structures rot, bulldozing what remained. Brownsville residents were tired of the neglect, tired of the fly-swarmed, trash-bag mountains. A few residents had taken that garbage into their own hands, and how could anyone blame them? The papers had called it a riot, but it was only after Brownsvillians had made the news for setting fire to their trash that the city had ramped up the garbage collection schedule.

So, the solution wasn't Black faces in high places: it was time to knock down the whole system. They could look toward Cuba, toward China—proof that the oppressed people of the world could carve their own path.

One Saturday in autumn, after the babies went home from Altogether Now Day Care, a woman and her son hiked up the stairs. Lina was happy to hear shoes tapping on the fresh wood; she and Walter had recently replaced several steps that had sunk like hammocks from age.

"Good afternoon, someone said y'all giving away free meals for the kids?" the woman said with a Midwestern lilt.

Lina had not seen them before. The boy's crown was no higher than his mother's waist. When he saw Lina, his lower lip protruded, his eyes narrowed, and he tightened his grip on his mother's arm as if *she* was the child.

"I'm Nellie Price and this is Wesley," she said, her voice high and pineapple sweet. On her curvaceous body, she wore a pink jumpsuit, a cotton sweater, and wide hoop earrings. A crucifix hung from her neck, and her hair blossomed like a black hyacinth, rising nearly a foot into the air.

Here was probably the world's most beautiful woman, Lina thought to herself—and there, the little boy at her side, the bittersweet evidence that she was already claimed by a man.

"You've come to the right place!" Lina said, waving them in. When it turned out there was nothing but a pot of plain rice in the fridge, she returned to the main room and, crouching beside the boy, asked him what he'd like her to cook. Both mother and son seemed embarrassed.

"How about some egg fried rice?" Lina suggested.

"We good with anything—we don't mean to cause trouble," Nellie said, tickling the crook of Wesley's neck.

Lina returned to the kitchen. Inspired by the various pots and sauces that the Wongs had left behind, she'd taken out a book from the public library called *The Easy Way to Chinese Cooking.*

She was surprised when, a few minutes later, Nellie and Wesley appeared in the kitchen doorway.

"Where you buy them sauces? Those are Chinese ingredients?"

"In the city. Got a store on Canal with all this stuff."

"All right now," Nellie said. "And I saw the sign that says this is a school. You the principal?"

"This is an alternative school. But you're the first to call me a principal." Lina smiled, certain Nellie was not from New York.

"And the books and art supplies out there—it's nice."

"Your son can use them! This space belongs to everyone in the community."

"You hear that, Wesley?" Nellie nudged her son. "Go and look at the books."

He wouldn't leave her side, and so she held him and fiddled with his ears. "I'd sure love to put Wesley in your school. I don't know if you'd accept a new student? They got him at P.S. 183 right now."

"Our Freedom School's not a government-sanctioned school. I wish it was. But he can come here after school and on weekends."

Amused by Nellie's curiosity, Lina dished the fried rice into two bowls, took them back to the table in the main room, and explained the school's origin story. Wesley ate tentatively at first, then rapidly, and Nellie replenished his bowl with spoonfuls from her own. Instead of eating, she looked around, absorbing the artwork on the walls and the charts outlining the Freedom School's values and principles. Then she pushed her bowl toward her son—and, giving his mother a woeful glance, he took it and mowed down the remainder.

Nellie touched Lina's naked ring finger. "You ain't married?"

Before Lina had a chance to respond, she continued. "My son has trouble with men who remind him of his dad. That's why we drove all the way here from Detroit."

They had been in Brooklyn for nine days, staying with a cousin who lived in Tilden Houses. Nellie didn't have any skills, or so she claimed, and didn't have a clue what she'd do about a job. "Well, I can do hair, but that's about it."

They stayed for the Decolonize Your Mind seminar that evening. The multigenerational group of students sat on chairs rescued from dumpsters, discussing *The Black Woman*. To Lina's surprise, it was the boldest ideas that captivated Nellie the most, that prompted her to hum in agreement, as if beneath her pretty exterior, her girlish sweetness, there was already a militant guerrilla ready to deploy for battle.

"I get what this lady Miss Kay Lindsey is writing," Nellie said at one point. "I used to be like most girls, thinking I needed a man to come save me, you know, 'a woman ain't nothing without her man.' But I don't think I need men no more."

Nellie had barely finished speaking when they all heard a loud clatter from down the hall. Lina ran to the bathroom and found that half the ceiling had collapsed, raining chunks of plaster on the toilet and on the sink counter. "Shit shit shit." The others hurried over to survey the damage.

Mr. Eugene shook his head. "The hell with paying rent for these conditions."

After the seminar finished, Nellie and her son lingered, helping Lina sweep up the plaster and tape bags to the ceiling.

"I hope all this craziness tonight don't keep y'all from coming back."

"Oh Lord, we love craziness. We fit right in," Nellie replied.

Lina laughed. Watching that long-limbed woman crouch on the floor with the dustpan in one hand and the splintering floor brush in the other, Lina wanted nothing more than to pull Nellie's body against her own and kiss her with a passion that no man on earth had ever felt or offered.

Instead, she saw them off to the door, handing Nellie her only umbrella and a container with the remaining fried rice.

Lina came up with the idea of designating a corner of the Freedom School as Nellie's salon. The services would have to be free of charge, but it would be a way for Nellie to build her name in the neighborhood. Nellie called it Mother Natural Salon, and she did hair, but also skin and nails. As she was always discovering coats and skirts laid out on the fences in other Brooklyn neighborhoods, she also built up an attractive rack of clothes that she shared with any visitor in need of a new outfit. She groomed mailwomen, bus drivers, and men living on the streets, and soon she had a steady crop of visitors, all of them drawn as much by her sense of style as by the tenderness of her nimble fingers.

It took weeks of encouragement, but eventually Nellie convinced Lina to take a seat at Mother Natural Salon. Lina had been afraid of what Nellie's touch might awaken in her, but eventually she gave herself over to the pleasure of those fingers. Over the course of several hours, Nellie washed Lina's hair and braided it. Then she looked admiringly at Lina in the dumpster-salvaged mirror and gave Lina a peck on the cheek.

"You look beautiful," Nellie said. "Handsome."

"Hmm. I like handsome." Trying not to think about the softness of Nellie's lips, Lina stared at their reflections.

"Yeah. I know that about you," said Nellie, standing and removing the backward man's coat from Lina's shoulders.

"Oh yeah? What do you know about me?"

"I know you don't want no man."

"How you know that?"

"'Cause if you wanted a man, you'd take better care of your hair," Nellie chided, pinching Lina's shoulder, and yet there was something in the glimmer of Nellie's eyes that left Lina breathless.

— — —

The same week that the temperature dropped to the teens, the radiators at 78 and 80 Livonia both went cold. Shuffling around in multiple layers, Lina turned on the oven. Her fingers were so numb she was afraid that, chopping the vegetables, she'd hack off her thumb and add it to the soup. She canceled classes and spent all night monitoring the heat from the oven and checking in on the neighbors' children, and she left voice messages for Mr. Wong, demanding that he send someone to fix the boiler. At the end of the week, she decided, enough was enough.

She invited all the neighbors at 78 and 80 Livonia to a Freedom School town hall. About fifteen showed up, but many were nervous about withholding rent. Yes, they were sick of the conditions, but what if Mr. Wong threw them to the street?

Annetta Brown was one of these dissenters. "I have kids. You activists think this is fun and games, but I can't risk being put out."

"Sí, yo también tengo miedo," whispered someone else.

"He can't evict anyone," Lina countered. "We're protected by the law. He can't throw us out if we take him to court."

"I'm not taking chances," Annetta said. "We won't make it through the winter on the street."

It was Nellie, ultimately, who ended the standoff.

"You love your babies, Annetta," she said, stepping toward her. "I know what kind a mother you are—I see it in your eyes. You never put nothing before your babies." Nellie took Annetta's hands in her own and pressed them to her heart. "But you know as much as I do—this world don't love a Black woman's babies. It's not gonna give them what they deserve. That's why we got to fight for our babies, Annetta."

Annetta remained silent for a full minute. The room deliberated, neighbors whispering to neighbors.

"If I agree to this," Annetta said slowly, "and he kicks us out, you all just gonna let me fend for myself at that point?"

"It's not gonna happen," Lina said. "I promise we won't get kicked out."

They were unable to reach a consensus, but more than half the room was willing to strike, and by majority vote, it was decided: when Mr. Wong showed up on February 1, he wouldn't get no rent. He'd get a piece of their minds.

After everyone left, Wesley returned to Tilden Houses to eat supper with his cousins, and Lina and Nellie huddled in the kitchen, shivering as they drafted a list of demands: repairs to all cracked and caving ceilings, extermination of vermin, remediation of bathroom mold, and the replacement of malfunctioning boilers and radiators.

Nellie invited Lina to warm up in the car. Lina wasn't good in cars, but Nellie insisted. They crossed two avenues and located Nellie's Ford Galaxie, parallel-parked on Blake Avenue. It was the car in which she and her son had fled Detroit, leaving Wesley's father in the middle of the night and driving for ten hours. The trunk handle was broken, and someone had shattered the back left window a few months earlier, but the car still meant everything to Nellie.

After Lina settled into the passenger seat, Nellie flicked on the blinkers and put the car in gear. They drove, and Lina watched Nellie's fingers move with their usual ease, dexterity, and confidence. Desire knocked the wind out of her.

They drove and drove—Lina had no notion of which roads, which highways; she couldn't keep track; in the blow of the heater, she sweated copiously.

"Go slow for me," Lina whispered.

"You'll get sick if we go too slow."

They ended up on a beach somewhere, not Coney Island, but maybe the Rockaways or somewhere farther, on Long Island. They took a walk on the sand, and Lina had never been to a beach so clean. It was surrounded, it looked like, by rich white people's homes, and at first, she found it difficult to relax. But there was the moon, dangling like an egg yolk in the sky, and there was Nellie, who hooked her elbow through Lina's, and whose head bent so close, Lina could smell the coconut oil in her hair.

It was safely in the car with the heat turned up that she first dared to kiss Nellie. She leaned in slowly, tentatively, and Nellie waited for her. When her chapped lips at last met Nellie's soft ones, Nellie gently brushed back Lina's curls with her nails, took Lina's cheeks in her hands, and pulled her closer.

They drove home, shed their coats on the kitchen counter. "Let me warm you," Lina whispered, weaving her arms around Nellie's slim baby-blue jumpsuit, the fabric silky against her palm.

Under the thumping of the train, Lina's fingers grappled for the zipper, drew it down her back, Nellie's bare shoulders and breasts emerging like petals of a moonflower. Lina had wanted this so badly, she couldn't trust it was happening.

She kissed each soft curve of skin she had yet to meet. Removed her own three layers of turtlenecks in haste, pressed her chest to Nellie's breasts, held the small of Nellie's waist, her neck in Nellie's teeth.

And then, on the floor mattress, far as possible from Annetta's wall, Lina drank from the ocean of Nellie's wetness. She anchored Nellie's thighs as the tide rolled in.

Like usual, Mr. Wong showed up on the first of the month at the crack of dawn, announcing his arrival on Livonia Avenue by honking the horn of his Chevy until he'd woken every baby on the block.

This time, they were waiting. The tenants marched down to the sidewalk: Lina followed by Harry Eugene and Daddy J, the Jenkins siblings, Patricia Taylor and her eldest grandson, and another dozen renters from 80 Livonia. Young and old, Black and brown, coated, gloved, and scarved, they gathered around the car—motley figures and steady eyes, the teens channeling Panther stoicism, the elders just tired.

Mr. Wong's eyes flitted nervously from one face to the next, his butt still planted in the driver's seat. He rolled down his window, and Lina handed him the petition.

"What's all this?" he muttered.

"Mr. Wong, you don't get a cent until you fix these buildings up. We're on rent strike, and these are our demands."

He squinted, examining the list, his brow furrowed. In the nine years since they'd first met him, his stomach had thickened. His hair was graying in patches.

Eventually, he crumpled the paper and threw it over his shoulder into the back seat. "No, you people brought your problems with you." He nodded toward the second floor, where June and William watched intently from the window. He waved a hand at the orange banner. "Who are these people? They're not my tenants. What's the 'Freedom School'? It's a zoo. The buildings have problems 'cause you make trouble with these parties."

"The Freedom School ain't no zoo," said fifteen-year-old Jamie Taylor, angling his head toward the car window. "And it ain't no party. It's the Freedom School. The best school in Brownsville."

"I said no guests. This many people, something's gonna break."

"You're the one who packed us in here," said Mr. Eugene, stepping forward and rapping the car hood with his knuckles.

"That's right. And when you filled the restaurant with customers to eat Chinese food," added Evelyn Garcia, her arm around Lina, "did you complain then?"

"You ain't so different from the rest of them," said Patricia Taylor. "Leave Brownsville, then act like it still belongs to you."

Mr. Wong looked at all the faces now squeezing into the window to say their piece. "The building, the building is old now," he stuttered. "If you don't pay the rent, how am I supposed to make the repairs?"

"Man, you've been living off that rent for years," said Daddy J. "And you never gave a damn about these apartments!"

They spoke their minds, and Mr. Wong held up a palm as if it could stop the truth from reaching his ears. He turned on the engine.

"You people are crazy. I'm sending the marshal. If you don't have rent by tomorrow, you're evicted."

"Oh yeah?" Lina leaned her elbows on the lip of the window. He thought he could scare them, that they didn't understand the law. "You can't get a marshal without a court order. And you won't get that court order because we'll be in court. You're in violation of the housing code and the warranty of habitability statute. And we'll let the reporters know what kind of landlord you are. Either that, or you give us the building. We're already running it without you."

He shook his head and began rolling up the window before she had a chance to remove her elbows—and then he muttered something sharp and bitter, just loud enough that she heard.

"Fucking spic."

"Fucking bigot," she hurled back.

The glass shut, the motor growled, the tenants dodged out of the way, and Richard Wong careened down the street, turning south on East Ninety-Eighth with a screech.

THE CHINS

Richard hadn't seen the ancestors in thirty years, but then lightning struck the transmission lines, and the circuit breakers tripped, and Con Edison's backup plans failed, and New York City was plunged into darkness. July 13, 1977.

Next came those who knew the darkness best. He was in the living room when they arrived. They pooled over the furniture, folded themselves into the window curtains, and leered from the void of the dead TV. He sat in his lounge chair, smoothing out the Help Wanted section of the New York *Daily News*, struggling to make sense of it, a shivering candle on the table beside him. His children and his wife were asleep, but the rest of the city was awake and restless, taut with desperate desires, and he was part of that restlessness, that desperateness. He was in trouble.

The ancestors knew.

Why are you wasting time?

They took turns whispering.

That shark will take the roof over your family's head.

Don't you know in America there are rules? How come you thought you could be a landlord and you didn't know any of the rules?

You brought a wife from China and now you're going to put her on the street?

How come you still can't read English? Can't read English! Can't read Chinese!

How come you don't go to Chinatown to find a job?

He tried to ignore them, but the room filled up with a strange odor: the smell of wet soil and rotting apples. It made him dwell on his bad decisions.

Buying 78 and 80 Livonia Avenue from Arnold Cohen—that had been a stupid idea; he could see so now. Because the bank had refused to approve a mortgage for the tenements, he'd borrowed ten thousand from a scumbag who was charging him nearly 100 percent annual interest. He'd thought the rent from the building would allow him to pay the guy back, but then the tenants had gone on strike.

He'd been fired from the Wall Street lounge after nine years of loyalty. Mr. Connelly had called him to the office, he thought for a raise. Instead, he was sacked, and Mr. Connelly promoted the Jamaican man with the name Richard couldn't pronounce. Richard was beside himself. He felt he deserved the higher wage—needed it. He was behind on his payments to the lender, and the collateral on the loan was the East Flatbush house.

Forgetting that the fridge had been off for hours, the food rotten and the beer lukewarm, he grabbed a Budweiser from the door.

You drink while your baba suffers. What kind of son is that?

Ancestors drip-dropped from the kitchen sink faucet, oozed from the rice cooker, bubbled up from the bamboo vase.

Your baba needs a knee replacement. That's what the doctor says. But you never do anything for him.

You should wonder what happened to your mother.

You don't know what happened to your own mother?

When she stopped writing the letters, what did you do? You drank a beer.

Richard slumped into a chair at the kitchen table and held his head in his hands.

What kind of father are you? Your son doesn't respect you.

"I tried!" Richard cried into the dark. "I tried to teach him things. The kid's too sensitive."

The boy is smarter than you. He knows you're stupid.

"I know! I know! I know!" He had known this for a long time. "Don't tell me what I already know!"

Richard knew he was running out of time. He hadn't told Foon Wah about losing the Wall Street job. For two weeks he'd pretended to drive to work, when really he was bound for a pay phone booth on a deserted street in Red Hook. So far, he'd called forty-five realties. The phone always grew greasy with his sweat, and not a single agency took interest in buying the Livonia tenements.

A few days after the power returned, he found the humility to take the train to Chinatown. Telling himself it would only be a temporary arrangement, he folded back his sleeves and walked to Columbus Park, where his second cousins played handball. Delighted to see him, the cousins invited him into the game. He played, intending to ask them where he might find a job.

These cousins, who worked as cooks and lived their lives within the radius of Mott Street, treated him like the peasants in China had; they thought he was a big man because his father was a donor to the association and because he lived across the bridge. He found it difficult to disillusion them. Before he knew what he was doing, he proposed a feast. They walked to Wo Hop, ordered enough dishes for a banquet, and got drunk. When he slapped their shoulders and assured them he could take the subway home in his sleep, they probably thought he was a happy and wealthy man. Instead, he walked to the Brooklyn Bridge.

He glanced up at Manhattan's skyscrapers, but their flashy jewelry no longer interested him. Instead, he peered at the darker Brooklyn side: the abandoned factories, the Brooklyn Navy Yard devoid of workers, the swellings of trees below a starless sky. Back in the day, Richard remembered, a man with a willingness to sweat could find work along those piers, or in any number of factories.

But he'd been too late for all that.

Richard climbed up onto the parapet. With a grunt, he pulled himself up so that he stood on the edge of a beam, the traffic roaring below.

He dared himself to jump.

A braver man might have done it. Wasn't that what bridges were for?

Sightseeing, and jumping. In the '30s, one of the Brownsville boys' fathers had thrown himself off the Brooklyn Bridge so his wife could collect aid from the state.

But he was too much of a coward.

Richard walked all the way to Flatbush Avenue with his soles aching, his graying hair in disarray. He continued past the flashing neon lights of Junior's and the Williamsburgh Savings Bank Tower, all the way to Grand Army Plaza with its mold-green Civil War heroes splattered with pigeon shit. Brooklyn belonged to the underworld: squeegee men waiting to ambush cars with mops, muggers sticking up pedestrians in broad daylight, perverts, pedophiles, flashers.

His head throbbed. He sat on the steps of the library, dreading his return home.

And then he remembered. A number he had memorized long ago. He hadn't talked to Steeplechase in years, though sometimes he heard rumors about his shady deals. Jack, however, knew everyone in real estate across the five boroughs. He would surely have the answer.

Richard hurried over to a pay phone on Eastern Parkway. He began to shake so badly he nearly dropped the receiver. Then he heard laughter—a woman's and a man's, and a television set.

"Hello? Who's this?"

"Richard—Richard from the Brownsville Boys Club," he stuttered. "Jack?"

"Richie Wong? Wow, is this really Richie Wong?"

"It's been a long time." Richard swallowed, trying to remain calm. "How's the family?"

"Well, Richie, it sure has been a while. The wife and I split. She took the kid. I got a girlfriend, Marla, she's with me right now. Say, where you calling from? I live in Woodhaven, you should come over and have a beer."

"I'm on a pay phone. Can I ask you a favor?"

"Sure, Richie. What can I help you with?"

"It's a sale. A property sale."

"You and Foo Foo moving out of East Flatbush?"

"No . . . I'm talking about the properties on Livonia I bought from Arnie."

"Ooh, that's bad, Rich," Jack sighed. "You're not gonna find a buyer for those. Just skip your property taxes and the city will take them from you."

"I . . ." Richard closed his eyes. "I need to sell. I need the money, Jack, or I'm going to lose my house."

"Oh boy, oh boy." Jack cleared his throat. "Let me think."

Richard sucked his teeth, waited, aware he had no backup plan.

"Actually, I know one . . . one firm. They might help you out. I'm going to give you a number, you got something to write with?"

He didn't. He'd have to scratch it somewhere, like a vandal. He took his keys and etched the number on the metal of the phone booth door.

"Don't ask them too many questions, all right?"

"What's that mean?"

"Nothing. Just sign the papers. They won't screw you, I give you my word."

Swiftly, Richard called the new number, hoping against reason that they, too, would answer at nine o'clock at night.

His luck was in the house.

"I'm calling to sell a property—I got this number from Jack Schmidt," Richard said.

"I need you to call another number," said a woman's voice. "Are you ready?"

He scratched down the second number, dialed it—the same lady picked up.

"And your name?"

"Richard Ch—" He stopped himself mid-speech. "Richard Wong."

"Please hold."

It must have been five minutes before he heard another voice. An old man's voice—sagacious, almost aristocratic.

"Thank you, Mr. Wong, and what kind of properties do you speak of?"

"Two buildings in Brooklyn. Fourteen apartments total." He gave the addresses and his home phone number. It was the first time any agency had taken down his information, and he was giddy with relief.

"We shall deliberate and then return your call, Mr. Wong."

"That's swell—and what's the company name?"

The old man laughed softly, as if this was funny. Richard heard a trickling in the background, perhaps the sound of a fish tank.

"Just call us the Leviathans."

"The Leviathans?"

"That's right, the Leviathans."

Foon Wah knew Richard had lost his job. She went to the lounge to meet Mr. Connelly and have her hunches confirmed. Yet even after this, she decided to say nothing. She'd already learned it was a useless exercise to confront her husband.

Whenever she'd asked him about the buildings on Livonia Avenue—why the loan man called, why the tenants left long messages—he would launch into a series of rebukes. She didn't know anything about the real estate business, he'd bark.

"You're wasteful," he'd often shout at her in Toisanese. "Always spending my money. Like a spoiled child."

Now that he'd lost his job, she hoped that if she kept quiet, he might resolve the issue on his own, maybe come home with his eyes wide, exclaiming about a fantastic new opportunity.

For three weeks, she kept her mouth shut.

Then one night, he berated her the moment he entered the house.

"Too many shoes," he said in Toisanese. "How come there's so many shoes?"

He hung up his hat and coat, then proceeded to the fridge. He'd long ago stopped offering her a kiss, and it was better this way, without them pretending to be the husband and wife in an American movie.

He slammed his fist on the freezer door. "You didn't buy beer."

She was, at that moment, spooning beef rice into bowls. Jason was seasoning the eggplant, Jackie setting out the chopsticks and napkins. With the two older girls married off, the house felt empty. Koon Lai crept over to his chair and put a napkin in the neck of his shirt.

"Jason, go to the market and buy your baba a beer," said Foon Wah. Richard took a seat at the head of the table and helped himself to the potatoes.

Instead of running the errand, Jason opened the fridge, removed two glass bottles of Coke, popped the caps, and put one bottle on his father's place mat.

"I didn't ask for a damn Coke!" Richard shouted.

Jason flopped into his own chair, drank his Coke.

Foon Wah didn't intend to show it that evening, but she was angry. In fact, she had been angry for a long time but was practiced at swallowing it, the way you swallow ginkgo soup for months during a famine. While cooking, she never complained about her wrists, which throbbed with pain from the years spent cramped at the sweatshop sewing machine. And while she sometimes thought she would be driven insane by the whining electric music Jason played on his record player, she only ever muttered that he should turn down the music and study. He was seventeen now and she was increasingly worried about him, that he would inherit his father's troubles with money.

For the most part, she had accepted the facts of her life. She could have been her best friend Mee Lai, married to a man twice her age. Yet sometimes she fancied that she was among those who the last president referred to as the "chim mak ge ai o su hou ngang jen." She'd read about it in the *Sing Tao Daily*: "The Great Silent Majority."

Much quieter than the drugged and long-haired bak gui, the slovenly and menacing hak gui, the hak gui women living off the government dole, the bak gui girls throwing their bras in trash cans. The Great Silent Majority suffered and persevered in silence.

Foon Wah heaped a second portion of beef rice onto Richard's plate, but his carping resumed.

"You didn't iron my uniform," Richard groused. He always spoke in Toisanese when criticizing her, even though she could have understood the same words in English. "I looked like a mess at work."

She put the spatula back in the pan, folded her hands in her lap, and stared at her bowl, a posture he might have read as remorse or shame.

And then she spoke.

"You no job." Her English words were barely audible, but Jason and Jackie looked up from their plates. Richard continued stuffing his mouth.

Perhaps the sound of her own voice gave her courage. She knew the language, yes. She had taken the night class at the library, studying alongside the Puerto Rican mothers. She had read the dictionary every night, and she always flipped through the deck of flash cards when she sat on the toilet. Almost thirty years of this, and you know more than you let on.

"No job." She lifted her eyes from the plate and looked right at him. "No job. Like a bum."

Now he'd heard her.

For a moment Richard was as still as marble, his fork lifted halfway to his mouth. Then he dropped the fork, pressed his hands onto the table, and slowly pushed himself up to standing.

"You calling me a bum? I'm a bum, because I served this country? Because every week I pay two mortgage bills?"

"Daddy," pleaded Jackie.

"Mou tou. To lok hui," muttered Koon Lai, waving his hand.

"This is my house! I bought this house!"

Foon Wah did not flinch. They were past the point of no return.

She would suffer whatever the consequences—and she would speak back to her husband if she felt like it. The time had come to end the silence.

"If anyone thinks I'm a bum," Richard raged, "they can—"

"They keep the hak gui," Foon Wah interrupted. "But not you."

Richard seized his Coke bottle and threw it to the floor by Foon Wah's feet. The bottle shattered, and pieces of glass whizzed across the kitchen.

"Aiya!" Koon Lai wailed. Jackie screamed. Jason's chair clattered to the floor.

They looked down at the scattered, sea-green fragments, large and small. Some had fallen centimeters from Foon Wah's feet.

"Get the hell out of here!" Jason shouted at Richard. "Get out of here now!"

Her husband's left hand trembled. Koon Lai put his face in his hands.

"Get out of here!" Jason cried again, and his voice was strange, both a man's and a boy's, low and angry, but also breaking, tearful. His fists were clenched, but she knew he didn't know how to use them. Full-grown, her son was taller than Richard, but also lean, gaunt; he'd resisted all of Richard's efforts to toughen him up, and all of Foon Wah's attempts to beef up his frame. Yet she had never seen Jason this angry before, and for a moment she wondered if he would hurt his father, and she was afraid.

Richard glanced at his son. He grabbed his coat, stuffed his feet in his leather shoes, and left through the front door.

Foon Wah gripped the napkin in her lap.

Jason was still standing, the others sitting, frozen. Then Jackie rose from her chair, swept up the glass, and put her arms around Foon Wah's shoulders.

Foon Wah couldn't help but push her daughter away.

"Eat your dinner," she said, at which Jackie began to cry. Koon Lai continued to sit with his hands over his face, avoiding Foon Wah's eyes. She pitied him.

"Eat your dinner," Foon Wah repeated. "Sit down. Don't waste your food. Children in China are starving."

They understood this refrain of hers as a call to order. Jackie slunk back to her seat, and slowly, they picked up their spoons and chopsticks, chewing in silence.

Foon Wah strained to hear, above the clinking of cutlery, her husband's footsteps on the porch outside. She wondered when he would be returning, and she hoped she would be asleep when he did.

Quietly, Foon Wah pushed back her chair, folded her napkin beside her plate, and took herself to bed. There were dishes to do, laundry to fold, and yet for once, she would neglect them.

She had done them, unthanked and unpaid, for thirty years, and she was tired.

Based on his writing portfolio, Jason was accepted to Columbia University on full scholarship. The news gave Foon Wah and Richard a distraction from their bitterness, and for Jason, it was the best escape. To get from East Flatbush to Columbia, he had to walk half a mile, take a bus, and ride two different trains—a two-hour commute each way. Decades earlier, Robert Moses had ignored a proposal to build a subway line down Flatbush Avenue, forever condemning the residents of East Flatbush to isolation. But Jason didn't mind the inconvenience. The distance gave him an excuse to stay out late.

The night of the shattered bottle had taught him something. Of course, there'd been a moment when he'd feared he'd fallen into some kind of trap. That his father had conjured the son he'd always wanted—a man's man, capable of fighting with his fists and toppling chairs to the ground. And yet what ultimately had thrilled him that night was not confronting his father. It was locking him out.

After his mother had left the table, Jason had bolted all the house doors. Three hours later, a summer storm had engulfed the neighborhood, and his father had rung the doorbell. Jason had enjoyed disregarding it. He'd imagined his father collapsing, resigned, onto one of the wet chairs on the porch, sleeping there with his hat over his face. Or maybe: walking to the subway, hoping to book a Midtown hotel, only to fall asleep on the train and ride it all the way to the Bronx and back. Like a bum.

But the fantasy had been short-lived. His mother had risen to admit his father. Jason had stood at the top of the stairs and watched her: barefoot and frail, wearing her lilac pajamas and without her lipstick and blush. A woman who had come across the world to serve others' whims, to catch others' spit.

Jason was indignant on her behalf, but in the weeks ahead, every time he tried to ask how she was feeling, she would change the subject, or nitpick, or send Jason to complete a chore. She would never leave their father, this much was clear. No matter how cruel he was, no matter how belligerent. He hated how easily she accepted this mediocrity. Now knowing the peace of a home without his father, he was loath to be home at all.

Matriculating at Columbia also gave him the opportunity to explore Manhattan on his own. He frequented the standing room section of Avery Fisher Hall, spent hours roaming in the Metropolitan Museum of Art, and attended performances of Chekhov and Ibsen in the little black box theaters of the cobblestoned West Village. And he was not alone; people came to New York from all corners of the country and the world seeking songs, poetry, and music, craving a life of the mind.

Of course, the city was also bankrupt. He skirted around the men and women who wore blankets in lieu of coats, whose bodies smelled of urine and who wore the thinnest flip-flops on their swollen purple feet. He never stopped to tell strangers the time, and always avoided the last train car.

In his sophomore year, Jason went to a poetry reading in the Lower East Side. Wishing to delay his return to Brooklyn, he lingered for the after-party in the garden, nursing a half-filled plastic cup of red wine and listening to the poets expound on Neo-Expressionism. Socializing with writers was more difficult than he'd expected. They barely glanced at him, and he wondered if this was because they assumed he had nothing witty to say. He was adrift in his thoughts when someone poked his knee.

"Smoke?"

He turned. The woman leaning against the fence was young and petite, but with impressively muscled biceps and black hair cropped boyishly short. She wore jean shorts and a tank top that revealed her midriff, including a belly ring with a dangling pendant the shape of the Tree of Life. And she was Chinese, a "jook seing" like him, one hand on her thigh, the other holding out a cigarette.

"Oh. No thank you."

"I'm Gina." She took a puff. "You're new. So where are you from?" She raised a jaunty eyebrow.

Understanding the joke, he nodded. "The *Mayflower*. You?"

She smirked. "Are you a poet?"

"I don't know," he laughed. She blew out her smoke, waited for him to change his mind. "I write, I guess."

"What did you think of the reading?"

"They were great," he said, eager now. No one else had asked his opinion. "Like that second guy? Chester. He was so good. Sounds like freaking T. S. Eliot."

"Is T. S. Eliot your favorite poet?"

"I mean, I don't know if I have a favorite . . . Sylvia Plath is awesome. Also Ezra Pound, Allen Ginsberg, Walt Whitman, Emily Dickinson . . ." She was nodding as he listed them, her eyes on a water tower across the street. She kept nodding like he was supposed to continue. "And Rilke . . . and Ashbery . . . and William Carlos Williams . . ."

"What about Li Po?"

"Who?"

She rolled her eyes. "Tell me you know Tu Fu?"

"Tu who?"

"Poor boy." She sighed and looked disappointed. He was starting to reply when a white man with a mohawk scooped the cigarette from her hand.

"I'm heading back to Beloved," the man said. From the smell, Jason decided the man's beautiful, handcrafted patch pants had never been laundered.

"Make me a bowl of lentils and don't let Jimmy eat it," she answered.

Jason waited anxiously for the man to depart, then followed her to the snack table.

"So tell me who I should read."

"Read like you want to know yourself." She stopped suddenly and turned to him, their bodies nearly brushing. "Like you're not just studying how to be a bak gui."

He was thrown by this. His mother tongue on her lips. Her indictment. The pendant dangling from her belly. He blinked. Looked around, but no one was watching them.

"You're a student?" she asked.

"Columbia."

"Okay, no excuse. They're in Butler Library. Li Po, Tu Fu, Li Ch'ing Chao."

"Are you also at Columbia?"

"I'm a Columbia dropout." She stuffed a handful of Doo Dads in her mouth and looked right at him without a hint of shame. Her parents had to be dead, he thought. How else to explain her existence?

She dug into the pocket of her shorts. "Come to this next week."

A typed flyer. A hand-drawn guitar, paintbrush, and Chinese opera mask.

Basement Workshop Arts Extravaganza.

He thought about her in the days that followed, imagining the ring in her belly. When he made it to the Basement Workshop—said to have once run out of a Chinatown basement, but now located on the twelfth floor of a loft building on Lafayette Street—he found himself surrounded by jook seing in bell-bottoms, with hair to their waists and anti-war buttons up and down their jackets. He fit in well there, and he'd never fit in anywhere.

Gina stood out in the crowd. She was another level of rebel: jook seing in leather and fishnets. She seemed pleased to see him—she grabbed his hand and pulled him onto the floor next to her. They watched the widely ranging art show, which included everything from children's fingerprint paintings to modern dance, from silk screen prints to a haunting set of portrait photographs by Gina herself. Next, contributors to *Yellow Peril* magazine read poems and essays from their latest issue. They spoke of racism and colonialism—of their anger, loneliness, and search for self. He understood every line.

The night deepened, and the crowd thinned as some of the Basement Workshop members headed to the subway station. He wasn't ready to leave, but he'd already missed dinner, and he knew his mother would be worried.

"This is when the goody-goodies go home," Gina quipped.

"Won't your ba be mad?" Jason whispered.

"Ba's in the loony bin. Mom's in prison."

"Wait, are you serious?"

"I live ten blocks from here. Alphabet City."

He'd never ventured to Alphabet City before. But if she lived there, perhaps it wasn't as dangerous as people said.

"In a squatter house. I don't know if you're looking, but we're trying to fill our extra room."

"Oh. Well, can I at least make sure you get home all right?"

They both knew it was funny that he offered, but she humored him.

Alphabet City was a menagerie of half-collapsed tenements and vacant lots. Some lots had been converted to gardens, their fences decorated with roses and beads. He told her that he'd loved her photograph of a blind Chinese elder who lived in the A train tunnel, and she nodded, seeming to appreciate his compliment, explaining how she'd met the man. In one garden on Avenue D, a naked white girl with dreadlocks bathed herself with a hose. Gina waved at her; Jason looked away.

They reached "Beloved House," a commune of some sort, ten

or eleven of them in an abandoned building without electricity or stairs. Gina and her housemates had installed canvas tarps to climb from floor to floor; they tapped electricity from the lampposts. The wall paint peeled like tree bark.

He pretended not to be crestfallen when she introduced him to her boyfriend, Jim Gallagher. He was sitting on the edge of a mattress with a guitar in his lap, and he seemed intensely focused on his new composition. Next, they climbed to the roof to meet "the poets"—the decked-out punk he'd seen at the party, and Angelo, who was Filipino. They were passing a joint and discussing Edward Said's *Orientalism*, but by then Jason was tired.

She showed him the free room. They were standing beside the mattress when she began unbuttoning his shirt. He looked at her, then at the cracked door of the room, his heart pounding in her hands.

"Jim?" he whispered.

"Relax. We're not the monogamous type."

He shivered as her cold fingers grazed his chest. Considered stopping her, of demanding something more for himself. Yet he had waited forever to be in someone's hands. When her fingers meandered down and stroked the crotch of his jeans, he lost his breath.

She removed her tank top. Beneath it she wore a lace bra, daintier than he would have imagined. He looked away again, and then back at them, her small cups. He ran his hand across her back, not knowing what was allowed.

She unhooked herself, took his hands and molded them over her breasts. And once he was situated there, she returned her hand to his jeans, unzipped the fly, felt him through his silly cotton briefs. It felt like playing with electric sockets; their bodies had buttons, levers, the capacity to shock. She was cold and methodical, without kisses, as if teaching him choreography for a play.

And then, quite suddenly, something shifted: she turned around, pressed her back against his bare skin, cupped her hands over his hands. No longer leading him; surrendering. She had pinned her small body against him. She had even shut her eyes, leaving him to see and touch her angles. And gradually, Jason did so like a man long starved, biting back the urge to chew her crisp black hair. They were no longer cold. They were hot and hurried, all instinct and need.

He had worried, at various times earlier that evening, that she saw him as a little brother. Now that felt like the most colonized thought he'd had yet. He could smell her body odor, at once unappealing and intoxicating. Then she drew his hand farther down, diving beneath the folds of her underwear. He felt the curls of thicker hair, and below it, a landscape of caves and coral—slick and glossy, he imagined, as an ocean bed.

He feared himself, he wanted to know the rules, but her low moaning seemed to say that there were none.

For several months, he forgot about the Met and the black box theaters and went to Beloved House to make love with Gina—and to study. He read the books and watched the tapes she set in front of him, became obsessed with Nam June Paik's TV art and Yayoi Kusama's polka-dotted nudes. And she studied *him*, and sometimes took his picture on her Canon when he wasn't looking. If he left the room to urinate, she picked up his books and read the notes he had written in the margins. It was flattering to be the object of someone's gaze in this way. To not always be the gazer. He had never felt so aware of himself as a body and as a person. Her questions required him to explain himself, and the more he talked, the more he felt he knew himself. He was proud to see who he was becoming.

He found a job at a bookstore near school and didn't tell his parents about his intentions to move to Beloved House until he was clomping down the staircase with one arm around his typewriter and the other holding a suitcase packed with clothes and books. He'd never needed much.

"Where you go?" his mother asked in English.

"I got an apartment."

She was horrified. What did he mean, what apartment? With

who? He was so young, just nineteen—who would cook for him and make sure he ate? He would probably eat cornflakes for breakfast, lunch, and dinner. He always messed up the laundry by forgetting to put in the soap, so how would he wash his clothes?

"Look what you're doing to your ma," his father said. "When's the last time you thought about anyone except yourself?"

Jason disregarded his father and argued half-heartedly with his mother. He was past caring what they thought. Only his grandfather's reaction disturbed him. Koon Lai's raisiny face clouded over, and he shrank into his chair like he might someday dissolve into it.

Beloved House held a communal dinner that night in Jason's welcome. The beans and rice ran out quickly, but the beer and music kept coming, and once inebriated, the housemates took turns relating the time and place of their favorite one-night stands, then the day and streets where they'd been mugged. He chewed on Angelo's sunflower seeds and tried to shake off the image of Jackie, Yia Yia, and his parents sitting joylessly around a table crammed end to end with plates of fish cakes and pork ribs.

Beloved House was a slapdash, janky construction, exposing them to the changing of the seasons, the drafts of winter and the smacking wetness of summer. It was an archeology site, littered with remnants of the past twenty artists who had come and gone with those seasons. Roaches squirmed in the corners of the dish strainer, squiggles of corkscrew pasta fell from the kitchen ceiling, and the shower curtain was always molding over and sticking to itself, so that Jason never managed to stretch it to its full length. The first month of his stay, they suffered a two-week gas outage. Jason spent those weeks eating Breyers ice cream and cereal, just as his mother had predicted. But it was better this way, he thought: to live in a house that continually reminded you of your animalness, your vulnerability to the elements.

About a year into his stay at Beloved House, Gina met someone at Club 57. Jason never learned his name, let alone his ethnicity—only that he had a Volkswagen. She set out with him on a cross-country road trip. She said they would return in six weeks, but six weeks turned into six months, and when they got back to New York she stayed with him, somewhere in Queens. When Gina finally dropped by Beloved House, she fought with Jim for hours and barely spoke to Jason at all, which made it obvious that in the hierarchy of her polyamory, Jason was at the bottom.

Going home was impossible. He couldn't bear to return to his mother's disappointment, his father's violence, his grandfather's ceaseless grief. He spent most of his time squirreled away in his room, writing poems about outcasts who wandered in shadowed, predawn Hopperesque streets or, like Li Po, drank *alone, under the moon*. The ink of spoiled pens dripped like hoisin, stained his fingers. Sometimes he only had the energy to lie in a ball on his mattress, paralyzed with the fear of unending lonesomeness.

During these months, only his grandfather visited him. Koon Lai would appear on the fire escape, wearing the gray suit that smelled of mothballs, and he'd spread a handkerchief on the dirty window ledge and sit there for hours with his thin knees crossed. He'd listen to his grandson moan into a pillow, and he'd say, "Go home and visit your mother." Sometimes he'd unwrap a dried plum and offer it to the boy.

But Jason couldn't hear or see him. All he felt was a lingering warmth that softened him like a bowl of mushroom jook on a winter day.

It took some time before he called home and learned Koon Lai was dead.

SADIE

Sadie arrived at the 99 Cents store on Rockaway Avenue determined to find Mr. William and his nurse, even if it meant spending
the whole day in Mr. Pierre Henry's dollar store. Mr. Henry didn't
mind. He gave her a plastic chair to sit on. She showed her gratitude
by fetching two orders of saltfish and bake from a takeout spot on
Rutland Road.

But neither Mr. William nor the nurse showed, and though Sadie
came back the following day to wait, they did not turn up then either. Sadie tore a page from her notebook, wrote a message with her
number, and asked Mr. Henry to deliver it to Mr. William if he ever
came by.

Three days later, the twinkle of her ringtone caught her with a mouth
full of toothpaste.

"Hello?" she gurgled.

"Hello?" said a voice raspy as sandpaper.

"Mr. William!"

She spat into the sink, wiped her mouth, and dashed back to her
bedroom.

"Pauline gave me your letter. I remember you. They said you've
been looking for me. But the thing is, these days, I don't leave the

house. And I don't know if you would feel comfortable inside my apartment. I understand a young woman might not feel right coming into a stranger's apartment."

"I'd love to come over!"

"Yeah?"

She scribbled down his address on a Post-it, then asked if there was anything he needed.

"Anything I need?" he sounded confused. "What do you mean, like things I . . . I need?"

"Or anything you want!" she laughed. "I don't know, a pint of ice cream. Whatever you feel like!"

She was not a reporter this time; she could afford to be generous.

She showed up two days later to his one-bedroom apartment in Tilden Houses. A baseball game, Rays vs. Yankees, murmured on the old Sony, and James Brown records lined the shelves. There were framed pictures on every wall, mostly of his sisters and their kids. "My pride and joy," he called his nieces—both in nursing school. His mother was gone. His little brother, gone. With the stroke having permanently weakened the left side of his face, his expressions were all half smiles, half frowns. The exception: when he spoke about his brother. Then, his face unified in a grimace—eyebrows begging, lips bowed.

"I'm a young man. You know, I had a stroke at forty-six," he said. "But I have lived too much."

He'd gotten better at wheeling around the house, so he took care of himself in the mornings. The nurse wouldn't arrive until noon. Mr. William sat in his wheelchair, and Sadie perched on the edge of the brown recliner. His temperament seemed different from when they'd met in the store, and he was grateful that she'd delivered on his request: a single cannoli from Little Italy. He'd been craving one for months.

"I never met your grandfather. Mr. Wong. They said he was the landlord who wanted the buildings burned. That's how it was back then, all the landlords burned property for money."

"I've been trying to find proof that my grandfather was definitely involved."

"I'm the proof. Take it from someone who was there in '78."

"Do you remember the day it happened?"

"Remember?" he scoffed. The grimace returned. "My life changed on that day."

His mouth puckered like he'd tasted something sour.

"Because they used us. That's how it is. Soon as you're born, they teach you to destroy yourself. You probably don't understand."

Sadie closed her notebook. Folded her hands. Leaned farther back in the recliner.

"We were just kids. Me and my brother, here in the old Sneaker. My brother was just six, seven years old. A man drove up, said he'd pay us one hundred dollars if we torched two buildings. He had four milk jugs in his car trunk, all of them filled with gasoline. Told us to pour the gas in the halls of those two buildings, light them up with a match. And he picked the right boys for the job. We were always doing acrobatic shit. Dumpster diving. We had no problem jumping out of second-floor windows.

"I don't know who that man was. Maybe Mr. Wong, or maybe Mr. Wong sent someone to do his dirty work. I never found out. Just knew this man was the devil in the garden with the apple. And we bit.

"We were in the *Daily News*: two Brownsville kids, William and Francis Joyner, arrested for torching Livonia. We told the cops someone paid us, but they never found the guy. Cops sent us home, enrolled us in a youth program, and that was the last time I played with fire. I couldn't stop thinking about these people. These people who couldn't care less if we blew ourselves up. I don't mean Chinese people, I mean all of them—it don't matter. They would take a Brownsville child's innocence before they took responsibility."

Sadie listened without speaking. Her heart was in her stomach.

He nodded to one of the medical certificates on the wall. It was his own.

"I was an ambulance driver. Twenty years on the job. For Kings County Hospital. Bullet wounds, strangulation, I've seen it all. A boy tried to decapitate his sister. I tell you, I've seen it all. But I had to. My job was to take people *away* from that mess. Take them to heal. That's why I signed up. Because at some point I realized: the last thing they want is you *serving* your people."

She nodded slowly, understanding.

"But my brother, he never *got it*. He was relieved we didn't end up in juvie, but he didn't know what he'd done. Just kept getting in deeper and deeper shit—thought he was impressing me. I don't think my brother even finished elementary school. And the thing is, I did that to him. That's what weighs on me. That and the people in the building. You know, I didn't think. I saw that hundred dollars like it was in neon lights."

Sadie wished she could do more than watch, wished she knew him well enough to squeeze his hand.

She touched the arm of the wheelchair.

"Mr. William, it wasn't your fault. You were just a kid."

His eyelids were red. She wanted to take away the weight—to take the blame on herself, even if she still didn't know the full story.

"It was the man who paid you," she continued. "He was a *real* person. Maybe my grandfather. My grandfather did it, not you."

"When you told me who you were, in Mr. Henry's store, I was angry." He looked directly at her. "But then with you searching for me, I knew you needed the truth."

LINA

Lina woke up on her mother's couch.

She was thirty-four years old, her dreams destroyed, and—she suddenly remembered—a murderer.

Nellie had found her. Had taken her to her mother's place at five a.m. Mami had pressed a cold towel soaked in alcoholado to Lina's head, smeared the burns with Vicks VapoRub, and tried to make her talk, but Lina only turned away into the cushion.

She had always been the strong one, but the night of the fire, Lina had fallen to her knees on the hot sidewalk and wept. That was when the trucks arrived, and the roof collapsed and the EMTs loaded three bodies into an ambulance. All around, the neighbors moaned and wheezed, and the old woman who'd lost her brother screamed into the smoke-filled sky, asking for the Lord to take her too.

Lina was still on the sidewalk, forehead to the cement, when she felt Nellie's arms around her.

"I'm a murderer," she cried.

"No, baby."

"It's my fault."

In the morning, then, Lina lay on her mother's couch and yet was not really present—she was stuck in the black hole behind her eyes. There, a little girl with burned legs howled in pain, and an old man danced, and Annetta in her bonnet wailed, *You done pushed that Mr. Wong!*

Lina sat up on the couch, wincing when fabric brushed the burns on her elbows and legs, and she peeked out the window blinds. She was back at her mother's place in Van Dyke, on the twelfth floor. Danny, Cindy, and Sofia and her kids had moved out.

Lina thought to herself that maybe she wasn't a revolutionary. She was just delusional, and the neighborhood would have been better off without her. She knew what it was like to lose a brother. That someone else had lost a brother on her account, she felt, was beyond forgiveness.

Weeks passed like this. Lina adjusted to living with her mother again. Morning cheek kisses and prayers to the Virgin. Plastic-covered furniture, vases of fake roses. No elbows on the table, no locked bedroom doors, no privacy. As winter came around, the hum of muddy aguinaldos on the record player. Irresistible bowls of arroz con dulce.

Van Dyke Houses was different. No longer was the lawn perfect as the crinkle cuts in an Easter basket. Now, she noticed holes in the hallway windows and trash scattered across the courtyard. The shopkeepers had installed gates over the stores, and at night the kids tagged them with gang signs.

In her bedroom, Nellie would braid Lina's hair. She'd talk about Wesley, who wanted to be an artist—"and we know where he got that from," she'd say, bending over to kiss Lina when Mami Isabella was not in earshot. Lina would pretend to listen, but her mind kept returning behind her eyes. It was like living inside a snow globe, except instead of snow, she was aswirl in ash.

Nellie thought they needed to get out of Brownsville. "Oh!" Nellie exclaimed one evening. "Let's go to Coney Island!"

"Why?"

"I've still never been."

Before Lina could object, she was dragged to the car and driven down the Belt Parkway, down to Astroland. They rode the Ferris wheel, and at the pinnacle, Nellie kissed her. The next week, Nellie drove them to a park in the Bronx and goaded Lina to throw bread to the ducks.

For many months, it was Nellie's love alone that kept Lina alive—a love stolen in shadowy spaces, muted so as not to draw the attention of relatives: her head, resting on Nellie's lap in Lincoln Terrace Park on a fall afternoon, the air full of sweetness and decay; the mornings, waking up together in the back seat of the car, cold coffee in the cup holder.

It was all she lived for, and that something so precious could require such furtiveness didn't seem right. Lina had not much left to lose, and she was willing to risk everything for what held her to life.

So, Lina sat with her mother at the kitchen table, two hands in two hands. She looked into the eyes of beautiful, withering Isabella with her silver Indian braids, her rosary beads, who every day patted her stomach and wondered aloud, "¿Estoy demasiado gorda, niña? ¿O es esto lo que le pasa a la cintura cuando tienes cinco bebés?"

Lina squeezed those hands. Hands that, each day at church, joined in a prayer for Lina's recovery. She didn't believe her mother would throw her out—Mami was too soft for that—but she was afraid of breaking her mother's heart.

"Mami. ¿Te gusta Nellie?"

"Sí."

Her mother slipped away from Lina's hands, poured them each a cup of café.

Lina exhaled. "La amo."

"Sí," her mother nodded, breathing in the steam of the café. She still did not understand, Lina thought, and to make her understand would be a kind of violence. A shattering.

"La amo," Lina repeated, her voice shaking. And then: "La amo como un hombre ama a su esposa."

Her mother stirred the sugar.

"No puedo evitarlo," Lina added, then swallowed.

For a while, neither woman said anything. The spoon rang against the side of the mug.

"I know, mija," she finally said, and her bony shoulders rose in a shrug. A tiny smile flickered across her lips, light and fleeting as a breeze in a lace curtain.

"Lo sé desde hace mucho tiempo."

She lifted Lina's chin. "If you are happy, I am happy."

It was then that Lina's tears finally came. Delayed as a fire truck. Gushing like an unscrewed fire hydrant.

She took a job at the Head Start program. Brought home the bacon. This was all her family had ever asked of her, after all: to be a little more normal. To not turn everything into "algo político." She could still help the community, but in quieter, tamer ways. Change was slow. It was time she accepted this as truth, time to be grateful that she was alive, she had a salary, her family ate three meals a day. Not everyone was so fortunate.

At least that's what she thought the world was trying to tell her. The women who smiled nervously at her, then lowered their eyes and hurried away. The young men who quickly shoved their hands in their pockets. She was so deep in her head those years, it took her a while to realize something else was going on in the community.

She was visiting Annie, her old friend and high school crush, when she figured it out. Annie was a sweet soul, a daydreamer. She still kept her hair straight and bobbed, with a little bow ribbon, and when that hound dog from Bed-Stuy got her pregnant, she'd been excited to be a mother. She'd miscarried, and ever since then, she'd been different—drinking, it was rumored. Still, Lina went to Brownsville Houses to wish Annie a happy fortieth birthday, and that's when she first heard it, the *it* that had invaded the neighborhood. It was crackling on the cooker.

"Lina, you ain't yourself anymore. I ain't either," Annie said wistfully. "But what I got here is gonna make you feel *good*, I promise you that."

Lina caught a glimpse of the stove. She saw chunks of it, glowing white like hardened Domino Sugar.

"Girl, no way in hell."

She refused to do it, refused to watch Annie do it, and left soon after, her only regret that she hadn't knocked that pan right off the stove.

The unraveling began quietly. Smokers hiding in the staircases, zip-lock bags traded in hallways, brown baggies dropped from windows, young women with blisters on their lips. The projects were rank with the smell of burning plastic. Most young users avoided her, afraid she'd give them a dressing-down, but one evening, Lina was walking on Mother Gaston—the sidewalk littered with vials—when she spotted Hank, that smart, quiet boy whom she'd taught at J.H.S. 271 fifteen years earlier. He was a grown man now, and as they neared each other, she could tell something was wrong: his clothes soiled, his chin sharp as a wedge, his eyes bulging.

"Give me what you got."

He grabbed her shoulder, pressed her to the wall, put a gun to her temple.

"Hank! Don't you know me?"

"Give me your money, lady, or I'll shoot your brains out."

She had four dollars and her mother's prescription pills. He took these and left her there, with bruise marks on her neck. Once again, she felt herself to blame. If the Freedom School had lived, it would have saved him.

Had it lived, she thought, there would be a Freedom School on every block by now. Instead, every block had a crack house. One night, Hank attacked the addicts in the Blake Avenue crack house with a screwdriver, then started breaking into other peoples' homes. The melee ended when a tenant across the street shot Hank in the face. Lina attended the family's burial wearing sunglasses.

The next public victim was Denise Scott. Lina was the one who found her motionless and blue-faced on the sidewalk, her two-year-old boy Tyrell in tears, shaking her shoulders with his tiny hands.

Annie thought she could handle her new medicine, but within a year she had sold all her furniture, all her clothes. Her refrigerator was empty, and she slept on her apartment's brown floor—all for that one ziplock bag. When Lina visited, she found Annie out of supply, curled in a corner by her living room window, a sliver of her former self. Lina kneeled beside her friend and held her bony hand.

"Annie," Lina said, fighting the itch in her eyes. "You got to get help."

"I got to stop," Annie whispered. She lacked the energy to sit up. "But I can't, girlie. I can't go back there."

"Back where?"

"To the world."

She watched her people forget their faith, forget each other, forget themselves. On summer days when tempers boiled over, gunshots echoed through the courtyards. Addicts dropped their kids off at her Head Start program, and so did their dealers.

"It's a job," one of these young parents told her. "The Chinese wash underwear. The Italians work the docks. If I don't sell, someone else will."

As deeply as she disagreed, she felt helpless to persuade them otherwise. All she could do was bolt the door after each child's arrival.

She attended more funerals of former students, while others were sent up the river to a different kind of death. Brownsville even got its own Express bus—straight to Rikers. Two hours of nausea and security checks so you could talk with your loved one for thirty minutes.

Walter's little sister Tammy was found dead in a basement in the Bronx. The way the news talked about it was almost a second murder. Everyone said Walter, now almost thirty years old, had tried to take his own life when he heard the news. He had not succeeded, but Lina could not muster the strength to visit Walter in the hospital or attend Tammy's funeral. She mourned by fasting for two weeks with her window blinds closed, and the news channel became her access point to the outside world.

Ronald was a convincing actor, she thought. The president could make it seem like he was the savior, the benevolent father, when he was the one fueling the cartels. Demonizing the babies. Stripping her people of every means of survival.

Nellie's son Wesley grew older, but he remained an outsider. He stayed in the apartment all day, drawing cartoons in a notebook. Sure the universe would punish her if she eased up, Nellie wouldn't let him out of her sight.

"Let's move somewhere else," she urged Lina one night in the back seat of the car. "Atlanta. St. Louis. Anywhere's better than here."

Lina asked hesitantly, "They got Puerto Ricans over there?"

"We'll drive until we find 'em."

She knew Nellie was getting frustrated, but Lina couldn't imagine leaving her mother, and there was no way her mother would give up her people in New York.

And the truth was, Lina herself was unsure. It was hard to say if this was love for Brownsville or fear of the world beyond. She'd never left the city. But if the white world was so determined to strangle Brownsville, how long would she and Nellie make it, on their own, on the outside?

Wesley wanted to see *The Prince of Darkness* at the Kings. On one summer day, Nellie finally let him, and the quiet teenager with the heavy brow ridge and the old man's lips took the bus to Flatbush for the matinee. Deciding to save the change for a day his mother really needed it, he skipped popcorn but did enjoy seating himself right next to the air-conditioning vent.

He liked horror movies and had collected *The Exorcist*, *The Texas Chain Saw Massacre*, and *Eraserhead* on VHS. They made Brownsville look decent enough by comparison. It was the uncanniness of a rom-com that spooked him, reminding him of all he didn't have.

After the credits rolled, he took the bus back to Brownsville, stopping by Motor City Salon to assure his mother everything had gone all right.

Back at Tilden, he rode the elevator with a teen he knew. Wesley nodded, but the young man was too distracted to take note. The teen wore a red bandanna and was anxiously fingering the cross that hung from his neck. When the elevator opened on floor eight, another boy with a blue scarf over his face lifted a Glock 9 mm and tore a hole in the neck of the wrong person.

Wesley shrieked. Crumpled to the floor.

His blood dripped through the crack between the elevator and floor eight.

Nellie went to the hospital without calling Lina, and Lina followed on the bus as soon as word reached her.

But he was already in the morgue when she arrived. Lina stared at Wesley's soft face, and in death, he didn't look like an old man at all. He had always been just a child.

There was no funeral. Lina paid for the tombstone in Cypress Hills. *A loving son. 1969–1986.* She thought about adding "stepson," but did not know how to ask Nellie for this.

Nellie slept all day in Lina's bed and wouldn't eat. Lina tried to comfort her, but there was nothing to be said.

At night, when Lina was sleeping, Nellie would slip out and drive to the cemetery. Then she began missing appointments at the salon. She couldn't offer stories or ask questions the way she used to, and everything Lina said dissolved in the haze of her eyes.

One morning, Lina woke up and found Nellie in the bathroom, holding a towel to her left foot. The cloth was soaked through with blood, and on the side of her foot dangled a loose flap of skin big as a quarter. She was still wearing her jacket and hat.

"Shit shit shit!" Lina gasped, squatting beside Nellie. "What happened?"

"The car has a flat," Nellie said in no more than a whisper. "But I had to go to the cemetery."

Lina was confused. "What do you mean? You walked there?"

Nellie said nothing. She wrapped her foot in toilet paper.

"That looks bad! I'll take you to the hospital!"

Nellie turned her head away. "No," she mumbled. "I'm fine. It's my fault."

Lina looked at Nellie, still not understanding. "How'd you cut your foot?" She surveyed the bathroom. "What shoes did you wear?"

It took her a moment to realize Nellie's shoes were still on the rack in Lina's bedroom closet.

"Babe, did you . . . ?" But she stopped because she saw it all in Nellie's eyes: her lover had walked to the cemetery barefoot. Three miles of bare skin against the glass-strewn streets of Brooklyn. Heels stained by cigarette bums. Toes sliced by beer caps and tuna can lids.

One night, she didn't come home. Lina called Nellie's cousin, the salon, some friends, but no one had seen her. She searched Nellie's favorite spots, asked the neighbors, the dealers.

And then she had no choice but to dial the police.

Lina would tell many people in the years that followed that the ones we love and lose survive in us and become a part of us, and that when we, too, are gone, they persist even still—because we, too, will live through those who love us and outlive us. Back in the day, there was a Jewish tailor on Sutter Avenue with Russian nesting dolls on the windowsill, she'd say. Those pretty wood dolls fit one inside the other, baby inside mami, mami inside abuela, abuela inside bis-abuela. Love makes a nesting doll out of all of us.

She'd say this without telling them that as you grow older and older, with all those many dolls crammed inside you, it becomes difficult to breathe.

Eventually, the NYPD found Nellie in her car under a highway in Long Island, her forehead on the wheel, a vacuum cleaner pipe hooked from the exhaust through a crack in the rear window.

THE CHINS

One month before he departed, Foon Wah and Koon Lai sat at the kitchen table, eating cornflakes with Del Monte fruit cocktail.

"Look, this group organizes trips to China," she said, pointing to an ad in the paper. "A four-week trip. Do you want to visit Toisan?" But Koon Lai did not answer, though his eyes wandered toward the ad.

Things had been different in China. In China, the house was always full. Foon Wah felt she had suffered the loss of her family not once, but twice: coming to America, and now, because her American children had forgotten her. Her three daughters had married and bought homes outside the city, and her baby boy had abandoned her.

Worst of all, it was the beginning of August, a month devoid of holidays. Holidays were the exception to her loneliness, for with the approach of holidays, her children began to involuntarily salivate at the thought of turkey stuffed with ham-speckled sticky rice and the memory of warm brown fat gao swelling in the steamers. Then, her children came like dogs sniffing their way back, stomachs against intellects, and the house was stuffed to its capacity, everyone clustered around the table and saying little to one another except to pass the no mai fan, pass the mo gu gai pein, consumed in the pleasure of eating. It was during holidays that she concluded that to be Chinese was to be only happy when in the flock.

She tried to sublimate these feelings into the task of caring for Koon Lai—brewing his gen mai cha, making sure he had enough light to read the *Sing Tao Daily*. When he went out for his morning walk, she helped him put on his shoes, though he was embarrassed every time, and reminded him to bring his cane. At least on the days he went out, he could look at the neighbors' front yards. The Georges always said good day to him, and Mrs. George had a flourishing garden full of all kinds of vegetables, which reminded Koon Lai of his mother's garden in Chin village.

On rainy days, however, he barely spoke at all, and Foon Wah became especially attentive, trying to draw him into conversation.

"One thousand dollars is not bad. We can go to Beijing, and then to Canton."

Even though most of her immediate family had already died, or else had fled to Hong Kong or Australia, she had been wanting to go back. She wondered what had happened to her best friend Mee Lai, with her thick eyebrows and caustic wit and clumsy hands that could never sew a fine line. She didn't know Mee Lai's address, and they hadn't spoken in forty years. Foon Wah would have liked to find her friend, and to bring oranges to the hill in Gui Lin where she had buried her mother.

Koon Lai lifted the soft pink and yellow cubes of the fruit cocktail, without rind or seed or stem, or much by way of flavor to differentiate them. He thought of his own mother smiling as she fed herself a bowl of jook, and beneath her skirt, those tiny shoes shaped like the triangle cookies in the Jewish bakeries. Hamantaschen feet. He thought of his wife, with whom he had spent only one night of his life, though their correspondence had lasted fifty years. Their letters had been polite, but not meaningful, and he had sometimes wondered if she'd met another man—if this was the reason she'd repeatedly turned down his offers to bring her to America.

The truth was, he had not felt strongly one way or the other, and so he had sent her the money she'd asked for, for as long as she'd asked, and when the letters stopped, he'd understood she was in the ground. It was in the dullness that followed that he realized how much they had always remained strangers to each other.

It seemed to him that someone should have tossed him out long ago, swept him into the yard like a pile of fish bones. Everything terrified him. Even the sight of an apple struck him with the fear of losing more teeth. At seventy-eight, Koon Lai tried to remember how old his father and grandfather had been when they'd died. Had growing old, for them, been so humiliating?

Foon Wah tried to pour the rest of the fruit cocktail in his bowl, but Koon Lai waved her away. "Bou le."

He watched her, feeling guilty for his distraction. What had she said? Something about going back to China? Something about fruit cocktail? "Hou hiak!" he exclaimed, to thank her for the snack, to thank her for everything—he could never repay the debt. Then he read to her a few items of news from the *Sing Tao Daily*, the agreeable ones.

1981八月一號

政府批准美國史上最大的減稅計劃

警察將打擊毒品銷售

美國和中國加強貿易關係

August 1, 1981: tax cuts in the U.S., police to fight drug sales, increased trade between China and America—yes, things were improving now that the red emperor was dead. Koon Lai had heard there'd been a public shaming of the Red Guard members who'd killed his brother. And yet, it hardly seemed like enough. The Communists now claimed the late Mao had been "70 percent right" and "30 percent wrong," but they continued to exalt his name.

Sometimes in his bitterness, he didn't feel like reading the newspaper, he didn't feel like doing anything, and yet nevertheless he went on sleeping and eating, eating and sleeping out of nothing but fear.

According to the New York section of the *Sing Tao Daily*, a government official named Robert Moses had just died at the age of

ninety-two. The newspaper said he'd been in decline for a much longer period—had suffered from deafness for years but refused to use
a hearing aid, in complete denial about his deterioration. That man
Moses was just like the red emperor, Koon Lai thought. Hiding his
many ailments, Mao had ruled far longer than he was fit. And so had
his son Richard, it occurred to Koon Lai, when he had long ago lost
his authority to command. Dun Ho refused to hear the doctors who
said he was too old to smoke a pack of cigarettes a day and eat bacon
for breakfast and duck blood for lunch. And the fifty-four-year-old
looked bad for his age: semi-bald with side hair, hands dry and
splotchy, belly overhanging his pants. He still yelled at Foon Wah,
but needed her help clipping his toenails. At least he had accepted
the job at Wo Hop.

To make up for his own uselessness and his son's foolishness,
Koon Lai did what he could to lighten Foon Wah's burden. He ate
less, reused the same glassware, washed his underwear by hand. Yet
with neither his ancestors nor his descendants in reach, he had no
purpose. It might have been different if they had kept the restaurant
open. Or earlier: if he had beaten the restlessness out of his son.
Sometimes, Koon Lai felt himself to blame for the stillness in their
house. Rendered immobile by regret, he would sit on the couch for
hours, unable to lift a limb.

Foon Wah finished her cereal, then drank the remaining Lactaid
milk. She pulled a section of the *Sing Tao Daily* toward herself.

"The Chinese Citizens Association is arranging a trip to China,"
she said again, in case Koon Lai hadn't heard. "One thousand dollars."

"You go," he said, holding the paper over his face so that she
wouldn't see his expression. "I am too old. You go, Foon Wah."

"Okay," she said, playing along. "One day, I'll go."

That autumn, Koon Lai dragged a stool to the middle of his bedroom
and looped a belt around his neck.

It was how his father-in-law had taken his life. The Americans
shot their brains out and the Japanese sliced open their guts, but not

so with the Chinese. They believed in tidy suicides. Hanging was preferable because it did not allow the opportunity to scream for help.

Before ascending the stool, he stripped the bed himself, though his bad leg ached as he bent over to tug the fitted sheet from its corners. Then he packed his clothes into the same maroon suitcase that he'd brought over from Canton in 1923. Perhaps Foon Wah would find somewhere to donate them. He drew up a will that left his remaining savings to Richard and Foon Wah, and he threw his dentures, toothbrush, worn-out slippers, and the wrappers of three dried plums into the waste bin. Only then did he dress himself in his best trousers, painfully ascend, tie himself to the overhead fan, and jump.

Foon Wah discovered him the next morning. She had come upstairs to see why he was late for breakfast, then opened the door and found the light off and the shades still pulled. The room was sparsely furnished with a red rug, a mahogany chest, and an alarm clock with the numbers blinking. Perhaps it was Daylight Savings Day already, and she had forgotten.

In the gloom, she saw the old suitcase, the folded bedsheets. For a moment, she worried he had lost his mind and gone out into the cold morning without telling her. It took her several seconds to realize Koon Lai was there—he was such a small, thin man that, dangling in the middle of the dark room, he looked like nothing more than a shadow of the coat stand.

With a cry, she fell to her knees.

In the *Sing Tao Daily*, they posted an obituary and an invitation to the funeral and told no one outside the immediate family that it had been a suicide. "Heart attack," they would say if someone asked.

Though he had long stopped taking the train to Chinatown for the association meetings, Koon Lai still had many friends. They hobbled over to the Wah Wing Sang Funeral Home on Mulberry Street, leaning on the arms of their sons, most of them shriveled and hard of hearing, with thinning hair or no hair. They told Richard and Foon Wah that Koon Lai had been the most outstanding man of his generation, that he had helped them secure the loan with which they had launched their business or procured the papers to bring over their wives and children. Richard thanked each one of them in Toisanese with his hands pressed together in the old way.

Jennifer, Julie, and Jackie drove in from the suburbs with their husbands. Jason appeared on foot, about twenty minutes late. They'd had trouble contacting him at first—the phone number he'd provided was no longer in service—but thankfully he'd called from a pay phone the day before the funeral. He arrived wearing a black T-shirt and skinny jeans, and Foon Wah thought he looked more haggard and cadaverous than the man in the coffin. His hair reached his waist, and his legs moved with a tight suaveness that Foon Wah feared meant he'd been with many women. Richard looked their son up and down, scrunching his nose at the skunk smell.

"You're late," he said. "Maybe you should have visited when your grandfather was still alive."

Foon Wah grabbed Jason's arm before he could walk out.

Some families spent a fortune to send bones to China for burial, but Koon Lai had indicated in his will that this would be unnecessary. He'd already purchased a plot for himself at a cemetery in Ridgewood, Queens. A procession of funeral cars crossed the Manhattan Bridge and took Atlantic Avenue to the city's eastern end. Then the guests followed the undertaker up a muddy path between two rows of tombstones to the hole in the frosted earth where Koon Lai was to be deposited.

"It's like a diorama of the city," Richard grumbled in English—to whom exactly, Foon Wah wasn't sure. "The Puerto Ricans get the squares down by the street, the bak gui are on the mountain with giant headstones, and the Chinese? The Chinese get the porta potties." He lined up next to Foon Wah in the first row of mourners at the edge of the burial pit and, shivering, accepted the flowers handed to him by the undertaker's assistant. "My dad. Still and always a cheapskate."

"Shut up," Foon Wah snapped in English.

Richard swallowed. He bent over and peered six feet down at his father's casket.

They left Koon Lai in the earth and went back to Chinatown to eat, but at the banquet hall, Foon Wah ordered tripe stew, forgetting Koon Lai would not be there to enjoy it. And when they returned home, she withdrew an extra hanger from the closet for Koon Lai's coat. It took the rest of winter to shed all the other habits, like heating his morning jook and his afternoon cha or looking out the window to assess whether he could take a walk.

She ruminated. Wondered whether she could have prevented it. Believed she could have tried harder. She should have insisted Richard drive his father to the association so he could see how much he was valued there. Or paid for Koon Lai's ticket back to China. Like his walks, it would have forced him out of his head, into the world, so that he could witness the growth and progress finally happening in his country after so many years of starvation and bloodshed.

She busied herself preparing for the Ting Ming holiday—*Cemetery Day*, she renamed it for her children, since they had forgotten so much Toisanese over the years. The second weekend of April, she insisted the entire family drive out to Ridgewood to take offerings to Koon Lai and pay their respects. They gathered at the Cypress Hills Cemetery, and Foon Wah laid out bowls of boiled chicken, pork, and sugared gelatin on a blanket in front of the grave. She directed Jason to dig holes for the potted flowers and taught her daughters how to light a fire in the metal bucket for the burning of fake money.

It was windy that morning. They watched the fake money crackling, curling, and withering into black ash. Pieces of gold paper occasionally rose out of the can and fluttered across the cemetery. The wind swept them in Foon Wah's direction; they kept smacking her midriff. She caught them against her belly and redelivered them to the fire pail.

"He wants to share with you, Ma," Jennifer said.

Foon Wah nodded, smiling, and her daughters watched as tears minnowed down her cheeks.

SADIE

Milk jugs filled with gasoline. That's what Mr. William had said. And that's what the cops had discovered in the rubble at 2100 Marcy Place in the Bronx, according to a news article from 1973.

Sadie had been hunting for a name, a human being. She needed to know who had paid Mr. William to burn the buildings. Yet instead of a name, she was developing an intricate spiderweb of addresses, of which 78 Livonia Avenue was just one node. Her web was a morass of defunct real estate entities, LLCs, false business addresses, and dead people. A man named Ethan Griffiths was listed on a loan taken out by 78 Livonia Avenue LLC, and Griffiths was loosely connected to a number of other men and properties, including several in the Bronx. She had visited the Fire Department Public Records Unit again and discovered that five of the Bronx buildings in her web had perished in fires.

She researched Ethan Griffiths and some of the other names. Hard to figure out who they were, since they'd died years earlier, though quite a few appeared to have worked in real estate. One business address kept repeating: 1058 Avenue Y, in South Brooklyn. She noticed the men did not share an ethnicity—their surnames were Anglo-Saxon, German, Jewish, Italian, Irish. This had not been a mob family, and this had not been one borough's secret—the operation had blanketed New York.

In the archives of *The Village Voice*, she read about arson rings. Landlords would over-insure their properties and throw kickbacks to an insurance adjuster. After a landlord commissioned a "torch" to burn a building, the adjuster would assess the damages in the owner's favor. Sadie searched for a database with fire insurance application records, but neither the Fire Department nor the Department of Finance had kept one.

There was only one door left: visit the nodes in person.

In May, she took the subway to 1058 Avenue Y in Sheepshead Bay. It was only a few miles from Coney Island, ocean salt on the breeze, and it looked almost suburban, a world apart from Brownsville's dense NYCHA complexes and the brownstones of Park Slope.

Approaching the address, Sadie found herself standing outside a trim yellow townhouse. According to the silver plaque on the door, 1058 Avenue Y was a children's dentist office. She frowned. But she had come all this way, and she had to find out what she could.

Sadie rang the doorbell. She was buzzed into a waiting room with toys all over the floor and a wallpaper of pink and blue teddy bears. A few families—mostly Eastern European, one Chinese—awaited their appointments, their toddlers crawling on the rug.

"Are you sixteen?" the receptionist asked, glancing at Sadie. "Dr. Lipschutz only sees patients under sixteen."

"Dr. Lipschutz," Sadie repeated. *Edward Lipschutz!* That was one of the names from the web! "Uh, is he available to speak between patients? Briefly?"

"His schedule is packed today. Is there something I can help you with?"

Sadie glanced over her shoulder. One toddler pushed a train along a wood track. Another tapped at a rainbow xylophone.

"What about Mr. Griffiths," Sadie asked. "Is Mr. Griffiths available?"

"Mr. Griffiths?" A look of surprise flickered across the woman's

face. "Hold on." She stood up and crossed to an inner door, then disappeared.

The woman returned.

"If you're looking for Mark, I'm sorry to tell you, but he passed
away last September."

"Oh, I'm so sorry to hear that," Sadie said, exaggerating her dis-
tress, though she couldn't recall the name Mark. Was Mark related
to Ethan Griffiths? She had promised herself not to lie to sources
anymore, but this wasn't even a source—this was just someone in
the way of a source.

"That's terrible news about Ethan." *Fuck.* "I mean Mark."

The woman tilted her head.

"Anyway, do you think I can wish the family condolences? My
parents were . . . friends with Mark."

Sadie could tell the lady wasn't convinced.

"What's your name?" she finally said, reaching for a notepad.

"Sadie . . . Sadie Wong."

"I'll tell Aaron you stopped by," the woman replied, and she
turned back to her computer to indicate the conversation was over.

Sadie made for the door and hurried across the street. Sitting on
the steps of another townhouse, she opened her laptop, pulled up
ACRIS, and entered "Mark Griffiths" into the search database. One
property came up, a home just a couple of miles away. It appeared
the property had been transferred from Mark Griffiths to Aaron Griffiths earlier that year. Also, she found an obituary she hadn't seen
before, for Ethan Griffiths—"survived by two sons, Mark and Baine,
and one grandson, Aaron," it said.

This, she concluded, was how it broke down:

1. Ethan Griffiths had been involved in 78 Livonia Avenue
   LLC. Ethan was dead.
2. Ethan had a son, Mark. Mark, the lady had said, was dead.
3. Mark had a son, Aaron. Aaron was on the deed for 9090
   Eighty-Fourth Street.

"That's where I'm going on my treasure hunt!" Sadie muttered to herself.

She rode the B1 to Dyker Heights, famous for its McMansions—at least that's what her father had always called them. When she was small, her father had taken her there in the winter to see the gargantuan Christmas decorations: homes lit up like Disney castles, their yards stuffed with flocks of lighted reindeers and human-size nutcracker soldiers. In December, it was hard to believe anyone could actually live in those homes, but in spring they had a neat austerity that seemed to warn the passersby not to gawk, and certainly not to trespass.

She did so anyway—unlocked the bolt and walked right up the steps to 9090 Eighty-Fourth Street, then turned on her Olympus recorder. It was a stone-clad house with a large patio and a border of sturdy evergreen bushes. A minute after she rang the bell, a woman cracked the door. She was middle-aged and heavily made-up.

"Hi. Is Aaron Griffiths home?" Sadie asked.

"May I ask what business you have with him?"

The woman seemed suspicious from the start.

"I would love to speak with Aaron about 78 Livonia Avenue," Sadie said.

"Who are you?"

"I'm . . ." She was tempted to lie again, but feared compromising the integrity of the audio recording.

"I believe my grandfather was a business partner of Ethan Griffiths's."

At that, the lady was already closing the door. "Not interested," she said.

Sadie put her hand against the finished wood. The woman raised her eyebrows.

"I know you're not interested but . . ."

"Let go of the door." The woman slammed it shut.

Sadie wondered what she was supposed to do now. Hoping to map the route to another spot on her web, she reached into her back pocket, only to discover her iPhone was dead.

"Damn it."

At that moment, a black SUV drifted down the street, and the automated gate of the Griffiths house opened to admit it. The car rolled into the yard, parking in the driveway to the left of the house. Sadie shoved the dead phone back into her jeans.

"Can I help you?" a man said, lowering the window.

A voice fit for radio, clean of origin.

"Are you Aaron?" she asked as she approached. "I was wondering if you might have a moment to talk about a few properties." He was a forty-something, clean-shaven white man in a navy-blue suit and tie, his hair slicked back with pomade—handsome in a '90s razor commercial type of way.

"Who do you represent?"

"I think my grandfather sold your . . . your grandfather some property. Maybe you know his name. Richard Wong?"

"No, I don't know that name," he said, and he glanced at his Rolex. "And it's been a long day, so."

He closed the window, emerged from the car, and, avoiding her eyes, headed toward the front steps.

She scrambled to think of something to catch his attention.

"Do you know about the arson ring?" she called out. "Our grandfathers were part of an arson ring. I thought you might want to know about it."

He turned to her again, his jaw tensed, and she thought she saw a glint of fear in his eyes.

"Are you a high school student?"

"I'm twenty-four."

"Is this some kind of practical joke?"

"No!"

"Where's the hidden camera?"

"I'm being serious."

"I don't know what you're talking about." He shook his head with repugnance, and opened the front door with his keys.

"Well," she said, following him up the steps. "Shouldn't I at least tell you—"

"You're trespassing. Get off my property or I'm calling the police."
He let himself in.

"Please!" She darted after him, propping the door open with her hand. "I know it's disturbing, but we really need to talk about this."

He did not slam the door in her face like the lady had, and she found herself stumbling into the front room.

She had never done this before—physically trespassed inside a house. At least Tyrell had held the door open.

The fineness of his McMansion chilled her. High ceilings, lacquered wood floors, mahogany stairs, carved balusters, Persian rugs, and cold enough to warrant a sweater.

He marched into another room. The lady—his wife or mother, Sadie wasn't sure—watched in horror from the stairs.

"If your grandfather was Ethan Griffiths," Sadie called after him, "he might know about these two properties that my grandfather sold in Brownsville to an entity called 78 Livonia LLC. All I want to do is work with you to figure out what—"

He had come back with his jacket off, his small eyes boring into her, and a gun.

"What the fuck?"

He was pointing it at her from about ten feet away. "Get out of my house."

"Oh my god," she cried, scooting toward the door. She was staring at the gun in his hands, and then she was deep within her head, watching a film: of herself staring at the gun in his hands. "What the literal fuck!"

"I'm not trying to hurt you," he said coolly. "You're trespassing, and under the Castle Law, it's legal to protect my property."

She stumbled down the stoop, grappled with the lock on the metal gate, and ran down the block. He had the semiautomatic pointed at her until she'd rounded the corner.

"What the literal, literal fuck!" she gasped once he was out of sight. She leaned her back against someone else's wall and tried to take a deep breath. Tears came to her eyes. She slid down to the concrete.

"What the fuck! Oh my god!"

She was only twenty-four. She wanted to be home in the arms of her mother. Her mother who loved her, despite all her tempestuousness.

She struggled to her feet and tried to remember the way home.

"Fuck!" she cried to the sky, laughing, as she walked toward the nearest subway station. "Oh my god!"

All the way home, she relived the experience. She saw the moment Aaron Griffiths had pointed the gun. The amber glow of the wood floors. The woman on the staircase. Swirled in these thoughts, she almost missed her stop on the F.

And yet, after she'd spent the evening cuddling with her mother, after she'd eaten her father's rice cakes and lap chiang, she saw her trip to South Brooklyn had been, from journalistic standards at least, a failure.

Sadie stayed up till four a.m. that night, writing down what she did know. She composed an article, though one poorly written and full of holes and question marks.

Then she thought about the draft email that had been sitting in her account for weeks, one she hadn't had the bravery to finish. She added a few more lines to the email, attached the unfinished article, and, holding her breath, hit the send button.

LINA

The school's auditorium was so stuffy it was like breathing through a sponge. They had gathered there on a sweltering Saturday in July to find out who had won the Request for Proposal for the development of the Livonia Avenue lot. In the front row sat the deputy mayor of housing and economic development with two of her commissioners. The community board members were assembled behind them, along with Jean Bernard and his associates. Lina sat in the back among about twenty Brownsville residents.

All the middle rows of the auditorium remained empty, and this, to Lina, signified that once again the mayor's team had failed to conduct sufficient outreach. She'd seen her people on the walk over. Everyone was out on the basketball courts and in the playgrounds eating Klondike bars with no idea what was about to go down at Teachers Preparatory High.

An image appeared on the screen above the deputy mayor, but it was not from their community land trust's RFP submission. With smiling brown people strolling on the sidewalk, it was a picturesque sketch of an off-white building bordered by birch trees. In the left-hand corner: the Bernard & Company logo.

"This will be upzoned to R7, allowing for fifty-three units of below-market housing—that's one hundred percent *affordable housing*—along with much-needed community facility space on the ground floor," explained the commissioner of the Department of Housing Preservation and Development.

The Bernard & Company group applauded. Lina's Wesley Price Community Land Trust activists cursed under their breaths and crossed their arms. Tyrell sighed, and Lina heard the creak of his wooden auditorium chair as he shifted restlessly.

But of course, the city would never hand them their land on a silver platter. The world had never worked that way.

"Now just to be clear, this project isn't fully approved yet," the commissioner said. "It will first have to go through the *extensive* democratic vetting process known as ULURP—the Uniform Land Use Review Procedure."

Someone shouted from the back row. "What the hell is that?"

"ULURP. ULURP will give your community board, the borough president, the City Planning Commission, and finally, the city council an opportunity to weigh in and vote on the project. But we are really confident about the proposal, given our city's true need for affordable housing . . ."

"Affordable to who?" Tyrell bellowed, his hands cupped on either side of his mouth, his voice echoing throughout the auditorium.

Smiling, the deputy mayor asked the HPD commissioner to hand over the mic.

"This is a fantastic question," said the deputy mayor. She was young, blond, and pretty: Jennifer Aniston with her hair in a high bun. She clicked to a new slide, and an elaborate chart appeared on the screen.

Units Per AMI Level	2–4 Person Household
30% AMI—10%	($17,300–$25,900)
40% AMI—15%	($25,900–$34,500)
50% AMI—15%	($34,500–$43,200)
60% AMI—40%	($43,200–$51,800)
80% AMI—20%	($60,400–$69,000)

The residents craned their necks toward the screen, trying to make sense of all those numbers. Lina had studied up on the "Area Median Income" stuff about ten years earlier—AMI referred to the median income of the metropolitan area—but she knew the majority of community members had never been taught the jargon. Her younger neighbor José chuckled and shook his head.

"I should've stayed in school," he muttered, and Lina, feeling a sudden wave of protectiveness, grabbed his forearm.

"They don't teach this in high school."

"What's all that mean?" Ms. Dorothy called out, her lazy eye and "awake" eye, for that's what she called them, pointing in two directions. The Alabaman was one of Lina's biggest supporters and served as vice president of the CLT board.

Aniston explained the chart, her voice pitched high like she was speaking to children. "Every single unit—I repeat, *every single unit*—will be *affordable* housing. And affordable to a range of incomes, but *all* below market rate."

What she didn't say, Lina thought, was that almost a third of Brownsville's residents made less than $15,000 a year—and would be too poor to qualify for the majority of these so-called "affordable" units.

Yet Lina's biggest problem wasn't with who might be moving into the building. It was the fact that outsiders still made all the decisions.

"A question!"

It was the booming voice of Mr. Trevor, head of Trevor LDC, the minority-owned development company that Lina had intended to partner with.

"Yes, yes, you, sir, in the back." The HPD commissioner nodded.

"This was supposed to be the Wesley Price Community Land Trust Cultural Center," Mr. Trevor proclaimed, his voice soaring as if he were the one with the mic, though he was only standing with his arms crossed. "This was supposed to be land owned by and for the community, and built up by community residents—not by Bernard and Company."

"And we don't need more housing here!" yelled Ms. Freda, the gardener on the CLT board. "We need green space and cultural enrichment for the kids in this neighborhood!"

"Thank you for your questions. We agree that—"

"We need developers from the community hiring workers from the community!"

"Okay. Let me address everybody's questions." The commissioner's voice quivered, and Lina could see he was already getting flustered. He needed Aniston to run the show. But Aniston had walked off the stage, was whispering with Mr. Bernard.

"Let me—let me just address everybody's questions," the commissioner attempted again. "The Wesley Price Community Land Trust team did submit a very strong proposal, but ultimately there were a range of factors that led the RFP selection team to move forward with the Bernard and Company proposal. But we're glad to say there's a lot of similarities between these two visions."

"Hell no." It was Ms. Keesha Jones, the community land trust secretary. She was a young woman, but looked exhausted as she rose to her feet. "Y'all just come in here and tell us what to do and then y'all leave. I was at every single community meeting. Did you listen to us, or did you just come up with your own thing and pretend you were listening to us?"

"You're not listening to *them*," retorted a voice from the front of the hall. It was Mrs. Jameson, who, a whole year since their argument at the precinct, still considered Lina her enemy. "You want answers to your questions, you have to give the city people a chance to talk."

"Oh Lord," Lina said under her breath, and as a cacophony of new voices joined the fray, she suppressed a laugh. The commissioner tried to speak, then gave up and, wiping the sweat off his brow with a kerchief, handed the mic to Aniston, who also struggled to gain the crowd's attention.

Lina took it all in, and the warring factions summoned up her memories of the occupation at the board of education in '66. She'd had all the energy in the world at twenty-two—had even taken the mic herself. She did not feel motivated to speak now as she had then, but she still prized the crowd's resistance. Gathering feeling and strength, the people empowered one another. Sometimes they spoke in unison, and sometimes they voiced multiple perspectives. Either way, it was better than slicing everyone up, seating them at little tables, and forcing them to identify neighborhood "assets."

"Remember," Aniston said. "Nothing is final yet."

A half-truth, Lina thought. The community board's vote was nonbinding. Ultimately, it was the City Planning Commission and the city council's vote that mattered—and even if the residents protested for the rest of the year, there was only a small chance these bodies would say no to one of the mayor's shiny projects.

She felt a hand on her shoulder.

"I'm sorry," Tyrell whispered, shaking his head. "This was our land."

"This is the new Brooklyn," she replied.

Back in the day, the city had worked with the churches and with the grassroots organizations. Now, luxury developers were having a grand old time in Bed-Stuy and East New York, and the city preferred them as partners. She knew this, and she felt almost angry with herself for participating at all, for granting legitimacy to a contest in which she'd been sure to lose.

"I guess it's time to get organizing," Tyrell said when they got to the sidewalk, clapping his hands. "Get the community out at some of these hearings."

To be young, she thought. Young and inexhaustible. She looked away from him.

"ULURP's a sham," she muttered. "It won't matter if the community board votes no. As long as the city council wants it, they'll pass the project."

"Damn." Standing with his hands on his hips, he waited for her to say something more.

"So, Ms. Lina, what do we do?"

But she didn't have an answer.

"My knees are killing me and I gotta lie down."

She took hold of her cane and trudged ahead.

At three a.m., she gave up on sleep and slumped into the living room chair. She wrapped herself in her mother's crocheted blanket and stared at the mural—at that big frizzy head with the lopsided beret. Little Lina in leather.

A few months after Nellie took her life, Lina had questioned the value of her own existence. This was once the shock had begun to dissipate, and she'd found herself back in her body, in her mother's bed, with two bowls of arroz con dulce growing cold on the bedside table.

But as always, there was no privacy in her mother's house, and a lot of prayer. And knowing her well, her mother enlisted not only Sofia, Danny, and Cindy, but also Father Powis and Reverend Oliver and Nick Parson, and even the Sunday school teacher from San Juan whom her mother pitied because he'd been crushing on Lina for two decades—anyone who could give Lina a reason to heal, *to live*.

An idea suddenly came to the arthritic Lina in the chair. A crazy idea, crazy as some of young Lina's crazy ideas. After the fire, she had promised herself to do all things by the book, to never get the courts involved or put anyone at risk again. But here she was, seventy-one years old, neck stiff and shoulders aching, and hatching a plan that could get her put away.

At six a.m., she shook off the crazy idea, rose and ate her oatmeal, emptied the leak bucket under the sink, and sat down at the Dell monitor as usual.

But she couldn't take it any longer.

"None of this shit!" she shouted at the screen. She couldn't just sit there, waiting around for this email or that email, feeling like she was already dead herself.

She would have to be crazy.

She put on gardening gloves, a raincoat, and rain boots to protect herself. Then she went down to the yard keeper's supply closet to borrow the handheld electric grass trimmer, a pair of large wire clippers, and several heavy-duty garbage bags. The grass of Brownsville Houses could go one day without a trimming, and NYCHA had plenty of garbage bags to spare.

Appropriating the grass trimmer as a cane, Lina marched the half mile down Livonia to the lot. Once she'd arrived, she trimmed around the sidewalk—there were ferns growing in the cement cracks—and then used the wire clippers to cut a hole in the fence large enough to climb through.

Real old school, she thought. They could definitely throw her in a cell at the Seventy-Third.

Half an hour later, however, Lina had trimmed a patch of the lot, and no one had come to bother her but the block cat. When a deli down the street opened, she left the lot and bought the cat a pack of turkey cold cuts, then sat down on a stoop across the street.

"Hermanita," she whispered as the cat nibbled on the turkey. "Are you Miss Freedom? Or are you Miss Freedom's grandbaby?"

She thought about what was next. After trimming, she'd need to bag all the trash—old beer cans, chunks of Styrofoam packaging, pizza plates. There were so many hypodermic needles, you'd think they grew on the trees. Yet she was already fatigued. The work was difficult for her legs, and being in that space jerked her back to those times. When the train passed by, she thought about those nights when she'd fallen asleep to its midnight rumble. The smell of soy sauce in the walls. And of course, Grandma, in the building next door, sitting all day at her window. After her brother died in the fire, she'd lived only a few more months.

In the nineties, Lina had tried a couple of healing regimens to help with the nightmares. She'd seen an acupuncturist, but without much result. She'd visited a psychologist who specialized in trauma and accepted patients on a sliding scale—a white man. He had told her it was "time to move on from your past," and she didn't appreciate hearing those words out of his mouth.

It always seemed to Lina that there were two types of people in

America: the people who forgot and the people who remembered. The forgetting ones didn't dare recall the things they'd done to others' bodies. They amputated the memory, and their bodies appeared healthy and fit, at least to others. They couldn't tell their children, so their children, too, inherited the amnesia. These children were the ones who faced forward, who climbed the fastest, who thought they could escape history. Born from denial, they graduated into the heights of power.

The children of the remembering remained weighted. They bore the memory of centuries.

So no, she hadn't healed. Her body refused. And it seemed to her that if she let herself heal, the truth would cease to exist. After all, why had Sadie Chin come after her? Because the story of the fire lived only in the mouths of its victims.

Lina stood up again and resumed trimming the yard. Her knees begged her to give up the enterprise altogether, to go home and never get up from her chair—but to hell with her knees, because she had work to do. This was just the start, and the following week, she'd find a mower. She'd get rid of that mini fridge and the two car tires in the back right corner. After that, she'd buy planters for vegetables. And how about some solar panels! Why not bring Brownsville into the future, make it the greenest neighborhood in all of New York City?

Even as she was getting excited, she reminded herself that she was crazy, and that she had to do this alone. That way, she alone would suffer any negative consequences. This would be her one-woman show, her resistance art, and even if they locked her up and bulldozed the garden for the Bernard & Company development, at least they would have to crush what she'd made with her own hands.

"Lock up who?"

At the sound of the voice, Lina nearly had a heart attack. She turned around and found Tyrell standing outside the metal fence.

"Ty!" she yelped, gripping her chest. "How you knew I was here?"

"Well." He took a deep breath. "It's a long story. When I got up this morning, I decided to check on you. And you didn't answer your door. So I thought about what you'd want me to do, and I thought you'd want me to eat breakfast. So I went out and got a bacon, egg, and cheese. But that bacon, egg, and cheese didn't come with enough ketchup, and like usual, Tima finished the ketchup last week and didn't bother to tell no one. So I went to the deli, and on my way home, I ran into Floyd. And Floyd told me he saw you this morning. He said you stole the grass clipper and went down Livonia."

"The man is a snitch," Lina replied, but she was chuckling as she shook her head. She sat on the mini fridge, depleted by the worsening heat.

"So who's getting locked up?" He raised his eyebrow, gripping the hexagons of the wire fence.

"Me! Was I talking to myself? I guess I'm losing my marbles."

"Whatcha doing here at eight o'clock in the morning?"

"What does it look like I'm doing?"

Tyrell shook his head in disbelief, but instead of abandoning her to her obsession, the skinny kid ducked through the hole she'd cut in the fence.

"Don't come in here!"

He sauntered over, kicking the trash and needles out of his way.

"You think I'm leaving you here by yourself so those cops can come lock you up, huh?"

She was about to make a clever retort, but then she thought about what he'd said and had to smile.

Tyrell had turned around.

"Hey Melvin!" he bellowed. "Melvin!"

She realized then that Melvin was on the other side of the street, squinting toward the lot as he stumbled along. He was still wearing that Mickey Mouse T-shirt along with shoes three sizes too big for him.

"I see you, man!" Melvin called back, and he crossed the street toward them.

"Melvin, how you been?"

Melvin nodded at Tyrell and leaned his forehead against the wire fence. "You got a dollar to help me get some pizza tonight?"

"You give me a hand with this trash for a few hours," Tyrell said, pointing to the heavy-duty garbage bags, "I'll pay you fifty."

"Fifty cents?" Melvin asked.

"Fifty bucks."

"Tyrell!" Lina cried.

"No sweat. Yesterday was payday," Tyrell whispered back.

"No, nuh-uh." Lina raised herself off the mini fridge and grabbed Tyrell's arm. "I ain't letting no one get hurt or arrested. I can't deal with that no more."

"No one said me or Melvin had to. What we do with our time is our business," Tyrell replied. "At least I employ the neighborhood. At union wages too."

Over the next hour, Melvin and Tyrell filled up three heavy-duty garbage bags with junk. Lina wanted to tear the implements out of their hands, but she was feeling dizzy from the heat, her limbs swollen and rigid as tree trunks. She sat back down on the rusted top of the mini fridge, baffled by her frailty. Back in the '70s, everyone had written zines about sweat equity, but had any of them considered what they would do when they were all old and gray and just too damn tired?

"Ms. Lina, you had a good idea," Tyrell said as he trimmed the rest of the lot. "But we need to get eyes on this site. Let's make a press release, send it out to the New York *Daily News, Our Time Press*, to Brian at *New Gotham.* And we follow our plan, at least the garden part. Get Ms. Freda and the others to work their magic. Then we get the whole community out here for a big rally. Take the 3 train, march to city hall."

"We can't involve the whole community," she replied. "There are people in this community on parole. Kids one arrest away from Sing Sing. They can lock me up, it don't matter—I'm gonna die soon anyway."

"We'll be careful. You know I always am," he insisted, and he crouched in front of her and fixed her with a look. "Come on, Ms. Lina, listen to me this time, all right? How you gonna sustain a community land trust without the community involved? You taught me that. We got to reach as many people as possible."

She answered with a snort and looked away. "Last time I listened to you, I was talking to that fraud Sadie Chin."

"Yeah." Tyrell poked the side of his cheek with his tongue. "And that was my bad."

"'Cause you had the hots for her."

"I'm sorry."

They laughed, but there was enough sense to his words that when he and Melvin took a lunch break, she was still thinking about the idea.

Eventually, nature called, and with a groan she raised herself to her feet and went down Livonia to the church to use the women's room. On her way back, she noticed two boys she knew from Brownsville Houses hollering curses up at a second-floor apartment in Marcus Garvey Village.

"What y'all doing?"

"Nothing." They shifted their eyes to the sidewalk.

"Nothing? I can hear y'all down the block and you telling me you doing nothing?"

"We . . . chilling." They shrugged and, always fidgety, the boy named Kenny kicked a beer can across the street.

"Kenny, you still got beef with that Marcus Garvey kid?"

"Me? Nah."

"Boys, I got something better for you to be doing."

She took them down the avenue to the hardware store and asked them to pick out two colors of paint and a block of wood, promising pay worth their time if they made a sign for the garden.

An hour later, the boys had applied a layer of blue to the board, and Tyrell and Melvin had removed every scrap of trash from the lot.

"This is starting to look like a real nice slab of real estate," Lina declared. "A nice beef steak. I know the mayor would love to throw it to his hungry dogs!"

But in all honesty, she was feeling good. It was the first time since the Freedom School that she'd gotten her hands so dirty.

"This is what I want you to write," Lina said, leaning over next to the boys. She noticed their knees were covered in paint and hoped their parents wouldn't be angry. "Wesley Price Community Land Trust. I'm going to help you spell it."

"W-E-S-L-E-Y," the other boy, Jeremiah, interjected.

"That's good, Jeremiah."

"It's like Wesley Gibson from the game *Wanted: Weapons of Fate*," he said.

"Wait! You naming the garden after Wesley Gibson?" Kenny exclaimed, looking up at Lina.

"Let's put the *W* here!" Jeremiah directed. The two boys embarked on the assignment.

There was something about Jeremiah's precision that reminded her of Tyrell. She hoped Jeremiah would be the kind of man to eat his yogurt, as she probably wouldn't be around to ensure he did.

Two weeks later, someone reported the break in the fence to 311, and Lina returned to the lot to find the fence patched, the boys' sign confiscated, and a bunch of city notices warning that fines would be assessed for future break-ins. She busted her way back in, and that afternoon a team of Brownsville's best gardeners arrived to help her prepare the soil. Some time later, the city repaired the fence again, threatening fines of an even higher amount if the trespasser was caught in the act, and Lina decided to buy her own wire cutters. She couldn't have Floyd, the Brownsville Houses janitor, snitching to the Seventy-Third.

Her gardeners were teaching her things. Funny how one could be seventy-one years old and still have so much to learn. Ms. Freda had caught Lina pulling out the dandelions—she said they had medicinal properties and could be harvested later.

"Don't you worry, 'cause those dandelions have deep roots," Ms.

Freda had reassured her. "When you pull them out at the top, you ain't getting rid of the taproot."

Ms. Freda ate her own plants and had much to teach others about health and wellness. She helped Lina start her own collard greens patch, and instructed her to also leave alone the mycelia, the worms, and the ants. Over time, Lina realized that maybe the lot hadn't been abandoned all those years. It was home to fellow creatures, and they'd been taking care of her land all that time—their land, our land, *the* land. She was trying to adjust the way she spoke about it, trying not to sound so possessive. Ms. Freda was part Cherokee and insisted they honor New York's Indigenous history.

"This land don't belong to Black folk," Ms. Freda would often remind Lina. "Not the Puerto Ricans, not the Jewish, not the Dutch. This land belongs to no one."

"I know, Ms. Freda," Lina would say. "This was Lenape land."

"But this ain't Lenape land either, Ms. Lina. The Native people didn't think about land like that. Nobody owned it. Land can't be owned, just like humans can't be owned."

It wasn't the first time Lina had heard that ownership was a European concept, invented to divide and conquer, to enrich the few at the expense of the masses, but it made her chuckle to think how many years she'd expended playing tug-of-war over a made-up thing. How many years spent trying to convince Richard Wong, then the city, to turn over the deed.

She respected the dandelions for their resilience. If she and her people in the 'Ville could be like dandelions, it wouldn't matter how many times they had to climb back from death. They'd keep on. She admired the mycelium fungi, too, the way they held together all the plants under the soil, and also the ants—how they worked in tandem. She took inspiration from these creatures, the reminder that she wasn't meant to work alone. Guilt could do that to a person, make you too self-reliant, afraid of asking others for anything, terrified of letting them down.

In September, she organized a community barbecue in the lot. A crazy barbecue—no permits, no license. Mr. Trevor brought his grill set from home, and Lina purchased all the hot dogs at the Associated. Tyrell invited everyone in the neighborhood, and all the members of BYTE came, along with residents of each NYCHA complex in Brownsville. Ms. Freda led the teenagers around the garden and gave them herbs to put on their tongues. Ricky, Lina's downstairs neighbor, showed up mid-smoke, and Lina promptly took the Newport loosie from his mouth and ground it into the dirt.

After everyone had helped themselves to the food, Lina sat on a plastic chair and watched her beautiful people. Now that there'd been articles about her lot in the *Brooklyn Eagle* and *Our Time Press*, she was less nervous about the police. It would reflect badly on the Seventy-Third Precinct and on the mayor's administration if they were to start making arrests. And yet she was still sure that they would lose the lot once the ULURP process finished. She needed to figure out how to explain why it mattered that they had planted a garden, even a temporary one, and come together for the barbecue.

The sun was setting, and Lina, sucking on a sage leaf, remembered how at this time of day, she'd lean out of the windows of the restaurant-slash-apartment-slash-Freedom School to take in all the color. The sky would have the rawness of sushi.

In the fading light, she looked over the party—at Tyrell, José, his aunt, Ms. Dorothy, Greg Trevor—even at Lou, her little brother.

Lou?

Usually she saw him only in her dreams.

The young man was sitting on a crate with the BYTE boys, and he looked exactly as she'd always remembered him: hair buzzed short, the faint traces of a mustache. His elbows were like hers—ashy volcanoes. He smiled at the other boys' jokes and said nothing. He'd always been the shy one.

She'd felt remorseful for so long, but seeing him there, chewing on a hot dog, she felt okay.

— — —

In the end, the police did smell the smoke, and Lina sent her people scattering before the cops had a chance to check IDs. She took responsibility for the trespassing and the party. Offering them lemonade and a few hot dogs, she kissed the cops' asses as much as her dignity allowed. They ate the hot dogs while writing out a ticket for $2,150 in fines.

She came home relieved that nothing worse had happened. In this optimistic mood, Lina put away the leftovers, then sat down at the Dell monitor to check her email.

There were no new messages, the inbox empty except for that one email she'd received several months earlier. She had refused to open it, but she had not deleted it either.

She opened the email, then opened herself to its offering.

THE CHINS

After the undertakers of the Wah Wing Sang Funeral Corporation buried Koon Lai in the earth, Jason left Beloved House. He rented a studio in Inwood where he could read in peace—Hawthorne and Tu Fu, T. S. Eliot and Li Ch'ing Chao. He stocked the fridge with mustard and mayo as well as hoisin, oyster sauce, lap chiang, and every Asian vegetable he could find at the Korean market down the street: the gnome-like baby bok choy, the snakish Chinese eggplant, the rubbery tree-ear fungi.

Each day he thought of Koon Lai, who, he realized, had been only nineteen years old—three years younger than Jason—when he'd crossed the world. Watching himself stir bean curd in a pan, Jason wondered if his hands, squarish and clay red, looked like his yia yia's hands in the Chinatown restaurant where he'd first labored.

Jason had always felt suffocated by the family memory of the old country, and his parents had wielded their sacrifice like some sort of blackmail, but now he felt mostly wonder and regret.

He continued to work at the bookstore on the Upper West Side. When they first met, Rachel Rabinovich was just the girl who frequently browsed in the fiction section without buying anything. She wore large glasses and oversize shirts in faded colors, along with jeans with big holes, the white threads strung across the knees like strings spanning the sound hole of a guitar. Her bell-bottomed legs were somehow both gawky and graceful, like the rickety stilts of flamingos at the Brooklyn Zoo.

When she asked for a job, they became coworkers. They talked about favorite books and childhood pets. She'd grown up in Connecticut with two dogs and two cats, and she'd even owned a horse named Bronco for a couple of years. Her parents, she admitted apologetically, "have way too much money."

He'd once had a turtle who lived in a plastic bin, but in two weeks it had starved itself to death. He'd never ridden a horse, but sometimes as a child he'd worn his Davy Crockett coonskin hat and jumped around with his mother's broom. As he told her these things, he expected her to laugh, but instead she listened intently and pressed him for more details—did the broom-horse have a name?

They shared something in common: a reticence about the hard facts of their lives. They said little about their prior relationships, their families, their educations, or future ambitions. Fantasies, imaginary worlds sufficed. It was only on the second anniversary of Koon Lai's suicide, when Jason broke down crying in the foreign language section and she held him, without even knowing what had broken him, and listened to him, without forcing her opinions on him, that he realized he was in love.

So the white-girl craze continues, he could imagine Macon joking. Macon had moved to the West Coast for medical school, and they had fallen out of touch. And Macon would have been right, of course, but there was also something different this time, something so wholesome, Jason could only compare it to the day he had met Macon, the moment his friend had poked a water gun through the fence of his backyard.

Eventually he decided to invite Rachel out for dinner, and not to the places he usually went—not the two-dollar burrito joint or the Chinese takeout place with the tiled walls that made him think of a public restroom. Someplace nice, like the Italian restaurant on Amsterdam Avenue, where men and women sat at small wooden tables and spoke in whispers, by candlelight, drinking wine and eating crab cakes and arugula salad.

The day he finally asked her, it was pouring rain, and they were walking to the A train under his umbrella. She blushed and took off her glasses, wiping them with the sleeve of her coat. "Yeah. We can go Dutch."

A takeout container floated by in the gutter. He could smell both the wetness of the tree and the firewood burning in somebody's townhouse, and he wished he had a house with a hearth, so that he could take her inside to warm and dry her.

The day of their first date, he wore his best blazer, a collared button-down, and khakis. She arrived in her same torn jeans and wool sweater. A waiter showed them to a table, and Jason examined the menu, trying to recall the Italian words he had taught himself in preparation. They placed their order, but then a strange sculpture of shrimp and mushrooms appeared, something they hadn't asked for. He nearly panicked, but Rachel explained that it was an "amuse-bouche," compliments of the chef, no charge.

At dinner, Rachel told him that her family used to live in the Bronx, that her grandparents had run a clothing store on Grand Concourse, but that her parents had raised her in the suburbs. She'd always wanted to move back to the city that her family had abandoned—to reclaim her New York heritage. Then, at the end of high school, she'd met a musician ten years older than her, and she had followed him to New York, living with him for three years in an unheated Queens apartment until she realized that he hated her— lusted for her, needed her, for months refused to let her leave, but hated everything that made her who she was.

Jason told her about his family. How he had left home, how Beloved House had become a disappointment. Something about the earnestness, the attentiveness of her face, her intertwined hands, kept drawing out his most private thoughts. He could see her absorbing all of it into the wells of her deep-set eyes, as if she might take his contemplations home, lay them between two paper towels like maple leaves, and preserve them for years—for a day when she was gray and wrinkled.

A few weeks later, they saw *Splash* at Cinema Village. She kissed him there, in the glow of the screen, while Daryl Hannah kissed Tom Hanks.

Everything had been rapture after that. When they were not together, he collected anecdotes to relate to her, poems to read to her, insights to share. The new impulse competed with his urge to write. He found that much of what used to make it onto the pages of his notebook he now relayed first to her, and he didn't care as much about his writing as he cared about the continuation of their real, embodied counterpoint.

He felt the world watching and straining to understand. The man who sold the movie tickets at the cinema looked from face to face with interest, then winked; the bead-draped hippies blew them kisses; an old white lady on the A train frowned at them for three stops, but looked away when he returned her glare. When Rachel invited him up to her apartment for the first time, her roommate glanced sideways at Rachel, as if surprised that *he* was the Jason of whom she'd "heard so much about." It irked him.

It was not until the roommate had left and they'd made love in her narrow twin bed that they finally spoke of the subject. As if impelled by the same question, they held up their arms and considered their skin side by side. His arms were tan and hairless; hers, pale and hairy and lined with prominent veins that branched like ivy vines.

"Will your family be upset?" she whispered.

Madly in love, he wrapped his arms around her, pulled her against his chest.

After that, he found himself referring to his Chineseness with growing regularity. With most bak gui, he avoided the subject, not wanting to draw attention to what was already the first thing on their minds. It was different with Rachel. He explained that the Laughing Buddha was not actually Buddha, but the Fat Guy, a different, happy deity who ate too much. He told her how Chinese people were obsessed with giving gifts, how if you give a gift to a Chinese person, it will spiral into a never-ending gift-giving war. Then he took her around Chinatown and introduced her to derng, *sticky rice in bamboo leaves*, and fu ga, *bittermelon*, which—with her love for black coffee and the darkest of chocolates—became her new favorite vegetable. He also warned her not to stick her chopsticks straight into a bowl of rice; he didn't know why this was taboo, but it had been impressed upon him so many times that the sight of erect chopsticks still awoke in him genuine feelings of terror.

During the summer, they walked the city together: the natural woods of Inwood Park, the Ramble Stone Arch, the cobblestoned streets of Sutton Place. Then winter came again, and they huddled together in his room and read aloud Maxine Hong Kingston and Chaim Potok and Shakespeare, their bodies swaddled in down comforters. Or they partook in long conversations about the postmodernists punctuated by syncopated kisses, conversations that swirled across the room until they no longer felt the need for radiators, blankets, or clothes.

He felt it a kind of miracle that their two stories had converged so perfectly. After the endless running away that had been their lives up to that point, they'd each taken sanctuary in the other.

He wanted her for life. A future with Rachel, one they would construct carefully from scratch—that was all he needed. After two years in secrecy, he asked if he could take her home.

Thanksgiving was Richard's favorite holiday. He liked the story: the cowboys devoured Indian corn, the Indians noshed on Pilgrim biscuits, and everyone made a friend. Eat another man's food and suddenly you respect him a little more. A lifetime in the restaurant business, and Richard knew this to be a fact.

It was Richard's favorite holiday because his children respected it as *his* holiday. No matter what was happening at the homes of

the son-in-laws' families, his girls understood they and their grandchildren were required to come home for Thanksgiving. Nothing
brought him more joy than the sight of his grandkids: Stacy and
Emily, Frank and Amanda, Dennis and Patrick.

At fifty-eight, Richard found life at home with Foon Wah was a
monotonous cycle through the same tired rituals they'd invented
decades earlier. The prior year he'd injured his back at Wo Hop and
retired on SSI, and so, for the first time in his life, he wasn't running
around like a chicken with its head cut off, trying to support the
family. His children were old enough to take care of themselves, and
he'd settled with the loan shark and paid off the East Flatbush mortgage. He had left a lot of things to the past, though sometimes he
had to sit in front of the TV for hours to keep himself from vomiting
up the memories.

Yet there was something strangely off about this Thanksgiving.
Foon Wah had been on edge all week. He'd assumed she was anxious
about the cooking, but on Thursday when his daughters' families arrived, his girls behaved strangely, too, disappearing together into the
master bedroom and closing the door. When he barged in and asked
why they had hijacked his room, they exchanged glances. "Uh . . .
planning Christmas presents, Daddy. Don't come in."

He hoped it was some womanly matter best resolved by women.
Returning to his recliner in the living room, Richard let Frank and
Emily scramble up his legs, and he bounced them up and down like
he was one of those coin-operated horses in Sunset Park. Next, he
took Amanda in his arms, blew air into her belly, and let her soar the
sky above his head.

His daughters' husbands plopped down on the couch to watch
the football game. He had acquired three impressive sons: a police officer, a bank manager, and a pharmacist. With these family-
oriented, well-paid jook seing in his house, he could almost put out
of mind the fact that his own son was late.

His girls returned from the bedroom, laughing and seeming at
ease. Julie helped Foon Wah carve the turkey, Jackie gave Emily a

piggyback ride, and Jennifer opened the window so they wouldn't melt from the oven heat.

"Jackie, did you hear Jason is coming with his girlfriend?" asked Jennifer.

When Richard heard her, all sounds fell away: the football game, the children's squeals, the rumble in his belly—everything hushed, like he'd turned the volume low.

"What girlfriend?" he said, but the girls didn't seem to hear him.

"Yeah. They should be here soon," Jackie said.

"Do you know what her name is?" asked Julie.

"I think Rachel?"

"Rachel," repeated Richard.

"Rabinovich," Jennifer added.

"Rachel Rabinovich!" Richard gasped. "That's a Jewish name."

"I think she's bringing rainbow cookies."

"Jason's got a Jewish girlfriend!" he exclaimed, not knowing whether to laugh or to scoff.

"They're serious," said Jennifer. "They're living together."

"They're engaged," added Jackie.

All three of his daughters avoided his eyes.

Amanda, Frank, and Emily disbanded, bored because their grandfather had stopped bouncing. Sammy, the banker son-in-law, handed Richard an an tat and told him to eat it. Reflexively, he lifted the crust to his mouth. The kids attacked Uncle Johnny with the couch pillows; their shrieks filled the silence.

They had known. They had all known and had kept the news from him.

"That son of a bitch."

"Daddy, the kids."

"Son of a bitch!" He pushed back the footrest, rose to his feet, checked his pockets for a cigarette, and crossed the room in the direction of the porch.

"This is Jason, Daddy," said Jackie, touching his elbow. "You know

Jason. You'll never change his mind. And if you say no, you'll never see him again."

Richard grabbed his coat and pushed open the porch door, letting it rattle behind him. He leaned on the railing and smoked, as cowboys or as country peasants do, and a strange blend of sweet and bitter filled his mouth: tobacco mixed with the an tat's custard. He squinted down the street at the driveways crammed with the cars of visiting families. Dance music played from a stereo. These Haitians understood they had a day off from work, but who knows how many could cook the traditional Thanksgiving foods, Richard thought. Most likely they were stewing goat and red snapper like usual.

Though, he couldn't deny it: the street smelled pretty good.

Jackie was right, of course. Jason did not care what he thought. And that had always been what was wrong with his son: not a whit of respect for what his parents felt or had to say. Made a disgrace of them, went around in flip-flops looking like a goddamn queer. No serious job, spent all his time reading poems. What was he supposed to tell people, his only son was marrying a bak gui?

He was angry, but then, it felt almost disingenuous, as if he were only pretending to be angry because this is what they had all come to expect. That made him furious in a different way: Did they think he was so backward, so traditional, so Chinese that he couldn't accept a Jew? He who had grown up with Jews!

What they didn't know, what they didn't need to know, and what he'd never told anyone, was that he'd loved a Jewish girl once. But that had been another time.

Then he saw them. They were approaching on foot; they must have taken the train and walked the mile from the station, hand in hand. Jason and his girl threaded in and out of the lampposts' glow. Richard felt there was something uncanny about the picture they made—how, from a distance, they resembled each other: both lean, with long dark hair; both wearing shabby hats and plaid scarves.

Startled by this mirage, he lit another cigarette. And then a kind of softness took him. He only knew that there was something those two young people possessed that he did not. They were coming to him, afraid, but hoping that he might recognize what had flowered between them, that he'd treat it with tenderness.

They were two houses away. It was dark, and she had not seen him yet, but Jason had. His son stiffened upon recognition.

His son feared that when they reached the porch, Richard would be obnoxious, that he wouldn't look Rachel in the eye, that all through dinner, he'd berate Jason for his life choices. That he didn't understand times were changing.

But his son underestimated him.

"Oh ho ho! That must be Rachel!" Richard called out. He flung the cigarette nub across the lawn, and Jason raised a tentative hand. They reached the steps. "Welcome, welcome!" Richard said, opening his arms wide, and when Rachel reached the top of the stoop, he gathered her bewildered frame into his arms and kissed her cold cheek with all the warmth of a big fat zayde.

He could tell they were perplexed. He led them through the door into the warmth of the kitchen. The table was covered end-to-end with dishes—turkey and sweet potato, yes, but also shrimp in lobster sauce and no mai fan, probably things the girl had not expected to see on Thanksgiving night. When dinner began, he enjoyed the awe on her face as a maze of reaching hands, spoons, and chopsticks crisscrossed like vines in the canopy of a rainforest. Foon Wah ran back and forth pouring apple juice into cups, reheating dishes, and cutting the meat into bites for the grandchildren, while his daughters' husbands shoveled food into their mouths like unabashed teenagers.

"I grew up in Brownsville. You heard of that neighborhood? Just northeast of here. Back then it was a Jewish neighborhood," he explained to Rachel. "My friends called me the 'honorary Jew.' They even taught me the prayers—Ba-rook, ell-you-hay-new, Adam-noy..."

She laughed in appreciation. He still remembered the melodies:

"Ay-ya-yay-yay-yay," he sang, swaying slightly like he'd seen the rabbis do in the synagogues, delighted as she covered her mouth to stifle another giggle.

"They called me the 'shabbos goy.' I was useful because I wasn't Jewish. Every Saturday, if I stood on the street, I could make five cents an apartment 'cause these Jews couldn't do anything on a Saturday—they'd have me light the candles, light the stove, and then they'd pay me. But on Saturdays, they can't touch money either, so they'd lift the tablecloth and there'd be pennies for me on the table. They'd plan it out in advance. And I could make half a dollar a week that way."

And then, because he was also still Chinese and the head of his house, he urged her to eat and spooned the best cut of fish onto her plate.

"I've always known it. Jews and Chinese are the same kind of people," he rambled on while the women washed the dishes—all but Rachel, who he insisted sit beside him. "Number one, they're ambitious. Back where they're from, everyone was poor, so they came over here. Number two," and he counted these off with his fingers, as Rachel laughed, "they're good with money and they're stingy, so everyone hates them."

His daughters brought the vanilla ice cream to the table, then a pumpkin pie, an apple pie, and a bowl of ji ma wu.

"Number three, education. Study, study, study. Because they came here with nothing, and they want only one thing: to get to the top." He patted Rachel's knee. "The Jews and the Chinese. More American than all the others put together."

SADIE & LINA

Sadie was stunned at the sight: the corner lot on Livonia Avenue looked completely different than it had the prior year when she'd first visited. It had become a community garden, bourgeoning with herbs and flowers.

Ms. Lina stood in the middle of the garden, waiting for Sadie. She leaned on a shovel and surveyed the land. Without her beret, her short silver curls gleamed in the sun, and she looked to Sadie like the Roman statue of Minerva—god of wisdom, justice, and war—that guarded Thirty-Fourth Street's Herald Square with her spear and shield.

Sadie approached, leaning her forehead against the fence.

"Ms. Lina?"

Ms. Lina turned. She frowned, then waved her in, and Sadie climbed through the body-size hole in the wire.

As she approached, Sadie could feel a change occurring in Ms. Lina's body. A tightening. A growing heaviness. Like she had just schlepped from one end of the city to the other with all her life in her bags.

They stood next to each other. Sadie could hear the pop of balls at the Betsy Head Park handball court. At first, she felt Ms. Lina's silence as coldness. Then she realized Ms. Lina was waiting for her to speak.

Sadie breathed in, preparing herself.

"Ms. Lina, thank you for meeting me here," she said, turning to face her. "I want to apologize for going to your house and not telling you that I was his granddaughter. That was invasive and . . . and manipulative."

Ms. Lina listened, her eyes lowered.

"Basically, I lied so I . . . so I wouldn't have to deal with whatever the truth was. Or maybe because I wanted to figure everything out on my own. It was wrong. I know I betrayed your trust and I don't really deserve it back. I'm sorry."

Feeling not at all sure that her apology sufficed, Sadie looked at her canvas sneakers, at the soil.

"I appreciate that," said the voice of the elder, and when Sadie lifted her head, their eyes met. "And I appreciate the work you've done. The research."

Ms. Lina's eyes were brown, same as Sadie's. The deep brown upon brown of their mixed families. And though Ms. Lina's eyes had seen the fire, seen the neighborhood's rise and fall, they were rich and unfaded. Afraid that she might spoil the moment, Sadie didn't move. It was Ms. Lina who eventually broke the gaze, taking a handkerchief out of her jeans and wiping the back of her neck.

"You're missing some of the details," she said. "I can help you finish this report. But I have to ask you. How do you plan to use it?"

"In whatever way you'd like me to."

Putting the kerchief back in her pocket, Ms. Lina nodded.

It was September but still too hot. They sat on the bench, the air thickening with each minute, shadows of leaves printed on Sadie's face. Lina would do what she needed to. The girl was not gloating; she was trying to make amends.

"I thought your grandpa still owned the building. No one told us it had been sold. We saw eviction notices on the doors, but they didn't look real—we thought maybe Mr. Wong was trying to intimidate us. In fact, we prepared for another protest because we didn't see any of it as legitimate.

"I used to think it was your grandfather behind all those tricks, but after reading your document, I don't know. You show how 78 Livonia LLC is connected to all those burned-down buildings in the South Bronx, and I know how the Bronx burned back then. Worse than Brownsville."

"I wish I could figure out exactly who these people were," said Sadie, and Lina wished the same.

"Did your grandpa know he was selling to arsonists?"

"I don't know. And I don't know if I'll be able to figure it out. But if he did . . ." Sadie paused. "Shouldn't my family think about how to hold ourselves accountable?"

"Hmm." A question she'd let Sadie answer on her own.

"I'm just not sure what accountability would look like." Sadie traced a knot on the bench with her finger. "An apology? Money? But my family isn't wealthy. Middle class, for sure."

"Where's your family these days?"

"My grandmother lives in Chinatown in a co-op apartment. And my parents have a brownstone in Park Slope, and two of my aunts have houses in Long Island, and another has a home in Jersey. And the homes are valuable. Like, property values went up and we benefited, while all these other people were pushed out of the city. But I also don't think I can convince my relatives to give away their homes."

"I know." Lina was imagining all the extra rooms in those suburban homes, then counting the number of people like Melvin who could have used a roof over their head.

"And I mean, it would trigger family memories—of China. My grandma always said the Communists would take away middle-class people's property, and if they resisted, they could be killed or sent to prison."

"Well, this isn't Communist China."

Lina could see Sadie spiraling. Getting lost in questions about process. Letting guilt conduct the train.

"Miss Sadie, Brownsville deserves reparations for all the evils done to it. And it wasn't just your grandpa."

Sadie nodded and swallowed whatever was happening in her throat.

"But I'm not asking to flip the ladder upside down, put your people at the bottom and my people at the top. It's much bigger than that. We got to bring the whole thing down. This country has enough resources to ensure every person has a home. That's the America I want to live in. We don't need your guilt, you understand me, we need y'all working full-time for *that* America."

Sadie's brows settled.

"Y'all showed up in this white supremacist country and tried to get as close to white as possible. God knows some of my people have too. And I believe in financial reparations, but I don't want people thinking they can pay us off, and that's it. I don't want to give people permission to forget. This country needs to remember the whole story—not just the version where they're the heroes. And if we want a better world for our children, a world that's not burning, and I mean burning in both senses, 'cause . . ." Lina wiped the sweat puddling on her temples. "It's real hot today."

"We can go inside if you're uncomfortable!"

"Let's go to St. Paul's church—they got air-conditioning. But let me just say this. What I want is for everyone in your communities to treat us like family. No more 'that ain't my problem' and 'them white folks said I'm better'—and 'we're always the victims, we're never wrong.' No, no: you go to bat for me. No more safety just for some—reaping the benefits of this country without taking responsibility for the injustice. No, we fight side by side. Will you do that, Miss Sadie?"

THE CHINS

There could be no doubt about it: the baby in the Polaroid was a Chinese. That thick black hair, moon cheeks, eyes big but unmistakably Chinese in their shape—it was clear the Chinese genes had won. They probably would win every time, Richard thought as he sat on the porch. Popping a grape in his mouth, he once again studied the pictures that Jason had brought from the hospital. Especially if the father was Chinese. With the father's genes, Chinese conquers all.

He lifted his head, peered out over the street, and smelled stew chicken from Mrs. Rose Louis's kitchen. Mrs. George was bent over in the garden next door. "Garden looks great. Big tomatoes this year!" he called to her, and she thanked him and waved, smiling beneath her sun hat. He liked the Georges, his longtime neighbors. A Black family, but the nicest people, and they'd raised their kids well. The boy, Jason's old friend, had moved to California to become a doctor.

He chuckled, thinking about a time, about a year earlier, when some cousins had visited from Taiwan. They ran a computer company and clearly, they thought they were big shots, the way they bragged endlessly about the price of their suits and their wives' jewelry. Yet on their way through the yard into Richard's house, they had all frozen at the sight of Mrs. George. His cousin's wife had put her hand to her mouth and turned to Foon Wah, crying, "Hak gui! Hak gui!"

Richard and Foon Wah had quickly ushered the cousins inside, but for months after, they could not stop laughing about it. That's how it was with the Chinese in the east, Richard had thought to himself that day: they believed they were modern and fancy, but they'd been breeding with their sisters for a thousand years. When he'd told them that his son had married a Jewish woman, the cousins asked for the details of the assumed business transaction between Richard and the Jewish parents. This, too, had made him laugh out loud.

With these memories, he felt a deep satisfaction, and he popped another grape into his mouth, slouching with his belly turned up like the Laughing Buddha. He was not Richard anymore; he was a bronze statue in an ancestral temple. He stared in front of him, thoughtless as if outside time, like he was floating beyond his porch and beyond Mrs. George's garden and down the street, maybe all the way down Kings Highway to Ocean Parkway, to Coney Island, into the Atlantic. His arms and legs felt weightless, like he was sinking in water. But he wasn't afraid. Not even as he felt himself fall onto the porch floor and then below it and then beyond it.

Mrs. George made a sound like a bird's high-pitched tweet. He heard the cat-meow of the rusty iron gate, and then Mrs. George was upon him, smelling like the grass on her hands and apron, lifting him up from the armpits. He could feel her fingers in what had become the malleable putty of his flesh. Foon Wah was also on the porch, and the two old women were trying to put him back in the chair. He knew it was an impossible task because he was already on his way somewhere else.

And then he was unconscious, and this was surprising and a bit terrifying, how quickly that thing called consciousness slipped away, like he had accidentally dropped it onto the subway tracks. His wife was still there, and his daughter Jennifer, sitting across from him in a very cold hospital room, Jennifer insisting that Foon Wah borrow her sweater. Then Julie and Jackie arrived, which meant this was serious. He probably looked as awful as he felt, like he was splitting into strands of kelp, loose skin flapping around the bones, tubes poking from the paper nightgown. Three Jamaican nurses fussed with him, whispering about a stroke and oxygen deficiency. At some point his wife nodded off in the chair. Her head hung heavily on her neck like that of a hanged man's, like his father strung up on the ceiling light. And suddenly he was afraid, because his father stood up and began chastising him, like Richard was a boy who, thinking himself invincible, had jumped off the jungle gym only to fall and break a bone—his father scolding: *You see what happens when you eat too much duck blood?*

At last, Jason appeared. Yes, that was the final portent: his son, here to show Richard to the door. Jason was standing right at the side of the bed, the bed that was more like an operating table, like the one on which Foon Wah had given birth to his four children, only now Richard was moving in the opposite direction. Back into the dark. His son waited, looking a little impatient, and Richard wished he could be a bit less obvious about it.

In truth, he was glad for his son. His son was alive and happy and a father now. He even had a bak gui wife.

In the coffin, dusted in talcum powder, Richard looked like a bak gui—finally white, as if with death ascending.

His children stayed for a week to arrange the details: Jennifer chose the casket, Julie reserved the banquet hall, Jackie phoned the relatives, and Jason delivered Richard's best suit and tie to the funeral home. Foon Wah busied herself with the obituary, printing, in elegant calligraphy, their Chinese names in order of gender and age. His funeral on Mulberry Street was well attended. People still remembered his importance in the family tree: first son of first son of first son of first son of first son, he never remembered how many times. There were some old Jewish friends from the Brownsville Boys Club, various Chinese relatives, and random Chinese hangers-on—he didn't recognize a lot of them. Maybe they just went through the funeral part to get drunk at the banquet. There was his daughter-in-law,

Rachel, peeking at him and then at the lump of hair cocooned in her arms, perhaps comparing his face to her daughter's. There were the older grandkids, hungrily eyeing the boiled chicken on the sacrificial altar, and so many wall bouquets his daughters had to rent an extra limo just to transport the flowers to the cemetery.

Jennifer had selected one of the priciest: Green-Wood Cemetery, where Richard used to take them for picnics. But it all went by too quickly: they dumped him in the ground, bowed and threw flowers on his casket, then got back in the car and drove away. He thought they should have been grateful that he'd had the generosity to die in June, not in the middle of the freezing winter like his father. And because it was spring, his decomposed flesh would fertilize the soil.

For a whole year, Richard waited anxiously for Cemetery Day. At last they returned, and they bore gifts: money for the underworld's vending machines and a feast of sesame gelatin, boiled chicken, and pork chops. Then they left again, taking the food with them. But how could food be an offering to him if the living were also going to eat it? Unless food has a spirit that had already made it up—or down—to him? And during all those years he'd visited his father's grave, had he been eating food with the spirit sucked out of it?

"When you come next April, make sure you bring a beer!" he hollered, but no one paid attention.

Thanks to Jennifer's generosity, he now reclined with the Anglos of yore, with the Ebbets of Ebbets Field, the Chadwicks of Chadwick Avenue. So maybe the bak gui had not moved away from Brooklyn after all: they'd reestablished themselves here, conquering the hill with elaborate sarcophagi and swelling obelisks.

"Hello and peekaboo," he joked. "So, here's where all you bak gui went! Bak gui—it means 'white ghost'! You get it?"

He laughed, but the earth hushed him. Lonely, he found himself yearning for his fellow gravemates' attention. He hoped that the bak gui of yore would initiate him into their underground club with its thick and pungent lounges, its rotten, acrid delicacies.

"I'm sorry for the noise, gentlemen!" he joked. "These Chinamen don't know the difference between a restaurant and a graveyard!"

He waited for their welcome, ready to withstand the hazing.

The day of the funeral could have been her wedding day, the murmuring crowd escorting her from Ng to Chin village. The bride is only important because the crowd makes her so, conferring an honor on her temporary homelessness. Not since those nuptials had she felt so rootless. Walking forward on the arm of first son of first son of first son of first son of first son of first son, her steps as careful as they'd been on her wedding day, she almost forgot that Mulberry Street was the street of death.

In the months that followed, Foon Wah, now sixty-three, sold the East Flatbush house. Its value had appreciated, and she was able to buy a co-op apartment in Chinatown and use the remainder to purchase a four-week travel package. Nowadays, a person could take a Chinese airline all the way from New York to Beijing. The attendants would not be bak gui ladies, but bilingual Chinese girls in bright lipstick and trim red-and-white uniforms, and instead of uncooked leaves soaked in oil and vinegar, the plane would serve dumplings and beef chiang fun.

During the eighteen-hour flight, her bottom grew sore, her knees ached, and her little bladder forced her to the washroom a dozen times. When she finally looked out the window and made out the contours of her homeland, she was moved to tears.

It was her homeland, and yet much of it was new to her. She'd never been to Beijing. The city's subways were much cleaner than New York's, its highways wide and faultless. She and the other expatriates on the trip stayed in a fancy hotel with bidets and faucets that turned on with a wave of the hand. Residents still hung their laundry on the balconies, but she could see through the windows that many households now owned color TVs.

The travel package came with a tour of the China World Shopping Arcade, a day of sailing on the translucent lake at the Summer

Palace, and a bus trip to the Great Wall. Foon Wah finally saw with her own eyes all the gilded, pretty objects that she had once read about as a schoolgirl. She especially liked the old hutong villages with their stone houses and cobbled roofs, where the people still traveled by rickshaw and where old ladies shucked corn in the doorways of their homes.

She was perplexed by the tour guide, a young man who spoke both Mandarin and Cantonese fluently, and who had been born to a Cantonese mother but had grown up in Beijing. Each day, he extolled the many great things that the Communist Party had done. The Communists had built factories, roads, bridges, and dams. They had practically eliminated illiteracy, had vastly reduced poverty, had doubled life expectancy. She wondered if all this was true, and how much of the progress had taken place before trade resumed with America.

Their next stop was Canton City. Skyscrapers had replaced the old bricks, there was electricity and running water, and her people dressed like Westerners, in pants and T-shirts. They took a bus to Gui Lin, to the mountains where she'd hid with her siblings from the bombs. The government had designated the caves a national jewel, and signs along the paths reminded tourists not to spit or throw their trash in the lake. The village where they'd taken refuge and where her mother had died was no longer there; the Party had razed the homes, and in its place, there was a travel resort, offering tourists access to hot springs and massage. She could not find the graveyard with her mother's tombstone, but she hadn't really expected to.

From the window of her taxi to Toisan, she beheld the peasant huts, the vegetable patches, the rice fields, and the children running in the dirt. Yet still, something was different: the people looked better fed and their skin clearer. She learned from the taxi driver that, along with a new and bigger school, the government had built a hospital with thirty cots. As they passed it, she marveled at its three stories, and at the mini ambulances lined up outside.

When they reached her father's village, two women dashed out to the gate to receive her. They so much resembled Foon Wah's cousins

Di Di and Moi Moi that it was only when they called out, "Gu Po!" that she realized they were Di Di's and Moi Moi's children.

In the hovel, her cousins greeted her in the doorway. They had transformed into toothless old ladies with white hair. Were it not for her hair dye, wrinkle cream, and regular dentist appointments, Foon Wah would have looked much the same. They took Foon Wah's arms while their daughters pushed sandals onto her feet and a cup of dandelion tea into her palms. There was another woman there, struggling to break through the crowd of cousins, and with one glance at the bushy-browed face, Foon Wah knew who it was.

"Aiya—Mee Lai?"

She and Mee Lai grabbed each other like they would otherwise fall down, then held each other at arm's length, both trembling, gasping, exclaiming with glee.

"You came all the way from Lew village?"

"Lew village? Ay, no! I was only there two years!"

"He died?"

"I threw him away, the drunk!"

Foon Wah laughed. They all did.

"Ni to! Ni to!" the daughters cooed, leading Foon Wah to the couch.

The daughters brought the older women four bowls of mushroom chestnut soup. Staring at one another through the steam, incredulous that they were all still alive, and overwhelmed by what time had given and taken from each, the older women sat in a circle.

"But you have been alone all this time? No children?"

"I remarried," said Mee Lai between slurps. "My second husband died two years ago. We have three kids—they're in the city." Grasping Foon Wah's wrist, she bent forward to explain.

"After the Communists took over, you could get a divorce. The Communists got rid of many of the old practices!" she exclaimed. "The Women's Federation told me about the new marriage law. They took me to a class so I could teach others. I used to travel around, teaching women about the marriage law. I went to see an eye doctor, and he gave me some glasses. And then I married the eye doctor! Chor Jung—a year younger than me! A very good man. But he had liver problems, died two years ago."

For almost fifty years, Foon Wah had believed her friend trapped in an unhappy marriage with that fat man in Lew village. She had imagined Mee Lai suffering to remind herself that she was the lucky one. Yet in all that time, Mee Lai had been free.

Foon Wah was glad for this, of course.

"And you!" cried Mee Lai, nudging Foon Wah. "You with that handsome American brother. I still remember his name—Chin Dun Ho!"

Foon Wah nodded, looking down at her feet.

"With a husband so pretty," Mee Lai laughed, "you wish you are the first to die!"

One thing hadn't changed: the respect accorded to those who had gone to America. Her cousins' children followed her around, anticipating her every need. When she slipped them heng bou, they pressed their hands together, bowing and murmuring with gratitude. A ten-dollar bill was worth fifty yuan, and Foon Wah knew they probably imagined she was a wealthy woman. She considered trying to dissuade them of this notion but realized her attempts would be futile. Never in a million years could they dream of buying a travel package to fly across the world. And her body was weak, pampered—she had been sitting on porcelain toilets for so long that she found it near impossible to squat over the trench in the woods.

It moved her to watch the women in the kitchen debone a fish just the way she liked to, to hear them hum their approval the way she did, and to see the old women's feet, in their open sandals, curling toe over toe, just like hers. Many of the men and children had left for America, Hong Kong, Taiwan, or Sydney, and her cousins complained that hardly anyone lived in Ng village anymore. Only ghosts.

She thought endlessly about her ghosts. Her ghosts in China, her ghosts in Brooklyn. On the third day, she asked a relative to take her on the back of his motorbike to Chin village. When they arrived, the

Chin villagers poured forward to greet her. She wanted to cry; everyone's country lilt was so exactly like Koon Lai's. Those who still remained in Chin village were Koon Lai's distant kin, second and third cousins, their bloodlines untouched by the blessing and the curse of America. In the house where Richard had been raised, Foon Wah burned incense and bowed at the altar. She then asked to be taken to the area where Koon Lai's prized new house had stood. But there was nothing there, not even the structure's remains: the Communists had instructed the villagers to dismantle the ruins and plant a pumpkin patch in its place.

"But the canal," the cousin added when he perceived her disappointment. "Your father-in-law built the canal. They still use it. You want us to take you to it?"

She smiled, declining with a quick shake of her head.

At the end of her journey, she felt it a great privilege to be old and to have caught a glimpse of how the world continues after one has left it. To realize that life is like the best of Chinese movies: a series of sweet heartbreaks that move in no particular direction.

Still, she began to miss a bowl of cornflakes, and to tire of squatting in trenches. At the end of those four weeks, she was ready to go home.

JASON

When his daughter shut the door of her bedroom and lived for days on LUNA Bars despite the carefully prepared meals he cooked for her, Jason thought of his younger self. How he'd taken off with his typewriter, wanting nothing to do with his parents. It brought him some comfort to think maybe she'd inherited her intensity from him—and one day she'd grow up and, like him, find someone who made her a little less severe.

He returned to this line of thought often, and it was easier than thinking about the other part: that the things she'd said in the kitchen on Halloween had upset him. She thought he didn't care what had happened to the Livonia Avenue restaurant building and to the people who had lived in it, but that was not the case.

He was deeply disturbed to hear there had been a fire, that people had been hurt. But his father had sold the building and never looked back. What happened after the sale was not his family's business, Jason felt.

But then, there were people in Brownsville who still remembered his father. Who believed he'd been responsible for this calamity.

Perhaps Sadie was right. He was still running. His father's past was the last thing he wanted to think about.

All spring and summer, as his daughter dug into the history of the Livonia Avenue lot, Jason chewed over how he could help. His own days were slow and solitary. He wrote in the morning, and in the afternoons he worked as an associate editor for *Verbena Press*. Often, he'd reflect on how lucky he was to do what he loved, to eat well, and to feel safe. In the evenings, he cooked and ate with Rachel, and they read aloud Ibsen or Chekhov, or else they played the game where one of them read a line from a book and the other had to guess the author. He cherished the quiet, for as a child, quiet was all he had ever wanted. To hear Rachel hum along to Billy Joel, or Brian Lehrer ponder the questions of the day, or the chirping of the sparrow out the window—that was enough for him.

In the early '90s, when they'd moved to Park Slope—Rachel's parents had bought the brownstone on their behalf—Jason had been a bit anxious about returning to Brooklyn. Then he'd realized that the new Brooklyn wasn't anything like the old one. Maybe it was Park Slope, or maybe it was the era. He never stopped double-checking the locks on the door, but as Sadie got older, he could be okay if she went to a party and didn't come back until after midnight.

But it was also true that Brooklyn had lost something. Its people. Neighbors had disappeared from the block, and he didn't particularly like the entitled ones who'd replaced them. There was a certain Brooklyn stoop culture on the wane. He missed the days when he could just sidle up to Macon's place, throw a stuffed animal at the window, and that was all it took to get a friend's attention.

It was thus a big surprise to him when, one weekend in October, Macon George friended him on Facebook. As soon as Jason accepted the friend request, Macon sent him a message.

Oct. 10, 2015, 10:23 p.m.

Jason! Jason Chin. I'm realizing how my many nicknames for you won't really fly in the 21st century, but Jason, it's good to be writing you. I'm sorry I've been out of touch for so many years. You might not believe it, but I still have your wedding picture

and your daughter's birth announcement. I saved them and
have been meaning to reconnect for a long time. I don't know
if you're still in Manhattan. How is Rachel? How old is your
daughter now? Are you already an empty nester? I'm coming
to Brooklyn in a couple of weeks to help my mother move to a
nursing home. Is it possible you'd like to meet?

Jason immediately invited Macon to the Park Slope brownstone.
It wasn't until he'd received Macon's message that he understood
how deeply he regretted their growing apart.

Jason pored over his friend's profile page. Macon still lived in Los
Angeles and was a surgeon at UCLA—chief of the division of cardiac
surgery.

He scrolled until he found a photo. Macon, though balding, was
unmistakable. He wore a suit and stood with his arm around another
Black man, the latter with salt-and-pepper muttonchops. *Twenty
years of partnership with Thomas Collins*, the caption said. *And now,
my husband.*

"Husband," Jason mumbled to himself, removing his reading
glasses. He smiled at the screen until his eyes began to water. "Husband," he repeated to himself, again and again, as if the word, like a
magician's handkerchief cloth, might yank invisible things into view,
bring back all the many memories Jason had forgotten or suppressed.

The day before Macon's visit, Jason bought more junk food than
he'd ever brought into the brownstone: Drake's Devil Dogs, several
boxes of Jell-O pudding, and four Hostess fruit pies in different fla-
vors, which he sliced into quarters as if they were sampling fancy
cheeses. He wanted to pay homage to the old days, even if it spiked
their blood sugar levels.

"You chopped your hair," Macon pointed out.

"And you have none left!" Jason replied, and guffawing, they
brought each other in for a hug. Toned and glowing from the California sun, Macon was fit. Jason tried to remember the last time he'd

hugged Macon, and could only recall the skinny boy he'd chased on the jungle gym.

Rachel and Sadie were at work, so for several hours, the two men sat on the living room couch, tasting and sometimes spitting out their formerly favorite snacks, impressed by their own disgust. Macon told Jason about Thomas, who was an actor, and about their wedding at the Hollywood Bowl.

"Give Mrs. Chin my best. She was always a sweet lady."

"She has heart troubles. I'm taking her to the doctor Saturday. She'll be happy to hear about you."

"My mom thought Mrs. Chin had moved far away."

"Just to Manhattan Chinatown."

"Well, that's far away to Mom." Macon chuckled. "My mom won't leave Brooklyn. I keep trying to get her out to LA, but she's too attached. That's why we had to settle with this East New York nursing home. But I need to ask you, Jason." Macon leaned in, a sly grin on his face that reminded Jason of the old, untoned Macon. "Am I in the right Brooklyn? Where did all the white people come from?"

They both laughed, and Jason was glad he still had a friend who could see this. Sometimes, spending time with Park Slope neighbors or his colleagues at *Verbena Press*, he felt as if he'd only dreamed the Brooklyn of his adolescence. And yet Macon's comment also made him a tad defensive, for wasn't Rachel part of that white arrival? If he could have filled the city with carbon copies of Rachel, he would have.

He thought of Sadie, then. He was proud of her for all her research into the history of the Livonia Avenue restaurant. He was also ashamed that she had come to need so little from him. Jason wondered what Macon would have done in his place.

"You know what Sadie found out?" Jason said to him. "The building in Brownsville where my family's restaurant used to be—it burned down in the late '70s."

"Oh yeah? What happened?"

"It's not clear." He was already having second thoughts about bringing up the subject. "After my dad closed the restaurant, he rented it to tenants, then sold the building. But right after the sale, there was a fire. There are people in Brownsville who think my father burned it down."

"Did he?"

Macon's sly grin reappeared, but this time Jason was taken aback.

"Wait—you're not seriously asking me, are you?"

Macon's head wobbled with hesitation. "Your dad *was* something."

"He was," Jason agreed.

"Temperamental."

"Yep."

"And, I'm sorry, Jason—he was, you know, a bit, uh . . ."

"Racist. Absolutely. I know."

"And all the time, ranting about those tenants. Saying he hoped they'd go to hell."

"Why don't I remember that?"

"Maybe you blocked it out. He would be screaming it in and out of the doors. My parents and I could hear from the porch. He was older by then. Maybe you'd already left."

When he went to Chinatown that Saturday to take his mother to the doctor, he had a secret mission. On arriving, he found her ready to go, wearing a purple peacoat and jade earrings. As always, she was a stickler for presentation. Pressing down the Velcro of her Mary Janes, he guided her into the wheelchair. The sun was out, and on Mott Street, he pushed her slowly so she could take in the sights.

Chinatown had changed. There were more white people on the street than Chinese, it seemed to him. A Japanese creperie shop and a Taiwanese ice cream parlor had replaced the old Toisanese pottery and dried fungi stores. A few homeless Chinese men sat on flattened cardboard outside a shuttered dim sum restaurant.

"Hon Ngin Gai change a lot," Jason leaned down and said into her ear.

"All the new immigrants are from Fujian Province," his mother replied in Toisanese. "The Fujianese are poor!"

"No, I mean this." He pointed at the creperie. "All these fancy shops."

His mother shrugged in the wheelchair. "Hon Ngin Gai hou gi," she said back.

Jason frowned. Even his own mother—with all her prejudices, her Republican leanings, her habit of projecting the word *Fujianese* like it was a cuss—was concerned about rising rents.

They reached the medical offices and took the elevator to the third floor. Jason sat beside his mother as a nurse recorded her vitals. Dr. Zhen, the young heart specialist, spoke Mandarin but no Cantonese, and they all agreed it was best if they just communicated in English. Dr. Zhen said she wanted to up the dose on the A-fib medication, and that his mother ought to come for another appointment in a month. From all this it seemed to Jason, though Dr. Zhen didn't say so directly, that his mother was declining.

When he thought of her dying, he felt wrapped in a silence that was deeper than the quiet he'd grown used to in the brownstone. Perhaps he should have been overcome with guilt, that long neglected but innate sense of filial piety finally welling up in him, so that at last, for her sake, he'd leave his life as a writer and become a lawyer, and renounce salads, and visit his sisters more often. But the feeling wasn't guilt.

What he was experiencing was something more like the anticipation of displacement, for even though he was so safe, so secure, in the brownstone that he owned with Rachel's parents' money, his mother's death would be yet another disappearance, the hardest of all. With her, it felt as if the world from which he came—a world of homegrown bean sprouts and rooftop pigeon cages, of hawthorn candy and Hostess fruit pies, of backyard barbecues and blackouts— would vanish entirely.

— — —

When they returned to her apartment, he helped her move to the couch, where she promptly fell asleep. Jason lifted his mother's feet so she could lie back properly, then repositioned her head.

"Oh, I go to sleep?" she said, laughing at herself.

"Don't worry—take a nap. I'll wash the dishes," he said, covering her with a blanket.

Within a few minutes, his mother's mouth was hanging open, and she was snoring at regular intervals.

This was just as he had hoped.

He crept to the cupboard by the window. It was an old wood cabinet with clunky shelves and no sliders. With a little tug to the left and a little to the right, he wiggled the bottom drawer until he'd opened it just wide enough to peek at its contents.

He withdrew a folder. Riffling through the papers, he found a yellowing rectangle from the Immigration and Naturalization Service.

Name: Dun Ho Wong	Occupation: Student	Age: Eight Years
Origin: Canton, China	Destination: New York City, New York	
Physical marks and peculiarities: Mole outer corner right eyebrow		

Next, he discovered his father's discharge papers from the U.S. Navy, the regal script rendered so heavily that it was now no more than a smear of black ink. And he noticed his grandpa's death certificate: *1903. Retired. Restaurant Owner. Suicide.*

He reached the change-of-name form next.

At a special term, part two, of the Civil Court of the City of New York, at the Court House thereof, 111 Centre Street, Borough of Manhattan, on Seventeenth of June, in the Year Nineteen Sixty-Six,

In the Matter of Application of DUN HO WONG and FOON WAH WONG on behalf of themselves and their children for leave to change their names to RICHARD DUN HO CHIN, FOON WAH CHIN, JENNIFER CHIN, JULIE CHIN, JACKIE CHIN, JASON CHIN . . .

For years, it seemed, his family had wrapped and unwrapped itself in disguise. Why, for instance, had his father bought the house on Livonia using the name Richard Wong—at least according to that deed Sadie had obtained—when one year prior, he'd changed his name to Chin? Had he forgotten his new name? Was he trying to hide himself still?

Jason continued to search. He found a bankruptcy filing, a utility bill, a mortgage note. He opened boxes, poured out folders, and closed the window so the drilling outside wouldn't disturb his mother's sleep. Then he noticed a folder marked "78 Livonia"—within it, a flaking piece of paper.

> THIS INDENTURE, made the ninth day of August, nineteen hundred and seventy-eight

> BETWEEN

> WONG DUN HO, also known as RICHARD WONG, residing at 5534 East 52th Street, Brooklyn, New York

> Party of the first part, and

> 78 Livonia Avenue LLC
> Party of the second part

> Witnesseth, that the party of the first part, in consideration of ten thousand dollars and other valuable considerations paid by the party of the second part, does hereby grant and release unto the party of the second part . . .

A record of the building's sale, Jason realized.

And there was something else in the folder: a handwritten petition from about two years earlier—January 25, 1976.

To Richard Wong:

We are writing to inform you that the tenants of 78 and 80 Livonia Avenue will not pay rent until The Demands, detailed below, are completely addressed. For years we have endured egregious conditions in violation of the city's housing code law, and our requests for repairs have been repeatedly ignored. It is our right to live in decent conditions, and your responsibility to ensure them. Until then, we will save our rent in an escrow account.

THE DEMANDS

1. Full restoration of all cracked and caving ceilings, including the 78 Livonia 2L Bathroom, 78 Livonia 1R Kitchen, 80 Livonia Avenue 3L Bedroom, and 80 Livonia 3R Kitchen.

2. Extermination of rats and roaches in both buildings.

3. Removal of mold on ceilings/window frames in the bathrooms on all floors of both buildings.

4. Replacement of malfunctioning boilers and radiators.

We make these demands from necessity and because they are our human rights. The Universal Declaration of Human Rights adopted by the United Nations states that "Everyone has the right to a standard of living adequate for the health and well-being of himself and of his family, including food, clothing, housing and medical care and the right to security."

We await your response and action.

Cosigned:

Lina Rodriguez Armstrong
Harry Eugene
John Coleman
Sam Jenkins
Sylvia Jenkins
Patricia Taylor
Ria Quincy
Evelina Garcia
Louise Rivera
Paul Laguerre
Benoit Laguerre
Mr. and Mrs. Reynolds

Jason held the papers to his chest, then stuck them back in the folder and tucked the folder in his bag to bring to Sadie. This was the most concrete evidence yet. His father had been unable to take care of the building, as shown by the tenants' letter. And so he had sold it.

But where were the address books?

Jason wondered if he was looking in the wrong drawer. Maybe his mother still kept her address books within close reach, by the dial-up phone, in the coffee table by the couch. He crept back over to her, holding his breath as she continued to snore.

In the coffee-table drawer, he found three timeworn address books. Skimming through each of them, he recognized some of the names—his dad's old friend Alan Friedman, for instance, and the Hoffmans from Kings Highway.

Then, finally, the one he had been looking for: his father's broker. *718-599-2939.*

This was who Sadie needed to talk to.

JASON & SADIE

Squeezed between nurses, PT specialists, and wheelchairs, Sadie and Jason rode an elevator to the fifth floor of the Yorkville Rehabilitation and Nursing Center. Surrounded by beeping machines and the perpetual murmur of *Law & Order*, patients languished in dim lighting. At the end of the hall, they found the PT room—and near the stress balls, Jack Schmidt.

Though it had been years since they'd last seen each other, and Jack had shriveled to half his former size, Jason recognized Jack immediately. Sadie was amused by how harmless the little man looked in his khaki shorts, T-shirt, and Mets hat. As he stretched his legs with a resistance band, she saw flabs of arm flesh riddled with melanoma.

He smiled widely as they approached, dropping the band.

"Correct me if I'm Wong, but that looks like the Wong family!"

Sadie tried not to choke. The nurse said they could take Jack to lunch.

"I took a fall. A bad one. At least I'm not dead like your pa!" he said as Jason wheeled him to the elevator, and then he looked at Sadie and grinned. "She's a beautiful girl. A beautiful girl, looks just like Foo Foo. And my boy Jason! You're getting older. You look just like your dad." With his good arm he reached out and patted Jason's stomach.

Jason looked down at himself, self-conscious.

"But you don't sound like him," Jack added. "You sound made for radio. Went to a fancy school and got rid of your Brooklyn accent, huh? Columbia, right?"

Sadie decided it was time to come to her father's rescue.

"So, Jack, how long have you been here?"

"Two months? Three months? Who knows?" Schmidt raised his hands in the air. "My nephew had me committed. You're young, but wait and see. You'll start going backward until you're in the cradle."

They took the elevator to the cafeteria on the sixth floor and found seats at an empty table. In the corner, a few seniors played dominoes and checkers. Sadie wondered what her grandfather would have been like at Jack's age, had he survived. She'd heard that Richard had been gregarious, an extrovert—cruel when he wanted to be, charming when he needed to be.

The nurse brought them each a tray containing a ham sandwich, a plastic bag of apple slices, and a chocolate Ensure.

"What about Foo Foo? Your mother okay?"

"She's doing well. She's living in Chinatown."

"God bless her. You know I loved eating at your mother's. Chow mein, lo mein, shrimp in that cream sauce—Foo Foo was the best cook in Brownsville. Now I eat garbage," he said, pointing to the tray.

According to Jack's nephew, who had answered his uncle's old number the prior week, Jack had lost all his money in dicey real estate moves. He'd had to sell his house and move in with the nephew, who had taken care of him until Jack fell on the street and broke his hip.

"That house, your house in Brownsville. Your house in East Flatbush too. I found them for your dad!" Jack exclaimed. "Did you know that?"

"Yeah, he was grateful to you for that."

"Well, I never had anything against the Chinese," Schmidt said with an innocent shrug. "And I knew how to hook Richie up with the right people. Some owners didn't want to sell to a Chinese back then, can you believe that? But times have changed. Now the Chinese own half the city."

Sadie glanced at her father and tried not to laugh. Of course, a millennial had to put up with this sort of Greatest Generation blather if she wanted access to the past. "That's actually something we'd like to talk about," Sadie said, scooting her chair closer to Jack and lowering her voice. "I wanted to ask you about the buildings on Livonia—78 and 80 Livonia Avenue. Do you remember when my grandfather bought them?"

"Oh, I didn't sell him *those*. Arnie Cohen gave them to him. For zilch. The neighborhood was falling apart by then."

"But then he sold them off, in 1978. To this group called 78 Livonia Avenue LLC. Do you remember?"

It took Jack a moment. Then the grin disappeared from his face.

"Oh." A piece of ham was caught in his fingers like a detached tongue. "That?" His eyes rolled to a corner of the room, searching for his nurse. "I can't talk about that."

"Why not?"

Schmidt frowned.

"Your grandpa would turn over in his grave."

Sadie thought of the times she'd gone with her mother to synagogue for the High Holy Days, the way the Jews would rock forward and back while knocking their fists against their chests: *For sins we have committed against you under duress or willingly . . . For the sins we have committed against you with knowledge and with deceit . . . For the sin we have committed against you by a bribe-taking or a bribe-giving.* It was a prayer that could last for ten minutes—a plea for forgiveness for every possible transgression, and it was said repeatedly during Yom Kippur.

"Teshuvah," Sadie remembered. "That's how you say it, right?"

The word *Teshuvah* impacted the old man. He blinked, placed the tongue of ham back on his plate.

They waited in silence.

Jack tapped the table with his pointer finger, as if he were trying to make a more emphatic gesture but lacked the strength.

"There were some bad people in the game." He glanced at Jason. "People thought I played dirty, but nothing like these guys." He looked around, but no one was in earshot. "Your dad was in a fix, so I gave him their number."

"There was a fire," Sadie asserted. "People died."

"Died?" Jack scowled. He looked like he was going to spit on his food. "No one died!"

"An older man. Three people were hospitalized for serious injuries. And everyone else lost all they had."

"Load of shit. They would have emptied the building first."

Jason rummaged through his bag, took out the folder, and handed Jack the petition from Lina Rodriguez Armstrong and the other Livonia Avenue tenants. "All these people were still living there. They refused to leave."

Jack took the petition and squinted at it with his Steeplechase grin flipped completely upside down. Sadie took out her Olympus and hit the record button.

THE CHINS

Richard had not heard back from the Leviathans. He'd waited for months, dialing the number repeatedly, always getting a busy signal. He needed to sell the buildings—to get out of the loan. The loan shark was calling every day, threatening to take the East Flatbush house.

Richard looked up the Leviathans' number in the white pages. He got it into his head that if he met the Leviathans, man-to-man, he might be able to convince them. Sometimes people heard the Chinese surname and misjudged him, but Richard could always win them over in person. The phone number matched an office in Sheepshead Bay. He drove down to Avenue Y one morning and scanned the streets until he located the right building, a small yellow townhouse with an office on the downstairs floor.

DR. EDWARD LIPSCHUTZ, PEDIATRIC DENTISTRY, the sign said. Undeterred, thinking perhaps this Edward Lipschutz shared the space with the Leviathans, he parked and rang the bell. Someone came to the door—a knockout of a girl, maybe in her twenties, in a miniskirt and heels. She let him into a small room with teddy bear wallpaper and a bunch of toys on the floor.

"Are you making an appointment for your child?" she asked, returning behind her desk, and immediately, he recognized her voice;

it was the woman who'd answered his initial call to the Leviathans. She had a Russian or Polish accent.

"I'm here for the Leviathans," he said. "About my properties."

She looked at him sharply.

"Wait."

He followed her swaying hips until they disappeared behind a door. A few minutes later she reemerged and led him to a small office at the back. Richard sat in a chair and looked around. On the left wall hung a 1943 air force medal with a plunging eagle engraved in the bronze. A tropical fish tank gurgled by the right wall, and above it hung a framed letter of gratitude from the local police precinct. He thought about what he should say to ingratiate himself. Maybe Mr. Leviathan had served in the air force.

Through the wall, he heard two male voices—he recognized the older, baritone voice.

"That guy who keeps calling?" said a younger man. "He showed up. Mila put him in the office."

"That's fine. I'll speak with him."

From the voice alone, Richard had decided that the old man was compassionate and would be sympathetic.

"Did we hear from Tuchman?" the older voice inquired.

"He called yesterday."

"And?"

"Second-rate. They're small, worth pennies. And too much attention."

"What kind of attention?"

"The tenants had a rally, called in the press. They still have a case going in court."

Richard's chest tightened.

The old man chuckled. "I thought Tuchman liked Brownsville."

Another pause.

"What about Abe?"

"Abe will sign if you want him to."

"And that kid. That kid who did Southern Boulevard?"

"No sign of him."

Richard struggled to decipher the meaning of these last exchanges, but then the doorknob turned. Richard grabbed the newspaper on the adjacent chair and held it to his face.

The two men stood in the doorway—a younger man wearing shades, with thin lips and a chin smooth as marble, and an older one, short and rotund, with small, kindly eyes swallowed in the wrinkles of his forehead. Richard got to his feet to shake their hands, but the young man sidestepped him, slipping into a chair in the corner of the office.

Richard eagerly seized the older man's hand.

"Sir, it's a pleasure."

"Call me Rich, Mr. Wong."

"Rich? Well, look at that—I'm Rich too! Richard Wong!"

"Oh?"

They both sat down, Richard in front of the mahogany desk and the old man behind it, while the younger man looked on from the corner, his arms folded in front of him.

"And your ribbon," Richard continued, pointing to the air force accolade on the wall. "I was a man of the navy myself. Trained down at Key West."

"Thank you for your service."

"And yours, sir. The air force—that's swell. You might know a few of the fellows I grew up with. I was a member of the Brownsville Boys Club."

"Richard." Mr. Leviathan cleared his throat. "My apologies, but let me save you some time. I don't think we're interested in your properties..."

"Really, I'll take any price!" Richard interrupted, raising his voice, ready to beg now. He leaned his elbow on the old man's desk. "Honestly, sir, I got myself in a bad situation. I lost my job. I'm looking to keep a roof over my wife's head. I took a bad loan, and my house is on the line. I just need to pay back this guy—I'm not looking to benefit."

Mr. Leviathan sat with his hands in his lap and something like pity in his face. Richard could still see the young man out of the corner of his eye, but he tried his best to ignore him. Something about that youngster in his black shades made Richard's neck itch.

"Sounds like a difficult situation, Mr. Wong," said Mr. Leviathan.

"Any price, any conditions," Richard repeated, and then, embarrassed, he leaned back and tried to make a joke out of it. "Tough times, this economy, right? We're all down on our luck—even the Mets. I don't know if you're a fan?"

"You really are quite the Brooklyn boy, Mr. Wong."

Richard laughed, wiping the perspiration off his forehead. He had never fallen so low. His pants were too short, he realized now; he could see the dry skin above his ankle socks.

"And I regret that I can't help you," Mr. Leviathan continued. "But there really is nothing I can do."

"I see," Richard muttered, crumpling into the chair. What could he say? All was lost.

He heard the young man stand up, and then Mr. Leviathan rose, the flesh of his white throat jiggling, so that to Richard's eye, the old man resembled a giant toad.

"I am sorry we cannot help you," he said. "I'll have to ask my son to escort you out now."

"Is that right."

Realizing that they were waiting for him, Richard rose to his feet. The young man opened the door to the lobby and waited for him to pass through it, and for a moment, Richard felt a wave of déjà vu, like he'd seen the young man before. Taking in his tight lips, his hairless chin, Richard tried to recall if they'd run into each other someplace else. Perhaps the man frequented the diner on Wall Street. Or perhaps he'd gone to school with Jennifer or Julie.

"Have we . . . ?" Richard began.

But the truth was that Richard Chin had never met this young man before, and there was no reason for déjà vu other than the fact that throughout his life, Richard had met many such men—men from whom Richard had found he always needed to get something, who always possessed in plenty what he lacked, and who could give him, or withhold from him, whatever he desired the most. And in truth, though Richard hated the *coloreds* and the *spics*, as he still called them, he hated the young man even more. This kid was the reason he was on the killing floor to begin with—chinks and coons, thrown together like chickens in cages in a Chinatown slaughterhouse, tearing at each other's feathers for a glimmer of sunlight, a taste of corn.

"Mr. Wong!" the old man called from behind. "In fact, please wait a moment—I've changed my mind."

Richard turned around, and the old man sighed, as if sympathy had suddenly overwhelmed him. "I can't help but feel your story touches me. I really can't see much use for these properties but perhaps we can work something out."

Richard jumped back, grabbed the old man's hand, and shook it with vigor.

"Thank you. Thank you!"

"Of course, we'll be evicting the tenants. There will need to be some serious renovations."

"The buildings are rent stabilized, sir."

"That is not a problem. We have our workarounds."

"That's very good, sir."

"I just need you to understand one thing, Richard."

"Yes, sir?"

Richard straightened into military posture.

"Once the deed is signed, it's signed. You have nothing to do with those properties anymore."

Richard nodded, but the elation dripped off his face, and he felt a hole growing in his stomach. He knew, though he couldn't admit it to himself, that something was wrong.

But, he told himself, he had no other option.

"Mr. Leviathan," he muttered, again reaching out his hand.

"Excuse me?" Mr. Leviathan stood up slowly, frowning.

"Mr. Leviathan?"

"Oh, right, right," the old man chuckled, giving his hand. "Yes, yes, Mr. Wong. Thank you for your business."

"Thank *you*, Mr. Leviathan."

He departed, willing himself not to think about it. He didn't want to know what type of "workarounds" they had to remove rent stabilized tenants, or what kind of designs they had for crappy buildings like his.

Yet there was one image he couldn't get out of his mind: that of the meat factories in Chinatown, where the air reeked of blood, bone, and musty feathers. He saw the butchers swinging their cleavers, the chickens clucking frantically within their cages. His whole life he'd been a chicken in that factory, he thought, and now he'd be the one to escape.

It happened only a couple of weeks later. He saw the piece in the *Daily News*.

He did not know who he could tell—not his father or Foon Wah, not his daughters, and least of all his son. He sat in the lounge chair, flipping channels so quickly that the actors could not finish their first syllables.

He decided to start waiting tables at Wo Hop, on Mott Street in Chinatown. All those years, whenever his father had suggested the idea, he'd wanted to grab a sizzling pot of chicken broth and dump it on his baba's head, but now he recognized his senselessness. Even with the properties off his hands, he needed the money.

For several weeks, he went nowhere except Mott Street.

And then one day, he knew he had to go to Brownsville. He needed confirmation that he hadn't dreamed the whole thing.

He drove on Pitkin past the shuttered glory of the Pitkin Loew's, then past what used to be Kishke King. Everything he'd known was gone. The knish sellers, the Belmont fruit venders, the Fortunoff furniture store. He drove by Nanny Goat Park, but where were all the baseball players? Where were all the goats? He remembered the young, bushy-headed Alan Friedman leaning down to be eye level with him.

We're a democracy, we make our own decisions, just like the American forefathers wrote in the Constitution. A Brownsville democracy. You want to be a member?

He drove past the projects, too many of them, the neighborhood just teeming with them, like it was turning into a graveyard, *gray, cold tombs*. The projects had killed Brownsville, he decided. If it weren't for the projects, the Jews would still be around. Canton Kitchen would be open. He wondered what life would have been like if they'd kept the restaurant. As a young man, he'd been so sick and tired of Canton Kitchen, and now it seemed to be the only place where he'd felt secure.

He circled closer, still unwilling, still bracing himself. Someone was living in their old house on Amboy Street and had hung up a blue, yellow, and black flag in the yard. This habit of the new immigrants was strange to him; never in his life could he imagine hoisting a Chinese flag in his American yard.

He was not ready, but there was nowhere left to go. Livonia Avenue waited for him—a ghost town, an abandoned village, burned and stripped to its foundations, sneakers swinging from the telephone wires, incomprehensible phrases spray-painted on the handball court walls.

This was it.

There they were.

The charred husks of what was. One tenement missing its rooftop. The other, its top two floors. Rafters exposed. Windows blown out. The CHOW MEIN HERE! sign gone. The sidewalk littered with scorched bricks. It smelled like the moratoriums on Mulberry Street, like incinerated bones, or like the musty bedroom upstairs on the day he'd found his wife on the floor and his father dangling from the ceiling.

A vandal had tagged, in orange: *Murderer!*

Richard felt sick. He clutched his stomach, held a hand over his mouth, and opened the car door to retch.

Lumps of half-digested beef lo mein fell in clumps to the concrete.

Wiping his mouth with his shirt, Richard got back in the car, closed the door, pressed the accelerator, and continued down the avenue. He found himself driving up Hopkinson to get a glimpse of the Betsy Head Park pool. The water looked like it had been sitting there for days, more a swamp than a pool. Leaves, twigs, and strips of bark floated on its surface, and soda bottles, plastic bags, and other trash littered the pool's side. In one corner, someone had clipped open the wire fence.

Richard parked the car, opened the door, and put his feet on the sidewalk.

He smelled marijuana. Then human piss. He walked to the hole in the fence, lowered his head, and ducked inside, scraping his arm on the wire.

No more or less dangerous than jumping off a bridge.

Richard sat by the edge of the pool, his knees to his chest, and cried.

LINA & SADIE

The City Planning Commission hearing fell on Valentine's Day, and Lina brought her people out in droves. They stormed the Department of City Planning in downtown Manhattan, packing the tiny hearing room and the sidewalk outside—sixty people in puffer jackets and beanies, each person holding a cardboard heart that proclaimed their love for Brownsville.

Brownsville Be Mine, one said.

I <3 CLTs!

Break Up With Bernard & Co.

Lina passed out printed copies of Sadie's article, published one month earlier, so that everyone could quote from it when they gave their testimony. It had been completed with the assistance of some more experienced reporters at *The Public Times*.

Brownsville, the South Bronx, and Corona, Queens, were the victims of a conspiracy that resulted in dozens of injuries and deaths. This criminal enterprise displaced hundreds of Black and brown New Yorkers and stymied local efforts to address poverty and build neighborhood power...

Even prior to *The Public Times*'s publication of the exposé, Lina had worked with one of June's lawyer friends to file a complaint against the Griffiths family. She'd hoped a court victory could provide funding for the Wesley Price Community Land Trust, but so far, the case wasn't going well; the Griffiths' lawyers had the judge on a string.

Still, when she went to speak at the podium, Lina told her story with passion. Recounting it to Sadie in private had made it easier to share in public. Her people shushed to hear it, and the dozen commissioners gave their attention.

The Freedom School. The smoke. The boys, Francis and William—Mr. William would testify next. How she'd almost lost her life. How she'd held herself responsible for so long. The victims and their families deserved reparations, she argued, and that meant returning the land to the people.

After her speech, as she looked into the commissioners' eyes and saw the consternation on their faces, she thought for a moment that they really had heard her and understood—that anything less than the CLT was a betrayal of the community yet again. If the commission stopped the Bernard & Co. project in its tracks, the city council would never get the chance to approve it.

Yet four weeks later, when she showed up for the vote, most of the commissioners acknowledged the CLT's demands, but they did not agree with Lina. They believed the Bernard & Co. project deserved approval, that Bernard & Co. had demonstrated a willingness to engage with the community, and that the company had offered an exceptional financial plan. The tally was two against, one abstention, and ten in favor of the project.

Time to shoot higher, she thought.

She and Tyrell organized an even bigger crowd for the city council vote two months later. Before entering the council chambers, they gathered on the granite steps of city hall for a rally. It was May but cool and damp, the air sweet and full of pollen. Excited children pumped signs in the air while José led the crowd in two chants: "From the

'Ville, never ran never will!" and "Community control now!" Seniors who had participated in the civil rights movement poured out in their Sunday best to strain their voices once again. Even Sadie Chin was there, and instead of carrying a notebook, she hoisted a sign that said, *Reparations for Brownsville!*

"If they vote yes," Lina said on a megaphone to the crowd, "then we win. If they vote no, then we still win. We win no matter what they say, 'cause we've shown them who we are. Brownsville *moves*. Brownsville's not a broken place with broken people. Brownsville is organized, and next time, they better watch out, 'cause we getting stronger, we getting louder, and we are powerful! We might not win this lot, we might not even win the next one, but we gonna get the one after that. And we will show the nation what community control looks like."

The crowd let out a resounding whoop.

"That's right! Let them hear you in Brooklyn!" Tyrell bellowed.

The group marched past the columns and ascended to the balcony of the council chambers. Below them, the fifty-one council members assembled for the stated meeting. The opening remarks took over an hour, and as the protestors in the balcony waited patiently for the vote on the Livonia project, they passed around a bag of cereal bars—until the security team heard the crunching sounds and took the food away.

When the Bernard & Co. project finally came up for a vote, the ten arrest-riskers readied themselves. Lina had brought lockboxes for six people who had already volunteered—herself, Ms. Cynthia, José, Ms. Keesha, Sadie, and Tyrell. As an official called the roll, the volunteers used plastic tubing to bind themselves to the balcony chairs and to each other; in this way, no one could be dragged off without the rest. Meanwhile, their whole group cheered for the council members who voted against, booed those who voted for, and finally halted the vote altogether, chorusing:

"Community control now! Community control now!"

"We say power! You say Brownsville!"

"Power!"

"Brownsville!"

"Power!"

"Brownsville!"

Eventually, the speaker of the council hollered up at the balcony. "Please respect your council members and let the vote proceed."

"Community control now! Community control now!"

"This is not a school cafeteria!" the chair of the Land Use committee barked up at them. "Please maintain decorum in the council chambers, or our security staff will remove you!"

The council sent fifteen security officers to escort the protestors out of the building. While most of the community members complied, the six arrest-riskers remained seated and bound to each other. They had become one entity, a centipede in blue jeans. They would not budge until the NYPD sliced the cords. An officer tried to drag Tyrell from one end, and he yelped in pain. "This is all on camera!" Sadie snapped, pointing to the press booth downstairs where several reporters were capturing the protest on their phones. The officers then left them alone and wired to the precinct for a cord-cutter.

Twenty minutes later, a troop of NYPD officers cut them apart, packed them into a police van with their hands zip-tied behind their backs, and had them fingerprinted and photographed at the precinct. But they had expected all this, had packed their medications and scrawled the lawyer hotline on their forearms. Lina and Sadie ended up in the same cell, where they fantasized about sesame chicken and pollo guisado and roti and chocolate and LUNA Bars.

About twenty-four hours later, they were back in Brownsville, holding their goodbye party for the garden in the lot, with Trini bread pudding and currant rolls for all. A local assemblywoman had asked the precinct to stand back, giving the party her unofficial sanction.

Lina was satisfied, at least enough to get up and do the whole thing over again for another lot on Livonia Avenue. The Bernard & Co. plan had passed, their occupation was all over the news, and Brownsville had once again put itself on the map.

— — —

In August, Brooklyn felt like the island it was: mornings clean and salty, afternoons slow and thick as the ocean. Brooklyn in summer smelled like the West Indies, though in winter, it had the bite of the Russian pale, the Polish shtetl.

Sadie loved her summer mornings. Each day she woke while the streets were still tranquil, and she biked from the brownstones to Brownsville to assist with the new community garden. The city had bulldozed the original one at 78 Livonia to prepare it for Bernard & Company's affordable housing complex, but the Parks Department had agreed to open an empty lot farther down the avenue for the community's use.

Sometimes, when Sadie arrived in the neighborhood on those early mornings, she felt like a child rising before dawn to gape at the mysterious boxes under a Christmas tree. There were still ghosts she wished she could speak to, and still many unanswered questions.

When it had become clear the lawsuit against the Griffiths would go nowhere, Sadie had quit her job at *New Gotham*. She needed to take a break from journalism—maybe for the time being, maybe forever. She was no longer sure it suited her, for she didn't just want to be witness to the life in her borough. She wanted to be entwined in it. To be at its service.

In the days after the protest, she joined the Wesley Price Community Land Trust Action Team and dedicated herself to the CLT's success. She shoveled compost, but she also helped launch a Kickstarter page and compile a list of vacant lots in the community. The team compensated her with Metro fare, and it meant delaying the day when she'd be able to live independently outside her parents' brownstone, but this was a small sacrifice.

At the community land trust meetings, she often ran into Tyrell. Watching him, listening to each wise thing he said, she still had feelings for him, despite herself. And now he was no longer her source.

But while he was not cold or cruel, he kept his distance—quite literally. At the meetings, he embraced the other members but was mindful to leave a few feet of space between the two of them. "I really appreciate what you've done for us," he said to her at one of these meetings, pressing his hands together with gratitude. She was pleased to hear him say it, and yet the compliment was airtight; it left no room to segue into all the things she really wanted to convey.

One day at the garden, he placed a hand on her shoulder. When she looked up, he was beaming, and she nearly fell through the earth.

"There's someone I want you to meet today," he said.

He turned around and waved at a young woman standing by the entrance. "Katrina, meet Sadie, the reporter who launched the investigation into the history of the lot. Sadie, meet my girlfriend."

The woman approached. Katrina wore a lilac wrap dress and from her sun hat gushed a bevy of braids with blue extensions. She was as tall as Tyrell and, Sadie thought, absolutely gorgeous.

"Katrina is a licensed nurse, and the founder of Brownsville Health Counsels," Tyrell added.

"I've heard a lot about you," said Katrina, reaching out her hand, a mothering note in her voice.

"It's great to meet you." Sadie tried to maintain her composure as she shook Katrina's hand. "So how long have you two been together?"

"Hmm, how long, babe?" Tyrell mused, smiling at Katrina. "Like a year, right?"

"Two years," Katrina answered.

"Off and on," Tyrell added. "This lady was always dumping my ass."

"Oh, shut up." Katrina knocked Tyrell's shoulder, and he laughed. "Ms. Sadie, you know how it is," she continued, talking girl-to-girl now. "I didn't know if this boy was serious."

"I'm always serious. When am I not serious?" Tyrell protested.

"You know what I mean."

"No I don't, I'm the most serious brother in Brownsville! Nah, but being serious"—he winked at Sadie—"I'm going back to school. Brooklyn College. Majoring in political science. Maybe one day I'll run for city council. You'll get me some good press, right?"

"If you deserve it." Sadie managed a smile.

There was something so lovely about the two of them that, inter-mixed with her heartbreak, Sadie felt relief. The fantasy would come to an end. Maybe Tyrell could see her turmoil, and this was his way of telling her to let go.

Sadie continued biking to Brownsville every day, and she watched the new lot transform from wasteland to urban farm. On the hottest day of the year, a bunch of gardeners announced they were heading to the Betsy Head Park pool. Sadie hadn't brought a bathing suit, but they insisted she purchase one on Pitkin Avenue and meet them in the water. As directed, she bought a suit, then followed a few shirtless boys all the way to Betsy Head Park. They passed handball courts, a lady selling ices, and a truck in front of which three Orthodox Jewish guys were bantering in Yiddish. For a moment, Sadie felt as if all the decades of the neighborhood's history were sliding into each other, as if she might turn around and see a Jewish deli owner gossiping with a Bangladeshi bodega man, a Jewish mobster bumping fists with a Bloods member, or Ms. Lina's block cat pawing her father's pet turtle. Perhaps when she reached the pool, she'd find her grand-father challenging the other children to a swimming race.

When they got to the bathhouse, she split from the boys and en-tered the women's changing room, slipping shyly out of her clothes and into the newly purchased one-piece. She trailed a group of laugh-ing young girls to the bathroom, where all the visitors were required to rinse themselves beneath the continuously blasting showerheads. Wet and shivering, Sadie followed the girls down the hall and in the direction of the laughter, the splashing, and the sunlight.

The concrete beneath her feet crackled with heat, and the pool was the too-blue of rock candy, a mirror to the sky above. The pool was gigantic and packed with people—not just young children, but also high schoolers whirling up enormous splashes, couples cud-dling, and men and women with infants strapped to their chests.

For a moment, she sat alone on the pool's edge with her feet in the water, and she watched the people. At the center of the pool, a group of teenagers played Monkey in the Middle with an empty milk gallon. A bunch of others attached themselves to a hand-to-shoulder human chain and waddled in a circle. Still others engaged in something like Marco Polo, a single "Yo!" substituting for "Polo." It was hard to tell where one game ended and another began, and her ears filled up with a smoothie of voices, reprimands, giggles, and shrieks. The lifeguards blew their whistles at regular intervals, and once every few minutes, a train hurtled across the elevated tracks behind the pool.

And then there was a Chinese boy.

He was very round-faced, small, and unselfconscious. He bounced on the balls of his feet and laughed with his mouth wide open, channels of mucus flowing from each nostril. He played Monkey in the Middle with the others, shouting "Over here!" when the milk carton soared, flopping his roly-poly body in the water. But when an adult voice, a woman's voice, on the side of the pool called out his name—"Tin Tin!"—he grabbed his nose dramatically and dropped beneath the surface of the pool. Sadie followed him under.

The water swallowed the cacophony. A blurry forest of legs surrounded her, all of them twisting, kicking, hopping—reveling in the seeming absence of gravity. Shattered sunlight warbled on the blue tile floor, and she saw bodies blurry and softly bobbing, and bubbles solid as glass beads. In this soundless, viscous place, it was like she had returned to the womb, become unborn, the hums and shouts of the present world so many years away.

Then she saw him: weaving through the forest of legs like a fish through seaweed. In the unborn world, his little arms churned the water with determination. He was harsh with his peers' legs; he jabbed the other children with his fingers, and some of them kicked and squirmed as he touched them.

Eventually he ran out of breath, and in a panic, returned to the surface.

Sadie rose for air and heard the boy's mother barking at him in the Fujianese dialect. She watched as he whined, as his face soured, and then as he surrendered, flapping his arms against the water to express his disappointment. He slunk over to the ramp and climbed the pool stairs, his head drooping like a heavy flower bulb. The young mother waited at the top step, ready to engulf him in a towel. Watching them, Sadie felt she knew the boy. Trying so hard to break away, battling forces even stronger than gravity. Willing and able to scratch others in that desperate quest to escape.

Sadie blinked, took a deep breath, and again plunged below the surface. She could see clearer below, in this folding across time, across space. She again expected others from the past to emerge— Jewish girls with pigtails chasing Black girls with box braids, her great-grandfather meditating with the rabbis on the pool floor. Some sort of alternate universe, where the land belonged to all of them, or to no one at all.

Sadie ran out of breath and returned to the surface of the pool, gasping.

ON SOLIDARITY—A NOTE FROM THE AUTHOR

If you seek to honor Brownsville and its residents' ongoing fight for equity and justice, consider supporting the work of local community organizers and artists. You can champion writers in Brownsville by donating to Power in the Pen (powerinthepenww.org), a grassroots nonprofit organization that holds a weekly writing workshop at the Brownsville Heritage House.

The NYC Community Land Trust movement is real and thriving. Learn more and get involved in your own neighborhood by visiting the New York City Community Land Initiative at nyccli.org.

Please be wary of any attempts by the real estate industry to commodify Brownsville's history and make a profit off its legacy. (You don't need to move to Brownsville to show your solidarity.)

ACKNOWLEDGMENTS

It took ten years, and the love and care of multiple communities, to write *Livonia Chow Mein*.

Above all, I am indebted to the residents of Brownsville who so generously offered me their stories and feedback. Ms. Cathie Wright-Lewis, Brownsville's homegrown novelist, teacher, and healer, pulled me through a portal with her historical, Afrofuturist novels: *Maurya's Seed, Passion's Pride*, and *Miracle*. These books taught me what hours in the library couldn't: what it *felt* like to survive white supremacy's ghettoization of Brownsville, and what it takes—spiritually—to persevere. Her feedback, based on both her knowledge of the craft and her deep commitment to Brownsville, greatly improved this manuscript.

Ms. Cathie welcomed me into Power in the Pen, which hosts a writing workshop at the Brownsville Heritage House (rent-free, thanks to the incredible Heritage House director, Ms. Miriam Robertson). Power in the Pen is ushering forth a bevy of powerful Black stories, stories of Brownsville and of the African diaspora. It's an essential organization in our inequitable and racially stratified borough, where race and geography over-determine access to publishing resources. Power in the Pen is changing this.

Moreover, I couldn't have asked for a more welcoming new family than I found in Power in the Pen. Ms. Andrea, Brother Ansel, Ms. Barbara, Ms. Betty, Ms. Beverly, Ms. Caroline, Ms. Carolyn, Ms. Celina, Ms. Chante, Ms. Christina, Ms. Dee Journey, Ms. Diamond, Ms. Diane,

Ms. Donna, Dr. Gail, Ms. Gerrie, Ms. Hyacinth, Ms. Huda, Ms. Katheann, Ms. Katonya, Brother King, Ms. Kwamina, Ms. Ladeeta, Ms. Linda (oh my dear Ms. Linda!), Ms. Margo, Ms. Niecy, Ms. Tayllor, Ms. Rosemary, Ms. Sasteh, Sankofa, Ms. Vanetta, Ms. Zainab, and so many other members: thank you for your trust and encouragement; thank you for raising my consciousness with your lived truths, your bravery, and your dedication to the pen.

I met Mr. James "Moe" Johnson, one of the original cofounders of Brownsville Old Timers Day, at the sixty-fifth anniversary of that tradition. Over the next seven years, he welcomed me into his heart and his home. Mr. Johnson taught me about 1940s and 1950s Brownsville—ball games at Nanny Goat Park, work at the slaughterhouse and the pickle factory, and interracial comradery in the Brownsville Boys Club. Most importantly, he shared his perspective on our society's ongoing, criminal neglect of the neighborhood.

I met Mr. Paul Chandler, a leader in the neighborhood's historic community control and tenants' rights movements, while I was reporting for *City Limits*. He and the late investigative journalist Wayne Barrett launched *The People's Voice*, an underground newspaper in Brownsville that exposed local government corruption. In our many conversations, Mr. Chandler helped me shape the character Lina, who would be his contemporary.

Three of the men I interviewed have since left this world—and while I regret that I could not share the final product with them, I feel profoundly blessed to have had the chance to meet them and record some of their stories.

It was Mr. Hank Trotman who remembered helping Jewish neighbors light stoves and put out candles on the Sabbath. He, too, brimmed with stories about the Boys Club, the Betsy Head Park pool, and the neighborhood's mobilization during World War II. A police officer as well as mentor and counselor to many, Mr. Trotman passed away in the summer of 2025.

When I met with Mr. William "Bill" Green, a local hero who brought crucial drug treatment programs to East Brooklyn while creating good-paying jobs for residents, he talked about relationships: between West Indian and African American Brooklynites, between Black leftists and China, and between younger and older Brownsvillians. Mr. Green passed away in 2022.

Mr. Herman McClain offered key details: what it felt like on the night of Martin Luther King Jr.'s assassination, the fish fry rent parties, life at Howard Houses, and the impact of the crack epidemic. A public servant and passionate athlete, he departed this life in January 2025.

I am grateful for Ms. Violet's time, though I ultimately did not include her stories; we agreed she had her own book to write.

I had the opportunity to interview multiple contemporary Brownsville leaders and neighborhood activists over the years, including Camara Jackson of Elite Learners, Lisa Kenner of the Van Dyke Houses Resident Association, Ronald Robertson of Brownsville Think Tank Matters, and Jonathan Bennett, whose father worked for the Brownsville Boys Club. During my reporting days, C. Aaron Hinton, Dionne Grayman, Renee Muir, Deron Johnston, Genese Morgan, and others contributed to my Brownsville education.

The late Carmen Vega-Rivera, a Loisaida-born, Bronx-based Nuyorican artist-activist, provided the initial seed for Lina's character—and inspired many generations of New Yorkers with her courage. The group she repped, Community Action for Safe Apartments (CASA), continues its bold fight for tenants' rights in the Southwest Bronx.

I first spent time in Brownsville as a high school student following my friend Nadiyah around her neighborhood, and she later welcomed me as a roommate and fed me her addictive Guyanese sorrel. I am still salivating. And my dear Natasha, Queens-born and Brownsville raised—thank you for keeping me accountable, for cheering me on, and for your absolutely priceless friendship.

Every weekend for most of my twenties, my grandmother Wun Kam Lew patiently combed through her ninety years to answer my questions about our family's history. I am forever grateful and missing her.

Dorothy Savitch and Howard Lew are the world's best parents. Because of them, I know the meaning of unconditional love. As classical musicians, they instilled in me what a writer needs most: discipline, stamina, a willingness to be one's own critic, and the stubbornness never to give up. They read and critiqued every draft of this book with an open mind and took me back in each time my savings dried up.

My aunt Linda preceded me as Lew family historian. For this project, she spent many hours searching for family documents and engaging Toisanese speakers to supplement my limited knowledge of the language. It was she who, many years ago, shared with me that her mother had come to the United States with reluctance. I've wanted to write this book ever since.

Aunt Nancy, my late uncle Peter, and my late uncle David shared stunning details from their Brooklyn childhoods. Thank you, Danny, for dinner in Hong Kong; that conversation challenged me to humanize my grandfather, and thank you, Uncle Gibbie, for feeding my imagination. Big heng bou for Jess, Sam, Greg, Jamie, Niki, and Robi! Last but not least, my late grandmother Fran, my late aunt Rhonda, and my uncle Michael helped me keep the lights on, asking for nothing in return.

And then there is learning to put words on paper. Kathy Collins and John P. McEneny set me on this path. Liz Howort has mentored me since high school. Rick Moody made the dream real. Billy Aronson was unfailing with his ALL CAPS encouragement. I'm grateful to my BHSEC professors, Brian Evenson and the Literary Arts department at Brown, Naoko Shibusawa's history class, and Jess Row, whose astute critique pushed me to rewrite the book.

When *Livonia* was still half-baked, the Asian American Writers' Workshop believed in its potential and assigned me a mentor—the outstanding author and truth-teller Lisa Ko. In these difficult times, she has been my guide and my inspiration. A big thanks also to Jyothi Natarajan, Yasmin Adele Majeed, and Millay Arts, and to the brilliant 2018, 2019, and 2020 Margin fellows.

Finally, the Rutgers-Newark MFA program took me out of a slump and to the finish line. My MFA thesis advisor, Akil Kumarasamy, helped me nail down what this book was really about. I received indispensable feedback and support from John Keene, Alice Elliott Dark, Naomi Jackson, and James Goodman. Michaeline Picaro Mann, Jack Tchen, and Kerry Hardy expanded my field of view, helping me locate my narrative in the larger story of Turtle Island and settler colonialism. A huge thanks to the Rutgers-Newark MFA classes of 2022, 2023, and 2024, especially Daniel Guberek and Noah Wilson, who read the entire last draft of this book with the most perceptive eyes, as well as Emily Lu Gao, Julia Silverstein, Ashley Bockholdt, Jessica Greene Camara, Lia Lewine, Onoriode Akporotu, Venus Green, Jo Telle, Luis Polanco, Daniel Pope, Sanjay Agnihotri, Cora Frazier, Shari Astalos, Zoe Dubno, Rebekah Sicari, Moon Young, Cynthia Ajuzie, and Patric Verrone.

This book exists because Jarrett Murphy and the *City Limits* team threw me into the field. I later joined the staff at New Economy Project—cofounders of the New York City Community Land Initiative. I'm so grateful to New Economy Project for showing me what transformative advocacy looks like, and a special thanks to Will for his insights on NYC housing finance policy.

Every writer prays for an agent and editor who will take up the long-incubating work as expertly as a nurse gathers an infant from a young mother's arms. My prayers were answered in Jim McCarthy, Dystel, Goderich & Bourret LLC, and the editors and staff at Simon & Schuster. Yahdon Israel, thank you for your brilliant suggestions and for clearing away the excess!

A number of books and documentaries were essential to this novel's creation; see abigailsavitchlew.com for a comprehensive list. My depiction of Lina's years teaching at J.H.S. 271 draws significantly from Charles S. Isaacs's firsthand account in *Inside Ocean Hill-Brownsville: A Teacher's Education, 1968–69*. I'm also indebted to Wendell E. Pritchett, Robert E. Barde, and Vivian Vázquez Irizarry.

For the Hebrew, Toisanese, and Nuyorican Spanish words in the book, I consulted Betty and Ralph Galarza, Stephen Poppel, the staff at the Chinese-American Planning Council's after-school program at P.S. 2, Stephen Hsiao-Yi Li's Taishanese Language Home, and Translation Services.

Natalie, only you would literally jump into the Betsy Head Park pool with me as part of my research! Thank you for your immeasurable love, and for keeping my eyes and ears open to the richness of the world. Emma, thank you for your indispensable comments on two drafts, your devotion to promoting this book, and for wading with me into the most essential political questions of our time. Alisa, your encouragement after that early draft meant everything. Riana, Claire, Phoebe, Vaith, Maxwell, Rose—you've gotten me through the ups and downs these ten years. Lorenzo, thank you for suggesting I start the book with the fire!

So many other friends and colleagues read drafts of this book and provided valuable feedback, among them Laura M., Mariel B., Clara K., Caroline T., the Panera Collective, Matthew M., and Michael M.

I wrote *Livonia* while suffering from OCD. This project might still be years away from completion if it weren't for Matt Wofsy, Dr. Evelyn Wong, Dr. Roy Jerome, Deborah Fatone, Dr. Alexa Myers, and my Obsessive Compulsive Anonymous family.

And finally: home.

Moo Moo, I appreciated the company in the predawn. Tasia, I love your powers of observation, your style, and your calm in tough times, and if there was a gift-giving war, you would definitely win. Thank you for adopting this awkward-as-hell only child as your big sis.

Darling, Cinderella Manny, Spider Manny . . . what words can capture what we have? You see me. You believe in me. I am yours after all the names roll by, forever after in the post-credits.